BOOK PUBLISHING CAREER DIRECTORY

Third Edition

BOOK PUBLISHING
CAREER
DIRECTORY

Third Edition

The Career Directory Series

Editor-In-Chief: Ronald W. Fry

The Career Press Inc.
PO Box 34,
Hawthorne, NJ 07507
1-800-CAREER-1
(IN NEW JERSEY: 201-427-0229)

The Career Directory Series

Book Publishing Career Directory, Third Edition
ISSN 0882-8261

Text edition (Paperback)   ISBN 0-934829-32-2
$26.95

Text edition (Cloth)   ISBN 0-934829-42-X
$34.95

Text editions of this Directory may be ordered by mail or phone directly from the publisher. To order by mail, please include price as noted above, $2.50 handling per order, plus $1.00 for each book ordered. (New Jersey residents please add 6% sales tax.) Send to:

The Career Press Inc.
62 Beverly Rd., PO Box 34,
Hawthorne, NJ 07507

Or call Toll-Free 1-800-CAREER-1 (in New Jersey: 201-427-0229) to order using your VISA or Mastercard or for further information on all books published or distributed by The Career Press.

TABLE OF CONTENTS

SECTION II: DEPARTMENTS & AREAS OF SPECIALIZATION

Our Heartfelt Thanks To...

• The many contributors who, while fulfilling their own significant job responsibilities, somehow found the time to write the articles—those invaluable bits of advice—we believe are the core of this Directory. We commend them for the concern they've shown for you—the aspiring professionals some of them may even eventually hire!

• Their staffs, who often helped with the research, dealt with our editors to make sure all the materials arrived on time and handled the many details endemic to such an undertaking.

• Parker Ladd, Chuck McMahon and the rest of the staff of the Association of American Publishers, the primary industry trade association for book publishers (to which, you'll find, many of our authors refer). They were instrumental in the earliest stages of this project, helping with advice, information and recommendations for contributing authors. Without their help, it would have been far more difficult to attract the top professionals who donated their time, experience and advice to this (and the two previous) edition.

• Diane Moore, executive director of the Art Director's Club, who recommended the professionals who wrote the chapters on art and design in all three editions of this volume (plus those who contributed to our Advertising and Magazines volumes, as well). Details of the ADC's many student-related programs are included in Appendix A.

• To make this brand-new third edition as comprehensive as possible, we added a number of new topics (and authors). Unfortunately, this required that some excellent articles written for the first or second editions be dropped, solely to keep this <u>Directory</u> at a manageable size. Our thanks to those professionals whose articles were omitted from this edition—for their help from the beginning of this project, their recommendations regarding additional topics and authors for this new edition and their kind understanding of editorial necessities.

• Many other top executives were unable, because of time constraints or other pressing commitments, to add articles to this year's edition, though they then worked with us to get other authors, looked over galleys or suggested important new topics. Our thanks to all of them—and a warning that they will be the first called as we prepare our fourth edition!

• The many publishing companies that provided the detailed information—more than ever before—on internships, training programs, employment contacts, and, most important, entry-level job opportunities. (See the *Job Opportunities Databank* for this exclusive data.) We thank each of them for helping us gather this information for you.

• The many people at The Career Press and our supplier companies who worked long hours compiling this data, editing articles, proofreading and doing all the other things necessary to complete a volume of this size and complexity. We thank all of them for their time, efforts and invaluable contributions: Dick Start, John Fitzpatrick, Carol Setzer, Jim Horn, Harvey Kraft, Scott Zipper, Abby Whitlan, Roberta Kopper, Tam Mossman, Tom Stein, Joe Zipper, Carol Start, Bill Killpatrick, Cy Chaiken, Michelle Gluckow, and all the folks at Words at Work, Book Mart Press and L'Escape Artistes.

Thank you—all of you—my friends.

Ronald W. Fry
President
The Career Press Inc.

Getting The Most Out
Of Your Directory

Despite its notorious reputation for underpaying the editors, salespeople, advertising, design, promotion and production pros who toil in its vineyards, the book publishing industry has, nevertheless, always been what employment counselors call a "glamour" industry, Consequently (and despite all those greenback drawbacks), there is usually an ample supply of qualified candidates willing to work for pennies, but a shortage of actual entry-level jobs.

This Book Publishing Career Directory, now in its third edition, was specifically created to help *you* break out of the pack hunting for one of those jobs. It won't just tell you how to get a first job in a publishing house—because *how* to get a job is only one aspect of the complex learning process you will need to go through, a process that includes learning about yourself, the book publishing business in general (it *is* radically different from newspapers or magazines), and key publishing houses and job specializations in particular.

It's a process of discovering *what* you want to do, *where* you want to do it, and then, and *only* then, *how* to break down the publisher's front door. This Directory is, therefore, a compendium of *all* the resources you'll need to make the *series* of decisions necessary to get that first job ...or to give you a better understanding of the book business so you can move on from your first job.

And it's written by the pros—20 of the top people in book publishing today. Articles and advice written specifically for this volume and directed specifically to *you*.

But why shouldn't we include information on magazines and newspapers, too? Aren't *they* involved in "publishing" (and pay better, to boot!)? Doesn't that make them pretty similar? Not by a long shot. Although some of the departments and job descriptions *sound* similar, these publishing worlds are as different as any other industries, despite their all having "publishing" in their names. Being an editor at Random House won't help you learn the ins-and-outs of Conde Nast and won't prepare you very well for editing *The New York Times*, either. Even given these differences, some have tried to lump all three industries into a single "publishing career guide." The result, unfortunately, is a book that gives short shrift to all three industries. (The other problem in virtually all such volumes we've seen is that they're invariably written by a freelance writer who's never worked for a book publisher, magazine or newspaper!)

So, in the first edition of this Directory, we made the decision to limit all of the information and articles to book publishing. For those interested in the world of magazines, we prepared the Magazines Career Directory, the third edition of which is also now available.

And, in response to the many students who wrote us asking about opportunities in newspaper publishing—those of you interested in becoming the next Hildy Johnson—we added a new volume to our Career Directory Series, the Newspapers Career Directory, which is now available in a brand-new second edition.

If you're sure you want to be in "editorial," but don't know the differences between the editorial functions at a magazine, newspaper and book publishing house, these three volumes will help you explore all three industries before you make the mistake of breaking into the wrong one! There is not significant movement between these industries, so knowing the differences and moving in the right direction from the very start of your career are extremely important.

HOW TO USE THIS DIRECTORY

Anyway, to return to those of you interested in *book* publishing. We've attempted to organize this Directory in such a way that reading it is a logical, step-by-step, educational progression.

The Introduction by Richard Snyder, Chairman of Simon & Schuster, and Section I (chapters 1-7) offer an overview of the industry as well as a look at some specialized areas of publishing—university presses, electronic publishing plus three brand-new articles on religious publishing, scientific/technical/medical publishing and opportunities at book clubs. It also includes an excellent article for those of you hoping to get a publishing internship.

Sections II offers more detailed discussions of the major areas of job specialization (in the order in which they appear)—Advertising; Art & Design; coming up on the Business or Financial side; Editorial (three articles: on elhi—elementary/high school—publishing, college and Trade book publishing); Production; Public Relations; Marketing & Sales (again, for elhi, college and Trade book publishers); and Subsidiary Rights. The nineteen chapters in these sections were written by top leaders in each field.

After studying these sections, you should be well on your way to deciding exactly *what* you want to do—Section III will help you figure out *how* to go about getting your first chance to *do* it. It includes a detailed Job Search Process that will take you through evaluating yourself and potential employers, preparing resumes and cover letters, the interview process and, finally, sifting the job offers.

Section IV is your *Job Opportunities Databank*, including listings of hundreds of publishing houses throughout the United States and Canada. Most of these listings include information on internships, training programs, key contacts, even actual and expected entry-level job listings. This information is exclusive to this <u>Directory</u>, gathered through our own surveys of these publishers.

Finally, Section V consists of three appendices—(A) book publishing trade organizations; (B) trade publications; and (C) book publishing courses—more important information to make sure you get exactly the right first job in publishing.

DISAGREEMENTS AND REDUNDANCIES

You'll discover as you read through the many articles in this volume that <u>the authors don't agree on everything!</u> In fact, you'll find certain instances where they rather vehemently *dis*agree, including their basic advice on breaking into the business, whether to work for one of the big New York Trade publishers (Simon & Schuster, Random House, etc.) or start at a smaller, more specialized company, and more.

What's going on here? How do you know who to listen to? Frankly, no one has all the answers, let alone all the *right* answers. Such occasional disagreement is only to be expected given the varied career paths and experiences our contributors have gone through in so many different departments at so many varied houses. We also think it's important that *you* realize there isn't always one way in, one way to do a job, one place to work, one way to think. We have occasionally inserted "Editor's Notes" into the body of articles to refer you to other chapters or sections where you can find related, though perhaps contradictory, advice or information.

On the other hand, you will occasionally find repetitious advice—on interviewing techniques, how to break in, etc.—from article to article. (Reviewers especially please note!) <u>We are aware of this duplication and have purposefully not edited out such repetitious advice.</u> Why?

Not everyone will read every page of this book—the young man who fancies himself the next Sam Vaughan might never make it through the Production or Publicity articles (although he should!). Someone just "thumbing through" may entirely miss an important piece of advice if it's in only one section or chapter.

And second, although we believe the job search process included in our staff-written Section III "covers all the basics," if the advice is sound and correct, we're sure it can't be repeated often *enough*.

THE GOAL WE SET...AND ACCOMPLISHED

When we began this project in 1985, students we queried indicated an intense need for a <u>guide to resources</u>—articles and advice on every aspect of the book publishing business by the practitioners out there doing the work, listings of major publishers (with then-unavailable information like who to talk to, potential openings, educational requirements, specific titles, etc.), the trade organizations to contact, the trade magazines to read, where to take courses, etc.

The overwhelmingly positive reaction to the first and second editions of this volume proved that we had achieved our initial goal: To produce the most comprehensive, all-inclusive guide to book publishing for entry-level people ever published.

We feel confident that with this third edition we have succeeded in the more difficult goal we set for ourselves this time: To make the best book on getting into book publishing even better.

Most of all, we hope it helps *you* get exactly the job you want in this exciting business.

Good luck!

Why Publishing Needs You

By

Richard E. Snyder, President, Publishing/Information
Gulf + Western Inc.

And

Chairman and Chief Executive Officer
Simon & Schuster Inc.

Publishing is often called the "accidental" profession, and, in my case, it certainly was serendipitous. When I was discharged from the army in 1958, I went straight to my father's office, fully prepared to begin a long and happy career in the family business. But after only a few minutes chat, he suddenly stood up and escorted me to the door—"Better a son than a partner" was his philosophy.

Later, walking up Fifth Avenue, I ran into an Army buddy. I invited him to have lunch, but he was on his way to a job interview. Rather than face a solitary lunch, I tagged along. To make a long story short, the next day I started work at Doubleday.

A few years later I joined Simon & Schuster, where I've been ever since. In all that time, I haven't had a moment's regret that I chose publishing—or rather, publishing chose me.

Publishing is unique, and there is real joy inherent in the process of making books. Even today, in an age of mass entertainment and electronic delivery of all kinds of information, books continue to challenge points of view, make people think and stimulate change in our social structure. Works such as Alan Bloom's <u>The Closing of the American Mind</u> or Richard Rhodes' <u>The Making of the Atomic Bomb</u> affirm the lasting power of the book. As a publisher and as a human being, I find this extremely gratifying.

The thrill of publishing a book like <u>The Closing of the American Mind</u> is not one that happens every day in publishing, but there *is* everyday joy of another kind—the kind that comes from working with creative, talented people, literate people who love books, who share books.

But joy, as we all come to realize sooner or later in life, is not without responsibility. As a publisher, one has a dual obligation—social responsibility and the need to make a profit.

Yes, It's A Joy, But A Business, Too

Let's not overlook the fact that publishing is a business—and these days, it's a big business. The consumer book market is a $2.9 billion market and growing. The education market for books and learning materials is easily double that. And the booming information industry represents a $15 billion market.

Simon & Schuster, with sales in excess of $1 billion, has operations in each of those markets. In an era of increasing consolidation and globalization, large publishers have an advantage. In our case, our size allows for economies of scale and gives us the resources to compete in an increasingly sophisticated and competitive marketplace. It also puts us in the forefront on issues of social responsibility. And even though we are large, the entrepreneurial spirit still flourishes in our publishing units.

Over the years, Simon & Schuster has published many authors of widely differing points of view, reflecting not only the rich variety of thought and opinion in our society but among our editorial staff as well. We have many imprints under the Simon & Schuster corporate umbrella—each not only reflects the tastes, interests and beliefs of its editors, but also what its editors believe will sell.

And A Business That Needs You

Editors, production people, designers, publicists, sales representatives—these are only some of the hundreds of people needed to do the job of publishing. To stay vital, a good publisher must constantly renew and replenish, nurture and train the wealth of talent needed to drive the company. I believe it is crucial for our industry to make an effort to attract the best and most able of our young people. Each generation brings with it its own point of view, a unique understanding of its common experience. In the publishing world, we value that infusion of new thought, and we need it to succeed.

If you're reading this book, you probably are considering a career in publishing. I hope you will give it a try. Your energy, your ideas and your enthusiasm will revitalize us, recharge our batteries. It will, after all, be a member of your generation who will be tuned in to the important voices of the 21st century, who will discover and publish the Alan Bloom of tomorrow.

Whatever career you ultimately decide to pursue, I have only one piece of advice that I'll share with you, one that's been important to me over the years: Working hard is important—it's 90% of the game—but having fun while you work should be that last 10%. That, for me, has been the true joy of working in publishing.

RICHARD E. SNYDER

Mr. Snyder was named president of the Publishing/Information operations of Gulf + Western Inc. when they were restructured in March 1985.

He joined Simon & Schuster in 1961, was appointed director of sales in 1964, director of marketing in 1967 and executive vice president in charge of all publishing operations in 1969. He became the president of the company in 1975, chief executive officer in 1979 and chairman in 1981.

Mr. Snyder was born on April 6, 1933, in New York City. He received a B.A. degree from Tufts University in 1955 and started his publishing career with Doubleday & Company Inc. in 1957, after serving two years in the U.S. Army.

Mr. Snyder has been a member of the board of directors of the Association of American Publishers and currently is a vice chairman of the board of directors for the National Book Awards. He also was chairman of the Publishers Committee for the 48th Inernational PEN Congress and is co-chairman of the PEN 1988 Benefit Committee.

SECTION I

Overview Of The Book Business

CHAPTER ONE

Have I Got A Career For You!

By

Ken McCormick, Senior Consulting Editor
Doubleday & Co.

Let's start at the very beginning. You've come to New York City to get a job in publishing. You know one fellow/girl from college whose been in New York for a year, but they work in a totally different business. You can count on your friend to teach you how to get around town, but he/she knows *NOTHING* about publishing. What do you do *now*?

I know a man—let's call him "Joe"—who came to New York years ago under similar circumstances. He's now a veteran in the business, even something of an institution, but back then he was just another scared kid from out of town trying to break into the big-time world of New York publishing. One night not so long ago, we started talking about how bleak it must be for someone starting out in this business without any connection to anyone in publishing. We traded stories of how *we* had gotten our starts in the business. While I thought Joe was romanticizing his tale then, I now suspect his story happens more often than any of us think. Perhaps hearing his experiences will make *you* feel a little less alone as you start trodding the cold streets of Manhattan, hoping that someone, *some*where, will introduce *you* to some publishing guru.

"It was terrible," he began. "I'd come to New York—with a brand-new diploma from the University of Texas—to get into publishing. I didn't know a soul in New York. But I had heard of *Publishers Weekly* at school, so I went to the library and read a couple of current issues. There was one piece about a big guy in the business—Alec Blanton of MacMillan. His picture made him look like a human being and, it turned out, he was a graduate of my *alma mater*."

"I marched to his office on Madison Avenue and told his secretary I had a message for him. (I didn't *really* have a *message* as much as some news I hoped would establish some tentative connection between us: A rather legendary journalism professor at Texas had just had quite an honor bestowed on him. I hoped that he knew, or at least *had heard of*, this professor. It wasn't the greatest connection ever invented, but I hoped it would at least get me in the door and give me a chance to talk with him.)

"The secretary took my name. Minutes later, a big, jovial man came out, looked me over, and asked, 'So what happened to Professor Franklin? I don't read the alumni news as much as I should.'

"It turned out that Professor Franklin was one of his idols. Connection established! He invited me into his office. It wasn't a big or showy place, but from the papers, half-read manuscripts and books strewn around—and the picture of Maxwell Perkins prominently centered on one wall—you got the distinct sense that a lot of important work went on there...*publishing* work.

"My 'pre-planning' had consisted of creating the story to get in the door. Now that I was actually in his office, I wasn't sure how to get the conversation going. In literature class, I'd read quite a bit of Thomas Wolfe, who had, as it turned out, just died. So I took the chance and asked if he had known him. He had. In fact, he felt Wolfe was one of our great novelists. So we talked about Wolfe. Eventually, the conversation returned to Professor Franklin. By the time we talked about *him* for a while, my new 'friend' was virtually glowing.

"The phone rang. 'I'm with someone now,' he said. 'I'll call you back in a few minutes'. A few minutes!—it was time to take the bull by the horns. So, as he hung up, I told him why I had *really* wanted to see him: I wanted him to give me a *job*.

"Mr. Blanton leaned forward and smiled, 'You want a job, and I don't have one for you. But go and see George Shively at Stokes. He's a good guy, and he likes young people'. I asked him if I could use his name. He said I could, shook my hand, and was reaching for the phone (to call Mr. Shively???) as I left the office.

"George Shively was a doll, though he was working for a publishing house I'd never heard of. Unfortunately, I got the same story—no jobs open. But *he* referred me to a lady at Simon & Schuster. And *she* referred me to someone else...who referred me to yet another editor. And so it went. No one had a job for me, but everyone passed me on to someone else. Within a week, I had seen *seven* people.

"The last conversation took a slightly different turn. 'Get right up to the Colony Bookshop,' this editor advised. 'They called me yesterday looking to hire somebody.' I practically ran uptown...and got the job. It wasn't exactly what I had hoped for. But in a single week, I *had* met seven people—seven big-time professionals who turned out to be friendly and helpful—and landed my first job in publishing. Seven people whom I hadn't known at all seven days before."

Joe and I continued to reminisce for the greater part of an evening. But that story is the one most pertinent to those of you who are trying to emulate Joe's success and get a first job in publishing. What does it all mean? None of the people Joe spoke with had known him before he walked in the door. And few of them knew many of the others with whom Joe had spoken. But each of them had *heart*. Each of them had been willing to take the time to speak with a newcomer and offer his or her help and advice. It says, I think, some nice things about the nice people who work in this business of book publishing.

HOW TO START A SUCCESSFUL PUBLISHING CAREER

In the Job Search section of this volume, you'll find detailed advice on writing resumes and cover letters, interviewing, following up, and more. Read them carefully. In addition, once you have a better idea of the area of publishing or specialization you want to get into, you can study the pertinent chapter(s) by the top professional who's written about that area for this Career Directory. Each of them discusses the requisite educational and/or extracurricular preparation you need to land that first job. (One piece of advice with which my colleagues may or may not agree: you might not be able to get that perfect first job, the one doing what you always wanted to do. I suggest you take *any* responsible job offered you by a good, respectable house and then work within the company to get to the job/area/specialization you want. There's a lot of competition out there—people are looking for jobs and publishers are always seeking talented job candidates. So get in the door—you have a better chance of moving around once you're already part of the company.

Once you've landed a job—no matter how lowly—it's important to realize that your publishing education *has just begun*. Borrow *Publisher's Weekly* (or subscribe to it yourself) and read it every week, the ads as well as the articles. Learn the difference between Trade publishing (books you can buy in a bookshop) and Educational publishing (books which are primarily textbooks). Scientific publishing is another field, religious publishing another, and so on. All special fields All important areas to learn about.

In 1928, when I started in publishing, there were 5,000 different titles published. In the past year, there were about 43,000 titles published—5,000 was too few, and 43,000 is too many. Help find ways to enable the publisher you are working for do the best possible job on the fewest number of books and still make money. Remember: You are in business; no one is subsidizing your house—it must make money to survive.

How To Help Your House

Whether you're at the top of the employment ladder or have just taken a first job as a clerk or a secretarial assistant (it pays you a salary that pays the rent!), you should be looking for ways to help your house...a search that will often, not incidentally, wind up helping *you* and *your* career, too.

Read magazines. When you see a story or an article by someone who hasn't been published in the book field, write to the author. Tell him or her how much you enjoyed the piece and ask if they have an idea for a novel or non-fiction book.

If they are any good, they *will* have an idea, possibly lots of them. Ask them to send you copies of whatever they've written that might work as a book. Or just synopses of their ideas. Read everything and start corresponding with the author. Encourage them. Keep copies of every such letter. Why do all this? Because sooner or later, you'll find a Joy Cowley.

My wife read *Short Story International* and came across a short story by Joy Cowley, a writer from New Zealand. My wife had never heard of her before, but wrote her a letter and, in return, got part of a novel. She read it, liked it and encouraged the editorial board at Doubleday to offer Joy a book contract. As a result of my wife's aggressive search for ways to help

Doubleday, we eventually published four books by Mrs. Cowley. This kind of editorial sleuthing is going on all the time at any good publishing house.

When do you stop your publishing education? The answer is: never. Even if you've reach the "top of the ladder" and no longer attend courses or seminars for yourself, you'll still attend Denver or Radcliffe...but as a teacher. It's essential to *pass on* what you've learned.

When Is It Time To Move On?

Most publishers give a raise every six months—a nominal raise, that is. You may not see a big increase for a while, so if a job that looks interesting opens up at another publisher, you may want to consider it. But think about the <u>house</u> you're currently working for, not just the job you currently have. Make sure you want to change <u>houses</u>, and not just jobs. If you do decide to leave, ask your potential employer for a reasonable increase, but don't price yourself out of the market. And before you make the switch, ask someone whose advice you trust whether *they* think you should.

When I was a young man in publishing I seemed to be surrounded by tall trees. I saw no possibility of getting anywhere. I went to our sales manager (Frank Henry, a wonderful guy with a hearty laugh) and asked "Is there any future for me at Doubleday?" He suddenly became very serious "Stay," he advised. "In about two years, the whole climate here will change, and there really will be a job for you—one a lot better than you have now." Now he was the sales manager and I was in the editorial department, but I sensed that I could trust his advice and that he knew what he was talking about. I stayed.

Now, unbeknownst to *me*, a mere toiler in the editorial vineyards, two red hot people at Doubleday were in the wrong jobs One, Dan Longwell, went to *Time* magazine and helped start *LIFE*. The other, Malcolm Johnson, was really a scientific publisher. He left for a very good house where his knowledge of scientific publishing would push him along. Those two moves opened up two "holes" and gave me an unexpected chance (we *were* in the depths of the Depression, and there weren't a lot of openings). Good houses—and Doubleday was and is one of those— usually look to their own people to fill an opening before searching "on the outside." I was promoted.

Every once in a while, I shiver when I think of the mistake I would have made if I'd given in to my small pessimism about my future. In two years everything *did* change and I got a break. (And I eventually became editor-in-chief!) Thank God for the Frank Henrys of this world.

Use this <u>Book Publishing Career Directory</u> to expand your current knowledge of publishing and, perhaps more importantly, to expand the areas of possibilities you're able to consider. Look at the chapter on working for a *university press*. What incredible changes have taken place there in the last few years! More and more of their books are competing with Trade publishing houses. The University of Nebraska Press, for example, has a very hot paperback line. Many of Wallace Stegner's best books are in that series. Learn more about what university presses are doing *now*, as opposed to what they *used* to do.

Think about <u>scientific publishing</u>, especially if you're technically-inclined or trained. Or working for a <u>book club</u> or in the fast-growing area of <u>religious publishing</u>. Or for one of the many <u>educational publishers</u>.

And even if you are hoping to break into Trade publishing, you can find *lots* of opportunities in areas besides editorial! Consider marketing, sales, promotion...or subsidiary rights, advertising, public relations, production. You'll find interesting and informative articles on all these areas of specialization (and more) in the pages that follow. Don't pass them by—you might learn about an area you never even considered before and find a totally unexpected career opportunity.

Don't think your search is confined to New York. Regional publishing has grown wildly, if not always profitably. When I was a high school and college student in Oregon, there was one struggling book publisher in Portland, another in San Francisco. But that was *it* for West Coast publishing. Now there are book publishers in Seattle, Portland, a number around San Francisco and Los Angeles, and many more all over the country.

So "Happy Publishing." If you want a career in book publishing, it's out there for you. Learn to type well, have a ravishing appetite for books, and be endlessly aggressive about not stepping on other people's hands (or toes).

Good luck. And smile...no matter *how* apprehensive you are.

KEN McCORMICK

In his nearly 60 years in book publishing, Mr. McCormick has worked with a group of famous authors far too numerous to list in full, among them: Sir Rudolph Bing, Noel Coward, William O. Douglas, Edna Ferber, Arthur Hailey, W. Somerset Maugham, Lowell Thomas, Leon Uris, Louis Nizer, Pierre Salinger, Irving Stone, Robert F. Kennedy, and many others.

Beginning his career at the Doubleday Bookshop in New York's Pennsylvania Station in 1930, he worked at a number of their book outlets before being appointed promotion manager in 1933. He joined the Editorial department in 1935, becoming associate editor in 1937, editor-in-chief in 1942, and vice president in 1948. Since 1971 he has been a senior consultant editor with the company and, since 1973, has fulfilled similar responsibilities at the Franklin Library.

Mr. McCormick has been active throughout his career in numerous industry organizations. He is a former director of the American Book Publishers Council, served several years as chairman of their Committee on Reading Development, and has taught creative writing at Columbia University.

Mr. McCormick is married to the former Anne Hutchens, who works in the subsidiary rights department of Alfred A. Knopf publishers. They live in New York City.

CHAPTER TWO

The Book Club: Selling Books By Mail

By

**Maron L. Waxman, Director-Book Development
Book-of-the-Month Club**

A book club is a publishing enterprise and, at first glance, offers many of the same career opportunities as any publishing house. But from another angle, it is also a bookstore. This combined role—publisher and bookseller—means that book clubs place more emphasis on selling and marketing books than on creating and editing them.

Not only is a book club a retail operation, it is a <u>direct mail</u> retail operation, which places a premium on the attractive and straightforward presentation of books, good service and good deals to keep book club members enrolled. The 1980's have seen a tremendous expansion in the products people can buy by mail, as well as a growing sophistication on the part of both sellers and customers. Book clubs are part of this expansion and offer you a chance to enter a challenging and not entirely well-charted field.

So you can consider a book club a kind of mail order bookstore that regularly offers its members a selection of several hundred books In comparison, however, even a relatively small bookstore stocks two to three *thousand* titles. How can book clubs attract and hold members? By being highly personal and often highly specialized. Although they offer only a fraction of the books available at any one time, the books they do offer are usually those in which club members are especially interested; specialized clubs like the Teacher Book Club often offer books that aren't available in general bookstores at all. This is, I think, the formula of every successful book club: It knows its members' interests and constantly strives to select and offer books that appeal specifically to them.

If directly addressing a highly interested group of readers and selecting books for them from a variety of sources appeals to you, book clubs are a rewarding place to work. Here's a look at the day-to-day workings of the various departments in a club, so that, given your skills and background, you can evaluate whether book clubs may be the place for you.

THE EDITORIAL STAFF

Like every publishing enterprise, book clubs begin with books.

The books come from publishers, who usually submit them in manuscript form. To give you an idea of the number of submissions, the Book-of-the-Month Club, one of the largest general clubs, receives about 5,000 books a year. While this is only a small percentage of the 50,000 or so titles published annually, it is still a great many books to consider.

Editorial Evaluation

Each submission is read many months before publication and evaluated by editors for content, reader appeal, the author's past performance and just plain "pleasure value." Both large and small clubs use **outside readers**—frequently because they have special fields of knowledge—in addition to **staff editors** for such evaluations. A side note: If you like to read a variety of books or have a special interest, freelance reading for a book club is a pleasant way to hone your editorial judgment and gain hard-to-come-by manuscript experience.

When the editors decide they like a book enough for the club, they call the publisher's Subsidiary Rights department and make an offer. If more than one club is interested in a book — the latest James Michener novel or the hottest new diet tome—there may be a lively back-and-forth auction.

Book Clubs Vs. Publishing Houses

Up to now this sounds like a job description for any editor. What are the differences between an editorial position at a book club and one at a publishing house?

First, book club editors are reading books that have already been contracted by a publisher and will be published. They are not deciding, as most editors do, *whether* a book should be published.

Second, book club editors almost never do manuscript editing. They may make suggestions about length, titles, jackets, etc.—suggesting, for example, that a glossary be added to a technical book—but they do not work with authors to shape the book. A few specialized clubs do create books for their members, because many publishers find such specialized titles unprofitable to produce. These books are still not edited by book club staff members, however. Only the concepts and editorial direction come from the club editors; the books are produced by book packaging companies.

Finally, book club editors rarely deal directly with authors and agents or the vast numbers of manuscripts and proposals authors and agents send to publishers.

On the other hand, book club editors (or managers) are responsible for their club's performance and, like the booksellers they are, are aware, almost on a day-to-day basis, of how well their selections are selling. Clubs are expected to maintain a steady rate of sales from month to month, and it is the editors' job to put together the monthly list that will maintain sales at the budgeted level.

The editors are also closely involved with the bulletins and the manner in which the books they have selected are presented in them. Working with the writers and designers, they are thus able to "speak" directly to their readers. So while book club editors are held more accountable for the performance of their lists than most trade editors, they can also address their readers in a much more personal way.

Breaking In: Editorial Assistant

The entry-level job is **editorial assistant**. Assistants have research and clerical duties and read manuscript submissions. They are remarkably free of the heavy typing and filing load most publishing editorial assistants carry, because book club editors do not have extensive correspondence. As assistants gain experience in learning what club members enjoy, they will be recognized, promoted and given more responsibility, but usually the only two jobs in the department are editor and assistant.

For the candidate interested in learning about direct mail and marketing, book clubs, since they are small, offer a marvelous opportunity to see the entire operation at work and to be closely involved with editors, the creative departments and marketing.

THE CREATIVE DEPARTMENTS

Once the editors have made their decisions about which books to offer their members and when to offer them, the books must be presented to the members. This is done through monthly bulletins, often fifteen a year. The Book-of-the-Month Club is credited with having invented the 15-month year, which features the original twelve plus spring, summer, and fall; many other clubs have followed suit. In producing the "monthly" bulletins, which may run to 24 pages, with several inserts and all kinds of artwork, the club becomes a magazine publisher of sorts.

Writing Promotional Copy

The **copywriters** write the descriptions of the books to be covered in the current bulletin, working with the editors and from galleys to create full-scale reviews or information-crammed 100- to 200-word summaries. These reviews and summaries are vital to the sale of the books, for the bulletin is the only vehicle the club can use to interest its members in a particular title. The members cannot hold the book in their hands, read the publisher's glowing jacket copy or skim a few sentences to see whether the story moves along, as they can in a bookstore.

Copywriters usually have some experience in advertising or publicity before coming to a club; the exacting schedules do not allow much time for training. Over the years copywriters develop specialties and, in a company that has several clubs, may become the voice of one club. Small clubs may use freelance copywriters.

Editorial Production

In editorial production, a staff of **copy editors/proofreaders** reads and edits all the copy for accuracy, style, grammar and punctuation. Copy editors can be seen hurrying all over the club, checking copy and layouts and keeping everything on schedule. They are responsible for coordinating the copywriters' text and the designers' layouts and keeping the entire production process on schedule. Again, book clubs do not usually hire beginners in this department—the time pressures are too great to allow for training.

Career Opportunities

In terms of career paths, editorial assistants may move into copywriting and copy editing jobs; copywriters and copy editors may become editors.

For the candidate who wants heavy-duty experience in copy editing and book-related copywriting, clubs offer excellent opportunities. Book publishers do not have many staff jobs in these areas, preferring to use freelancers. Here is an excellent chance to learn highly-portable skills that can be used in advertising, magazines and other areas of publishing.

The Art Department

The Art department at a book club also offers excellent opportunities for entry-level people. With bulletins and brochures going out every three and a half weeks, there is a tremendous amount of design, layout and paste-up work. Each *Book-of-the-Month Club News* —our "monthly" bulletin—features more than one hundred titles. To publicize and present these books, the Art department uses photographs, original art, public domain artwork, display type and, sometimes, art created by members of the department. Each featured book must be treated individually, with a layout suited to its style and contents. Again, the importance of the bulletins—the clubs' only chance to sell our list—cannot be over-emphasized.

The pace is fast, the books varied—anything from the new supplement to the Oxford English Dictionary to the latest Berke Breathed cartoon collection—and, in addition to the regular bulletins, there are direct-mail pieces that are mailed by the thousands to enroll new members. These, too, are designed on staff (though sometimes by art people working in the Marketing department). Because mailing pieces are vital to book clubs, both to enroll new members and to continue to entice active members, they have to be inviting and attractive. All art techniques are used, and designers have frequent chances to work in full color and utilize a range of display types and graphic devices. Promotional pieces can also take many forms— postcards, stickers, fold-up mailers, letters, etc.

For the beginning designer, book clubs are a superb opportunity. Students and interns are hired on a freelance basis and often graduate to full staff jobs. First assignments may be photographic enlargements and reductions or simple paste-ups, but within a year the beginner will probably be promoted to **junior designer,** with responsibilities for full page design. Because the staff is small, supervision—and thus the chance to learn—is continuous. Because the work is varied and constant, beginners are able to try their hands at many techniques and work in many mediums. For the aspiring designer, book clubs can be a highly stimulating training ground in an area where few book publishing houses maintain more than a one- or two-person staff and freelance almost all hands-on artwork.

THE MARKETING DEPARTMENT

The Marketing department of a book club is a highly sophisticated and knowledgeable group, equipped with computer printouts on every aspect of the clubs' members—what books they bought, how frequently they bought them, what magazines they read, as well as the usual age, income and occupation demographic profile. Using this information, the Marketing department seeks to attract new members from previously successful or experimental new sources, find out what kinds of book offers result in the most active members and uncover new interests to which the club might cater.

At a publishing house, the first marketing effort is actually directed at a middleman, the bookstore. Bookstores, *not* readers, are the publisher's primary customers. While the publisher's Marketing department will publicize and advertise its books through print, radio and television ads, the audiences they reach have little in common, except that they were reading, listening to or watching a particular newspaper or radio or TV program that day. Seldom does a general publishing house directly address its readers.

Thus book clubs offer the candidate interested in marketing more well-defined tasks and provide better tools—in the form of highly-individual and well-analyzed buying patterns—to accomplish them.

The marketing function at book clubs has three goals: With the club executives and editors, they seek out new members by trying new lists and new advertising media, put together the best possible combination of attractive but cost-effective offers and test new approaches, even new clubs. This multifaceted effort involves the department staff and its outside advertising agencies in the development of promotional materials. At a large book club, marketing is a sizable department, with assistants working on research and the general run of entry-level duties. At a very large club like mine, the Marketing department has an entire range of creative people—copywriters, copy editors/proofreaders, designers—and there is time to hire and train beginners who are on a career track.

Marketing is an active area, accelerating under the twin drives of increased interest in direct mail and ever more-sophisticated computer reporting. At a book club there is more to be learned about book buyers as individuals than at almost any other publishing or bookselling enterprise. There is a wealth of data, the chance to use this information experimentally and creatively, and a quick reaction to all marketing efforts. In short, for the candidate interested in direct mail marketing, book clubs are an excellent training ground.

BOOK CLUBS' SPECIAL NICHE

There is no question that book clubs occupy a special niche in publishing, somewhat removed from the all-out merchandising of major book chains and the scramble to acquire and publish books at traditional publishing houses. For editors there is the rare chance to read books—both critically and for pleasure—that reflect the interest of the club member and to deal with an audience seriously interested in books. For copywriters, copy editors and designers, there are staff jobs in areas that are freelanced in most publishing houses. For marketing candidates, there is the bright new world of direct mail, with sophisticated computer assistance and a clearly-defined task.

Even the big book clubs are rather small by publishing company standards, however, and there are not a great many entry-level jobs. Turnover tends to be a little slower than in the industry in general. But there are internships at the larger clubs, so a student, especially one in art, can get an inside peek before he or she decides to sign on for the duration.

Book clubs provide a special pleasure to both their members and the people who work at them. If this brief overview has intrigued you, you should take a look at them as a promising area of opportunity.

MARON L. WAXMAN

Prior to her current position, Ms. Waxman was executive editor at Scribners and Macmillan, in both the trade and educational divisions. A lecturer at the CUNY Institute for Publishing, she has also taught at the NYU Center for Publishing and several writers' conferences. She holds a bachelor's degree from Tufts University and a master's from Columbia.

CHAPTER THREE

Electronic Publishing: What Is It? And Is It For You?

By

Gary Craig, Program Director
Wiley Electronic Publishing
John Wiley & Sons, Inc. Publishers

"ELECTRONIC PUBLISHING DEPARTMENT, PLEASE"

If you walk into a publishing house and ask for the "electronic publishing" department, you'll get a variety of responses. Sometimes you'll be referred to the production department, sometimes to the data processing department, sometimes to a software product group. Most often, they won't even know what you're talking about!

I guess that qualifies electronic publishing as a "leading edge" area of publishing. And if that's the case, there is a very big question any potential job applicant must ask: What is my tolerance for interruption, uncertainty, and rapid change of direction?

"Regular" publishing is fairly predictable: When you accept a position, at any level, you will enter a functioning environment. The major activities have an operational structure, and the people already there will have little difficulty in passing on to you the details of "how we do it here." (You may immediately want to change "how we do it here", but that's standard—every new employee is expected to contribute to improving the process.)

But when you join an "electronic publishing" area, you will be conducting business and, at the same time, inventing the way that business is done. In the course of doing so, you will frequently have to abandon many procedural approaches that, it turns out, do not work—not because they don't get your own work done, but because they are in conflict with other in-house systems, financial reporting requirements, or even the company's long-term view of itself.

You will find, even if you enter at an administrative level, that you are expected to help "sell" your own department's operations to the rest of the company; in fact, how well you do that may determine how long your job exists.

If you are motivated by work alone, if you believe you would be uncomfortable in a position where you must simultaneously keep the work moving and keep a company-wide perspective, if you are happiest when you come to work at nine, leave at five, and erase the job from your mind 'til the following morning, please read no further—electronic publishing is too exciting to be treated that way. It needs people who are excited by its potential to change the way people think about knowledge and information. It requires a commitment, not only of labor but of ideas, plus a generalist's vision of where our society as a whole is going.

ELECTRONIC PUBLISHING AT WILEY

We see electronic publishing as a piece of the company's philosophy, an affirmation that a traditional company (we have been in business since 1807) can respond to change. It is not, therefore, an activity or even a department, but rather an idea against which a whole spectrum of activities and opportunities are tested.

If we accept a book manuscript on a diskette, rather than on paper, we have made a decision to change the company—handling that project will demand different kinds of people and different procedures.

If we have been publishing, for decades, a standard handbook, whose main audience is now using computers to do the majority of their work, we have to decide whether we should offer them that same information in a form which lives in the machine, instead of in a dog-eared book on the shelf.

If we have an opportunity to publish a reference work that is extremely valuable to the marketplace, but only if it can be updated very frequently, we know in advance we cannot approach it conventionally—it takes a long time to make a "regular" book. If we decide to do the book at all, we'll have to seriously consider publishing it electronically.

If we want to publish a reference work that is simply too large to squeeze into a book, we must look at electronic publishing as the only way we can deliver the information to the customers.

If we are publishing some information that is invariably used in conjunction with a computer program, it is probably not reasonable for us to print that information in a book; we should provide the information in the form which integrates directly with that program.

Internally, electronic publishing is how we streamline our publishing process and shorten, as much as possible, the interval between when we receive an author's original material and when we can get it into the hands (or machines) of our customers. And externally, it offers us dozens of options for matching our product—very exactly—to our customers' needs; the more we can do *that*, the more solid will be our position in the markets we serve.

BUT WHAT ABOUT THE COMPUTERS?

Yes, we do depend on computers. In fact, some of us even use them. But please don't get the idea that electronic publishing jobs are computer jobs.

Do you like to work on a computer? Good—you will be able to identify with the customers for electronically-delivered products.

Do you like to write programs? Good—you are probably a very logical thinker, and electronic publishing requires some very systematic activities. But if you come to my department, you'll never write a BASIC program (although you'll be a big help when we have to buy some programming outside).

Are you motivated by disorder? Good—electronic publishing offers so many design and implementation options that every project begins by looking like utter chaos; the computer is a frighteningly powerful tool which, in fact, can do anything you ask—it requires considerable mental discipline to decide *what* you should ask it to do.

WHY DOES ELECTRONIC PUBLISHING EXIST?

Is it just a novelty? After all, publishing is publishing; it just means getting some kind of information from its author to some other person. *How* that is done never did matter very much—nailing information to doors of churches, writing it on scrolls, even writing letters—all these things accomplished the desired result.

For more than five hundred years, we've been doing it in these packages called books. Books are perfectly nice products, and they should be—the book as a delivery vehicle has been evolving during those hundreds of years, with refinement after refinement contributing to the design in response to customer needs. It's probably your own positive feelings about books which have led you to consider publishing as a career in the first place.

Books, however, have some limitations as all-purpose, information delivery packages:

1) *Size*—you can only glue so many sheets of papers together in a binding.

2) *Weight*—have you ever tried to lift an unabridged dictionary?

3) *Timeliness*—information is often two or three years old by the time it is finally published in print.

4) *Labor-intensiveness*—human labor is about the most expensive commodity around; building this cost into the price of the product sometimes places the publication beyond the reach of its audience.

5) *Non-transferability*—if you have information in print and you want to use it in a computer or word processor, you will probably have to type it all over again.

On the other hand, information—considered in machine-readable form—can take on a great variety of forms:

1) It can be created by the author using his or her own computer, sent to the publisher, edited and otherwise manipulated, and then sent—again in machine-readable

form—straight to a compositor who will convert it into typographic-appearing output that can be used as the "mechanical" (original) for a book.

2) It can be keyboarded once and then "loaded" onto a large computer, where customers access it by hooking their own computers to telephones and issuing commands. In this form, portions difficult to find in the printed form can be readily located in seconds.

3) It can be updated as often as needed, right up to the time manufacturing (or "loading") begins. Often, this last-minute updating capability adds considerable value to the product.

4) It can be delivered to a customer in exactly the machine-readable format the customer needs, possibly for use in the customer's own computer or electronic "workstation."

5) It can be easily merged with information from other publications to create new or enhanced products.

6) It can be made more valuable by combining it with a software product that gives the customer the ability to manipulate and rearrange it in various ways.

And on and on, limited only by imagination and marketplace acceptance!

ELECTRONIC PUBLISHING PRODUCTS

Here are some specific products you'll find:

A **directory** of a certain body of names and addresses, accompanied by descriptive information about those contacts. The same information may exist in print, but online it can be searched, manipulated ("all the addresses with CHEMISTRY in their names," for example), and labels ordered containing just the names you want.

References to all articles in nearly a thousand different journals and magazines. These "bibliographic" databases are the mainstay of the industry—they have been around for a long time, and many people think they are the only kind of online product.

The **full text of entire magazines or journals**. Not only are the references available, but the entire article as well. Portions or the entire text can be easily inspected, extracted or printed. Printing is also sometimes done "offline" and mailed later, at a lower cost.

Financial databases, containing details of a company's structure and business activities—its sales, locations, management names, information about branch offices, stock prices, credit status, etc. These are among the most expensive databases, because they support some decision-making which has the potential for very high profit.

Scientific data collections, sold online as databases, but also licensed to the manufacturers of laboratory equipment for integration with the software delivered to the purchaser of the instrument. Industry has always sold hardware combinations; the idea of selling a data collection (or "library") as part of an installed equipment sale is a newer but growing area.

Consumer databases of things like hotel accommodations, airline flight schedules, games, and other general interest databases, usually sold at reduced prices during the host systems' off-peak time (evenings, weekends). These online offerings are usually more "user friendly." The search and retrieval options are more limited, presented through Chinese restaurant-like "menus" of selection options (one from column A, one from column B, etc.).

Data collections from printed works such as handbooks. Often the data is sold integrated with software that not only delivers the data to the user but also offers various graphic display and manipulation options (chemical drawings, x/y axis charts, graphic displays specific to particular technical professions). This field is just getting started and is one of the more technical areas, since graphics are generally more complex than plain text. It is also one of the most exciting areas.

Estimates vary, but there are around 4,000 online products now, a ten-fold increase in the last five years or so.

THE KINDS OF JOBS AVAILABLE IN ELECTRONIC PUBLISHING

While looking at specific jobs, you should also be aware of the several different kinds of companies involved in the chain of events we are calling "electronic publishing". You will also need to know a few terms:

Publishers

The traditional book publisher is often still distributing in printed form the information that is electronically published. In fact, many or all of each product's expenses are often charged to the printed version, with the additional "electronic" income being regarded as "other income"—nice to have, of course, but not the driving reason for the existence of the publication.

Program director/publisher/acquisitions editor

Built on the similar position in conventional publishing, this is the person who negotiates contracts, does strategic planning, has bottom-line responsibility for the department or division, and, in general, is responsible for the business decisions. Previous experience in performing the same job for printed publications would, of course, be relevant, but so would an extremely broad exposure to many publishing areas—remember, electronic publishing is important because it takes new looks at traditional publishing.

Product manager

This person may have a variety of titles. The role usually includes primary responsibility for awareness of the marketplace (or marketplaces) where the product's audience is found. The skills are the same basic ones used by all marketers—knowledge of mailing lists, attendance at trade shows, cultivated networks of personal contacts, etc. Product management usually includes ultimate responsibility for the success or failure of the product, including negotiations with others (in-house and outside) whose actions may affect that success. At this stage of the game, libraries and major corporations are the most important customers, so having been a user of databases or computer systems in one of those environments would be a big help in identifying customers' needs and in relating to those customers.

Technical administrator/database administrator

This person is the main "computer type" in the group. Databases must be designed, host system capabilities must be understood, and, with the help of the product manager and others, translated into functional products. In addition, databases that are already "online" (that is, currently available through host systems) must be supported—tapes must be shipped out periodically, online data must be inspected, quality of the information must be sustained, and some means must exist for keeping track of the numerous magnetic tapes, documentation, and other odds and ends. Usually the technical administrator either does or supervises this activity.

Customer support (aka "hotline") person

This person is frequently the main customer contact, or at least is responsible for administering customer support. This is a critical position, and one in which the right person can gain considerable personal acclaim and gratitude by performing it well. The problem with online databases is that they don't actually exist—there is nothing you can show the customer, nothing to which the customer can react at the personal level. Rather, you are selling the *potential* of answering questions, of finding information. You can only succeed through continuous contact with the customers, thoughtful analysis of their specific needs and problems, and the cultivation of their personal loyalty to both yourself and your product. Interpersonal skills, obviously, are the key ingredient; teaching experience helps, too.

Sales manager

Just as in other fields, the sales manager has one main responsibility—to bring in sales dollars. To do this, the sales manager must devise just the right combination of tactics and personnel to ensure that sales forecasts are met. Often, the sales manager's compensation is directly related to the sales dollars which come in. There is little credit for "trying hard"—results are the key criterion. In the case of databases, this is a difficult assignment, because sales in growth areas are very difficult to forecast, and there is little past experience that is applicable to this particular sort of product. The customers' learning curve is also a factor—you cannot bring in real sales until the customers understand the product sufficiently to know when it meets their needs, and there are few proven tactics for speeding up this learning curve.

Host Systems

A host system is simply a company that operates a huge computer facility, one which not only stores large masses of information (databases), but also maintains hundreds of incoming telephone lines, and supports the programs which allow the customers at the other ends of those telephone lines to access particular databases. In effect (though the actual business arrangements vary), the publisher rents a part of the host system's computer in order to give its customers a place to use the publication (database). The host system also owns the software that lets customers make inquiries against the database; part of the cost of using the information is shared with the host as a fee for that software.

Producer contact/producer liaison

This function is critical. The publisher is the source of a specific database, but the host system is selling a service consisting of its own unique combination of databases and system capabilities that distinguishes it from its competitors. The producer liaison constantly balances the sometimes conflicting needs of the publishers with those of the host system. Typically, one such person is responsible for a group of publishers whose products are complementary. His or her role includes the packaging of those databases into a coherent "product family" to be marketed as part of the host system's package.

Sales manager

Very similar to the publisher's sales manager. In this case, the product being sold is the host system's package of services.

Customer support

Even more important—and considerably more difficult—than at a publishing house. The publisher only has to answer questions about one or two databases—the host system's customer support person must be knowledgeable about hundreds of databases, each with its own quirks. This person is an extremely skilled online "searcher," a skill usually learned in a school of library science or through years of experience in searching databases at, for example, a busy corporate or university library. The more frequently a person searches, the better his or her online support skills. In general, technical search questions come to the host system, while questions about the content of a database are directed to the publisher.

Networks

Though computers can easily "talk" to each other over standard, voice grade telephone lines, it is expensive to use standard long distance lines for this purpose. Therefore, this type of communication is usually done via a separate system, one that transmits only digital information between computers. The network is usually reached by dialing a local "node" (really just a local telephone number) that connects to the larger network. Usually the user of an "online" database pays a single charge to the host system; the host system then pays out a portion of this money to the publisher and to the network.

The positions available in network firms are beyond the scope of this article; networks are really a specialized kind of computer service bureau, not a deliberate part of the publishing process.

Other Positions At Publishers

Publishers operate offices in which they must employ an army of secretaries, receptionists, administrative assistants, and other support staff. The electronic publishing group is no exception. However, in the case of electronic publishing, you will find that these positions offer a greater than average potential for either career advancement or job enhancement. Aptitudes for handling customer questions, using databases, helping with trade show arrangements, handling unconventional record keeping assignments, etc., are quickly recognized and supported by managers—there is simply too great a variety of work needed in this field to expect that it will fall cleanly into standard "job descriptions".

WHAT I LOOK FOR IN APPLICANTS

As in any job, previous experience is always an advantage. But since electronic publishing is brand new, few applicants come in with really relevant experience.

On the other hand, an applicant's handling of the interview itself is critical. Any staff member will spend a great deal of time explaining things—design ideas to other staff, product features to customers, what work we need done to outside contractors. So I am always looking for people who have a full command of the language, who can express not only general ideas, but can develop an idea using specific, relevant examples, and have the knack of choosing exactly the right word. Electronic publishing extends the power of words geometrically, so someone in the field must have a healthy respect for it.

I also look for a person who gets excited about doing something new. *I* still get excited about electronic publishing, and I want people in the group who share that enthusiasm.

I also look for at least minimal computer literacy, especially in a work context. I want people who regard the computer as a helpful appliance, not as a number cruncher or data handling machine. The ability to relate to an inanimate device through a keyboard should feel very natural—in an odd way, I feel that a pianist has this same sense of interaction, giving selected instructions through a keyboard and producing something amazing by doing so.

I would be impressed by someone who has been a project leader. Any kind of project—community service, school, scientific research—that requires managing a large number of events over a fairly long time span. Electronic publishing projects tend to get rather complicated—I want people who are stimulated by projects of this scale.

HOW TO FIND THE OPPORTUNITIES

1) Take a look at the journals where database products are advertised (*Online, Online Review,* and *Database* are good starting places). Look at the ads and the articles—you will get a feel for the kinds of issues which are important to our customers.

2) Review the catalogs of the major host systems. (DIALOG, BRS and MEAD DATA are some of the main ones serving libraries; also look at THE SOURCE, COMPUSERVE, and GENIE—these host systems are more consumer-oriented.)

3) Do some reading about the various electronic mail systems. These systems are increasingly being used as the distribution means (directly or through connections to other systems) for online information of many kinds.

4) Go to your librarian, specifically the reference librarian. Librarians are currently the primary market for online databases, and they know all about them. Ask the librarian how databases are used, which ones are important, why they are important, how they handle the charges they have to pay for using them, how they deal with the clients whose questions require the use of a database, and any other questions you can think of. Not only will you learn a great deal about databases, but the ease with which you are able to do such an interview will be a test of your aptitude for dealing with this kind of customer.

5) Be an online client yourself—ask the librarian if you can request a "search" on some part of the online database world. See how it feels to be a client. (There may be a charge for this—think of it as a career investment.)

6) Get yourself a password to one of the easier systems (see above for the list). Browse around in the system, see how much information you can discover. If you find you are able to do it instinctively, without looking at the instructions very often, you probably have a very good feel for using online information. If you enjoy the experience, electronic publishing may be the very thing for you!

Gary Craig is program director of Wiley's electronic publishing group, under the company's scientific and technical publishing area. He joined the company in 1978 as library sales manager, and his initial exposure to online information was his work in developing the database containing all of Wiley's product information, supporting catalogs, newsletters, and other marketing needs. When he learned in 1981 that an electronic publishing group was being formed, he eagerly volunteered to handle the marketing for that unit, and a few years later was given the job of running the group.

Before coming to Wiley, he worked at McGraw-Hill and Harcourt Brace Jovanovich in several areas, including management of domestic and foreign sales and as director of international advertising. He majored in both English and journalism and did additional graduate work in dramatic arts.

Mr. Craig is active in several industry associations, and speaks frequently on subjects related to the development and marketing of electronic publications. He is also the author of several published articles in these areas.

CHAPTER FOUR

The Mission Of Religious Publishing

By

Steve Halliday, Editor
Multnomah Press

Publishing might seem like a strange business for people who revere a text that warns "Of making many books there is no end, and much study wearies the body."

But strange or not—and despite the warning from the biblical book Ecclesiastes—religious publishing is big business these days. It's estimated that 150 million religious books were purchased in the United States alone last year, and that nearly 2,500 new religious titles made their way into bookstores. Add to that the estimated 100 million Bibles that Americans bought in 1986, and it quickly becomes clear that religious publishing is booming.

Religious books and products seem to be everywhere. Where do they all come from?

The 1987 Literary Market Place: The Directory of American Book Publishing lists 48 Catholic publishers, five Islamic, 38 Jewish, 87 Protestant and 59 "others." While these numbers are not exact—many companies are listed in more than one category and others are not mentioned at all—the LMP listings nevertheless give a good sense of the size of today's religious publishing field.

But so what if it's big...and growing? "Secular" publishers are bigger still. Why make the choice to work in the religious publishing field when an even larger world awaits?

THE DISTINCTIVE ASPECTS OF RELIGIOUS PUBLISHING

Many make a career in religious publishing because—as hard as it is to imagine in these cynical times—they truly believe that what they publish is <u>true</u> and that it will significantly improve the lives of those who read it. Often their beliefs are reinforced by the mailman. "A couple of months ago, a wonderful thing happened to us," began a letter we received not long ago. "A package, forwarded to our new home in San Clemente, arrived from the Northwest. Inside, a book that, chapter by chapter, made us think. It made us realize that we had some changing to do. We are in the process of making those changes—changes in our priorities, our goals and minor changes in what we believe..."

Religious publishers sometimes point to a clearly-defined <u>mission</u> to explain their choice of career: They publish because they are convinced that's what they ought to do. In crasser (but I hope not irreverent) terms, they think of God as their ultimate boss. Evangelical Christians are especially prone to thinking in such terms. The Evangelical Christian Publishers Association—a publishing group of about 60 members—prints the following "Mission Statement" at the front of its 1987 membership handbook:

> The Evangelical Christian Publishers Association is an international, not-for-profit trade organization serving its industry by promoting excellence and professionalism, sharing relevant data, stimulating Christian fellowship, raising the effectiveness of member houses, and expanding the market for their products.

It doesn't take a major *Publisher's Weekly* poll to guess that not too many general trade publishers would say the same thing.

That's an important consideration to make when pondering whether religious publishing is right for you. While not all religious houses operate with those kinds of convictions, it's wise to find out whether the house you're considering *does*. If you join an organization which thrives on goals you don't share, each hour you remain there might seem agonizingly long... unless management senses your lack of enthusiasm and decides to summarily curtail those hours.

Religious publishers are generally small to medium-sized-except for the few giants in the field, such as Zondervan, Word and Thomas Nelson—and many consciously try to create a "family" atmosphere at the workplace. Editors know and talk to marketing people, marketers have lunch with bookkeepers, warehouse personnel drive to work with production people. Many of those committed to religious publishing simply like the "feel" of a smaller operation; they *like* thinking of it as "family." But just as some family temperaments are more pleasant than others, so are some publishing families more affable than others. Doing some preliminary research could spare you from walking into a divorce.

Last, the driving force behind religious publishers differs widely from house to house. Some are market-driven, others editorial-driven, still others management-driven. Some are business-minded, others ministry-minded. Some are controlled by outside boards (who can decide whether the press can or cannot do a certain book) or by stockholders, some are independent. Some are for-profit, others nonprofit. All these factors will greatly influence the kinds of books the company publishes, the style of management it utilizes, the market it serves, the type of person who works there and a host of other traits.

THE DEPARTMENTS IN A RELIGIOUS PUBLISHING HOUSE

So far I've stressed the uniqueness of religious publishing. But it is, after all, still publishing, and therefore has much in common with secular houses. The departmental division of labor found at most publishers generally holds true for religious publishers, as well: editorial, marketing, production, and bookkeeping.

Editorial Department

While every company has an editorial staff, those staffs may differ substantially from press to press in number and organization. Many houses have but one editor. There are six at Multnomah Press. A large company like Zondervan will have multiple positions (at last count: five trade editors and three academic editors in the book division—along with support staff and editorial assistants—and about five editors in the Bible division).

What those editors do will also vary according to company policy. Some groups use **acquisitions editors,** whose job is to scour the countryside for authors who can contribute to the success of the press. These editors do no hands-on work to the manuscripts they contract; once the book is in house, they're back out on the trail, searching for other prospects.

You might find all types of editors at a religious house—**manuscript editors, copy editors, senior editors, managing editors,** etc. But it's most likely you'll find a generalist, someone who does a little of everything—from contracting new manuscripts to line editing to copy editing to copy writing. That's another reason many professionals choose to stay in the field: the diversity of workload. Far from the sometimes crushing pressure of megapublishing in New York, editors of smaller religious houses can often look forward to some (not much) travel, discovering new authors, trying their hand at copy writing (sometimes trying it repeatedly) and a host of other tasks.

There's often a downside, however. In part because of the small size of most religious publishers, an editor should not look to become wealthy—salaries range from $15,000 to $30,000 a year, depending on the house and the kind of editorial tasks demanded.

Another minus on the ledger can also, occasionally, be regarded with some humor. It is unfortunately true that issues of faith, in addition to bringing hope and comfort, also attract crackpots, charlatans and oddballs. From time to time I receive an especially outrageous proposal that gets added to a special file devoted to such treasures. I have proposals describing a "direct connection between the crucifixion of Jesus Christ and the assassination of John F. Kennedy," books describing the prayers of common houseplants, a novel advocating the Christian virtues of snuffing drug dealers with poison dart guns, a book of odd verse billed as "a series of poems such as Christians seldom get a chance to read" and a few which are just plain incomprehensible: "A best-selling book is the focus of many, but who do we love? Global abstinence from mid-March through mid-April could virtually eradicate gonorrhea, and more. We have the scientific knowledge—but how do we communicate?"

An editor of religious titles must often wade through hundreds of such curiosities in order to find the single, unsolicited "gem" of a manuscript that is actually publishable. And unsolicited manuscripts do pour in—hundreds each month. Editors are often responsible to look them over (*hastily*, it happily turns out).

Editors of religious houses have a unique set of questions to ask when reviewing manuscripts for possible publication: Does this manuscript have a sense of integrity (not just, "will it sell?")? What are its biblical values (if it's a Christian house)? Is the author committed to our values? What is the "felt need" here? Normally, religious books must overcome the "so what" factor—they must hold out the promise of significantly improving the reader's life. Rarely does a religious publisher print something that "merely" entertains.

Preparation For A Career In Editorial

What kind of person makes a good religious books editor and what sort of background is helpful?

It's surprising to discover that many, if not most, editors in the religious field have little or no formal training in journalism or theology. At a recent informal meeting in Colorado of a dozen editors from various religious houses, only one had any training in journalism. Some were trained in English, others in business or something equally unrelated.

Many people get their start by working in bookstores—I don't know what the percentages are, but I would guess they're high.If you want to get into religious publishing, and you don't know where to begin, get a job at a religious bookstore. There are more than 3,400 such stores in one organization alone (the Christian Booksellers Association). Sweep floors, shelve books, wait on customers—it'll give you a feel for what's "hot" in the religious market, as well as for the kinds of questions that book buyers ask.

It's critical that you get a feel early on for what will work and what won't in the religious field. Editors are often considered the "priests" of their companies. Frequently they set the tone for what their press publishes—its style, substance and market. That's not to say they dictate what goes on! But they often do have a major voice in shaping the publishing program of a religious house.

Marketing Department

If editors are the priests of their companies, marketers might be considered the "prophets," for they must proclaim the virtues and strengths of the press's product.

Marketing considerations have become increasingly important to the success of any religious house in the past few years. More and more often, authors are more interested in the specific marketing plans for their books than about the press's editorial plans for the same manuscript. That's a significant change.

It would be wise for someone interested in the marketing side of religious publishing to get as much training in marketing and advertising as possible. Increasing sophistication of techniques and reliance on market surveys are fast becoming the norm; that wasn't true even ten years ago. Those who know how to apply modern marketing methods to a religious product will find far more open doors awaiting them than those who rely on native cleverness.

Still, young marketers must remember that certain rules and etiquettes that don't exist elsewhere apply in the religious world. Consumers have an ingrained sense that books of faith ought to reflect a higher moral standard than prevailing mores in the secular world. (That is why, for example, Jim and Tammy Fae Bakker made such rich fodder for headlines and wisecracks; people expect more from a personality espousing religion.) Many a marketer has taken a financial bath by forgetting this aspect of the business.

As in most areas, marketers generally draw a larger salary than do their editorial counterparts—perhaps 10-25% more. But again, you can expect lower pay in the religious field than in the general market. Many religious houses see themselves as "ministries," and exist not so much to make a profit as to get their message out. And that's reflected in pay scales. Those who believe in the message are often willing to pay the price. But if you're not one of the convinced, you'd probably be better off working elsewhere.

The Marketing department offers a wide variety of job opportunities. There are **telephone marketing specialists**—who sell to bookstores over the phone); **publicists**—who apprise periodicals of new releases, arrange for media interviews with published authors and, depending on their creativity, may perform many other informational tasks; **special markets coordinators, sales representatives** and **sales managers, advertising coordinators** and others. One way to find out about the workings of a particular Marketing department is to contact the publicist. While she or he is usually overworked, getting out information (and sometimes propaganda) is the substance of the job. So ask them—at least you'll learn how pleasant professionals can sound even when that's not their first inclination.

Production And Bookkeeping Departments

Production and bookkeeping functions are undoubtedly the publishing tasks most similar to their secular counterparts. If there is a "religious" way to keep ledgers and print books, I don't know what it would be. Still, working in a religious house may significantly effect both pay scales and working environments. The jobs are the same, as is the way they are performed, but the surroundings in which they are performed may make an enormous difference to the one doing them.

WHY WORK FOR A RELIGIOUS HOUSE?

Working for a religious book publisher is not for everyone. The pay is generally lower, as is the "status." While American society in general still gives a nod to issues of faith, it's usually a sleepy nod. Religion just doesn't seem as important to many people as it once did.

But for those who believe that human problems are truly spiritual problems and that the human soul is worth nourishing and strengthening through a healthy faith, religious publishing can furnish a vibrant and rewarding option. And to put uneasy minds at ease, I'm convinced of one thing: You won't starve.

STEVE HALLIDAY

In his current position, which he assumed in 1984, Mr. Halliday's duties include conceptual, substantive, and line-by-line editing, plus acquisitions within and administrative oversight of assigned book categories. He has directed several series, including "Living Theology," Authentic Christianity," "Classics of Faith and Devotion" and MP's booklet line. He was formerly editor for the Multnomah School of the Bible's monthly magazine, *Message.*

From 1980 to 1982, he was editor for the quarterly *Seminarian,* published by Bethel Theological Seminary. Concurrently (in 1981 & 1982) he was editor of *Diakrisis,* an occasional publication of their student senate. He began his career as education reporter for the *Beloit Daily News,* a Beloit, Wisconsin daily.

Mr. Halliday received his BA in journalism and Spanish from the University of Wisconsin-Eau Claire (Wisconsin) in 1979.

CHAPTER FIVE

The Special World of Scientific, Technical And Medical Publishing

By

Robert E. Baensch, Vice President of Marketing
Macmillan Publishing Company

Scientific, technical and medical publishing—**STM publishing** in the trade—is a fascinating and different kind of publishing. Why? First, because the information is made available in a variety of formats or packages (not just "books") to a broad spectrum of very special readers. Second, those readers (or markets) are further divided into numerous special segments with very distinct interests. For example, while engineers, in general, are a significant market, each area of engineering specialization—electrical, chemical, civil, mechanical, etc.—represents readers who are interested in completely different kinds of "engineering" information. Similarly, medical publishing breaks down into specific subject areas like surgery, nursing, etc. But then each of these groups is further divided into sub-specialties—e.g., cardiovascular, plastic or neurosurgeons, intensive care, geriatric or maternal/child nurses.

While assembling and publishing the great variety of information for even one broad category of specialists is, therefore, a daunting task, it is further complicated by the different "time value" placed on the information, which means it must be published in different formats. For example, new scientific, technical and/or medical research may be presented as speeches or lectures during meetings and then published as proceedings. Such research documentation may mature into journal or magazine articles, but it may also published as *monographs*, short books on specialized topics. A group of doctors or engineers may get together and write a handbook as a comprehensive reference work.

In order to stay current, publishers specializing in areas in which new research and new results are almost a daily occurence often need to release books in three-ring binders so that quarterly or semi-annual updates can be issued and inserted (without having to reprint the entire volume). Furthermore, the personal computer has provided two new physical formats for publishing information—the PC software diskette and the CD-ROM disc (Compact Disc Read Only Memory), which can store up to 250,000 pages of reference information.

THE EDITORIAL PROCESS

The **publisher** or **editorial director** determines the subject areas, type of publications and number of new books to be published each year. The **editor-in-chief, editors** and/or **sponsoring editors** then go out and find the authors who are most knowledgeable in and able to write about the special subject areas. The editors also rely on expert **advisors** and **editorial boards** in these specialized areas to help them select new topics and authors. The continuous challenge is to not simply stay current but actually stay *ahead* of new developments, a task complicated by the time constraints inherent in the publishing process.

The entry-level position is **editorial assistant**. Sponsoring editors usually join a house with a university science degree and have had at least a year or two experience as travelling sales representatives.

In Trade book publishing, the **literary or author's agent** maintains most of the immediate contact and correspondence with the authors. In professional and reference publishing, it is the editor and editorial assistant who establish and maintain contact with authors working on new manuscripts. They also manage the timing and the author's preparation of revised editions of previously-published books. (In contrast to Trade publishing, many STM reference works are revised every two or three years.—a "classic" handbooks may be in its second, fifth, fifteenth or twenty fifth edition.)

PRODUCTION AND DESIGN

Once the manuscript has been written, the **copy editor** and **designers** prepare the text for composition and printing. The Production department at an STM publisher faces many more challenges than a comparable department at a general trade house because of the detailed tables, graphs, charts and illustrations required in all of the books it publishes. They also tend to use computer-based composition systems more extensively—authors usually submit their manuscripts on diskettes. Desk top publishing or electronic publishing has opened new career opportunities in STM publishing houses because both their authors and their readers are computer literate.

Low printing quantities for individual books and journals are the rule at STM publishers—the typical house may release 30 to 50 new titles a year but print an average of only 1,750 copies of each. One reason is the very limited marketplaces for such specialized works. A book on open heart surgery cannot be marketed to the entire universe of 22,000 surgeons, just to 1,500 cardiovascular surgeons. A monograph on microcircuit design may only be of interest to 2,000 of 140,000 electrical & electronic engineers. Another important reason is the time factor—

most copies need to be sold within 18 months; after that, new research and developments in the field will invariably cause the publication to be out of date.

Entry-level production positions are **copy editor, production assistant** and **design assistant**. Computer literacy and word processing skills are mandatory.

MARKETING

For each book an STM publisher releases, the single segment of potential readers within the much larger general STM universe must be identified and reached, which often involves a variety of distribution channels. The printing quantities are small. The average list price high. The typical STM Marketing/Sales department that must contend with these facts of life consists of a team of specialists responsible for the following very different "marketing channels":

• *Sales representatives* who call on customers, libraries and bookstores and attend numerous special conventions and meetings. There are over 21,000 bookstores in the U.S.—only about 200 actually stock and sell STM books.

• *Telemarketing staffers* who call customers, bookstores and librarians to offer new titles, backlist titles of special interest or build subscription renewals.

• The *Direct Mail Marketing department*—the largest and most effective way of selling scientific, technical and medical books. Brochures, catalogs and a variety of special mailing pieces are created in this department and mailed out to targeted mailing lists.

• The *Advertising department* places space advertising to promote certain titles or groups of titles in the journals or magazines read by the targeted audiences. Again, it is a focused effort—promoting new books via a targeted vehicle, one that most effectively reaches only those individuals interested in the narrowly-focused subject matter.

• The *Public Relations department* tries to make sure that travelling authors attending or speaking at special meetings or conventions receive the appropriate backup information and promotion from the publisher to help generate sales. It is a way of developing added value visibility for a book at minimal cost to the publisher.

• *Conventions and conferences* always have exhibit space for publishers and manufacturers of equipment of interest to the target audience. It is important for publishers to exhibit at such shows—to sell books, meet with authors and hear about new subject areas for next year's books.

• The *International or Export Sales department* plays an especially important role because STM publishers enjoy the largest international sales volume. Whereas the average American publisher exports 6% of its books, the average STM publisher exports 27%. This is mainly because English is the international language for most scientific, technical and medical subject areas. And because scientists and doctors around the world are interested in the research and developments carried out in the United States.

Opportunities for entry-level jobs are greatest in the Marketing/Sales department. <u>Sales representative</u> is still the best entry into STM publishing (although many smaller houses use shared-commission, independent sales groups rather than in-house sales staff). The Direct Marketing department provides opportunities for <u>copywriters</u>, <u>graphic designers</u> and <u>product managers</u>. The <u>promotion manager</u> in a STM publishing house is expected to know all about cost-effective uses of the many mailing lists available. Due to the increasing expense of putting a salesperson on the road and the geographic spread of its bookstore customers, more STM publishers are developing telemarketing staffs to sell to stores and libraries by telephone.

OFFICE ADMINISTRATION AND DISTRIBUTION

Scientific, technical and medical publishing involves a large number of new and backlist titles—some STM publishers have as many as 3,000 to 5,000 titles in their catalogs, books that are sold as single copies to individuals. This means a lot of paperwork and record keeping—careful sales documentation, inventory control and cost accounting. Due to the sheer volume of paperwork, a micro-, mini- or even a mainframe computer will probably be utilized for accounting, royalty records, inventory control, customer files, mailing lists and other related documentation.

The larger STM publishing houses have employees in Accounting, Data Processing, Credit/Collections, Invoicing, Customer Service, Distribution and Warehouse departments. Some of the above functions are combined in the smaller publishing houses.

There are many entry-level positions in these service functions at STM publishers. And unlike the larger general trade houses, it *is* possible to move from the service area to marketing, sales or other departments.

UNIVERSITY PRESS AND PROFESSIONAL ASSOCIATIONS

Some university presses specialize in STM publishing and, therefore, offer excellent entry-level opportunities, so it would be a good idea to review the catalogs of the major university presses, such as Johns Hopkins, MIT, etc. *(Most of these are listed in the Job Opportunities Databank in Section IV of this volume—Ed.)*

Many of the professional associations and societies in the scientific, technical and medical areas have their own publishing programs. The American Medical Association, for example, has a larger journal and book publishing program than many commercial houses and the American Institute of Physics is a major publisher of both journals and books. So if a specific subject area within the STM community interests you, identify the pertinent associations and societies that exist and determine if they have a publishing program. A book like Gale Research's <u>Directory of Associations</u>, available in most medium-sized libraries, will help you. One does not have to be a member of such an organization to search out career opportunities within these very large professional publishing operations.

REFERENCES

Association of American Publishers, Professional and Scholarly Publishing Division, 220 East 23rd Street, New York, NY 10016

Association for Information and Image Management, 1100 Wayne Avenue, Silver Spring, MD 20910

EP&P, The Magazine for Electronic Publishing, Maclean Hunter Publishing Corp., 300 West Adams Street, Chicago, IL 60606

International Group of Scientific, Technical and Medical Publishers Association, Keizersgracht 462, 1016 GE Amsterdam, the Netherlands

Publish: The How-to Magazine of Desk Top Publishing, 501 Second Street, Ste. 600, San Francisco, CA 94107

Scholarly Publishing, University of Toronto Press, Toronto, Canada M5S 1A6

Small Press: The Magazine for Independent/Desk Top Publishing, 11 Ferry Lane West, Westport, CT 06880

Society for Scholarly Publishing, 2000 Florida Avenue NW, Suite 305, Washington, DC 20009

ROBERT E. BAENSCH

In his current position, Mr. Baensch is responsible for the review and development of marketing, research and new programs for all of Macmillan's publishing units, including the special USIA English Language Teaching By Broadcast project. The G. K. Hall Library Reference and Information Science Publishing Division also reports to him and he is responsible for the overall research and development of electronic publishing for Macmillan.

Previously, Mr. Baensch was vice president of marketing for the McGraw-Hill International Book Company and, from 1980 through 1982, the president of Springer-Verlag New York, Inc. He was vice president and director of Harper & Row's International Division for 12 years. He began his career at McGraw-Hill in 1960 as a sales representative and went on to be an editor, manager of the foreign rights department, editorial director of the International Division and, in 1967, manager of Information Systems Research and Development.

Mr. Baensch was chairman of the AAP international division and a former member of the AAP board of directors. He is currently chairman of the AAP professional and scholarly publishing division executive council. He was one of two U.S. delegates to the executive council and chairman of the education and training committee of the International Publishers Association from 1978-1982. He is currently chairman of the innovations committee for the International Group of Scientific, Technical and Medical Publishers.

He is presently on the faculty of the Center for Publishing at New York University, the University of Denver Publishing Institute and the Stanford University Publishing Program.

CHAPTER SIX

Working For A University Press

By

Herbert J. Addison, Vice President and Executive Editor
Oxford University Press

University presses differ from each other almost as much as commercial publishers differ from each other. But all university presses have the same basic publishing mission: to search out and publish works of scholarship that will contribute to the world of knowledge. Some presses do only such "scholarly" books. Others, however, publish a wide range of titles—some indistinguishable from those produced by the commercial houses—but still reserve some portions of their lists for scholarly books.

Many university presses began as vehicles for publishing the works of the faculties of their associated universities. As time passed, however, they began to reach beyond their own campuses in an effort to publish the best works they could find, wherever they were written. Today, it is not unusual for a local university press to compete with a distant one for a book by a professor who teaches just across campus.

To fund their growing editorial independence and survive the financial problems that many universities themselves now face in a period of stable enrollment and Federal cutbacks in education, university presses have had to become more financially independent. Some still receive subsidies from their parent institutions, but many must completely fund their own operations. The larger presses may even earn a surplus, which they use to fund future books...

and thus preserve their nonprofit status. Later we shall look at some of the problems university press people face as a result of today's financial realities.

As with all book publishers—commercial or nonprofit, large or small—university presses employ people in the four main areas of publishing: editorial, production, marketing, and finance. Let's look at the key jobs in each area and see how they differ (if they do) from similar jobs in commercial houses. We will also discuss the usual entry-level positions in each department.

THE EDITORIAL DEPARTMENT

The Sponsoring Editor

The publishing process begins when a university press finds an author with a publishable manuscript and signs a contract with him or her to publish it. The task of finding authors and signing book contracts is the responsibility of the **sponsoring editor**.

Sponsoring editors are usually assigned by academic discipline. In the larger university presses, an editor may work with authors in a single discipline; in smaller presses, the editor may well be responsible for several.

This method of assigning books and authors already suggests an important difference between sponsoring editors in university presses and acquisition editors at commercial houses: The sponsoring editor will be seeking manuscripts almost exclusively from college professors.

There is keen competition for authors even in the genteel world of university presses. Most press editors, therefore, can't afford to wait for manuscripts to arrive in the morning mail, so they frequently travel to university campuses in search of publishable manuscripts. The editor may make some appointments in advance, but will probably leave time to see professors without appointments—it's called "knocking on doors," and all good editors are skilled at finding out about a prospect's writing plans without wasting too much of either party's time.

Once a likely manuscript is found, the editor must decide if it merits publication. Most university press editors rely on expert academic reviewers to assess whether a manuscript is right for that press. The editor sends the reviewer the manuscript and a specific list of questions about it. The reviewer is generally paid an honorarium for his or her services.

If the reviewer thinks the manuscript worthy and recommends publication, the editor must then propose it to his superiors. Many university presses have a board of advisors—senior professors at the press's university who meet periodically to consider new proposals—whose imprimatur is needed on any book proposal before it goes to contract. They read the academic review the editor has commissioned for each book and will probably ask the editor about the book in the meeting. If they approve the proposal, the editor prepares the contract to send to the author.

The editor's job, seemingly done, actually begins in earnest when the author signs the contract. Reviewers frequently suggest revisions to strengthen the books they are sent: If a specific book is accepted by the board of advisors, they may have done so with the understanding that the author will incorporate the reviewer's suggestions. The editor will work with the author during this revision stage and may make his own constructive editorial suggestions as well.

Sometimes an editor will have only a portion of a manuscript to review but, because of competition from other presses for especially promising books from well-known professors, will have to make a decision on the basis of such a fragment. If the academic reviewer of the partial manuscript likes it and if the board of advisors approves it, the editor will probably be even more involved in the final development of such a manuscript than he would in the case of a complete manuscript submission.

Do sponsoring editors in university presses usually have degrees in the subject areas in which they work? How can someone who is responsible for finding publishable mathematics manuscripts do the job without being trained in math? There is no simple answer to either question. Many university press editors do have degrees in their assigned subjects, but many others do not. Even editors specializing in highly technical subjects may have liberal arts degrees. Some press directors feel, however, that a sure instinct for good authors and manuscripts is more important (and more necessary in almost all cases) than a degree in a given subject. A good editor soon learns the best schools in the assigned discipline, who are the important researchers, who are the reliable reviewers. By putting all this knowledge to work, an editor can succeed despite the lack of a relevant degree.

But for those seeking their first job as a sponsoring editor at a university press, having a degree in an appropriate subject area will probably be considered a plus. Some presses will hire people directly into a sponsoring editorial job without previous publishing experience. Others will hire the person at a lower level—as an **editorial assistant** to a sponsoring editor, perhaps, or as a **manuscript editor**—and then promote faster if the person does well.

The other publishing position that probably offers the best training for someone aspiring to a job as a sponsoring editor is that of **sales representative** for a college textbook publisher. Their work takes them to college campuses daily, and they have to learn about disciplines and curricula, even do some scouting for manuscripts for their companies. As we've seen, this kind of work is the basis for the work of a sponsoring editor.

When the sponsoring editor is satisfied that a manuscript under contract is sufficiently developed to be published, it is sent to the **manuscript editor**, whose functions we will discuss next.

The Manuscript Editor

Even the most meticulous academic author is likely to misspell words and commit grammatical miscues. It is the job of the manuscript editor—sometimes called the copy editor—to catch the misspellings, grammatical errors, and myriad other mistakes that invariably creep into even the best-prepared manuscripts. It is also fair to say that some academic authors need more than a little "light editing." In these cases, the manuscript editor may edit the work quite heavily, even rewrite portions that require it.

Besides such copy editing chores, the manuscript editor may also mark the manuscript for composition, which involves indicating the different elements on the manuscript—chapter titles, subheads in the text, illustrations, etc.—so that the compositor will set them correctly (in accordance with the design provided by the designer).

It is essential that the author see the edited manuscript before it is set in type, because it is always possible that inaccuracies were introduced in the editing phase. This is an especially important requirement for highly technical books where the substitution of a seemingly-synonymous word can drastically alter the author's meaning in the specialized language of that discipline.

Though authors may occasionally grumble about the intrusions of the manuscript editor, most are glad that their manuscripts passed through the hands of such a professional before they were printed and released for the world to read.

People often ask the same question of manuscript editors at university presses that they ask of sponsoring editors: Do you need a specific degree to work on specific books? It is less likely that a manuscript editor has a relevant degree. Most work on manuscripts that cover a range of disciplines.

Manuscript editors will frequently tend to specialize in a related group of disciplines, however—the physical sciences, humanities, or social sciences, for example. No matter which disciplines an editor works in, there is the pleasure of lifelong learning such work affords one. For the manuscript editor at a university press, a college education literally never ends.

The best training for the job of manuscript editor is to begin as an **editorial assistant**. This entry-level job involves learning how proofs flow between the compositor, the press, and the author, and keeping records of the flow of proofs, illustrations, and the other editorial elements that make up the finished book. Eventually editorial assistants begin to work on manuscripts and learn the editing skills necessary to move up.

When a manuscript has been edited, marked, and approved by the author, the manuscript editor sends it to the Production department.

THE PRODUCTION PROCESS

Production people work with outside suppliers—paper manufacturers, printers, and binders—to turn a manuscript into a finished book. The production function is nearly identical in a university press or commercial house—university press books can be as simple or complex as commercial books and require the same kind of skill to produce them well—so production jobs, therefore, are probably more like the same positions in a commercial house than any university press jobs.

Because so many university press books are important scholarly works expected to have lasting value, the production people pay special attention to the materials used in their books, especially the paper on which they're printed. Paper that contains acid from its original pulp will turn yellow and brittle over time. To be sure that their books will last, university press production people buy acid-free paper; many are beginning to indicate that specific books are on acid-free paper by printing a special symbol on the copyright page for quick reference by librarians.

The principle entry-level job in the Production department—the same as the commercial houses—is **production assistant**. It is the training ground that will enable you to acquire specific knowledge of the kinds of books that a given university press is doing and the skills needed to produce them.

Increasingly, candidates for production jobs are arriving with degrees from some of the fine colleges and universities that have programs in printing and production. This kind of degree is a definite advantage for those who are seeking production jobs in the larger university presses.

While the editors and production people have been preparing the manuscript and transforming it into final book form, the Marketing department staff has also been busy.

THE MARKETING DEPARTMENT

University press books are special: They require specialized marketing. As a general rule, they don't sell through the average bookstore in the same numbers as books from commercial houses. They *do* sell through college bookstores and through specialty bookstores in larger cities. But the major markets for university press books are libraries, institutions, and the world of academia—markets best reached through mail promotion, not via bookstores.

As a result of this necessary market focus, university presses usually have large Advertising and Promotion departments but may have no salaried sales force at all. (This is not true of *all* university presses. Some presses band together and share a salesperson. Others use commissioned sales representatives—who are paid for what they sell but otherwise cost the press nothing. Still others make arrangements with one of the large, commercial publishers. In this case, the commercial house's sales force takes on the books published by the university press and presents them to booksellers during their regular visits.)

To produce the many different mailing pieces directed at libraries and individual academics, most university presses need **advertising copywriters, graphic designers,** and **advertising managers** (who must know what mailing lists to buy for which kinds of books). Many of these same people will produce the advertisements that appear in scholarly journals and, in many cases, in the quality intellectual journals and magazines that may be utilized if a book is believed to have a broader audience.

Smaller university presses may use freelance people to produce the mailing pieces rather than incur the cost of a full-time staff. The larger presses, on the other hand, may have specific people on staff to perform each specialized task.

A few of the larger presses do have their own sales forces. These sales representatives call on bookstores and sell the new and backlist titles much as their counterparts at the commercial houses do. The principal difference between their roles is that the press representative will tend to call on the larger and better bookstores in major cities—as well as the larger university bookstores—where university press books have their greatest appeal.

The usual entry-level jobs in the Marketing department are **copywriter** and **sales representative.** For obvious reasons, there are more copywriter jobs open at any given time than sales jobs. Neither usually requires experience—though it can help getting into one of the larger presses—but both require a college degree.

THE FINANCIAL/ACCOUNTING DEPARTMENT

Most university presses have a Financial department or, at least, one person who is responsible for financial accounting and reporting. With the advent of computer billing and accounting, this person may also be responsible for the data processing functions. Any such position in the Financial department will almost always require a degree in accounting or finance.

THE PLEASURES OF A UNIVERSITY PRESS

Given all of the mobility that exists between publishing houses, I find one phenomenon most interesting: More people seem to move from commercial publishers to university presses than vice versa. While there's no empirical evidence to confirm the reason why, I think it likely that once someone has worked in the world of university press books, commercial publishing is much less attractive. The work is just as hard and the hours are just as long at a university press, but the intellectual rewards are greater.

There is something quite satisfying about working for an organization that is, first and foremost, committed to publishing books of unquestioned quality. The discussion in one of our editorial meetings is likely to sound something like this: "I know this book will not be a best seller, but it is an important book, so we should find a way of publishing it anyway."

Working for a university press will also keep you in touch with the academic world and, as I mentioned before, can constitute a kind of continuing college education. College professors are, as a general rule, stimulating authors whose books are a source of immense pride to those of us who work in the field.

But it should also be pointed out that the world of university presses is not all quiet browsing through scholarly manuscripts and afternoon teas with professors.

THE PROBLEMS OF UNIVERSITY PRESSES

University presses are chronically underfunded by their associated universities—if they are funded at all. They must find and publish the best scholarly works with modest budgets for people, production and marketing. As a result, university press people usually consider themselves overworked and underpaid. I won't comment on whether they are overworked. Who isn't? However, salaries in university presses vary widely, depending on the type of job and the location of the press. A press in a small university town may be able to attract good people at all levels for modest salaries. A press in a large city must compete with other publishers—including commercial houses—and will often pay equal starting salaries. But my guess is that the higher-level jobs in most university presses, regardless of location, probably pay somewhat less than equivalent jobs in commercial houses.

There is also intense competition between presses for the best scholarly works—this can drive up the cost of signing a given book, further straining the press's financial resources. In addition to the higher advances against royalties that might be necessary to sign-up an important new book, a press may have to commit to elaborate (and expensive) production and/or marketing efforts to insure the book's success. Working within the tight budget limitations which are the rule, rather than the exception, most presses must continually balance the desirability of any book against its cost...just like the commercial houses.

Despite these problems, university presses continue to attract some of the best people in the world of publishing. There is no reason to suppose that they will not go on doing so as long as they exist. And certainly a lot of us hope that they do.

HERBERT J. ADDISON

In his present position at Oxford University Press—one of the oldest university presses in the world—Mr. Addison is responsible for the Bible editorial program and for books on economics and business.

Prior to joining Oxford in 1978, Mr. Addison worked in commercial publishing, mostly on college textbooks. He began his career with Holt, Rinehart & Winston as a college traveler, was promoted first to sponsoring editor, then to editor-in-chief of the basic books unit. He later joined Thomas Y. Crowell Company as general manager of the College Textbook department. He has also worked for John Wiley & Sons as an executive editor in their College department.

He has a B.A. from the University of California at Berkeley and an M.A. from New York University.

CHAPTER SEVEN

Internships And Training Programs In Book Publishing

By

**Chester S. Logan, Consultant
(Formerly Vice President - Personnel
Harper & Row, Publishers, Inc.)**

If you want an accounting job in a publishing company, by all means get a good degree in accounting and try to acquire some experience in a leading public accounting firm.

If you aspire to a job in book production, some education and experience in the printing trades will improve your chances.

But if you're aiming at a job in the editorial or marketing functions of book publishing, your best credentials will be a good liberal arts education at the bachelor's degree level, some basic office skills, and a good measure of energy and curiosity.

What accounts for this difference? Publishers call it the <u>apprenticeship system</u>.

Traditionally, book publishers have considered hands-on, on-the-job experience the best way for neophytes to learn many of the basic functions of the business—particularly in editorial, design, and marketing. This apprenticeship system may seem old-fashioned compared to many other businesses, and in some ways it *is* inefficient, but no one has yet found a better way. Perhaps the survival of the apprenticeship tradition can be attributed to the fact that successful publishing depends so much on subjective judgment and taste, intuitive qualities that cannot be taught, but *can* be sharpened by experience. Of course, success in publishing also requires technical skills. Many of these skills can be learned on-the-job, but may be learned more quickly through structured training programs.

With all this in mind, let's look at the wide variety of training resources available to would-be and beginning publishers, and the internships that can speed up the process.

FORMAL TRAINING

Educational programs in publishing abound, and many of them provide valuable information and some technical training in the process and business of publishing. Some offer an overview of the industry, coupled with hands-on workshop experience. Examples of this are the summer institutes at several universities across the country (Radcliffe, Stanford, Howard, N.Y.U., University of Denver) and the Coalition of Publishers for Employment (COPE) course in New York City.

The university summer institutes introduce prospective publishing employees to the business as a whole. Students learn about the different kinds of book publishing and the work each requires. Many discover for the first time that there is more to publishing than editing fiction and non-fiction for the general reader. Summer institute students are better able to focus their job searches, because they have a better sense of where their own interests and abilities are likely to fit (as marketing assistants, editorial assistants, design trainees, etc.). A few learn that publishing isn't the business for them and thereby avoid future frustration and disappointment. Probably the greatest benefit these students gain is the opportunity to develop valuable contacts with the visiting lecturers, who are experienced professionals from the industry.

Several colleges have introduced degree programs in book publishing in recent years. They offer special bachelor's degrees or post-graduate certificates. These programs usually take an approach similar to the summer institutes, but cover these same topics in much greater depth. While it is too soon to know whether graduates of these programs fare better in their publishing careers than those with less specific education, the former certainly gain a perspective that can only help their future career decisions.

Many colleges offer non-credit courses on publishing subjects. Among these are general overviews of editorial or marketing processes, and technical instruction in topics such as copywriting and copy editing. These types of courses are especially useful for publishing employees who wish to enhance the knowledge and skills they are learning on the job. They are also helpful to those exploring career changes within the industry. Most publishing companies encourage employees to take such courses by providing tuition assistance.

TRAINING WITHIN THE COMPANY

Training and education within the company is usually called "in-house" training. The two main components of this kind of training are structured lectures and workshops and informal, day-by-day instruction from supervisors.

A few book publishing companies offer courses and seminars on a regular basis, but most offer them "as needed." In either case, the speakers and instructors are usually drawn from the ranks of professional employees in the company. They generally address the issues and practices that are most relevant to their own organizations. Some of these in-house courses may be very specific: how to prepare a manuscript for production, how to develop an advertising campaign, or how to prepare a budget and monitor results. However, the courses are more likely to be general, addressed to employees who want to understand better how the company operates and what goes on in other departments. Frequently the more general courses serve as orientation for new employees. In-house education of this sort varies widely from company to company, from much to none, and from structured to casual.

As with any other apprenticeship system, the most important training in publishing comes from the daily interaction of employees with their supervisors and colleagues. Much depends on the experience and style of the supervisors. Formal education outside and informal programs within the company are valuable supplements to the learning process, but most publishers agree that there is no substitute for learning by doing. More often than not, supervisors in publishing are willing to give new employees a considerable amount of independence to expand their range of responsibilities.

INTERNSHIPS

If you can get one, take it.

Internships vary widely. However, the one thing they have in common is the opportunity to work in a company and get firsthand exposure to the real world of publishing. As you'll see from the listings in the Job Opportunities Databank in the back of this volume, a number of book publishing companies offer internships, some regularly, others only occasionally. Some are formally organized to give the interns hands-on experience in a variety of basic functions. Others are less structured, giving interns the opportunity to assist professional managers and observe what goes on. Internships in the industry are *not* commonplace and there are many applicants for the limited number available. So how do you get one? The following four steps will give you a better shot:

Step #1: Start early. Don't wait until the end of the academic year, by which time most openings will have been filled.

Step #2: Write directly to the companies that interest you most. Start with the listings in the back of this <u>Career Directory</u>. To get even more detailed information on the publishers listed, see the brand-new volume available from the Career Press—<u>**Internships, Volume 2: Newspaper, Magazine and Book Publishing.**</u> And to find information on smaller publishers not included in either volume, use <u>Literary Marketplace</u>. Approach the people in charge of the publishing divisions that attract you. It is always a good idea to write to personnel departments, too—they may know of internships of which others in the company are unaware.

Step #3: Work with your college's career placement office. Find out about whether intern experience counts for degree credits. This is particularly important for unpaid internships because of federal employment regulations.

Step #4: Investigate foundations and independent intern programs. Some foundations have special programs for interns. For example, the Morehead Foundation sponsors a scholarship program at the University of North Carolina that features internships in a variety of industries, including publishing. The INROADS program for minorities has a very effective intern sponsorship program in a wide range of industries which, in the past few years, has included publishing. College and school career offices are the best source of information about these.

SO WHAT DO YOU DO?

There may be no substitute for the apprenticeship approach to careers in book publishing. Few people have achieved promotion or advancement because of degrees or certificates of learning. Nevertheless, the most successful people in publishing are those who add to their innate abilities a curiosity and knowledge of the complete process. This is where training and outside courses can add much to one's hands-on experience. This is also where those who have had college-level orientation education have a head start. And it is where those who have been so fortunate as to have some sort of internship experience are at a particular advantage.

The "Accidental Profession" welcomes you warmly. The next steps are up to you.

CHESTER S. LOGAN

Mr. Logan began his publishing career as a college textbook sales representative with the Oxford University Press after his 1951 graduation from Princeton. Since then, he has held editorial and marketing management positions at Oxford, Reinhold Publishing Corp. (now Van Nostrand-Reinhold), and Harper & Row. He directed the personnel function at Harper & Row from 1973 to 1987.

He has been active in the Association of American Publishers (AAP), including membership in the Education for Publishing Committee in 1977, and chairmanship of the College Division in 1969.

He has been president and chairman of COPE (Coalition of Publishers for Education), is a member of the advisory board of the American Reading Council and has lectured in publishing courses at the University of Denver, Howard University and New York University.

Mr. Logan's writings include contributions to The Accidental Profession (AAP, 1977) and The Business of Book Publishing (Westview Press, 1985).

SECTION II

Departments & Areas Of Specialization

CHAPTER EIGHT

Advertising—The Inspiration And The Aspiration

By

**Diane A. Kuppler-Weaver, Director-Advertising & Promotion
College Division, Prentice-Hall, Inc.
Simon & Schuster Higher Education Group**

What's the difference between joining a book publisher's Advertising department and going to work for an advertising agency?

Essentially the differences are minimal. At an ad agency, you might work on a range of products, from soup to nuts, while at a book publisher your product group—books—will remain the same. But the fundamental elements of advertising are identical wherever you are: to produce advertising that gets results.

One major difference, however, is that publishers more often hire individuals with little or no practical experience, whereas ad agencies generally prefer to hire individuals with proven ability (read, experience). So the Advertising department of a book publisher is an ideal place for most aspiring copywriters and designers to get their start.

The setup of individual Advertising departments, both within and among publishing houses, varies greatly, depending not only on the size of the house, but also on the size of the various publishing divisions. For example, a publisher's College Textbook Division might be much more profitable and thus larger than its Elhi (Elementary/High School) Division. A publisher with a large, successful college text product line might also have a large, in-house college advertising support staff. This is by no means a rule of thumb. Some publishers with productive divisions might have small advertising staffs that rely heavily on the services of outside freelance support.

So if you plan on pursuing a career in book publishing advertising, do some research: Identify each publisher's areas of specialization or particular strength (i.e., college texts, elhi texts, professional/trade or mass market books, etc.) to ascertain which area you feel best suited for and to gain a better idea of the areas where your greatest chances for opportunity lie.

WHAT DOES THE ADVERTISING DEPARTMENT DO?

Typical advertising functions in the publishing industry generally fall into one or both of the following categories:

A. ***To produce promotional advertising that generates qualified sales leads*** (that are then followed up with a sales call by the publisher's sales representative or an examination copy of the book being promoted)...Or

B. ***To produce advertising that generates either single or multiple order sales***. This kind of advertising assumes no follow-up sales call; the ad must make the sale by itself.

The publishing divisions most likely to produce the first type of advertising would be those involved with educational markets—college textbooks, elhi texts, and other educational/developmental kinds of learning materials.

Naturally, the audience for these products are educators—your own college, high school, or elementary teachers, for example. The types of promotional/advertising pieces that educators in these markets would be exposed to might include any of the following:

- Informational brochures
- Flyers
- Booklets with photos, artwork, or reproductions of sample pages from the text
- Catalogs
- Sales letters
- Educational wall posters, calendars, etc.
- Advertising in educational journals
- And any other related sales support literature

These pieces are usually informational in both tone and approach. The copy may or may not tend toward "hard-sell." However, the decision to "adopt" the text (a term publishers use to describe a school's or individual instructor's decision to order ten or more copies of a text for class use) is rarely made on the basis of the ad piece alone. Before an instructor will commit to using a new text in the classroom, he or she must first see it and thoroughly examine its content, tone, level, and approach. So the purpose of any ad for the educational market is primarily to inform. The way you inform, of course, can range from the very straightforward to the very creative.

The audience receiving the second kind of advertising might be the professional business person, persons involved in specific trades, or individuals with specific hobbies (i.e., photography, woodworking, flower arranging, personal computers, etc.), and, of course, the general public.

The types of advertising used to promote books to these audiences might include:

- Direct mail/direct response packages (including any or all of the following: 2-, 4-, 6- or 8-page sales letter, detailed brochure, premium offer, or card)
- Brochures
- Flyers
- Catalogs
- Space advertising (ads in newspapers, magazines, etc.)
- Point-of-purchase displays or promotion
- And any other type of promotional, attention-getting tools.

This type of advertising is also informational, but it is primarily attempting to elicit an immediate response: the purchase of the book by an individual.

These are just two of the most basic ways that books are promoted and advertised. There are many, many other options available and many areas where techniques used to promote books are "traded" from publishing division to publishing division.

ADVERTISING'S RELATIONSHIP TO OTHER DEPARTMENTS

Since advertising is so closely related to the marketing function, it is almost always included somewhere under the overall umbrella of a publisher's Marketing department. In fact, these two departments are integral to each other: Advertising depends on Marketing to supply the order to advertise, identify the target audience, and supply them with the information they need to accomplish the task. Marketing depends on Advertising to produce the vehicle(s) that will effectively inform the appropriate audience(s) that a new product is available and generate either sales leads or actual sales.

The degree to which the Marketing department dictates the form, format, and content of advertising pieces varies greatly from publisher to publisher, and even from division to division. Some Advertising departments have more freedom than others in planning and budgeting advertising. However, most are given a general advertising budget that is determined by the director of marketing and controlled by the advertising honcho.

Aside from the Marketing department, the Ad department will usually work closely with a number of other departments in a given division. Within the College Division, for example, the College Ad department would have considerable contact with the acquisition editors (who contract the books), the production editors (who transform the typewritten manuscripts into bound books), the Art department (where the book's pages are laid out and designed), and the authors themselves.

The advertising staff would also have contact with various outside vendors—printers, typesetters, illustrators, photographers, and other suppliers.

There may also be opportunities to travel to conventions, sales meetings, and trade shows, where advertising people can actually meet and talk to their audience.

OPPORTUNITIES IN THE ADVERTISING DEPARTMENT

The typical Advertising department may include any or all of the following job titles, depending on its size, its needs, and the number of new books it publishes each year:

Advertising director/advertising manager/promotion manager

These three titles are basically synonymous, varying in usage usually according to the size of the actual department (i.e., advertising director usually connotes a rather large department with several sub-levels, whereas advertising manager might connote a smaller department). Regardless of the particular title variation used, the individual in this position is in charge of the general operation and management of the department, responsible for maintaining the adver-tising budget and ensuring that department goals are met. This person must be knowledgeable in all phases of advertising, creative, and print production.

Asst. ad director/asst. ad manager/asst. promotion manager

Again, these titles are basically synonymous, varying only according to department size. The person serving in this capacity is usually considered as a backup to the head of the depart-ment and is responsible for department production and operations, general training and development, involvement in special projects, troubleshooting, and setting standards.

Naturally, neither of these two top positions is considered entry-level, but they are indeed positions to which an individual can aspire. Salary ranges, depending on department size and degree of responsibility, will range anywhere from $25,000 to $50,000 or more.

Copy chief

Responsible for setting and maintaining the quality of copy, planning and organizing the work, writer training and development; may become involved in some budgeting and may also maintain a freelance support network.

Art director

In charge of the daily operations of the design staff. Sets creative standards, performs budgeting duties, trains and develops staff, and may maintain a freelance support network.

These two positions usually require a strong familiarity with the publisher's product line and at least several years of practical and proven experience. They are also, of course, positions to which new copywriters or designers can aspire. Salaries range between $18,000 and $40,000.

Copy supervisor

Responsible for maintenance and approval of the workload of a small group of copywriters, whose writing responsibilities may or may not be specialized (e.g., technical writing, business book writing, etc.).

Design supervisor

Responsible for maintenance and approval of the workload of a small group of designers. May be involved in budgeting.

These positions usually require proven ability, a solid grasp of the fundamentals, and an ability to work well with people. They are growth positions with salaries ranging from $22,000 to $35,000.

Copywriter (entry-, intermediate- or senior-level)

Responsible for researching and writing advertising copy, which involves concept development and contact with a designer or art director, marketing manager, editor, and/or author.

Designer (entry-, intermediate- or senior-level)

Responsible for creating the layout and design for the advertising copy, which involves conceptual collaboration with the writer or copy chief, marketing manager, editor, and/or author.

Advertising space/journal writer

Responsible for researching and writing copy for space or journal ads; may involve concept development and journal research to target the best market.

These are the three most likely entry-level positions with considerable opportunity for advancement and growth. Starting salaries can range between $16,400 to $17,400 for entry-level, $18,000 to $23,000 for intermediate-level, and $23,000 to $27,000 for senior-level copywriters and designers.

Production assistant

Acts as a support person to the design staff and performs many design/production related duties.

Mechanical artist

Responsible for taking the elements of the designer's "dummy" (a rendering of what the printed piece will look like) and pasting them into position for the printer to photograph.

These three positions may be entry-level, but usually require some practical skill or knowledge. Salaries can range from $15,000 to $18,000, depending on skill.

Many Advertising departments may also have several miscellaneous support positions such as:

- *Budget coordinator/controller*—budget tracking and department book-keeping.

- _**Traffic controller/production manager**_—responsible for keeping track of the workflow in and out of the department.

- _**Sales support group manager**_—responsible for producing sales support material to be used by the marketing or field staff personnel.

- _**Freelance coordinator**_—responsible for keeping track of freelance work in and out of the department.

Once again, the range of responsibilities, accountabilities, and duties can vary significantly from division to division and publisher to publisher. When you are in an actual interview situation, ask as many questions as you can think of to get a good feel for the department and the opportunities you will be afforded.

HOW IS AN AD PIECE CREATED? THE COPY/DESIGN COLLABORATION

As most copywriters and designers would agree, there is no "typical day"—anything _can_, and usually _does_, happen! So to give you a better idea of what is involved in both the copy and design functions—the two most likely opportunities for an entry-level position—let's look at the step-by-step creation of a single ad for a new book.

A directive to produce the ad comes from Marketing. A copywriter and designer are assigned. The process begins with their joint pursuit of the single, most important selling idea and/or concept that should be used to promote the book.

Since an ad's mail (or drop) date is scheduled as close as possible to the book's availability date, the copywriter usually has to write about a book months before it is even printed. He or she must dig out the most important facts about the book and its marketing strategy by talking to the marketing people, calling the author, reading the book's preface, reviewing its table of contents, reading through a questionnaire form completed by the author, and, in many cases, (especially when the ad is intended to generate single copy sales) by actually looking at the typewritten pages.

After reviewing this material, the copywriter fleshes out the concepts and key selling ideas and creates benefit-oriented copy that will create attention, interest, desire, and the hoped-for action (to generate either sales leads or actual sales).

In much the same way that a copywriter communicates on a verbal level, the designer must convey the key ideas through visual devices, such as choice of typeface, color, use of artwork (photos, illustrations, examples), folds, use of white space, size, and visual tone.

Once the ad is written and designed, it is ready to be approved by whichever in-house or out-of-house persons a publisher's "approval policy process" dictates.

When the approvals are completed, the copy is returned to the designer to begin production. Now the pressure to meet the pre-determined drop date becomes even more intense. From this point on—until the day the piece goes to the printer—the copywriter/designer team will race the calendar to make sure that the ad mails on time.

The final, approved copy is sent to the typesetter and then proofread; mechanicals are built and then proofread; the ad is sent to the printer, who returns a "blueprint," which is proofread. (One mistake is too many.) And finally the finished, printed ad piece is delivered.

This whole process can take anywhere from days to weeks to months. What's more, during any phase of the writing, designing, or production of that single piece, the copywriter and designer might (and probably will) have several other projects in various stages of completion.

THE IDEAL ENTRY-LEVEL CANDIDATE HAS:

• Good organizational skills and the ability to handle a lot of volume and detail simultaneously.

• A genuine love of either writing or designing.

• A high energy level—anything can and will happen during a normal work day.

• The ability to think on one's feet—there are always times when you have to come up with a quick alternative or idea on the spot.

• A certain amount of poise and professionalism—especially if you will be dealing with people outside of the company. Every person with whom you interact views you as a representative of the company you work for.

• The ability to take criticism constructively—being creative is a highly personal process, but not everyone will love your ideas every time.

• The ability to manage stress and pressure—Advertising makes some pretty tough demands at times.

• A sincere willingness to learn, explore, and try out new ideas.

• A responsible, mature attitude—advertising always has deadlines that have to be met.

• Self-motivation, initiative and drive.

• The skills and desire to be a team player—the business of advertising always involves people working together toward a common goal.

• Good communication skills—you must be able to express your ideas clearly, regardless of whether they are verbal or visual.

• And last, but certainly not least in the publishing industry, a genuine love of books.

THE NECESSARY SKILLS AND APTITUDES

For A Copywriting Career:

1. B.A. or B.S. in any field, but preferably in advertising, communications, English, or journalism.

2. Any kind of writing experience—short stories, articles for the campus or school newspaper, literary magazine, yearbook, etc.

3. Any kind of advertising experience, whether through class assignments, an internship, or freelance activities.

4. Good writing and organization skills.

5. Good grammar and punctuation skills.

6. Research skills—the ability to pull out and organize the pertinent facts.

For A Design Career:

1. B.F.A. or B.A. in graphic design, communications design, or advertising design.

2. Practical production experience for the campus yearbook, newspaper, literary magazine, or any other publication.

3. Any part-time or freelance design experience.

4. Exposure to an agency or in-house Advertising department—either through coursework or a design internship.

NOTE: Knowledge of mechanical preparation and/or exposure to type selection and type specification should be considered helpful (the former even desirable), but not necessary.

The ideal candidate applying for either position should have a neat, clean, and carefully organized portfolio of samples, which can include both class projects and self-initiated ideas.

A FINAL ADVERTISEMENT

The business of advertising is certainly challenging, never dull, sometimes frustrating, but *always* interesting and rewarding. It's a vocation that affords you virtually unlimited opportunity for creativity and self expression in your work. The atmosphere is generally relaxed, but the energy level is high and the demands can be tough. In order to succeed you must be devoted to your craft and to constantly expanding and refining your skills. Ultimately, the successful copywriter evidences a good "design sense," and the successful designer has a good "copy sense." If you possess that, then the opportunities become even greater.

Ms. Kuppler-Weaver began her career as an arts and entertainment critic for a local newspaper and a cable television station, for which she also hosted a half-hour program on community affairs.

After joining Prentice-Hall in 1976 as a copywriter (in those days copywriters also designed their own ads), she quickly moved up the ranks to special projects writer/designer, supervisor in charge of both copy and design development, copy chief, assistant director, and in 1984, to director of college advertising. In the Spring of 1986, Ms. Kuppler-Weaver's responsibilities expanded to include overseeing Prentice-Hall's Higher Education Group Publicity Department.

Presently, she manages a 50-person staff consisting of designers, writers, supervisors, publicists and various support personnel. She is responsible for overseeing the production of some 900 individual pieces of advertising and promotion per year.

CHAPTER NINE

A Diversity Of Artistic Challenges

By

Zlata Paces, Vice President/Design Director
Macmillan Publishing Company

Book publishing is not the homogeneous business many of you probably think it is. Rather, it's an industry that encompasses a great diversity of products that are, for the most part, produced in book form—Trade books, reference books, children's (juvenile) books, professional books, dictionaries, college books, school books and more. While these may all be books, they differ radically in terms of design requirements (not to mention editorially, marketing-wise, etc.).

If you are interested in a career in book design, this is an important distinction, because while you will need to learn certain basic skills—those necessary just to become a competent designer—each of these specific book categories presents its own unique problems and a diversity of design challenges. Each of these challenges may well demand a variety of sophisticated design approaches. To see why this distinction is important, let's first look at the general or basic functions any book designer must fulfill.

THE FUNCTIONS OF A BOOK DESIGNER

The overriding concern of any book designer is an attempt to translate the overall (sometimes ephemeral) "concept" of a manuscript into a living, breathing, physical book. In order to achieve this objective, the book designer must responsibly carry out five more specific functions:

1. Decide on the size of the book (with the Production department).
2. Develop the overall look or style of the book.
3. Develop the typographic approach to the book.
4. If the book requires, choose illustrative materials—photographs, illustrations, tables, technical drawings, maps, etc.
5. Technically prepare the book for release to the Production department.

While these functions are, in a general sense, endemic to the design of any book, certain aspects of the overall design will tend to be emphasized or de-emphasized according to the specific book category. A brief look at some of the major categories should help to explain the disparate tasks a designer may have to undertake on books within each:

Trade Books (Fiction And Non-Fiction)

Emphasis is on cover design—trade book covers need to make an impact so the book, while on display among many other titles, will "jump off the shelf." Additional emphasis on good type design, readable typeface, well-proportioned type area, pleasing unit/chapter handling.

Reference Books

Sections within book must be well-defined; organization of material very important.

Dictionaries

Excellent layout and an interesting handling of spot art must be utilized to enhance the usually monotonous type requirements. (A good example of successful design—the Random House Dictionary.)

College Books

Like reference books, organization is very important. Type must be easy to read and categorize specific sections of the book.

Elhi (Elementary/High School Books)

Complicated by the variety of products—pupils' books, workbooks, teachers' guides, etc., all with different objectives, all demanding varied design skills and ideas. In general, layout is important—each book must be understandable and easy to follow for both students and teachers. Type legibility is a high priority. Depending on the specific subject, the designer may have to handle a great amount of visual materials on each page.

Children's/Juvenile

While a specific technical approach may apply, the overall concept of the book—and the handling of the elements that will achieve it—is usually a cooperative effort between the designer, illustrator, author and editor.

THE SETUP OF A TYPICAL ART DEPARTMENT

The Art department is a service department within any publishing operation, which means it must work in close cooperation with both editorial and production to visually interpret and practically achieve the editorial concept of each book.

While titles will tend to vary from publisher to publisher, a typical Art department setup would include an **art director** on top, a small number of **senior designers** and many more **designers** (and, probably, some **"board" people** to handle paste-ups, mechanicals, etc.).

The art director is the department head, responsible for the total visual output of the Art department, as well its budget, staff and, perhaps most important, deadlines. Compensation may range from $30,000 to $55,000 (or more).

A senior designer will be responsible for all of the design functions necessary to produce whatever specific books have been assigned to him or her. Salary would range from $17,000 to perhaps $33,000.

These two positions are those to which you should aspire—they are the professionals who have learned the necessary design and management skills to supervise a number of ongoing projects and the staff who help produce them. In some large houses, there may be some additional titles at this level of responsibility.The **associate director of design** (salary: $28,000 to $43,000) would work immediately under the art director. One or more **design managers** (salary: $25,000 to $40,000) would supervise a number of senior designers and designers.

In many houses, the entry-level job is called just **designer**, though once again, titles will vary quite a bit. In any case, this position requires no experience, but does require a good layout sense and a basic knowledge and understanding of design. Compensation would range from $14,000 to $22,000.

If you are hired by a publisher, with whatever title that entry-level position carries, you will probably start out doing mechanicals. If you are especially capable, you might be given some simple paging job and/or some uncomplicated type-specing (specifying the typeface, sizing, etc.) jobs.

As we've already seen, a designer's specific functions may vary quite radically from book to book, depending upon the type of book he or she is working on. But forgetting those nuances for now, each book must go through a similar routine.

First, the manuscript should be read by the designer so he or she begins to understand the intent of the book. Discussion follows between the art director (with or without the designer) and the Editorial and Production departments to clarify and codify their coordinated visual approach to the book.

Second, the Art department develops the art budget for the book.

Third, the Art department (having received budget approval) develops a design approach and prepares sample pages to illustrate the overall design, type selection, relative positioning of heads, subheads, captions, etc.

Fourth, when this approach has been approved (possibly after more discussion and some revisions), the actual "book work" begins: The manuscript is marked up and sent to be typeset. When type is received, the galleys are broken into pages (depending on the complexity of the book, this may be done directly at the typesetter's or in-house); dummies of the book are prepared, then adjusted after further input from editorial; and, finally, mechanicals are prepared. The book is ready to be released to the Production department.

There may also be a group within the Art department responsible for the photo/art research function. This group will be headed by a **research supervisor** (salary: $22,000 to $35,000); the entry-level position in this area is **research assistant** (salary: $14,500 to $27,000). Getting into this area would require a good eye and an intellectual knowledge of a variety of subjects, though a college degree is not necessary. A photographic background would be most helpful—as beginning duties would entail searching for photos—but a sense and knowledge of history is probably of paramount importance.

HOW TO BREAK INTO A PUBLISHER'S ART DEPARTMENT

A candidate looking for an entry-level design job should have a carefully-prepared, professional-quality portfolio, be self-assured (but not overly aggressive), have a pleasant personality that projects a sense of self-worth and an interest in both the creative and practical aspects of a design career. If you are solely interested in working "on the board," an art school degree is sufficient. Otherwise, I recommend college.

Some publishing companies hire summer interns in their art departments. I suggest you utilize the internship information in the *Job Opportunities Databank* in the back of this Career Directory to search them out (and the additional listings and information in the Career Press' brand-new volume, **Internships, Vol. 2: Newspaper, Magazine and Book Publishing**). Internships are scarce, but they offer an excellent chance to "get a feel" for the kind of everyday work you'll be asked to do in an entry-level design job.

The Importance Of The Portfolio

Wherever you apply and whatever you want to do in the field of design, a portfolio is an overriding necessity—many jobs will be won or lost strictly on the basis of its professionalism (or the lack thereof). It should be neatly organized and contain the following elements:

- A series of neatly-prepared **finished layouts**.
- A series of **rough layouts** ("thinking" layouts, rough comps, maybe some tighter comps) for at least two or three of the finished layouts included— this will show the art director the progress from concept to execution.
- A specification **(type-spec) sheet**.
- Xeroxes of some finished layouts with neatly marked **type specifications**.

- **Mechanicals**—some simple, one-color; some with overlays, color and break indication. These should be finished and professional-looking.
- The **dummy** of a small book with art and type areas indicated. If you are interested in children's books, you should include a dummy of an entire book.

A book designer is very involved with a great amount of type; therefore, an in-depth knowledge of type is definitely an asset when applying for a position in book design.

Where You're Headed

The layout, type and good design skills you will learn at your first job should enable you to function in any other field of design. It is up to you to recognize your talent and decide, after that initial year or two on the job, if there are other areas of design you may wish to pursue.

Moving (upward, hopefully!) to another publisher after a year or two (even three) at your first job is a good idea (unless you're very happy there and are being given increasing responsibilities). Such a move will normally allow you to take the skills you've learned and apply them in a different arena, perhaps to learn additional design methods or styles or to work on a variety of different books.

Progress from an entry-level position to senior designer or even art director may take anywhere from three to seven years (or more). To become a senior designer you must, of course, have mastered all the basic design skills. But you also must be able to handle a number of projects simultaneously and possess the supervisory skills necessary to oversee junior-level designers and the diplomatic skills to work effectively and efficiently with the Production and Editorial departments.

To become an art director—the top of the ladder—you must be capable of working under extreme and sometimes constant pressure, taking responsibility for your staff's work, controlling budgets, estimating the financial aspects involved with each book or program and, perhaps most important of all, delivering the products on time. You will need to acquire a complete working knowledge of production, printing processes, color judgment and estimating.

Talent Will Out

Make no mistake—no matter what school you attend, how many and varied your pre-interview preparations, how much you spend on your portfolio case, talent is really the prerequisite to any design job. Skills can be learned; talent must already exist. It's a hard, cold fact, but true.

But talent alone does not guarantee success, although talent combined with hard work and the determination to succeed no matter what can overcome any seemingly-insurmountable obstacle. I started in this business with a great handicap—I barely spoke English. It didn't stop me.

My first job was with a magazine. I was assigned to work on the 'back of the book" layout, probably the least exciting or challenging design job of all. But I didn't see it that way—to me, each new task was an invaluable learning experience. So I was very diligent and enthusiastically "attacked" every job assigned to me, no matter how basic.

In my hours away from work, I carefully studied all the leading magazines, especially their type design. I took issues of *Esquire, Ladies' Home Journal* and many others and prepared my own type specifications for each of their feature articles. Why did I do all this? Just to improve my knowledge of type and to become more aware of type design.

As my current title and responsibilities attest, this hard work paid off. So if you have the talent, remember: It may be a prerequisite, but it will only get you in the door. What other "rooms" you're able to visit, how long your "tour" takes and what "floor" you eventually wind up on is really up to your ambition and your own hard work. Take the chance—it's worth it!

ZLATA PACES

In her current position, Ms. Paces is responsible for creating over 200 books a year, including all phases of design—covers, texts, etc.—and typogrphy specification and purchasing. She received her B.A. from Hunter College. During her career, she has designed hundreds of magazines, promotion pieces and books, projects as diverse as the Girl Scout's Handbook and A History of the American Nation.

She currently teaches a course in book design at the Parsons School of Design.

CHAPTER TEN

The Business Of Books

By

John Sargent, Publisher—Juvenile Division
Simon & Schuster, Inc.

Do you picture yourself in a tweed jacket or skirt, strolling manicured grounds, immersed in important conversation with a literary czar? If so, and you're not willing to put in quite a few years first, flip right over to the editorial portion of this book. What this chapter will do is give you a run down of various business-oriented publishing career paths (general and specific), offer you some free advice (no doubt worth every penny) and encourage you to enter our field with high expectations and great enthusiasm.

WHY BUSINESS?

Starting a career on the business/accounting-side of the book publishing industry offers several advantages over starting in the more "publishing"-oriented side. Since the business side lacks the connotations of glamour inherent in the industry, entry-level and second-level jobs tend to pay more than their editorial or marketing counterparts. In addition, the business skills you'll learn are easily transferred to other departments, companies, even industries. A business manager for a college division of a large publishing house can easily transfer into the trade division. Likewise, a business manager in a trade division would be considered for a job as chief financial officer at a small independent company. And if you decide to get out of publishing, your business experience will serve you well in virtually any field you choose.

Given these two important advantages—higher pay and greater flexibility—why isn't everyone applying for that financial analyst opening?

Because jobs on the business side are not *publishing* jobs *per se*—your work will not generally involve you with books...at least, not the literary kind. Most people who go into publishing, myself included, do it for the love of books and the interesting people who work with them. An editorial assistant may slave away for five years typing and filing, earning a pittance, but he or she is involved with *books*. Few starting business jobs provide that satisfaction, but don't sell the business side short if you are looking at publishing as a *career*.

Before I zero in on the meat of the matter—entry-level positions and career paths—let's discuss two factors that argue persuasively for a business/accounting start in publishing.

Publishing, for better or worse, is shedding its gentlemanly image. With heavy consolidation in the industry, and the huge sums invested by corporations, the profit motive has emerged as the driving force. Publishing has become much more competitive at every level, from purchasing the publishing property through retail distribution of the product. Though many people in publishing still wince at the thought of books as "property" or "product," you'll hear these words more frequently as publishing becomes much like any other manufacturing industry—selling goods for the highest possible profit. Needless to say, in such a profit-driven environment, a background in business will be highly valued by management.

The second reason to start your publishing career in business is that you may be better at it! Publishing needs people with many types of talent, not just great editors or book designers. Just because you have no particular skill with the English language (witness these pages), ability to design or deep compassion for literature, do not forsake a career in one of the truly enjoyable industries. Analyze your abilities and concentrate on the areas in which you do well. If you are serious about a career in publishing, starting out as a superb analyst will be better in the long run than beginning as a mediocre editorial assistant.

CAREER PATHS

Before discussing the general types of jobs available, I want to give you some real-life specifics. In my own career, I have changed job descriptions (which can be different from changing titles) six times. In two cases, I could have predicted the next opportunity, but in four the changes came as a surprise. This is a common, delightful, though occasionally frustrating, aspect of the business end of publishing.

I provide here three actual career tracks: 1) my own first and in more detail, to help you realize what bias I bring to this article.; 2) an associate publisher who started in editorial and moved to the business side; and 3) a "pure" business career track. The latter two examples do not list company or personal names in order to protect the innocent.

My Own Career Path

Job Title	Years	Company/Division	Description
Sales Representative	1	D. Van Nostrand	College textbook sales
Sales Manager/Rep.	1	D. Van Nostrand	Managing plus selling
Student	1 1/2	Columbia	MBA Finance
Financial Analyst	3/4	Doubleday/Corporate	Generating financials, budgets
Cash Manager	3/4	Doubleday/Corporate	Investing and borrowing all corporate cash
Business Associate	2 1/2	Doubleday/Publishing	P&L analysis on books and authors, cost control and inventory
Financial Manager	1/2	Macmillan/Checkerboard Press (Juvenile)	Setting up a new acquisition as a stand alone division.
V.P. Finance & Administration	1/2	Macmillan/Checkerboard Press	A/R, credit, customer service, distribution, operations, finance and budgeting.
Publisher	Present	Simon & Schuster/Juvenile	Running a division, including editorial, marketing, sales, art, finance

After A Start In Editorial

Job Title	Years	Company/Division	Description
Editorial Assistant	3/4	Major trade publisher	Reviewing manuscripts, typing, filing
Corporate Research Analyst/Sr. Analyst	3	Major trade publisher	Strategic planning and analysis
Business Associate	1	Major trade publisher	P&L analysis, budgets, cost control
Managing Editor	3	Major trade publisher	Manuscript trafficking, production, editorial management
Associate Publisher	Present	Major trade publisher	Same as managing editor, with more editorial responsibilities

Straightforward Business Career Path

Job Title	Years	Company/Division	Description
CPA	3	Big 8 Accounting Firm	Auditing and Accounting
Student	2	Ivy League	MBA in Finance
Manager, Corporate	2 1/2	Major publisher	Financial analysis and budgeting
Operations Manager	1	Major publisher	Responsible for back office A/R, A/P, credit, mailroom
Divisional Controller-Retail	1	Major publisher	Responsible for all financial and accounting systems
Divisional Controller-Publishing	3/4	Major publisher	Same as above
Divisional VP-Finance & Administration	Present	Different major publisher	Responsible for distribution and all financial and information systems

SO WHERE AND WHAT ARE THE JOBS?

Now that you have seen a few specific examples, on to the generalities. The first question asked by most people going into the business side of anything is "Do I need an MBA?" In publishing, an MBA, while not a necessity, is becoming more and more valuable as a credential. But since many of the technical skills learned in business school do not directly apply to many of the business jobs in publishing, it is *only* a credential, not some magic wand that guarantees a management slot after two months on the job. Since the type of job that interests you will determine whether you should invest in an MBA, let me describe the basic options for a person looking to enter the business side of publishing. I will limit myself to fairly typical, large publishing houses, as that is where the majority of financial jobs will exist.

There are two types of business jobs in most publishing houses—for lack of any real definitions, I call them controller's jobs and business manager jobs. They are not mutually exclusive, and a well rounded individual could certainly have both types of jobs in a career. I have found, however, that most people move up through an organization as one or the other.

The Controller's Career Path

The controller's career path includes many entry-level positions. In this category I would put **warehouse jobs, customer service jobs, accounts receivable/payable clerks and supervisors, royalty accountants, corporate accountants, assistants in various financial departments (cash management, tax, controller's office etc.).** Most of these jobs will be accounting oriented and involve heavy number crunching through the first few promotions. If you do well in these jobs, the most likely progression through the organization would have you moving from super-vision of a small area to manager of a department (such as cashiers, billing, accounts receivable, royalty, payroll, mailroom, accounting.). The next logical step would be to assistant controller or assistant operations manager. After controller or operations manager, you would be in line for the top financial job in the company.

A second branch of the controller's career path would take you into the more technical financial areas: tax accounting, controller, cash management, or treasury. Though an entry-level position may not require it, for high level success an MBA would be an asset. Becoming a CPA would also be helpful in a number of these positions.

The Business Manager's Career Path

The business manager's career path offers more direct exposure to the publishing process. Typical entry-level jobs include **inventory analysis, data input, general ledger research, systems maintenance and variance analysis**. Most Business departments will have one or two MBA jobs and a number of operating jobs (tracking contracts, keeping data bases current, generating reports, reprinting books). In the Business department you will generally have more direct involvement with the books themselves and less bookkeeping work to do. Decisions on publishing and reprinting books, as well as strategic planning, are all based on financial projections. A typical career here would take you from an **analyst or assistant** job to a**ssistant manager or manager** of a specific function (inventory, for instance), and then on to **business manager**. After business manager, you would qualify to go into a corporate staff job, a corporate business manager job or a division manager position.

The "In-Between" Career Path

In addition to the controller and business manager career tracks, there are several jobs that fall in between and offer good access in either direction. Jobs in **financial analysis, strategic planning, research, and information systems** can typically lead to divisional jobs as business manager or in corporate financial work. Many companies now hire mostly MBAs for these jobs. The advantage of these positions is that you typically get to discover the workings of several divisions and gain exposure to a variety of management.

ADVICE, HINTS, HELP

I realize this discourse may be confusing, especially if you have no experience in a corporation. On the next, page, I have diagrammed the structure of a fairly typical large publishing house (the jobs shown are strictly business oriented) to give you a better idea of how all the positions I've discussed line up and interrelate. Remember: The structure at every house is different, so don't expect to ever find a company that looks exactly like the one I've diagrammed.

While the brief sketches of the various jobs associated with the numbers side of publishing are important, I also want to pass along some disparate pieces of advice gathered from the eight years I've spent in publishing:

- Learning profit and loss statements and balance sheets will always be useful in almost any career.

THE BUSINESS SIDE OF A TYPICAL LARGE PUBLISHING HOUSE

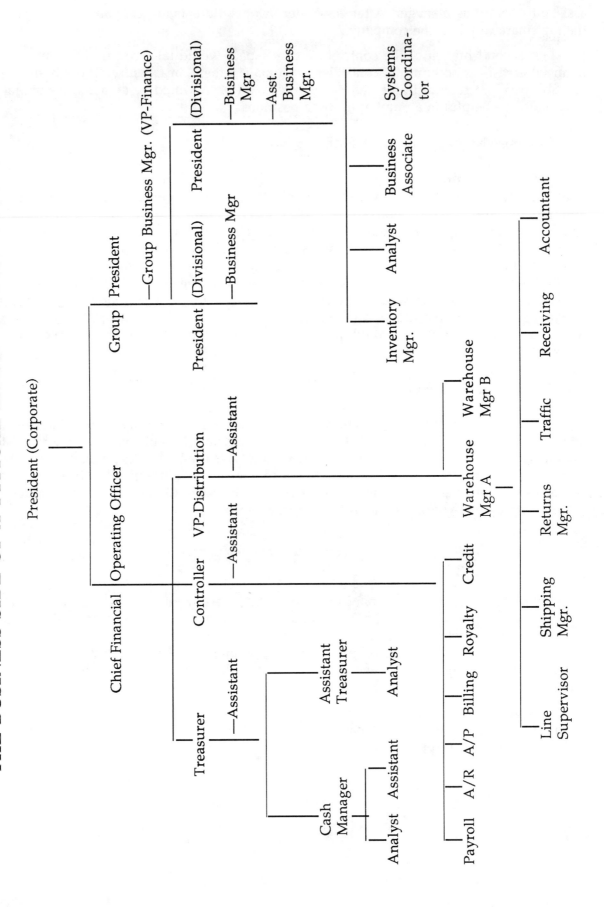

- Do not narrow your field by working in only one type of publishing operation. Working in bookclubs, bookstores or educational publishing (among others) can be valuable, even if your primary interest is publishing literary fiction.

- Do not hesitate to switch houses during your career if you are unhappy with your job.

- Some selling experience is invaluable, whether a part-time job in a bookstore or a full-time job as a rep.

- Do not expect to make a lot of money initially in publishing. At higher levels, publishing salaries are comparable to most companies. You will pay a price to work in this field, but a small price if you believe in enjoying what you do for a living.

Finally, a word about publishing as an industry. Books have enormous value, and producing them provides great satisfaction. Though publishing can prove frustrating to a business person, at the end of the day you have been involved with manufacturing something of intrinsic worth. That, and the people you will end up working with, make publishing a hell of a lot of fun.

CHAPTER ELEVEN

Editorial Opportunities In Elhi Publishing

By

Robert B. Stewart, Vice President/Editor-In-Chief
Prentice-Hall, Inc.—School Division
A Division of the Educational Group of Simon & Schuster, Inc.

Your undergraduate degree is recent vintage, and you have been "out of school" for two to four years, right? That practice teaching and summer camp counseling you did as a college student have paid off in your current job—teaching school. There are pluses and minuses to that, and recently you've begun to sort them out. The administrative hassles you could do without, and the lunch duty, and that occasional unruly kid you just can't reach.

On the other hand, you like the touch-and-go in the classroom as your students pick up on the activities you have devised for that lesson in phoenemes, or biomes, or square roots, or Kipling's imperialism. You have found the curriculum planning assignments more a fillip than a chore, and you look forward to the camaraderie of some like-minded colleagues. Although you've considered graduate school, you realize you just aren't ready to make the leap yet.

Have we got an idea for you? Yes, indeed. You're an ideal candidate for entering the highly-specialized field of elhi ('elementary/high school") educational publishing, whether you've been teaching third or tenth graders, and wherever you've been teaching in the U.S.A.

THE QUALIFICATIONS YOU THINK YOU NEED...AND DON'T

Do you have to be an English major? No, although it helps if you have at least a minor in the subject or, even better, a double major with another subject specialty.

Do you need newspaper/yearbook/literary magazine experience? No. The bookmaking aspects you'll learn on-the-job. But if you have done "literary work," by all means highlight it on your resume. If you enjoy using the written word as an effective means of communicating facts and concepts, you already have a key prerequisite for an editorial position.

Do you have to know how to type? No. Some of the top editors in the business are still original hunt-and-peck typists—and pretty speedy, too. But, like most things in life, the more skillfully you can prepare your work—neatly, quickly—the better. So typing helps. So does word processing experience in this new era of desktop publishing.

THE JOB APPROACH

Elhi publishers are continuously on the lookout for people like yourself, with subject area knowledge that's up-to-date, with a flair for organizing lessons and class activities, and with the savvy that can come only from managing a classroom. But you need to put all this on paper in a resume, for you won't be hired on good looks, good grades, or "personality" alone!

Check out the listings in the *Job Opportunities Databank* in the back of this Career Directory and the additional information available in Literary Market Place (LMP), which should be at your local library. Locate the elhi publishers in the geographic areas that you believe are feasible for you. New York City (and environs in New Jersey and Connecticut) has some of the biggest elhi publishers. But so do Boston and Chicago. And there are outposts elsewhere in Pennsylvania, Florida, Oklahoma, Texas, and California. Take your pick.

More important than geography, however, is the scope of the publishing operation and the business focus of the company. If you are teaching in the elementary area, certain publishers will appeal to you. (And you are probably already familiar with their products.) The same for high school. This is not to say that the field is split into two parts. It is not. There are a sizable number of K-12 (kindergarten through 12th grade) publishers. After all, the education market services a lot of K-12 kids (some 45 million), as well as their teachers and administrators.

A cover letter and standard resume are your "job passport." Compose your cover letter carefully. It's the first clue for the interviewer as to your facility with the language. Do not be too brief, but don't "oversell" either. One page will do nicely.

You can follow up with letters of reference, if requested, or samples of school materials you've devised. Expect a personal interview—it would be most unusual for a job offer to arrive from a publisher in the mail.

If all goes well at the interview, you may be given a test assignment. Here's a typical "test" which you would be expected to complete on your own for a specific deadline. The example is from the social studies area, but tests from other subject areas would be similar:

1. Analyze and evaluate the two attached 8th grade American history chapters. Comment on chapter structure, special features, writing style/reading

level, visual program, and questioning strategy. Choose the better of the two and justify your choice.

2. Write a classroom activity for an 8th grade American history text, using the cartoon herein. Assume the cartoon accompanies text material about the subject at hand.

3. Choose a topic from one of the two journalistic pieces attached. Write a high-interest feature (one manuscript page) for an 8th grade American history text.

4. Reorganize and edit the attached special feature on Peter Zenger by reducing the material to one or 1 1/2 manuscript pages and simplifying the content for a junior high audience, 7th - 8th grade reading level.

The test will provide your potential employer with a lot of good evidence of your budding writing/editing skills: how well you show an understanding of the needs and abilities of your target audience; how you apply your audience awareness in shaping material for exposition and for further interpretation; what you choose to highlight and to play down; and so forth. You will be judged also on the insight and judgment you display in your analysis of the various elements that come together to make an effective pedagogical tool.

THE ELHI PUBLISHING SCENE

The test is also of particular interest for what it reveals about the elhi publishing scene:

It is highly competitive and becoming more so as publishers scramble for market shares in a decade of gradually decreasing enrollments (an upturn in elementary schools is foreseen for the early 1990s).

Subject matter is determined by curriculum requirements, and it is safe to say that **the U.S. has a "consensus curriculum"** in that many states share the same educational goals and attempt to meet similar standards. If one could simultaneously visit an 8th grade American history class in Sioux Falls, South Dakota, another in Baton Rouge, Louisiana, and still another in Portland, Maine, one would find the same topic under discussion, the same overall historical storyline, and the same cast of historical personages. Therefore, to maintain a "competitive edge," your textbook must exhibit top quality work, editorial ingenuity, and extra-special visual/verbal appeal. You have to keep one jump ahead of the competition!

An elhi editor has to be flexible and talented, both as an editor of others' work but also as a writer/critic of his or her own material. Your subject expertise and pedagogical bent will stand you in good stead here, as you are already a good judge of what will attract a student's attention and hold it firmly as the necessary facts, opinions and ideas are expressed clearly and succinctly.

Sensitivity to readability is a "must" for an elhi editor, who should be familiar with both the strengths and weaknesses of the major reading formulas (Dale-Chall, Fry, Flesch), such measurements as the Cloze test, and how to make reading level compatible with the vocabulary and concept load of the subject being taught.

Sensitivity to controversial issues in the subject discipline, an ability to deal with conflicting viewpoints sensibly and resolutely, being alert to language and ideas appropriate to introduce into the classroom as well as relevant to the age and interest level of the students.

ELHI EDITING DIFFERS FROM TRADE AND COLLEGE EDITING

The test has even a further dimension of interest because it points up directly or by implication how elhi textbook editing differs from general Trade practices, even from editing college level textbooks.

First of all, elhi textbooks are designed to be revised—the initial time, dollar and talent investment is high—and a publisher wishes to undertake a project that will seize a market segment and expand it over time. The textbook will be kept current and valuable through repeated revision. (This is true also, though to a more limited degree, in college publishing, where the initial investment can be much more modest. It's not true of Trade publishing, except for reference works. No one, for example, expects John Updike to update his latest novel. If successful, it will be reprinted as is, repeatedly. A sequel may even be prepared. But no one would suggest a revised edition.)

The elhi editor plays a more central role in the development of the work than the editor in general Trade or even in college publishing. Curriculum requirements, market research needs, up-to-date subject matter research must all be brought together to form a book outline—even a detailed table of contents, in some cases—before authors are even chosen. (All this "backgrounding" isn't essential for the creation of an imaginative work, as Updike could testify. Nor would it be appropriate for the college professor-author with his specialized knowledge for advanced grade-level students, survey courses excepted.)

After choice of authors, the elhi editor must assign the writing workload (most elhi texts involve multiple authorship) and then follow up repeatedly on the progress made by the authors, staff and production editors, artists and designers. In short, the elhi editor must act like a general—decisively, seriously, fairly.

The elhi editor also functions as a prime coordinator between the textbook and the auxiliary materials—some for the teacher, some for students—that may accompany it. A teacher's guide to the text material is a must. In the past few years, these guides have become complex and elaborate teaching aids, actually day-to-day, step-by-step formulas for presenting the subject matter. Test items are also essential so that the teacher can evaluate student performance. Students are provided with workbooks in many subjects, with lab manuals in the sciences, and with games, activities and many other learning aids.

So the elhi editor—the general at the head of the troops—must function to keep the creative group moving ahead on many fronts. (All of this points up another significant difference from Trade and college editing. In the latter, supplements are more limited in scope—expectations are higher for instructors to choose and/or create their own backup materials. In the former, Mr. Updike would most certainly register surprise or even dismay at the prospect of supplying backup supplementary material for publication with his works.)

After the program is published, the elhi editor still plays an important role in the sales/marketing efforts that launch the textbook and its many auxiliaries into the marketplace. The editor will be called upon to describe the materials to the sales representatives—the special strengths of the program in content coverage, readability, pedagogy, and so on. Subsequently the editor may be involved in special presentations to customers—at state textbook adoption committees; at district, state, or national teachers' conventions; at local school district adoption proceedings, etc. Maybe this is not the glamorous life—author-editor lunches at well-known restaurants, TV talk shows, nationwide promotion tours—afforded some general Trade editors.

But it's stimulating and productive for the elhi editor, who can then add the results of this experience "in the field" to subject matter knowledge and prior teaching experience in order to improve revisions of existing textbooks and the development of future programs.

Not to be overlooked is the salary differential for elhi editors and those in general Trade. According to the AAP (Association of American Publishers), which conducts an annual compensation survey, staff editor jobs in educational publishing generally pay better than comparable level jobs in general Trade. For beginning editors up through senior editors, the differential is from 12% to 18% of annual compensation. In elhi editorial management, the differential can be even greater, which is basically a reflection of the size of an enterprise. In summary, the K-12 educational publishers of basal series and programs for required curriculum courses are major publishing houses with sizable in-house staffs. By contrast, the general Trade publishing scene has many more small "independents" than giants, and salary offerings are by necessity more modest.

TYPICAL ELHI CAREER PATHS

Publishing companies differ in the manner in which the editorial hierarchy is established and maintained. There are also differences in terminology for job titles, rates of advancement, and compensation. But the following career ladder is probably typical of both a medium-sized company (annual sales of $40 million) and a large one (sales topping $80 - $100 million).

Assistant editor—the entry-level position. With your qualifications and a successful interview and test assignment behind you, you could expect to begin your first job as an assistant to the other editors already assigned to the project team. You would be responsible for needed subject matter research and expected to be available for administrative tasks and minor writing/editing assignments. You might find yourself preparing and monitoring work flow charts, which is the swiftest way to become oriented to the complexities of an entire project's many parts and tasks. You could also be called upon to correlate the outline or table of contents of the project-in-progress with state or district curriculum guidelines.

Of course, you can expect to plunge into the editing/writing/rewriting matrix of the project alongside your fellow editors. You will find your energies divided between work done on your own and work done with others. But the results of both kinds of work will be shared with the group, so that within a few days on the job, you will begin to feel that you are an integral part of the project team.

If you have shown yourself capable and willing to assume greater responsibility, one to two years as an assistant editor should lead to the next step upward. As an **associate editor,** you will be responsible for preparing one or more auxiliary components for the project, as well as sharing responsibility with your colleagues for project assignments as needed. Because the auxiliary will be your "baby," you will be involved in all the aspects of bookmaking to which you've been exposed—art, production, manufacturing. As the key editor for the auxiliary component, you will be accountable for readability, sensitivity issues, and the coordination of materials with subject specialists and teacher reviewers.

Scope of responsibility increases as your experience adds up. You can look ahead, if all goes well, to **project editor** status, in which the student text—the chief revenue item—becomes your "baby."

At **senior editor** level, a number of textbooks or a series, developed grade-level by grade-level, would become your province.

The **executive editor** is in charge of the entire product line and is thus responsible for allocating all the talent, time and dollar resources properly to maintain an ever-growing, profitable product line.

Are there other related jobs in educational publishing for which you might qualify? A good question and a resounding "yes" to answer it. You may find a growing interest in preparing space advertising, promotional brochures, or other sales support materials. Speak to the Advertising department. Or a desire to undertake market research may catch your fancy. See the director of marketing. Or a hankering for direct field contact on an everyday basis could lead you into the sales rep or sales consultant category. See the sales manager. In summary, opportunities within the company will become visible to you in the normal course of events. The outcome depends on your motivation and skills potential, coupled with the needs and future plans of the publishing company.

THE GOOD, THE BAD, AND THE BEAUTIFUL

"All does not go well in the best of all possible worlds all of the time," as even the somewhat dense but good-natured Candide was able to advise his overly-sanguine tutor, Dr. Pangloss, by the end of Voltaire's classic novel. You should be prepared for very tough deadlines —tougher than those faced in general Trade or college publishing. Of the 50 states, some 22 confine textbook purchases to a list of approved books. And the rules for submission can be rigid and non-negotiable. In many cases, when textbook adoptions cover a three to four year time span, if a state deadline is missed, the publisher cannot submit an entry again for sale in the state until the next adoption date. You will quickly learn the state adoption priorities and internalize them.

The teamwork necessary for successful project development may not be your bag. Consensus is necessary to maintain a working homeostasis, so you may have to forego some of your favorite notions or private ambitions. This is a truism in business, speaking broadly, but is mentioned here because the nature of elhi editorial work demands ego flexibility and cooperative group endeavor.

The positive benefits of project teamwork more often than not outweigh the negatives. This has been demonstrated over and over again by the great number of project groups with members who stick together willingly through good times and bad to achieve the team goal: successful completion of an educational program of which the group can be proud. Healthy peer relationships based on mutual professional respect have been shown to be, year after year, one of the most satisfying aspects of an editorship in elhi publishing.

ROBERT B. STEWART

"Teaching, writing and editing come together functionally in my current job," declares the author, "and I'm hard put to think of a time in my worklife when these three roles didn't blend well."

Since he attained his current position in 1977, Mr. Stewart has been responsible for managing product development—editorial, art and production—in all content areas for which his division offered textbooks.

"These days the teaching is mostly coaching while the writing is pretty much 'business prose,'" he admits, "but the editing takes place every day in different subject areas and on many different levels with many different talents. Editing is truly the heart of the job.

"I came to publishing after college teaching. My first assignment was gargantuan—editing a best-selling, two-volume college text entitled <u>Civilization Past and Present</u> at Scott, Foresman & Co. It rivalled H.G. Wells' <u>Outline of History</u> in size and majesty. I was probably able to succeed solely through naivete and ambition—an unbeatable combination in youth."

A high school version of <u>Civilization</u> climaxed seven years at Scott, Foresman, followed by another seven years at Holt, Rinehart & Winston. He then decided to free-lance, soon finding himself "working both sides of the street as well as all the intersections—authoring a humanities program, doing filmstrips, writing, ghostwriting, trouble-shooting, editing, and more editing. All this led ultimately to editor-in-chiefship."

Stewart is an adjunct professor in New York University's summer publishing program and has been active on the education-for-publishing and research committees of the Association of American Publishers. Originally a Midwesterner and a graduate of the University of Chicago, he has spent most of his professional life on the East Coast "in that civilized enclave known as educational publishing."

CHAPTER TWELVE

Editorial Opportunities In College Publishing

By

John S.L. Holland, Managing Editor
The Dushkin Publishing Group, Inc.

College textbook publishing differs markedly from general trade book publishing —in its emphases, its atmosphere, its organization, its concerns, and, perhaps most important for anyone considering entering the field, in its job descriptions. Is textbook publishing as glamorous as trade publishing? The answer depends on what *you* call glamorous. If you have an intellectual bent, if you think it sounds exciting to work with professors, scholars, and specialists in a range of academic fields, if you enjoy the challenge of exploring new subjects, then college publishing may be for you. This chapter describes the responsibilities of the various positions found in most college textbook publishing houses.

COLLEGE ACQUISITION EDITOR

A **college acquisition editor** (salary $20,000 - $50,000) is usually selected from a textbook publisher's sales force, since the position requires a sense of how a book will sell. Selling books to professors is the best way to obtain this feel for the marketplace. (The campus bookstore manager, who actually purchases the books, does so only after a professor has decided to adopt a particular text for a class). In addition, a person with textbook sales experience already knows a number of professors, in whose ranks the acquisition editor finds authors.

As an acquisition editor, you solicit manuscripts—from college professors—read them, send them to other professors to review, suggest changes and reorganizations, and submit proposals to an editorial board. For some manuscripts, you will work closely with a **developmental editor** (see the next job description). You will probably concentrate on one or more disciplines—for example, history and art, English and geography, the social sciences, computer sciences. The subjects of the books you solicit are largely determined by the editor-in-chief, who may ask you to find an author for, say, a new introductory sociology book or a new volume in an existing history series. You will also be expected to discover or commission new books on your own initiative and to evaluate unsolicited manuscripts that are submitted to the publisher.

Once one of your books has been accepted for publication, you will help an author fulfill various obligations, such as obtaining permission for using material from other sources and providing roughly- drawn artwork. You will make sure that what the author has contracted for is submitted on time. You will arrange for the preparation of study guides, instructors' manuals, and any other ancillary material. You will present the book to the sales force at sales meetings and consult with the Promotion department about advertising and promoting the book. Your success as an acquisition editor depends on the success of your books and, often, on how well you have communicated with a developmental editor.

COLLEGE DEVELOPMENTAL EDITOR

A **college developmental editor** (salary $20,000 - $40,000) does just what the position title suggests—he or she "develops" a manuscript from its first, sometimes rough, stage until it is ready for final polishing by the **copy editor**. The **managing editor** usually gives a developmental editor a manuscript, reviews written by specialists in the field, and instructions on how to proceed: "You are responsible for checking the contents of each chapter to ensure that the proper topics are covered, making suggestions to the author about deleting or adding topics, enhancing the author's style where necessary or desirable, and correcting mistakes in grammar, syntax, and so on. You may have to reorganize material to achieve logic and clarity. You should see to it that the writing and exposition are at a suitable level for the intended audience. Try not to disturb the rhythm or the 'voice' of the writing."

These instructions leave a lot to the discretion and professional opinion of the editor. To make the necessary decisions, to rewrite whole sections or chapters—let alone discover and maintain an author's "rhythm"—require experience and breadth of knowledge. Thus being an inveterate reader is a key requirement for this job.

Developmental editors usually specialize in particular disciplines. They may have specialist knowledge to begin with or develop expertise on the job. But they *have* to know their fields. For example, they must be able to spot whether a psychology text meant for freshmen lacks crucial information on cognitive perspective.

As a developmental editor, you must be able to work closely and amicably with authors. You may have to obtain additional reviews after a manuscript has been rewritten or reorganized. You will be responsible for ensuring that permissions for reprinting material have been obtained. You will help the author draw up an index or give a professional indexer instructions.

Developmental editors are usually promoted from the ranks of college manuscript editors.

COLLEGE MANUSCRIPT EDITOR

A **college manuscript editor** (salary $17,000 - $35,000) edits in much the same way as a developmental editor, but is not usually expected to do heavy rewriting or restructuring or to commission reviews. Like a developmental editor, a manuscript editor is concerned with the writing style and the presentation of ideas. Both look out for—and repair—such faults as wordiness, jargon, awkward constructions, infelicities of style, and obscure or ambiguous wording. They may work with an **art editor** (see job description that follows) and **designer** to develop an art program (photos, drawings, graphs, maps). They see to it that "breathing spaces" (headings and subheads) help students absorb a large amount of information. They make sure that summaries *really* summarize and that end-of-chapter or workbook questions are actually answered in the text. In short, they act as surrogates for the student who will be learning from the text.

Probably the best preparation for becoming a manuscript editor is to have been a college copy editor.

COLLEGE COPY EDITOR

A **college copy editor** (salary $12,000 - $22,000) may be the *only* editor to review a manuscript or the second reader (after another editor). As a copy editor, you must spot and correct errors in spelling, punctuation, grammar, syntax, and usage. You must know your dictionaries and standard reference works and be able to use library services efficiently and check facts quickly. You are familiar with the Modern Language Association and the American Psychological Association documentation styles and know when to use them. You can proofread, using proofreading symbols; typemark a manuscript for typesetters to follow; compile a table of contents and other "front matter;" and copy edit an index.

Most copy editors are probably recent college graduates, and many have started in publishing as assistants or secretaries. Anyone applying for such a position should be familiar with the bibles of copy editors: The Chicago Manual of Style, 13th ed. (Chicago: U of Chicago P, 1982); The MLA Style Manual (New York: MLA, 1985); Words into Type, 3rd ed. (Englewood Cliffs: Prentice, 1974).

Other books on a copy editor's reading list are:

Cook, Clare Kehrwald. The MLA's Line by Line: How to Edit Your Own Writing. Boston: Houghton, 1985.

Coser, Lewis A., Charles Kadushin, and Walter W. Powell, Books: The Culture and Commerce of Publishing. New York: Basic, 1982.

Follett, Wilson. Modern American Usage: A Guide. New York: Hill, 1966.

While the descriptions and responsibilities of these four basic editorial positions are probably common to any college department or publisher, the specific titles may vary. Ask the interviewer to describe the duties of your job, since what I have called a manuscript editor may be called a copy editor at another house, and vice versa.

COLLEGE ART EDITOR

A final editorial position—**college art editor** (salary $12,000- $30,000)—is somewhat of a misnomer, since it combines editorial and graphic duties. This person selects illustrations to match the ideas and subjects discussed in a manuscript. The illustrations may be photographs, charts, graphs, maps, cartoons, or fine art reproductions. So an art editor must be imaginative, well-read, and knowledgeable about collections of graphic materials available for commercial use.

The art editor obtains permissions and negotiates fees, and is sometimes pressed into writing captions and credit lines. The person in this position must deal tactfully with authors and be willing to pursue their often vague leads. The art editor may have to travel to secure needed illustrations.

The art editor keys the illustrations to a text, sizes and crops illustrations, and often, under the supervision of an editor and designer, makes a dummy of the book, with blueprint illustrations in place to guide the printer. A good background in fine arts, applied arts or photography would be helpful in securing this position.

JOHN S. L. HOLLAND

Born, raised, and educated in the United Kingdom, John S.L. Holland worked in publishing in London and Sydney before coming to the United States in the 1960s. For 16 years he was a member of the College department of Harcourt Brace Jovanovich, Inc., in New York and San Diego. Currently he is managing editor of the Dushkin Publishing Group, Inc., in Guilford, Connecticut.

CHAPTER THIRTEEN

On Not Looking For A Job

By

Samuel S. Vaughan, Senior Vice President & Editor-Adult Trade Books
Random House, Inc.

Let's clear this up right away: I am crazy about this work. Luckily. Because it helps to be crazy.

The pay is poor at the bottom, middling in the middle, and almost no one gets rich at the top. The hours are nonsensical, roughly 9 - to - ridiculous, and the rewards and recognition are mostly hidden. Your work disappears into the work of others. Your ego must be subordinated to the ego of authors. Yet you must have and retain a sense of your own worth and character.

My advice to those of you faintly interested in book publishing: Go faint somewhere else. As one of my colleagues in another house remarked recently, we all get (far too many) calls from new people who think they "might" want to work in publishing. They seem to have no compunction about wasting an hour or two of our time while they try to make up their minds.

But if you (1) are crazy; (2) don't mind living vicariously off of others' fame; and (3) strongly desire to be underpaid and overworked...read on.

AN "OVERVIEW" OF TRADE BOOK PUBLISHING

"Trade" book publishing means the opposite of what "trade" means in magazine publishing. Trade *magazines* are for specialized audiences; most Trade *books* are for general audiences. Trade publishing is also sometimes called General Publishing.

Thus, a **trade or general editor** tends to be one who specializes in generalities. That is, I feel equipped to handle most fiction and "non-fiction" except books which require very considerable specialized knowledge. Some trade editors do have specialties: Judith Jones at Knopf and the ex-Dial editor Fran McCullough are known as cookbook specialists, in addition to their reputation for high-grade literary editing.

Five or six departments make up most publishing houses. They are: 1) editorial; 2) publicity and advertising; 3) sales and "marketing" (such terms vary in meaning but all are concerned with selling books); 4) art, design, and production (i.e., printing); 5) business and finance; and 6) rights selling.

Some houses are editorially-driven, to use the current expression. That is, editorial decisions—the opinions of the editors—come first. Other houses are marketing- or sales-driven; i.e., almost everything is decided first on the basis of its sales potential, as evaluated by the sales department. In a healthy house, I believe, both editorial voices and sales voices are respected. A house operated exclusively for or by its sales department could turn out to be purveyors of books as pure "merchandise;" a house operated exclusively by its editors could end up bankrupt.

HOW TO GO ABOUT GETTING INTO PUBLISHING

You go about. A great deal. Unless someone shoehorns you into a suddenly vacant desk with your name on it, you have to conduct a campaign.

To begin with, read. See the newspapers and trade magazines for any openings that are announced. Most aren't. They're filled from within or in a fast contact with the outside world. In a well-run, well-regulated world, a file of the best applicants would be regularly brought up-to-date and reached into the moment a chair became vacant. Nice idea, but not the way the world works. (Oh? You've noticed?) You have to apply and re-apply. Don't count on "The System."

Send a thoughtful resume and a short, polite, pointed cover letter to any of the editors in the publishing houses you want to try (see those listed in the back of this volume and in Literary Marketplace). Wait for them to respond, but don't wait *too* long. Tell them in the cover letter you'll follow up within two weeks—and do so, with a phone call. You're trying to get an interview—not a "job"—at this point.

Try to make each interview lead to others, so that nothing is ever a dead end. After doing your best in the interview, ask whether the interviewer has one or two people you should see. Use these recommendations as a springboard for other interviews. Drop a lot of pebbles into the pond. Make rings.

Publishing houses come in all sizes and shapes, so although you may not be right for one job, you could be ideal for another. Try to get The Right Chair (though you may need to take whatever's available just to get inside).

I am convinced that anyone who is any good can get a starting job in publishing, if they take the time and make the effort to devise a strategy to hit the houses and get the interviews…and can stay alive, fed, and sheltered while working to break in.

THE IDEAL PUBLISHING CANDIDATE…

…Is a person who likes some of the books he or she's read, loves others, and has forgotten many. A person who wants to enrich the culture and at the same time enrich the company; who can manage the seemingly at-odds objectives of commerce and literature. A private person willing to go public. (At first I found the alternating, conflicting demands of the work—working head down, in solitude, with words on paper—at odds with the requirement to express to others, inside and outside the house, my feelings for a manuscript, my enthusiasms, my reservations, my convictions, to "sell." But I learned first to live with the contradictions, then to enjoy them.) Someone who has done something extra, not just a young person who spent time in school.

I look for extracurricular effort and/or enthusiasm. I am not looking for freelance critics who want to tell me how imperfect most writing and most organizations are. Someone with energy, ideas, standards, follow-through, zest, flexibility. Attractive—not pretty or handsome, but someone whose caring is evident, whose willingness to contribute, cooperate and understand is natural.

THE ENTRY-LEVEL JOBS IN TRADE EDITORIAL

Usually hitting a typewriter, answering the phone, and volunteering to read and report on book submissions and proposals. Much of your reading will be done on your own time—on the bus or subway, at home.

Other entry-level "editorial" jobs might well occur in other parts of publishing—selling books at retail or on the road for a publisher; in dogsbody jobs in art and design, or writing copy for advertising and publicity departments (though these departments offer fulfilling publishing positions above the dog's level); putting labels on books sent to reviewers; "cleaning" (bringing up to date) mailing lists, etc.

In other words, you don't have to begin in editorial to become an editor; if you work in other publishing departments, your chances of being a well-prepared editor are even better.

But don't work in other parts of publishing overlong (more than 2 to 5 years) or until you are making such decent money in the "other" job that you won't want to or can't sacrifice that job to move into editorial.

I was a young sales manager. When offered a chance to become an editor—even a senior editor, as I was somewhat prematurely called then—it was, in many eyes, considered a step backward.

Why did I do it? Because I was asked. And because I was a fairly good sales manager and wanted to be a first class editor.

THE MONEY...OR LACK OF IT

Starting salaries in trade editorial range from $12,000 - $15,000. You can expect, in most well-organized companies, regular raises of 5% to 7%; raises accompanying a promotion will be 10 to 15% or better. Advancement is rapid or glacial, depending on you, the "corporate culture" —the tradition and temperament of the company—how well the company is doing, and whether you switch jobs or companies. Long-term, loyal employment was once said to be the norm; publishing people now change jobs with the rabbit-like affinity of advertising agency people.

How long should you do scut work before getting a promotion? One year, two years, or five—then you'll get promoted and still have some scut work to do. Every job is work, *real* work, in part. The lunches might be better, the books seem a little more selective (though they're not), but I still spent my first six years in publishing occasionally doing jobs I wasn't particularly crazy about.

Why? I wanted to learn publishing and had to make a living. I made some progress. Promotions came every two years, not always into what I wanted, but always representing a chance to move ahead. When I finally got where I wanted to be—into Editorial—I wasn't promoted again for ten years. But I had made it to the right place and, eventually, the promotions came.

The beginners I see today have a more urgent sense of time. Most will not go the distance. There is a decided difference between *being stuck* and *sticking it out*.

EDITORIAL JOB TITLES

They're grand, glorious, meaningful or meaningless. It all depends on the company.

You start as an **editorial assistant** or **assistant to an editor**. ("Secretaries" have disappeared ...as some bosses will sadly say, "And how!")

The next step is to **assistant editor,** then **associate editor,** then maybe **editor** or **senior editor,** then **executive or managing editor** (managing is usually more administrative than straight editing), then **associate publisher, editor-in-chief, president, publisher,** or some combination.

YOUR TYPICAL DAY WILL BE —

Atypical.

But it usually starts with coffee, getting your own and maybe someone else's—for your boss or the kid at the next desk or the first guest who has an appointment with your boss. You'll get good at getting coffee. And at opening the mail and trying to do something with it—sorting it for your boss's convenience, routing some of it elsewhere. Answering the phone. And the phone and the phone. Calls from agents, other bosses, the mailroom with misaddressed mail you've just re-routed. Your Mother. People trying to sell stocks.

Also, typing, filing, fetching, kvetching, chatting with the woman or man waiting with you for the Xerox machine to be fixed. Much talk.

Talking to your typewriter or word processor and to yourself. Some of us major in muttering.

Making lunch reservations for your boss. Calling the deli for yourself. Finding ways to tell your editor that anyone who (A) likes this manuscript or (B) does *not* like this manuscript is seriously brain deficient and wholly lacking in any kind of taste...except bad.

Dealing with a rich supply of questions from others in the firm and those friendly creatures called authors: What's the pub date of the new book by Gina LollaBallonga? How do you *spell* LollaBallonga—with one or two e's? Where is my contract? My check? Why is my book out of stock? Don't you people know what you're doing? Can I take you to dinner? (or) How about you taking *me* to dinner?

So you squeeze in a few personal calls (most firms limit them to no more than fifteen a day) and sweat out your landlord or the arrival of the TV or telephone installer. But each day *will* be different.

IS COLLEGE NECESSARY?

Avoiding the larger societal implications of that question, you should know that most people in publishing have a college education. No, let's put it this way: Most of us have been to some college, somewhere. Our education continues—or, for some of us, begins—when we get into book publishing. That's one of our main pleasures and rewards: You can't stop learning. Authors, editors, sales reps, other publishers, the books, magazines, newspapers, newsletters, radio and TV shows you scan constantly: All will teach you something. Maybe they'll teach you that there's too much communication and too little knowledge. Too much "news," too few trustworthy facts. Too many "features," not enough substance. Too many opinions, too little wisdom.

But you'll learn and re-learn to respect books, one of the oldest of the media.

And as soon as you figure you have learned enough, you'll put in for early retirement.

GRADUATE DEGREES?

Sometimes useful. It helps to know a good deal about something, but by and large you will not receive extra compensation for graduate degrees in the liberal arts. M.B.A.s, yes, of course, but we are not speaking here of the illiberal arts. One of the best trade editors, Lawrence Ashmead of Harper & Row, has a graduate degree in geology. He never edits books in geology.

IS ENGLISH NECESSARY? "I *LOVE* BOOKS!"

Fluency with the language—there are still some cities where English is the language of choice—is helpful, maybe essential. All of us have to write: letters, press releases, book jacket copy, catalogue copy, author biographies, memos. And it's nice to be able to do so and have them become intelligible when read from left to right. Still, publishing is *not* necessarily a place for writers—that is, those who want to be Writers above all else—but it *is* a place for people who can express themselves.

And if you love books, that's nice. Because that love will be severely tested.

The first thing you sell in a job is your time. Then your skills, talents or brains. And the first thing you sacrifice in publishing is time to read on your own, to read what you *want* to read. We are all *supposed* to read what other authors are writing, other houses publishing. The hard truth is that many of us become semi-literate, spending nearly all our reading time on the books we are engaged in helping to publish.

So there is some "sacrifice" involved. The solution is to try to find books to publish, to "work on," that you want to read in the first place (the first market test for us is in our own hearts and minds) and like even on re-reading. I am currently engaged in re-reading and editing novels by writers as splendid and diverse as William F. Buckley, Jr., Wallace Stegner, Winston Graham, Hannah Green and Bud Shrake. I don't mind *that* work a bit.

SO STOP LOOKING FOR A JOB.

If you want to "look in" on us, look first within yourself: for signs of a vocation, a calling, a compulsion, a commitment. This lunacy might or might not pay as well as selling insurance, bonds or your body. But ours is an unfailingly interesting line of work—grand or goofy or glorious at various times. And it's not for everybody.

But if you're beginning to believe it could be for you, welcome.

SAMUEL S. VAUGHAN

Before he accepted his current position at Random House in March, 1986, Mr. Vaughan spent his book publishing career at Doubleday & Company. He started there as an assistant selling "rights" and became advertising manager at 24; sales manager at 26; senior editor at 28; and, eventually, president, publisher and editor-in-chief over the next decades.

He was the the first chairman of the Education for Publishing Committee of the Association of American Publishers and was chairman of its General Books Council. Mr. Vaughan is a frequent lecturer at universities, did the Bowker Memorial Lecture, has written three books for children, two for adults, and extensively about publishing.

He went to Penn State and has four "ex-children" (all grown) who went to Brandeis, Berkeley, Coe, Lawrence, and Penn State.

Mr. Vaughan and the editors of this volume wish to express their special thanks to Ms. Angela Himsel and Mr. Jeff Cohen, two assistants at Random House who, according to Sam, "helped bring this manuscript closer to English and made sure I wasn't completely out of touch with *their* concepts of editorial reality."

CHAPTER FOURTEEN

Production: We Make Things Happen!

By

Lyman O. Louis, VP-Inventory & Manufacturing
MacMillan Publishing Company

Judging by the backgrounds of those people currently in production functions in publishing, advertising or printing, most attribute their positions to serendipity. This is certainly true in the book publishing area. Whether they're involved in producing books, records, catalogs, transparencies, disk programs, or other educational material—or all of the above!—the backgrounds of the production managers I've known or worked with seem to be as varied as the areas of the country from which they come.

But common to all production managers is strong logistical ability, good mathematical skills, pride in developing tangible products, and an ability to grasp technical details. Communication skills—written and verbal—are essential.

EDUCATIONAL REQUIREMENTS AND TRAINING OPPORTUNITIES

The educational backgrounds vary from specific degrees in printing management, operations analysis, production or industrial management to the more design-oriented majors. But liberal arts students with degrees in social sciences may be found working next to biology majors or those technically-trained pros mentioned above. Despite the variance, there is one key to success—a college degree.

Those graduates with degrees not specific to the production area frequently applied for or actually started out in other positions and later gravitated to production management to fulfill a desire to create—or disseminate on a large scale—art, ideas or products.

In many houses, preliminary, on-the-job training exists for students just out of college who impressed the interviewer with their communication skills, were involved in coursework that required a certain "comfort-level" with statistics and enjoyed keeping track of a lot of pieces going in different directions...simultaneously.

FUNCTIONS OF A PRODUCTION MANAGER

The specific functions which a production manager might perform would include the following: At an initial meeting, editors, marketing managers or others might present the seed of an idea for a new book, which will not become a reality for over a year; a college title for which several chapters already exist; or a trade book which is approaching reality, but with which production is not yet involved. At this stage, the production manager needs to determine costs and schedules. Where specifications (the essential ingredients of costs and schedules) do not exist. the production manager makes assumptions based on experience and further discussions with editors and marketing managers. Suppliers are called in to bid on the various facets of the job, from composition, film preparation, and separations, to printing, paper manufacturing, and binding.

Once the budgets have been approved, the final prices and vendors determined, and the specifications firmly established, the purchase orders are written. Then the production manager follows up to make sure all the many tasks and pieces are performed and received on time. Finally, the first copy of the book is delivered. And if the editors, designers and authors are pleased with the final result, the production manager holds a copy and enjoys that rare moment of satisfaction in a job well done.

The production function is complicated in that more than one job is going through at the same time. A given production manager might be responsible for from 20 to 50 jobs per year.

My own job is proof enough that production is complicated and that a "typical" day really doesn't exist. I often meet with my staff first thing in the morning to check on particular problems of interest to all. This might be followed by an interview of a potential new employee or a review of the progress on a new computerized estimating system. Before lunch I might prepare a productivity report for senior management or check on a couple of jobs that had presented some unique challenges or problems the day before.

After lunch a vendor might present a new proposal for a piece of equipment his company may be considering and we would discuss its applicability to our future requirements. This might be followed by a meeting with a senior manager of the School Division regarding some problems which have surfaced in a new math program they are developing or an editor in the College Division about a new psychology text. And so the day goes. Often I travel to visit various suppliers or monitor a job on press.

THERE ARE SUBSTANTIAL ENTRY-LEVEL OPPORTUNITIES

While the production function in a printing or publishing facility is not a *conspicuous* employment opportunity, it is fulfilling and rewarding...and there *are* substantial opportunities for people with the right skills.

Entry-level positions are typically **planning assistant**, **secretary**, **manufacturing assistant** or **estimating trainee**. Depending on the level at which you start and your ability, promotions should occur in six months, two years and five years. After five years, most entry-level people have become full **journeymen production managers**; many are **unit managers**. After eight years, it would not be unusual to be a **departmental manager** and part of the management team.

The particular assignments for each of these job titles will vary depending on the needs of a department and your own particular ability. However, you might initially be involved in preparing purchase orders, setting up meetings with vendors, making travel arrangements, logging material in and out, and/or beginning to request bid proposals and analyze bids, as well as controlling various components of a simple job as they move through the system.

Starting salaries vary by size of company and geography. Depending on experience and major, a beginning salary might be from $14,000 up to $18,000 in the New York market. Three to five years out, $25,000 might be a reasonable objective, with departmental management earning $40,000 and up. Clearly this varies according to situation, ability, opportunity, etc., but these salaries are probably fair estimates for larger companies in the New York market. These companies also tend to have better benefit programs, including health programs, employee investment funds, company stores, educational assistance packages, and many other programs which improve the salary considerations.

Certainly at our company—and many other houses—there is adequate exposure and remuneration for night school or seminar courses to fill in technical gaps that might exist in an otherwise suitable entry-level candidate's knowledge. Again, a college degree is preferred for virtually every position in order to afford the individual a reasonable chance for promotion and career advancement. (While exceptions may sometimes be made, the climb up the career Ladder will definitely be more difficult for non-degreed individuals.)

If all of this sounds like the kind of career you've been looking for, come join us! Production is an exciting and fulfilling occupation if you have energy, enthusiasm and the strong desire to "make things happen."

LYMAN O. LOUIS

Mr. Louis was formerly vice president-manufacturing for CBS Educational and Professional Publishing. A past president of the Seattle Club of Printing House Craftsmen, he was formerly an executive with the North Pacific Bank Note Company in Seattle. He is a member of the American Institute of Graphic Arts and a member and former chairman of the Publishers Committee of the Advisory Commission on Text Book Specifications.

Mr. Louis holds a B.A. in general business from the University of Washington and a B.S. in printing management from Carnegie-Mellon. He has taught at the Burnley School of Professional Arts and the Association of the Graphic Arts.

Listed in Who's Who, he is also chairman of the board of the Greater Westchester Youth Orchestra Association and a partner in Sugarbush Farms, which raises, trains, and leases show horses.

CHAPTER FIFTEEN

Book Publicity/Public Relations: It May Be Free, But Nobody Ever Said It Was Easy!

By

**Julia Knickerbocker, VP/Associate Publisher/Director of Public Relations
Simon & Schuster, Inc.**

I get people to do things for me for free. It's a great job, but, as you might imagine, a bit of a challenge!

THE PUBLICIST'S TASK—ATTENTION!

The task facing every book publisher's Publicity or Public Relations department is to draw attention to the books their house is launching, either through book reviews, print interviews with the author (separate from the normal book review page or section) and/or radio and television appearances. Many books need some combination of all of the above.

And though it might sound hard, it still *sounds* a lot easier than it really *is!* Unlike advertising—which is bought and paid for—the articles, reviews, appearances, mentions, etc. that the Public Relations department generates are, strictly speaking, free. They don't cost us anything except hard work. Which might be welcome news to the accountants, but is why our jobs are so challenging—when is the last time *you* got a total stranger to do something for you for *free*?

Public Relations Vs. Advertising

It's not difficult to call up a magazine and pay them whatever they charge to run an ad promoting your book. It's somewhat more involved to call a magazine *editor* and convince him or her to interview an author or feature the book or author in an article. Or to convince a particular *reviewer* or review medium, who can only feature a handful of the tens of thousands of books that are manufactured each year, to include yours in an upcoming issue or column.

While it's easier to pick up the phone and place an ad, it's a trifle more expensive—the cost of an average full page newspaper or consumer magazine ad these days is roughly $12,000. For <u>one</u> ad. For *that* kind of money, I can send an author to a dozen cities, get him onto 20 or 30 television shows, 30 to 40 radio shows, and probably generate an equal number of magazine and newspaper interviews and features. And I'd get the author far more exposure *that* way than the ad could ever *hope* to generate.

Despite the high (and going higher) cost of advertising, many companies, publishers included, use it extensively. Why? Because it is usually easy to discover whether or not a particular ad or series of ads has been successful. You can code each ad and trace every response, every sale it generates. Then you can total up the orders and see the kind of money made (or lost) as a result of each media placement.

How do you quantify the results of an author's appearance on the "Mornings At Nine" show in Des Moines, Iowa, or on the Style page of the *Oshkosh News*? Readers who go to a bookstore to buy a particular book don't usually tell the bookstore manager *why* they are buying it, let alone *where* they heard about it. And while you can trace the effect of such public relations efforts indirectly—why *else* did sales double in Des Moines that week?—you can rarely obtain the kind of solid, quantifiable sales figures that any businessman likes to be able to see and feel.

At the same time, no one can *buy* the kind of exposure a good publicist can generate for a book. While most of the largest and/or most progressive publishing houses now recognize the "power of publicity," I think Simon and Schuster is probably the most aggressive house in the industry in terms of publicity. S & S's top management views us, at least metaphorically, as the key component of their advertising effort. And, like the Advertising department, they expect us to achieve *real* results.

Luckily, although they sometimes seem to want a miracle a day, they do give us the books to do it with and the support staff to pull it off. The results we've achieved as a result of this corporate emphasis and support prove that they're right—<u>a solid, professional publicity effort can absolutely change the life of book</u>.

SOME PUBLIC RELATIONS SUCCESS STORIES

There's probably no book in existence that wouldn't sell more behind a professionally-mounted publicity effort. Of course, when your publishing house launches hundreds of books every year, as Simon & Schuster and just about every other major house does, you simply can't create a massive, concerted publicity drive for every single one. You don't have the time or the staff. So you have to pick out the ones that you think have the best shot....or those that will potentially benefit most from the right approach.

A recent example: <u>Secrets of the Temple: How the Federal Reserve Runs the Country</u> by William Greider, an 800-page tome on a subject that doesn't exactly get everyone's juices flowing like the latest James Michener paperweight. Yet we managed to book the author on the "Today" show and work to ensure that the topic was revealed as an important one to the average viewer, and an accessible one, too. I'm keeping my fingers crossed, but I think this and similar exposure may well propel it on to the best-seller charts.

Then again, some books don't *need* a big approach. Not every book lends itself to an author's tour, for example...though few *authors* would agree! Some are just purely review books, in which case we have to make sure the reviewers are aware of it and going to pay attention when it comes around. Others, like Bob Woodward's <u>Veil,</u> are so anticipated that all we have to do is schedule it right and make sure reviewers have the copies they need.

And some books need special treatment because of special circumstances. Carrie Fisher's novel, <u>Postcards From the Edge</u>, was a *really good novel,* not an autobiography, not a thinly-veiled <u>Mommie Dearest II.</u> I saw my job as making sure she and her book were taken seriously—because they deserved to be—and not consigned to that sometimes-condescending corner of the bookstores and the review columns reserved for "celebrity tell-alls."

The bottom line: You do as much as you can for each particular book and put your greatest effort (and time, our nemesis) into the books with the greatest potential.

TYPICAL PUBLIC RELATIONS DEPARTMENT SETUP

There are probably far fewer professionals in the Public Relations departments of most major houses than you would think. At Simon & Schuster, for example, I have a staff of 15...and we handle upwards of 300 titles a year.

We are officially part of the overall marketing effort—I report, for example, to Simon & Schuster's marketing director. The other departments we tend to work most closely with are: Advertising (we provide them will reviews and quotes they'll want to feature in their ads); Sales Promotion (who will occasionally do glitzy press kits that cost a fortune; they are *not* for every book); and Sales (to make sure books are out there—and in the right stores—when our publicity efforts take off).

Our department is set up in a three-tiered structure. At the top—the first tier—are myself (**director of public relations**), one **associate director** and one **assistant director**. Two **senior publicists** are the second tier. The remaining members of the department—**assistant publicists** and **assistants to the publicists** make up the third and final tier.

That's the corporate setup. From a practical, everyday standpoint, the department staffers are divided into four **publicity teams**. The entire list of books is divided up among these four teams, though not haphazardly. Rather than simply apportioning them equally, I tend to assign them according to each individual staffer's affinity. If one of my publicists were particularly good at promoting cookbooks, for example, I would assign him or her *all* the cookbooks. Since it's a subject he or she cared about, he or she might well do a better job with those books. Others might be great at fiction or politically oriented. While I feel any professional should be a capable generalist, and my staff all are, some are particularly talented, knowledgeable or interested in specific areas. Taking advantage of such individual talents is not just good management, it may well make a difference in the publicity effort and, therefore, the success of a book.

Publicity assistant is the entry-level position. You'll start out typing labels and releases, fielding phone calls for your boss (one of the publicists), and preparing bills (for authors' tours). When an author is out on tour, you'll be the one calling the newspapers, magazines, TV and radio stations the day before scheduled interviews to reconfirm the author's schedule. You may spend some time researching mailing lists that we may want to use to promote a specific book. (At S & S, we have 45 - 50 major consumer lists on our computer, but we occasionally need a whole new one—e.g., people interested in dance (for a new ballet book), gardeners (for The Vegetable In Your Life), etc.

After a little while—six months or so—you'll get a chance to arrange telephone interviews, maybe even make some television or radio bookings. For all this admittedly boring, "grunt" work, you will be paid the princely sum of $11,500 or so.

After a year (absolute minimum) or two (more likely), you'd be ready for promotion to **assistant to the publicist** (salary—$16,000 to $18,000). Here you will spend nearly all your time arranging bookings. A talented assistant can expect to be promoted to the next level—**senior publicist** (or, in some houses, just **publicist**)—in two to three years.

At Simon & Schuster, a senior publicist is the head of each of the four teams mentioned earlier. Each publicist or senior publicist (salary—$22,000 to $35,000) has probably five years experience (or more) and works with senior management (myself, the associate and assistant directors) to conceive the overall public relations program for each book assigned to their team. This includes everything from which media should receive initial galleys to whether a full-blown author's tour is advisable (as opposed to just local promotion). Is a press release required with each submission or just a thoughtful letter? Should direct mail be used? If so, are there any special lists that the book may require? Can the author supply us with specific ideas, lists of contacts, etc.?

Those publicists who reach senior management level may earn anywhere from $35,000 to nearly $100,000. An assistant or associate public relations director at a larger house would probably be in the $35,000 to $40,000 range. A public relations director at a smaller house might make the same or a little more. And the directors at the largest houses will probably earn a minimum of about $50,000, up to a top of very near $100,000.

THE IDEAL CANDIDATE FOR A PUBLISHING PUBLICITY CAREER

While your individual major is not too important, you must have a college degree. (I seem to see a preponderance of English majors, but that's *their* preference, not mine.) What *I* want is someone for whom books are already an important part of their lives, someone who already reads book reviews because they care about books. That's why I frequently ask candidates what books they read for their own pleasure—it's a quick way to find out if books are *really* important to them.

Experience in a book publishing company—summers, part-time during the school year, whatever—is important; it's a further sign to me that you want to get into book publishing publicity, *not* just find a public relations job anywhere. I therefore highly recommend internships. It's nice if you have attended one of the better-known publishing courses—the NYU summer course, Denver, Radcliffe, etc.—but isn't really essential if you evidence the right other credentials and attitude.

If you've done a lot of writing—reviews for a local newspaper or magazine, features, etc.—it's a very definite plus. And, of course, I'd like to see your best samples. A good publicist has to be able to communicate on all levels—written, verbal, even visual—so *any* evidence showing these skills will help you land that first job.

What should you be *like* to succeed in public relations at a book publishing house? First, you must have a very high energy level. Actually, given the high stress levels of the profession and the hours (long hours are the *rule*, not the exception), you need *inhuman* energy. Second, an ability to cope with infinite detail; it's one thing to book an author on a number of shows, but if you don't get the boring details right—what time, where, etc.—you won't survive. Third, you should have a near-infinite capacity to deal with frustration. You'll have to graciously accept an awful lot of "no's," be able to face and handle the rejection, persevere, and try another way.

ENTRY-LEVEL OPPORTUNITIES...
AND MOVING TO OTHER DEPARTMENTS

I don't believe entry-level public relations jobs at publishing houses are really at a premium. Many new employees are sure they want to be in book publishing but unsure of a particular department or specialization; so we get our share of entry-level people who start in our department and use it as a "stepping stone" to other jobs at Simon & Schuster. Sometimes a manager in some other department spies a particularly promising assistant publicist and initiates the transfer himself. (This is always done in a very straightforward way. If someone from another department wanted to "hire away" one of my staffers, they would tend to speak to me first. But it *does* happen, often to everyone's benefit.)

The result is that there tends to be a fair amount of turnover at the entry-level in our department. I suspect it's similar at other houses. Which means there are frequently openings for people who *do* actually want to get into book publishing publicity!

Moving to other departments in Simon & Schuster from a first job in the Public Relations department is not particularly difficult. Once you have a toehold here, you will find out about openings in other departments far more quickly than the general public and can move along to another area if you so desire and if the right opening exists. I don't know about policy or ease-of-transfer at other houses, but I suspect that if someone is really talented but wants a different job, the house would want to keep him or her in whatever capacity possible and would attempt to affect the necessary transfer.

WHY YOU SHOULD JOIN US!

Entry-level jobs in our field, as should be obvious from our previous discussion of job responsibilities for the assistants to the publicists, are far from glamorous. And not everyone can handle the hours, the pressure, the stress, or the rejection.

And it *can* be difficult and scary. When I first started, the thought of picking up a phone and talking to a total stranger was absolutely *terrifying*. And that was a major part of my job! I used to write out my first sentence so at least I'd *start* the conversation right.

You'll make mistakes, some of them horrifying. Twenty years ago, on my first job, I booked an author on two shows simultaneously—one taped, one live. Logistically, that was fine, but unfortunately, the author wound up appearing on two shows on competing networks in the *same time slot*. Neither the producers, the author, or my boss were particularly overjoyed.

But I still my job exciting, challenging and worth the effort. Every time I think I'm totally burned out and can't do it, something wonderful happens. But as much as I enjoy the whole range of public relations functions, I wouldn't want to do *any* of it in any other field, even though I know I'd be better paid. I just love books. I really do. And that's all I want to promote.

If *you* love books and really want to effect what happens to some you care about, come join us. You'll *love* it!

JULIA KNICKERBOCKER

Ms. Knickerbocker has been with Simon & Schuster since 1981. She was previously director of publicity and public relations at William Morrow & Co., which followed a previous 3-plus year stint at S & S as co-director of publicity (the department was much smaller then). She was also director of public relations for Mason and Lipscomb, now difunct, and Avon Paperbacks.

Ms. Knickerbocker began her career as a receptionist/proofreader for a small house, M. Evans and Co. The company had never had a public relations director, a job which Ms. Knickerbocker created for herself after two years there. She quickly developed a high-profile reputation—two of the books she promoted while on her first job were <u>Body Language</u> and <u>Open Marriage</u>.

She graduated from Radcliffe with a B.A. in English and is a member of the Women's Media Group and the Publishers Publicity Association; she was also on the board of the latter group. She lectures on her specialty at Stanford University every summer as part of their well-known Publishing Course.

CHAPTER SIXTEEN

Marketing And Sales Opportunities In Elhi Textbook Publishing

By

Fred Schilling, Director of Training
D. C. Heath and Company

Sales and marketing professionals in the elhi textbook industry are most often former classroom teachers and/or school administrators. In most instances, these educators have had highly successful teaching careers and, by serving on textbook selection committees, become known to textbook representatives and consultants as curriculum leaders.

Marketing and sales positions in the elhi industry provide excellent opportunities to apply one's professional educational experiences to a variety of instructional settings. School personnel look to the publishers, consultants and sales representatives for the instructional materials and textbooks they need to help them implement their school districts' curriculum objectives. A highly rewarding aspect of a marketing-sales career in elhi publishing is the collegial relationship that one is able to establish with the leading educators in one's sales territory.

THE ELHI INDUSTRY

In 1987, it is estimated that sales of elhi textbooks will exceed $1.6 billion. Language arts is the single largest segment of the elementary textbook market, accounting for over 50% of all expenditures; math textbooks run second, with 20% of the sales. The secondary textbook market remains slightly smaller than the elementary segment, with vocational education leading sales with 30% of the market, followed by combined language arts and math, at 29.1% and 17.4%, respectively. The most rapidly growing area in secondary sales continues to reflect the renewed emphasis on modern languages.

Today's market environment requires professionals representing publishers to become more aware and sensitive to the divergent needs of their customers. More and more textbooks and other instructional materials are measured against curriculum frameworks and courses of study developed by local school districts or state departments of education.

It is essential that elhi marketers be able to clearly demonstrate how their instructional materials complement these local or state criteria. Additionally, they must communicate emerging education trends back to the publisher to assure that product development is responsive and adapts to the changing needs in the elhi marketplace.

FUNCTIONAL STRUCTURING OF ELHI PUBLISHING HOUSES

Most elhi publishing houses are departmentalized according to function: editorial (which includes art and production); general administration (including manufacturing, distribution, human relations, finance and inventory control); and marketing/sales. Opportunities in editorial, manufacturing and production have been discussed in detail elsewhere in this publication. Staffing of general administration positions often requires different skills and educational credentials, such as an M.B.A., accounting degree or expertise in industrial relations.

Most often general managers have been promoted through a series of increasingly responsible marketing and sales or editorial positions. While this article focuses attention on the opportunities in marketing and sales, it is important to understand that a successful career in elhi publishing requires an intimate familiarity with the interdependencies, need for effective communication and interface between the various functions.

THE SCHOOL MARKETING & SALES STRUCTURE

Since the early 1980s, a number of acquisitions and mergers have led to a significant amount of consolidation in school publishing. This has enabled many of the larger publishers to group their business activities according to areas of specialization, creating operating divisions such as elementary, secondary and a supplemental print and software group. This type of organization allows publishers to become more focused and responsive to the needs of specific elhi market segments. Regardless of whether the publisher specializes in a specific market segment or publishes for grades K-12, the marketing and sales structure remains similar.

Director of marketing and/or national sales manager.

This position carries the authority and responsibility for directing field and other sales of text products; developing and executing advertising and promotion of these products (including space advertising, direct mail advertising, trade show and other marketing-related exhibits, sales staff selection and the definition of function and training for the sales staff); market planning and budgeting; cost control and profit generation; field service, including teacher training; and participating in product development or revision. If the publisher has created a national sales manager's position, it is this person who assumes authority and responsibility for the sales functions. Depending on the organization of the publisher, the national sales manager usually reports to the director of marketing. If the national sales manager and director of marketing divide responsibilities, then they would both probably report to the general manager.

MARKETING ORGANIZATION

<u>Product manager</u> positions are often filled by the most successful sales representatives, educational consultants, line sales managers, or, sometimes, by editors seeking to broaden their publishing background. Product managers report to the director of marketing.

The product manager develops an action-oriented marketing plan that carefully details all activities associated with the promotion and maintenance of the product line. While developing and executing this plan, he or she interfaces with the advertising and promotion department to develop both print and non-print sales support materials; works with the exhibit manager to plan convention and trade show activities to help gain national attention for the product line; interacts with the executive editor during the developmental stage to be certain authors and editors are sensitive to the needs of classroom teachers and other educators; coordinates market research activities to test the features, advantages and benefits of the product; provides forecasts and print quantities to inventory control; and acts as the home office liaison to the field sales force. Each product manager should be a true "product champion" and must be the most knowledgeable person in the company regarding his or her product line.

Advertising and promotion manager

The advertising and promotion manager most often reports to the director of marketing. In school publishing, the exhibit manager, advertising and promotion copywriters, creative director, public relations and communications functions are all usually found in this department. This is one of the few areas in the national marketing office where entry-level positions are sometimes filled with recent college graduates who lack teaching experience. Degrees in communication, journalism, advertising and marketing are helpful to the job candidate interested in this area of publishing. For a good, detailed explanation of this area—and the appropriate jobs—see Diane Kuppler-Weaver's article earlier in this volume (*chapter 8—Ed.*)

SALES ORGANIZATION

Most school publishers have organized their field sales and consultant staffs into four to six geographic sales regions, supported by regional offices. These offices are supervised by a **regional sales manager** or **regional general manager** who is in charge of the first line sales managers, educational consultants, regional marketing staff, secretarial and clerical support. Many companies operate their regional offices as profit centers, and the general manager operates his or her region as a microcosm of the national office.

First line sales manager

The **first line sales manager** is responsible for meeting the sales goal assigned to him or her by the regional manager, while staying within the expense budget. He or she provides field supervision and training for sales representatives and, in some companies, for educational consultants. He or she may also schedule sales-service and sales-support personnel. The sales managers design and implement sales plans, recruit and hire field personnel and help to train, plan and organize the activities of their subordinates. Sales managers are most often selected from the ranks of the most promising sales representatives or consultants. Organizational skills and proven leadership ability are traits associated with this position.

Sales representative or educational representative

This is considered to be an entry-level position for school publishing. (Despite the fact that "entry-level position" implies a place merely to *start* one's career, many men and women who have entered school publishing have found sales to be a worthy, lifelong professional career and remain sales representatives until retirement.) The sales representative is usually a former classroom teacher or administrator. Duties include presenting products and services to potential and existing accounts, actively selling products to meet sales goals, servicing the complete product line in a designated territory and providing inservice training to customer schools.

To accomplish these goals, the representative must learn as much as possible about his company's product line and the curriculum needs of the territory's customers...and how to match the two. He or she will attend local, state, regional and even national exhibits and provide for inservice training of teachers using his company's products. Careful records of everything he or she does must be maintained—these are forwarded to the regional or national office on a regular basis.

During a typical week, a sales representative will call by appointment on school administrators to determine if any of his or her products match areas where the school or school district is adopting new textbooks or other instructional materials. Depending on the size of the representative's territory, it will sometimes be necessary to travel overnight, as many as two or three times each week. It is not uncommon for representatives to be called upon to entertain key customers at dinner, lunch or other social activities.

Consultants

If the principal responsibility of the sales representative is to "sell the product," it might be said that the consultants' job is to "keep the product sold." School districts rely heavily on the publisher to provide inservice training and staff development activities to assure that their products are used properly. Consultants are most often product specialists who have gained a reputation for expertise in a certain discipline such as reading, mathematics or modern languages. They are usually former supervisors, department heads or classroom teachers who have demonstrated effective teaching techniques in a specific subject area.

The consultant introduces products and methodology to key educators to generate sales, provides inservice training to customers and reports market conditions, trends, and customer needs to management. Duties and responsibilities include organizing and conducting training workshops, visiting classrooms and demonstrating teaching techniques, training sales representatives in product knowledge, giving professional talks, attending exhibits and providing service to customers who have purchased the publisher's products. Consultants are often selected to fill sales management, product management and sometimes editorial positions. In most companies the consultant reports to the regional or line manager. Travel is often quite extensive and requires overnight trips two to four nights a week during the school year.

QUALIFICATIONS AND SUCCESS FACTORS

From the preceding discussion it should be evident that candidates must have a minimum of a bachelor's degree, although advanced degrees are preferred, especially for consultant positions. Teaching experience is clearly an advantage, especially for field sales and consulting positions. Salaries are competitive with the teaching profession and supplemented with a company car and bonus or commission incentive program.

Ideal candidates for entry-level field positions must have excellent verbal and written communication skills. They must be highly organized, possess the ability to prioritize tasks, maintain a balance between long-term and short-range goals while performing a variety of tasks simultaneously, enjoy working with people in both business and social settings, be willing to travel extensively and to work independently with a minimum of direct supervision.

FRED SCHILLING

Mr. Schilling began his career as a secondary teacher. He joined Holt, Rinehart & Winston's School Division in 1969 as a sales representative in the Midwest region. In 1976 he was appointed to a division sales management position in California and, from 1979 to 1981, held positions as director of marketing services and director of sales administration in New York.

In 1981 Mr. Schilling joined Open Court Publishing Company as vice president of marketing and sales. Since 1985 he has served as director of marketing and director of training for D. C. Heath and Company in Lexington, Massachusetts. He has been active in the AAP School Division, serving on a variety of state action committees.

CHAPTER SEVENTEEN

Launching A Sales Career In College Textbook Publishing

By

Donald W. Burden, Director of Marketing Services
McGraw-Hill Book Company

Professors anxiously awaiting your visit? This is probably a not-unwelcome switch from what you experienced as a student. And it will happen if you join the ranks as a successful field sales representative for a college textbook publishing house.

A career in college textbook publishing offers you a unique opportunity to cement a new relationship with those professors charged with the educational development of our valued student population. As a professional representative of an educational publisher, you'll be welcomed by professors who want to explore the contents of books that support their classroom and laboratory teaching.

COLLEGE PUBLISHING—A LOT MORE THAN "JUST" TEXTBOOKS

Today, textbook publishing is a major segment of the communication industry. The demand for knowledge is ever-increasing. The impact of today's technology challenges everyone to keep abreast of these changes as it impacts their career—their earning power and earning potential. Whether it be the latest surgical technique in a specialized field of medicine, a recently unearthed archaeological find, or a new management or economic theory, the need remains for a medium to detail this information to a knowledge-seeking market. A major resource for distributing this information is the textbook.

But college publishing, which many of you may still think of as "only" textbooks, now includes a vast assortment of materials needed to master a subject or develop skills for a specific professional career. The major college publishing houses publish not only textbooks but a wide assortment of other supplementary print materials—lab manuals for biology, chemistry, and physics; drill and practice audio tapes for foreign languages and music appreciation; software disks and documentation for engineering problems and calculations; practice working papers for accounting; and many more.

HOW COLLEGE PUBLISHING HOUSES ARE ORGANIZED

A textbook publishing company is generally divided into three departments: Editorial, EDP (Editing, Design and Production, not electronic data processing), and Marketing. A closer look at the inner workings of these departments will identify some of the career opportunities available to you. (*While the first of these is exhaustively covered by John Holland in his chapter on College Publishing Editorial Opportunities, we thought you might find this "view" of the editorial function from a marketing perspective instructive—Ed.*)

The Editorial Department

The Editorial department is directly charged with developing the content of textbooks and supplements. The key player or orchestrator of these functions is the **sponsoring editor,** who rates top billing at the publishing house. It is the editor who is the product developer and product champion, the one who continually seeks writers within the academic community who can synthesize the subject matter into a publishable manuscript. The editor needs to be sensitive to current trends in teaching, the leading academics (authors) molding the subject matter, and the competitive books either published or under development at other publishing houses. An editor assists authors in molding the content, size, and publishing plan or schedule for each textbook and its supplements. Key to an editor's success is developing a book that will ultimately sell into the marketplace.

The EDP Department

The EDP department, working in close concert with editors, is charged with preparing the manuscript for printing. It is this segment of the publishing partnership that is responsible for the line-by-line editing of the manuscript and designing it to insure that a sound educational design has been provided to compliment the material. Finally, the production team oversees the actual printing and binding of the textual material.

Enter The Marketing Department

Traditionally, it is within the Marketing department that most individuals begin their careers in textbook publishing. Except for those individuals within the EDP department, whose backgrounds are a composite of highly-trained technical expertise, the clear-cut entry-level position into textbook publishing is as a **field sales representative.** This is the training ground, the arena in which you learn about the environment that supports profitable publishing ventures.

YOUR JOB AS A COLLEGE FIELD SALES REPRESENTATIVE

A sales representative for a college textbook publisher is assigned a territory consisting of several colleges and universities. The boundaries of a territory will vary from one publishing house to another, generally depending on the number of books the publisher produces.

The basic job responsibilities of the sales representative are to contact college and university professors, administrators, and bookstore buyers and managers to sell and promote the publisher's list of books and supplements. Key to this basic objective is the need to explore and define markets for new books and products that need to be developed to maintain a publisher's growth commitment for the future. Reporting market trends and competitive information about books and authors is crucial to a sales representative's success. Identifying a professor as a potential author, encouraging and molding the professor to prepare a marketable manuscript, and eventually obtaining a contract for publication are other tasks commonly expected of a successful field representative.

Training

A new sales employee at a college textbook house can expect to participate in a structured training program in which he or she will learn the basic framework of the college curriculum, detailed product knowledge (including key components of each book), territorial management, and selling techniques. Throughout the first months as a sales representative, additional guidance and support is provided by a **field sales manager**. Working in close harmony, selling books and expanding upon the individual talents and desires of each sales representative, the field manager coaches each member of his or her sales team in the skills needed for sales success and/or eventual promotion to a position in field management, marketing/product management or editorial management. (Some individuals ultimately elect *not* to pursue a promotion, choosing instead to remain sales representatives. After a few years of learning the skills and the sales territory, the sales rep position can become quite lucrative, so promotion does not necessarily mean "greater" success. In general, the choices among these career paths will be determined in your second or third year as a field sales representative.)

Compensation

A highly motivated, successful college textbook sales representative is adequately compensated, depending upon his or her level of experience. Recent college graduates with limited prior work experience customarily start at a salary ranging from $18,000 - $22,500. New employees with extensive prior experience—often competitive publishing sales experience—command salaries of $25,000+, with the "+" depending upon past performance. With each promotion, salary increases generally range between 12 & 18 percent. In addition to this annual base salary, sales reps usually participate in some sort of commission, bonus, or incentive payment program. These programs are frequently supplemented by special sales campaigns throughout the year. To support your efforts to maximize sales and fulfill the basic requirements of the job, most publishers also provide expense monies and a company car plan.

WHAT YOU NEED TO GET HIRED AND SUCCEED

A successful college textbook sales representative possesses highly refined communication and organizational skills. Since verbal and written skills are key components of the job, demonstrable proficiency in these skills is crucial for a student seeking a sales career in college textbook publishing.

Intellectual curiosity, flexibility, and an entrepreneurial spirit are common traits among the most successful college textbook sales representatives.

Traveling is a big part of the job, so be ready to do so—reluctance to spend time on the road away from your home base will make it difficult to get that first job. If you secure a job knowing that you are reluctant to travel, this will eventually impact negatively upon your career in publishing.

The bulk of college sales representatives are hired from the vast pool of college graduates with (at least) a bachelor's degree in the arts, sciences, humanities, or business. While those of you with engineering or nursing degrees may still be hired, the bulk of successful publishing personalities do not evolve from these more specialized areas. While publishers welcome applications from successful M.B.A. candidates, this specialized degree is not crucial to employment; neither is it a guarantee of a successful publishing career. Some teaching or sales experience is generally looked upon favorably during the interviewing process.

Introductions to a publishing firm often evolve from faculty members, many of whom are authors for one house or another. These knowledgeable individuals are familiar with the publishing industry and the personalities who lend character to it. So their recommendations are valued and will usually lead to an interview and, if you possess the credentials and desire we like to see, eventual employment. A direct inquiry through the Marketing department of the publishing house is always encouraged. Few, if any, summer intern programs are currently available.

CAREER OPPORTUNITIES—EXPANDING AND INCREASING

For those sales representatives seeking a publishing career that encompasses more than a sales territory, the most frequently-trod career paths will lead first to **marketing manager, sponsoring editor,** or **field manager** positions. Both the marketing manager and sponsoring editor positions require relocation to the publisher's home office. On the other hand, the field manager will generally be located in a major metropolitan area that allows him or her easiest access to the group of sales representatives under his or her supervision.

Successful performance in these positions can result in increased responsibilities and promotion to **director of marketing services, editor-in-chief** or **regional manager.** From there, the common career path—short of the ultimate vice president position—will lead to **publisher** or **director of marketing.** Promotion from an editorial career track to a high level of responsibility in the marketing operation, and vice versa, are quite commonplace in most college publishing firms.

As the need for knowledge increases, the career opportunities for salespeople in college publishing will also increase. Books will remain a viable source of knowledge, but the art and science of book publishing will further expand beyond the confines of the printed textbook to include the dissemination of knowledge through electronic media.

Regardless of how knowledge is distributed, talents will be required and people gainfully employed to collect the information, mold it into comprehensible formats, and market it successfully and profitably.

And whatever new technologies impact the communications business, the fundamentals of publishing you will learn and practice as a college textbook sales representative will give you the basic sales skills and publishing knowledge that will insure you a rewarding career.

DONALD W. BURDEN

Mr. Burden has spent his entire publishing career with McGraw-Hill, starting as a college text sales representative in Southern California in 1963. In 1967 he was promoted to general manager of customer relations for McGraw Hill's Western Distribution Center in California. In 1974, he became district sales manager, responsible for nine Midwestern states.

He became a sponsoring editor in 1976 and was promoted to executive editor in 1979 before returning to the marketing area in his current position four years later.

Mr. Burden is an active member of the Association of American Publishers' Marketing Committee and the National Association of College Stores.

CHAPTER EIGHTEEN

Marketing And Selling Trade Books

By

Michael T. Pratt, VP-Marketing and Sales
Random House, Inc.

It is hard for me to imagine more rewarding careers in book publishing than those associated with marketing and sales. The people who perform in these areas, after all, are the ones who convince booksellers to make new books available to book readers; further, as you'll see in the chapters that follow, they create consumer demand for books through advertising, promotion and publicity. The men and women in marketing and sales, then, provide the final step in the long and complex process in publishing books.

Sales and marketing people in a consumer goods company like Procter & Gamble might "introduce" up to a dozen or so new products each year. In book publishing, the number of new books "launched" each year ranges from 250 for a medium-sized company to 500, 1,000 or more for the largest trade book publishers. The range is exciting and diverse, and includes fiction, general non-fiction, cookbooks, diet books, biographies and autobiographies, inspiration, history, finance and economics, and books of important current interest, such as environmental and political issues. Children's books are equally far-ranging, offering a world of words and pictures as diverse as a child's imagination.

Trade book publishers often describe themselves as being in the education and entertainment business. Recently, many of them have begun experimenting in non-book areas, most notably with video and audio cassettes. Now, we still offer readers advice on "how to" prepare a festive dinner or change the spark plugs in their car, but we also *show* them those same techniques on a television screen. And children can now watch <u>The Velveteen Rabbit</u> illustrated on their television screen while Meryl Streep, instead of Mom or Dad, narrates the story.

Audio cassettes are beginning to play a significant role in trade publishing. More and more people are choosing to listen to self-help, self-improvement and foreign language audio cassettes, as well as best selling fiction and non-fiction books on tape.

Trade publishing is no longer just trade book publishing. And the career opportunities are growing as fast as the business is changing.

THE TASK OF MARKETING—CREATE THE DEMAND

Someone has to convince booksellers that a publisher's new books (or video and audio cassettes) deserve a place on their shelves, a chance to find a life. This task—to "create the demand"—falls to each company's marketing people. And it involves far more than just "selling books" to the bookseller.

For example, the book's jacket (or cover) will be graphically designed to catch browsers' eyes. Posters and other in-store merchandising aids—such as displays which hold several copies of a book in a featured spot on a table, counter, or primary floor area—may also be utilized. Marketing people will design these displays to reflect the theme and the benefits of the books. Other creative devices—mobiles, shelf danglers, slit cards, etc.—may be devised in an ongoing process to attract the most attention to each book.

Generally, a marketing manager will work with the sales manager (and often the publisher as well) to determine which books need, or will most benefit from, special marketing attention. They will be responsible for creating a budget for the marketing plan, which may include author tours, advertising, and in-store merchandising aids. They must also consider how (or *if*) booksellers will respond to particular marketing devices...buying more copies than they otherwise would is one desirable response.

THE DEMAND FOR MARKETING AND SALES PEOPLE

Successful publishing requires the orchestrated and coordinated efforts of many people in a variety of different but interrelated jobs, and the marketing and sales staffs are certainly key to any such effort. These are also career fields which offer a number of exciting and rewarding opportunities.

Among the skilled professionals necessary in any book publisher's marketing department are **designers** and **copywriters**. They bring their separate talents to bear on creating attention-grabbing graphics and benefit-laden headlines. The natural background skills for entry-level positions in these areas are courses in design and journalism.

A **sales representative** is generally assigned to a specific geographic area (or "sales territory,") which will vary depending on the size of the publishing house and the number of sales representatives employed.

Typically, a publishing house will have 15-25 sales representatives. You can imagine that sales people assigned to a metropolitan area such as New York City, Los Angeles or Chicago will have lots of customers in their "home base" and will, therefore, have less overnight, out-of-town territory. The same is true of especially "bookish" cities like Boston, San Francisco and Washington, D.C. On the other hand, sales representatives in Cleveland, Kansas City, Atlanta, etc., will spend more nights in motels in order to cover the assigned accounts in their larger geographic territories.

The most common compensation is salary plus bonus. Most book publishers offer sales trainees a beginning salary in the $15,000 - $19,000 range, depending on the size and demands of the sales territory and the amount of related experience of the sales candidate. The bonus may be paid semi-annually or annually and is often based on sales performance in relation to established goals; in addition, it may often include other criteria, such as submitting weekly call reports and other administrative assignments on a timely basis. Bonuses may range from a few thousand to several thousand dollars annually.

An accomplished and enthusiastic representative will probably earn in excess of $20,000 annually in salary after three to five years of experience. A good sales manager or marketing manager would probably earn in excess of $50,000 and may exceed $75,000 or more, depending on the size of the company and the range of responsibilities and experience of the individual.

HOW TO PUT YOURSELF A STEP AHEAD
OF THE OTHER SALES CANDIDATES

The skills needed to become a sales representative are a sales aptitude and an interest in books. Some people find selling easy and natural. Others must develop such "natural" sales skills through some sort of training program, either at school or on-the-job. A liberal arts background, with a major in literature, communications, or business, is common among many successful salespeople I know. I think such "broad-based" training is probably best.

A summer or after-school job stocking book shelves or working as a cashier in a bookstore will generally be considered an advantage when you begin looking for a trade sales position. So would any previous sales experience. I've heard sales managers say they will teach a trainee how to sell, or help them learn to appreciate books, but they don't want to have to do *both*. So while either reading experience or sales experience is helpful, if you have both, and your communication skills are good, you should be in demand.

Sales managers admit they are at a loss to determine which candidates are psychologically fit for the job of sales representative. Selling books requires a degree of initiative and motivation that many people lack. Consider the salesperson living in Cincinnati, whose territory may include Ohio, West Virginia and Kentucky. His boss may be a regional sales manager living in Chicago or a New York-based sales manager. Selling books requires having the motivation to work on your own, without immediate supervision and without the on-hand support system that you will find in other fields. If you are not highly motivated and independent, forget it; if you *are* highly motivated and *enjoy* independence, you'll probably find this an exciting field.

WHAT YOU'LL BE DOING AS A TRADE BOOK SALES REPRESENTATIVE

Your "typical" day as a new sales representative will vary with the nature of the publishing house, but the following is not uncommon: You will prepare for each bookstore appointment by reviewing your list of new book titles, considering which ones do and do not have sales potential for that bookstore's market. You will also think of merchandising ideas that might help you sell those books into the store and help the bookseller sell them to his or her customers. (You'll study the author information, for example, to determine if there is a particular local tie-in you can exploit to generate interest.)

Once in the store, you'll review your new list of titles with your customer, making recommendations on titles and quantities. After you have secured your new book order, you will inventory the books already carried by that store to determine those that have sold out and need to be reordered. Most books are sold on a returnable basis, so you will also pull off the shelves any books which the bookseller has been unable to sell. Those will be shipped back to your company by the bookseller, usually for full credit. While more and more bookstores are beginning to use computers to keep track of inventory needs, the majority still do not, and the sales representatives need to assist their customers with this.

All of this may take two or three hours, or all day, depending on the length of your list and the size of the store. And every appointment—every bookstore—offers new and different experiences. Your next stop may be a similar kind of store in the same city, but with a different clientele, or one in another city whose customers are looking for a completely different selection of books.

And each time you finish an appointment, you have an opportunity to evaluate your efforts. Former sales representatives often tell me what they miss most about selling is the instant gratification, knowing *immediately* whether they accomplished their goals, each and every day. So many jobs do not offer this. In most non-sales positions, employees may wait for an annual, or perhaps semi-annual review, to see how they "measure up". The sales experience allows you to get immediate "feedback," feel good about yourself and your efforts, and identify areas for self-improvement...every day.

A CAREER ITSELF...AND GREAT TRAINING FOR MOVING UP

Many salespeople find selling an exciting and professional career; others view it as a first step in their career path. Where can it lead? In my view, the opportunities are virtually unlimited. A natural progression would include positions as a **regional sales supervisor, assistant sales manager, national sales manager, vice president of sales,** etc.

No job in publishing offers a knowledge base like that of the sales representative. Those jobs closest to consumers and booksellers—our customers—will *always* offer a continuing education of enormous value to a publisher. Wouldn't marketing decisions be enhanced if they came from someone with sales experience? Who else would know more about what would and would not entice booksellers and consumers? What graphic design or "look" in a book jacket would likely be more successful? The sales representatives see them all—the books and ideas of all publishers, every day, on the shelves of their booksellers' stores. No one else in the company has that opportunity.

An intelligent publishing house looks at its brightest sales representatives as consultants. A career in marketing is a natural enough extension from sales, and I would not discount the possibility of becoming an editor, a publisher, or even president of the company. If you are bright, motivated, and determined, sales experience will serve you well in whatever career path you choose in publishing.

Michael Pratt's career in the book publishing industry spans more than 20 years and followed a three-year stint in retailing. His first two years were spent with Westminster Press, where he sold religious and children's books in seven Midwestern states. This was followed by two years as a sales representative for Harper & Row Publishers, Inc.

In 1969, he began his career at Random House, where he is now the senior marketing executive. His positions there have included: sales representative; assistant sales manager; national field sales manager; national sales manager; director of trade marketing and sales; division vice president, trade marketing and sales; and corporate vice president, marketing and sales.

Mr. Pratt is a Midwesterner who grew up in Troy and Ashland, Ohio. His undergraduate liberal arts education was undertaken at Muskingum College, Ashland College and Temple University. He has taken various graduate courses and seminars from the American Management Association and the Wharton School of the University of Pennsylvania. He is included in Who's Who in America.

CHAPTER NINETEEN

Rights Aren't So "Subsidiary" Any More!

By

**Josephine Fagan, Director of Subsidiary Rights
Crown Publishers, Inc.**

Subsidiary Rights is an aspect of book publishing that has become increasingly important over the last decade or so. Twenty years ago, subsidiary rights *were* subsidiary to bookstore sales. Now it's possible to make *more* money from the sale of a book's subsidiary rights than from sales of the book! These rights can be crucial to the success of a book, a publishing list, even a company. Nevertheless, most people outside of publishing are not familiar with the concept of subsidiary rights or their importance to a publisher's health. So let's begin with a broad definition and then get on to specifics.

SUBSIDIARY RIGHTS—WHAT THEY'RE ALL ABOUT

Subsidiary rights involves selling your book—in part or in whole—to third parties who will then resell it to their customers. The most common and often-sold rights are **serial rights**, **book club rights** and **paperback rights**.

Serial Rights

Serial rights are book excerpts of varying lengths that are sold to another print medium —usually magazines, newspapers or newspaper syndicates (who then sell to local newspapers across the country). These rights are broken down into two categories—_first_ and _second_ serial rights.

First serial rights are excerpts that appear shortly before the actual publication of the book. They serve as "teasers" to the public and often help generate interest in the book that results in bookstore sales.

For example, several years ago my company published a first novel by a relatively unknown author. It was a "women's" novel that featured a glamorous heroine who is smart, beautiful, successful, etc., and who overcomes great personal trials to live, in the end, happily ever after. I'm sure you are familiar with the genre. Serial rights were sold to _Cosmopolitan_ magazine, which we believed the perfect vehicle. At least partially as a result of that sale, the book went on to become a major hardcover best seller.

More recently we published a college men's guide to women's colleges. First serial rights were sold to _Playboy_. Again, the perfect vehicle. The book went on to respectable trade sales.

First serial rights generally command higher fees (these can range up to tens of thousands of dollars depending on the book, the author's reputation, the magazine's or newspaper's circulation, etc.) because they provide the magazine or newspaper with a kind of exclusive scoop.

Second serial rights are excerpts that appear _after_ the book's publication, sometimes _considerably_ after. This type of excerpt provides a continuing source of income for the publisher and has significant publicity value in keeping a book in the public's consciousness. It is not terribly unusual to be able to sell second serial excerpts to a book that is several years old.

Book Club Rights

Book club rights involve selling the whole book to a club that will, in turn, sell it to their members through the mail at a discounted price. (_See the discussion of direct mail marketing and book clubs in the article by Marion Waxman of Book-of-the-Month Club earlier in this volume—Ed._) There are many book clubs, ranging from large, general interest clubs to those targeting audiences with very specific areas of interest.

The two major **general interest clubs** are Book-of-the-Month Club and the Literary Guild of America. Whichever of these two clubs buys the book will receive exclusive book club rights from the publisher, print its own edition and then market it to its members through the mail. You've probably seen the advertisements these clubs run in major publications to solicit new membership. Generally speaking, these clubs have thirteen or fourteen "cycles" per year when they send a bulletin to their members with the top new selections ("Main Selections"), a few other new books ("Alternates"), and a recap of their back list (books they have previously offered as mains or alternates but are continuing to sell).

The book club pays the publisher an advance against royalties (which can range from about $3000 to hundreds of thousands of dollars). This is paid to the publisher up front and then applied to the royalties which the contract specifies they are to receive. This income is generally shared 50/50 between the publisher and the author. On occasion, both Book-of-the-Month Club and the Literary Guild will be interested in the same title (a happenstance that causes Sub Rights directors and everybody else at the publisher's offices paroxysms of joy). In that case, an auction develops. The two clubs bid against each other until one drops out. The book is sold to the highest bidder.

And the bidding can reach unexpected highs. I recall one instance where the opening bid on a first novel by an unknown author was $5,000. After three days of bidding, it was ultimately sold for $75,000. Often, however, because of their different memberships and images, only one will be interested in licensing rights. This provides the rights seller with little leverage to force the advance money up.

The smaller **specialty clubs** (professional, science, history, nostalgia, etc.) operate in basically the same way, paying an advance against royalties and selling books to their members through the mail at discounted prices.

Paperback Rights

Paperback rights—the largest income potential (once in a while, *millions of dollars*) for the hardcover publisher and author, the most "glamorous" subsidiary right and the one with the highest frustration potential for the person selling them.

Paperback reprint rights are license agreements between the hardcover publisher and a paperback publisher who agrees to publish a paperback edition approximately one year after a book's initial hardcover publication. There are two kinds of paperbacks: **Trade paperbacks** are usually done in the same size and format as the hardcover edition and are sold primarily through the same outlet—bookstores. **Mass market paperbacks** are produced in rack-size (approximately 4" x 7") and are sold in numerous outlets in addition to bookstores—drugstores, airports, magazine stands, etc.). Because mass market paperbacks can be gotten into the market place in major quantities, paperback publishers will pay higher advances for these rights. In any event, the hardcover publisher is paid an advance and royalties that are shared with the author (a percentage basis stipulated in the author's contract).

The Paperback Auction

You may have heard or read about the **paperback auction**, which occurs when the hardcover publisher has a "hot" property—usually a book that has done very well in hardcover, is written by an author with a large following, or is the type of book that will perform well in paperback.

There are two kinds of auctions. One is an **open auction**, where no paperback publisher has established a minimum guaranteed bid (called a *"floor"*). The book is submitted simultaneously to several paperback publishers, a date is set for bidding, it is sold to the highest bidder on a "last-person-out" basis, and the hardcover publisher and author sit back and count the money.

In the other case, a book is either shown to one paperback publisher first or one of the publishers who receives a simultaneous submission establishes the "floor" bid. The auction begins at that point (say, $50,000), instead of at zero. The **floor holder** usually has the privilege of topping the highest bid received at the end of the auction by 10%.

The paperback auction can truly be the glamorous part of the rights seller's job. If the timing is right and everything comes together, there is a great deal of excitement and a lot of money to be made. But as in all other aspects of life, timing is critical. Should the book be sold early? Should the hardcover publisher wait and take a chance that the book will "break-out" in hardcover? Should it be auctioned at all or should it be sold to one interested party?

A couple of years ago, my company published a book that promised to be very, very hot, even though the author's name was not a household word. There was a lot of excited "talk" about it in the industry. We decided to sell the paperback rights early (more than two months before we published the hardcover edition) in an open auction. The results were very gratifying: The paperback rights were sold for more than $500,000.

Just recently, we published a first novel that clicked immediately in hardcover and began appearing on bestseller lists, including the *New York Times*, within three weeks of its arrival in bookstores. A mass market house had established a floor. When the book climbed to #5 on the *Times* bestseller list, we set the auction date for two weeks hence. The book then climbed to #3 and the stage seemed set for a giant auction. But the book went for just under $500,000.

This just proves that there are many variables that wind up coming into play. In this instance, the length of the book may have worked against it in the paperback auction—it was expensive to produce and hard to display in a standard-sized mass market rack.

In another instance, we published what could be called a "pop-psych" book. Initially it didn't look like a "mega"-book. We couldn't get a reprinter to pay even $25,000 for the rights. Then, for a variety of reasons, the book clicked in hardcover and became a nationwide bestseller. Reprint rights were then auctioned for more than $600,000. We also recently sold the reprint rights to a novel for $100,000 on a negotiated sale basis—no auction at all. And I just heard about a lucky rights director (not me, alas) who set a record for selling the reprint rights to a first novel...for $3.1 million. Needless to say, that doesn't happen very often. The variables and potential scenarios are almost limitless.

Unfortunately, not all books are immediately snapped up for paperback publication. There are many, many instances of hard-won, modest sales where the rights seller must cajole, convince, bombard and really *sell*, in the truest sense of the word. And there are many unfortunate instances where no amount of cajoling, convincing or bombarding works. At times, its like being a desk-bound Willy Loman.

The same auction fever—or difficulty—also applies to serial and book club rights. There can be high levels of frustration and rejection, but also major rewards and satisfactions in selling rights.

These three rights are the basic ones, the real "bread and butter" of most publishers' and authors' rights sales income. But subsidiary rights can take many other forms.

The Other Rights We Sell

Some of the more obvious are film and/or TV rights, large type editions or books on tape for the visually impaired, condensation rights, and hardcover reprint rights (where a specialty publisher will do a small hardcover printing of an out-of-print title). Publishers now even deal with other industries. Many now work with the toy industry, licensing three-dimensional character rights to a character from one of their books and cross-marketing it in both industries.

As technology continues to change, the list of rights sold continues to grow. We now have audio and video cassette rights, even the potential to sell a book to a software manufacturer. Who knows where it will end?

But as the field continues to expand, it is more important than ever that the rights seller be aware of developments in the rights business. Who is buying what and for how much? Is there a book similar to one of yours that has recently been sold? Who is looking for a certain type of book to fill a gap in his publishing program? Is there a new market out there that others are tapping and you're not? The better informed you are, the more likely you'll be successful.

THE SUBSIDIARY RIGHTS DEPARTMENT...AND YOUR PLACE IN IT

Now that we have defined the basic subsidiary rights, we can discuss how the department itself works and what your role in an entry-level position might be.

In small publishing houses, all of the rights may be sold by one or, at most, two individuals. Most large trade publishers—those producing over 300 new titles a year—have several people in the Rights department. The **director** oversees the entire operation and handles the actual selling of major titles. There may also be a **manager,** the second in command, with primary responsibilities for selling as well as some administrative duties. Other members of the department will also be selling and negotiating.

Often, under the supervision of the director or manager, one person will specialize in serial and film rights, another in book club and/or paperback rights, another in selling rights to the publisher's juvenile books, etc. And each person often has more than one area of expertise.

As is always the case in sales, it is important, even critical, to have a good professional relationship with one's customers. In publishing this means several phone conversations a week, frequent lunches, etc. When you are dealing with an almost infinite number of magazines and newspapers, many potential book clubs, and at least 15 viable paperback customers, it's absolutely necessary to specialize to some degree, particularly if you are selling more than 300 titles a year! If you spread yourself too thin, both books and customers are bound to be ignored. In some houses, foreign rights and domestic rights are handled in the same department, which requires even *greater* specialization. Some publishers assign titles—one person sells *all* the rights to his assigned titles. My own experience has been working with assigned *rights*—we have one person handling serial and film rights, another handling book club and paperback rights. Each person then has the time to develop good relationships with a finite number of people instead of a scatter-shot approach.

In most cases, each salesperson will either have his own assistant or share one with another member of the department. **These assistant positions are the entry-level spots**. The salary you can expect probably varies widely from company to company, but a safe guess is a starting salary in the low-to-mid-teens ($11,000 to perhaps $16,000).

The selling of rights is a high volume business. Each book is submitted in manuscript form to potential customers. If no sale is made or if new customers emerge, the book is resubmitted in bound galley form and then again in bound book form. So a publisher with 300 titles may need to handle up to 900 submissions a year to perhaps 100 potential customers. Reviews, press material and any other pertinent information and details are also submitted. The bottom line: voluminous correspondence which needs to be typed, filed, and recorded. This is the "donkey" work of the department and it is performed by the assistants. There is also a large amount of telephone contact, from inquiries to follow-up calls and troubleshooting (yes, there is often trouble). The assistant can and should be able to field and handle many, if not most, of these calls.

The work may sound tedious and heavily clerical, but it is really the best way to learn this aspect of the business. An intelligent, ambitious assistant can take a great load of work from the rights seller, really become familiar with the ins and outs of laying the groundwork for a sale and negotiating a deal and become familiar with the customers. It's the best preparation I can think of for an eventual career as a rights seller.

Since subsidiary rights is now an integral part of the marketing plan of any book, there is much contact with and feedback from almost every other department in the company—editorial, trade sales, publicity, promotion, advertising, production, art, etc. Each of these departments can provide the rights seller with invaluable information and selling tools necessary to his or her job.

So the rights seller (and the assistant), already visible in the publishing industry, also become highly visible within their own house. It never hurts to be recognized, particularly if you want to move up to the next level.

MOVING IN AND MOVING UP

It is very hard to predict a time frame for career advancement from an entry-level job in subsidiary rights. So much really depends on the individual company's policies. Do they groom and promote from within? Do they go outside for middle-level talent? Is it locked in at the top? Is the company's list growing at a rate that will require them to add staff? These are just some of the variables. Where you will be a year from now depends as much on *these* factors as on your own interest level, ambition and performance.

If you are good at your job, lucky enough to work for a company that promotes from within and with individuals who are willing to delegate authority and responsibility, after a year or so you should be able to start doing some submissions of your own, perhaps even some deal-making.

But there aren't *that* many top spots to go after. Publishing is really a very small industry, so subsidiary rights is a small piece of a small pie. And there is only *one* top rights person in each house. However, many of the skills you'll pick up working in rights are applicable to other areas of publishing—particularly the "feel" one can develop for a salable book. Lately, several subsidiary rights directors have been named president, publisher and associate publisher of major firms and are now running companies and buying properties instead of just selling them.

THE SUCCESSFUL "RIGHTS-SELLING" CANDIDATE

What qualities make for a good subsidiary rights candidate? You must enjoy people and be outgoing and enthusiastic. You will, after all, be trying to convince someone else to buy your product. You will need patience, not only because it may take a while for your career to progress, but because you may find yourself working on a sale for several months before you get positive results. You will rarely enjoy instant gratification. You also must love to read. To sell a book effectively you must have read it. Having read it, you might come up with an angle or a handle no one else has thought of. Be interested, be alert and try to be innovative in your approach.

Your customers may not buy one particular book but they'll remember you when you take the next book to them. Subsidiary rights is not all glamor, million dollar auctions, lunches and pizzazz. If you examine the careers of the major rights people, you will find that a lot of hard work, energy and persistence built their careers. That and *luck*—it never hurts to be in the right place at the right time—are the keys to subsidiary rights success.

Publishing is really an apprentice industry; so is the area of subsidiary rights. No one graduates from college and immediately starts selling rights. It takes time to familiarize yourself with the company, the list, the routines, the procedures, the customers.

But as Yogi Berra said, "You can observe a lot just by watchin'." And from the watchin' comes the doin'.

JOSEPHINE FAGAN

Ms. Fagan was promoted to director of subsidiary rights for Crown, which includes Clarkson N. Potter, Inc. and Harmony Books, in 1985. She had been manager of subsidiary rights for six years and prior to that was manager of copyrights and permissions. Ms. Fagan began her publishing career at Doubleday & Co., first in the Contracts department, later in the Adult Trade Editorial department.

SECTION III

The Job Search Process

CHAPTER TWENTY

Getting Started: Self Evaluation And Career Objectives

Getting a job may be a one-step, couple of weeks or months-long operation.

Starting, nurturing and developing a career (or even a series of careers) is a lifelong process.

What we'll be talking about in the four chapters that together form our Job Search Process are those basic steps to take, assumptions to make, things to think about if you want a job—especially a first job in book publishing. But when these steps—this process—are applied and expanded over a lifetime, most if not all of them are the same procedures, carried out over and over again, that are necessary to develop a successful, lifelong, professional career.

What does all this have to do with putting together a resume, writing a cover letter, heading off for interviews and the other "traditional" steps necessary to get a job? Whether your college graduation is just around the corner or a far-distant memory, you will continuously need to focus, evaluate and re-evaluate your response to the ever-changing challenge of your future: Just what do you want to do with the rest of your life? Whether you like it or not, you're all looking for that "entry-level opportunity."

You're already one or two steps ahead of the competition—you're sure (pretty sure?) you want to pursue a career in book publishing. By heeding the advice of the many professionals who have written chapters for this <u>Career Directory</u>—and utilizing the extensive industry and publisher information we've included—you're well on your way to fulfilling that dream. But there are some key decisions and time-consuming preparations to make if you want to transform that hopeful dream into a real, live publishing job.

The actual process of finding the right publishing house, the right career path and, most importantly, the right first job, begins long before you start mailing out resumes to potential employers. The choices and decisions you make now are not irrevocable, but this first job will have a definite impact on the career options you leave yourself. To help you make some of the right decisions and choices along the way (and avoid some of the most notable traps and pitfalls), the following chapters will lead you through a series of organized steps. If the entire job search process we are recommending here is properly executed, it will undoubtedly help you land exactly the job you want.

If you're currently in high school and hope, after college, to land a job in a publishing house, then attending the right college, choosing the right major and getting the summer work experience many publishers look for are all important steps. Read the section of this <u>Career Directory</u> that covers your job specialty—many of the contributors have recommended colleges or vocational schools they favor.

If you're hoping to jump right into the book publishing industry with*out* a college degree or other professional training, our best and only advice is—don't do it. As you'll soon see in the detailed information included in the *Job Opportunities Databank* in Section IV, there are not *that* many job openings for students without a college degree. Those that do exist are generally clerical and will only rarely lead to promising careers.

THE CONCEPT OF A JOB SEARCH PROCESS

These are the key steps in the detailed job search process we will cover in this and the following three chapters:

1. *Evaluating yourself*: Know thyself. What skills and abilities can you offer a prospective employer? What do you enjoy doing? What are your strengths and weaknesses? What do you *want* to do?

2. *Establishing your career objectives*: Where do you want to be next year, three years, five years from now? What do you ultimately want to accomplish in your career and your life?

3. *Creating a publisher target list*: How to prepare a "Hit List" of potential employers—researching them, matching their needs with your skills and starting your job search assault. Preparing publisher information sheets and evaluating your chances.

4. *Networking for success:* Learning how to utilize every contact, every friend, every relative and anyone else you can think of to break down the barriers facing any would-be publishing professional. How to organize your home office to keep track of your communications and stay on top of your job campaign.

5. *Preparing your resume:* How to encapsulate years of school and little actual work experience into a professional, selling resume. Learning when and how to use it.

6. *Preparing cover letters:* The many ordinary and the all-too-few extraordinary cover letters, the kind that land interviews and jobs.

7. Interviewing: How to make the interview process work for you—from the first "hello" to the first day on the job.

We won't try to kid you—it *is* a lot of work. To do it right, you have to get started early, probably quite a bit earlier than you'd planned. Frankly, we recommend beginning this process one full year prior to the day you plan to start work.

So if you're in college, the end of your junior year is the right time to begin your research and preparations. That should give you enough time during summer vacation to set up your files and begin your library research.

Whether you're in college or graduate school, one item may need to be planned even earlier—allowing enough free time in your schedule of classes for interview preparations and appointments. Waiting until your senior year to "make some time" is already too late. Searching for a full-time job is itself a full-time job! Though you're naturally restricted by your schedule, it's not difficult to plan ahead and prepare for your upcoming job search. Try to leave at least a couple of free mornings or afternoons a week. A day or even two without classes is even better.

Otherwise, you'll find yourself, crazed and distracted, trying to prepare for an interview in the ten-minute period between your 18th Century Literature lecture and your Creative Writing seminar. Not the best way to make a first impression and certainly not the way you want to approach an important meeting.

THE SELF-EVALUATION PROCESS

Plato had it right: "Know thyself." Learning about who you are, what you want to be, what you *can* be, are critical first steps in the job search process and, unfortunately, the ones most often ignored by job seekers everywhere, especially students eager to leave the ivy behind and plunge into the "real world." But avoiding this crucial self evaluation can hinder your progress and even damage some decent prospects.

Why? Because in order to land a job with a house at which you'll actually be happy, you need to be able to identify those publishers and/or job descriptions that best match your own skills, likes and strengths. The more you know about yourself, the more you'll bring to this process and the more accurate the "match-ups." You'll be able to structure your presentation (resume, cover letter, interviews) to stress your most marketable skills and talents (and, dare we say it, conveniently avoid your weaknesses?). Later, you'll be able to evaluate potential employers and job offers on the basis of your own needs and desires. This spells the difference between waking up in the morning ready to enthusiastically tackle a new day of challenges and shutting off the alarm in the hopes the day (and your job) will just disappear.

Creating Your Self-Evaluation Form

Take a sheet of lined notebook paper. Set up eight columns across the top—Strengths, Weaknesses, Skills, Hobbies, Courses, Experience, Likes, Dislikes.

Now, fill in each of these columns according to these guidelines:

Strengths: Describe personality traits you consider your strengths (and try to look at them as an employer would)—e.g., persistence, organization, ambition, intelligence, logic, assertiveness, aggression, leadership, etc.

Weaknesses: The traits you consider glaring weaknesses—e.g., impatience, conceit, etc. (And remember: Look at these as a potential employer would. Don't assume that the personal traits you consider weaknesses will necessarily be considered negatives in the business world. You may be "easily bored," a trait that led to lousy grades early on because teachers couldn't keep you interested in the subjects they were teaching. Well, many entrepreneurs need ever-changing challenges. Strength or weakness?)

Skills: Any skill you have, whether you think it's marketable or not. Everything from basic business skills—like typing, word processing and stenography—to computer, accounting or teaching experience and foreign language literacy. Don't forget possibly obscure but marketable skills like "good telephone voice."

Hobbies: The things you enjoy doing that, more than likely, have no overt connection to career objectives. These should be distinct from the skills listed above, and may include activities such as reading, games, travel, sports and the like. While these may not be marketable in any general sense, they may well be useful in specific circumstances. (If you love travel, you may be perfect for that editorial spot at the publishing house that specializes in producing travel books, atlases, etc. And your "hobbies" may just get it for you!)

Courses: All the general subject areas (history, literature, etc.) and/or specific courses you've taken which may be marketable (computer, business, marketing, economics, etc.), you really enjoyed, or both.

Experience: Just the specific functions you performed at any part-time (school year) or full-time (summer) jobs. Entries may include "General Office" (typing, filing, answering phones, etc.), "Sales," "Writing," "Research," etc.

Likes: List all your "likes," those important considerations that you haven't listed anywhere else yet. These might include the types of people you like to be with, the kind of environment you prefer (city, country, large places, small places, quiet, loud, fast-paced, slow-paced) and anything else which hasn't shown up somewhere on this form. However, try not to include entries which refer to specific jobs or companies. We'll list those on another form.

Dislikes: All the people, places and things you can easily live without.

Now assess the "marketability" of each item you've listed. (In other words, are some of your likes, skills or courses easier to match to a publishing job description, or do they have little to do with a specific job or publisher?) Mark highly marketable skills with an "H." Use "M" to characterize those skills which may be marketable in a particular set of circumstances, "L" for those with minimal potential application to any job. Some obvious examples: Typing, word processing and stenography are always marketable, so you'd mark them with an "H". Teaching, computer and accounting skills would also qualify as highly marketable. Similarly, if you listed high energy or perseverance as a strength, any advertising sales manager will find it a highly desirable trait. Speaking French, however, gets an "M." While not marketable in all job situations, it might well be a requirement for certain industries (e.g.,importing and exporting) or jobs (working on the English translations of Proust and liaisoning with the French publisher's staff).

Referring back to the same list, decide if you'd enjoy using your marketable skills or talents as part of your everyday job—"Y" for yes, "N" for no. You may type 80 words a minute but truly despise typing (or worry that stressing it too much will land you on the permanent clerical staff). If so, mark typing with an "N." (Keep one thing in mind—just because you dislike typing shouldn't mean you absolutely won't accept a job that requires it. Most do.)

Now, go over the entire form carefully. Look for inconsistencies. After you are satisfied that the form is as accurate as you can make it—and gotten over the shock of some of your honest answers—pass it along to a close friend or two. Ask *them* to check it for accuracy—you'll not only uncover areas you may have fudged a bit, but learn a great deal about what the rest of the world thinks of you. After they've completed their assessment of the person you've committed to paper, put the form aside for the time being.

ESTABLISHING YOUR CAREER OBJECTIVE(S)

For better or worse, you now know something more of who and what you are. But we've yet to establish and evaluate another important area—your overall needs, desires and goals. Where are you going? What do you want to accomplish?

If you're getting ready to graduate from college or graduate school, the next five years are the most critical period of your whole career. You need to make the initial transition from college to the workplace, establish yourself in a new and completely unfamiliar company environment and begin to build the professional credentials necessary to achieve your career goals.

If that strikes you as a pretty tall order, well, it *is*. Unless you've narrowly prepared yourself for a specific profession, you're probably most *ill*-prepared for any real job. Instead, you've (hopefully) learned some basic principles—research and analytical skills that are necessary for success at almost any level—and, more or less, how to think. But that's all. You probably don't have the faintest clue about how the book publishing business (let alone a specific house or department) functions or any of the specific information necessary to perform even the lowliest task.

It's tough to face, but face it you must: No matter what your college, major or degree, all you represent right now is potential. How you package that potential and what you eventually make of it is completely up to you. And it's an unfortunate fact that many houses will take a professional with barely a year or two experience over *any* newcomer, no matter how promising. Smaller publishers, especially, can rarely afford to hire someone who can't begin contributing immediately.

So you have to be prepared to take your comparatively modest skills and experience and package them in a way that will get you interviewed and hired. Quite a challenge.

There are a number of different ways to approach such a task. If you find yourself confused or unable to list such goals, you might want to check a few books in your local library that have more time to spend on the topic of "goal-oriented planning." Four that may help: 1) Your First Resume by Ronald W. Fry, our own attempt to simplify the entire job search process for first timers, available via the mail order coupon in the back of this volume; 2) The ubiqui-tous What Color is Your Parachute, still the Bible of the job search field (though if you find it absurdly complicated, you're not alone): 3) After College: The Business of Getting Jobs by Jack Falvey, a far more readable (though somewhat controversial) overview of the job search process; and 4) (by the same author) What's Next? Career Strategies After 35, for you post-35ers out there. The latter two books are also available from The Career Press.

YES, BUT IS BOOK PUBLISHING RIGHT FOR *YOU*?

Presuming you now have a much better idea of yourself and where you'd like to be—job-career- and life-wise in the foreseeable future—let's make sure some of your basic assumptions are right. We presume you purchased this Career Directory because you're considering a career in book publishing. Are you sure? Do you know enough about the industry to decide whether it's right for you? Probably not. Do you know enough about the two other major areas of publishing—magazines and newspapers—let alone the possibilities of getting involved in one of the peripheral areas, such as working with a literary agent? Doubtful. So start your research *now*—learn as much about the book business as you now know about yourself.

Start with the Introduction and Section I. These eight articles will give you an excellent overview of the book business, some very specialized (and growing) areas of the industry and some things to consider about yourself and publishing. This will give you a relatively simplified, though very necessary, understanding of just what people who work in book publishing actually do.

Other sources you should consider consulting to learn more about this business are listed in the various Appendices.

In Appendix A, we've listed all the trade organizations associated with the book publishing industry. While educational information available from these associations is often limited (and, for the most part, already a part of this Career Directory), you should certainly consider writing each of the pertinent associations, letting them know you're interested in a career in publishing and would appreciate whatever help and advice they're willing to impart. You'll find many sponsor seminars and conferences throughout the country, some of which you may be able to attend.

In Appendix B, we've listed the trade magazines dedicated to the highly specific interests of the book publishing and book selling communities. These magazines are generally not available at newsstands (unless you live in or near New York City), but you may be able to obtain back issues at your local library (most major libraries have extensive collections of such journals) or by writing to the magazines' circulation/subscription departments.

You may also try writing to the publishers and/or editors of these business publications. State in your cover letter what area of the business you're considering and ask them for whatever help and advice they can offer. But be specific. These are busy professionals and they do not have the time or the inclination to simply "tell me everything you can about book publishing."

If you can afford it now, we strongly suggest subscribing to *Publishers Weekly*, the major trade magazine for the book business—plus whichever of the other magazines are applicable to the specialty you're considering. If you can't subscribe to all of them, make it a point to regularly read the copies that arrive at your local public or college library.

These publications may well provide the most imaginative and far-reaching information for your job search. Even a quick perusal of an issue or two will give you an excellent "feel" for the industry. After reading only a few articles, you'll already get a handle on what's happening in the field and some of publishing's peculiar and particular jargon. Later, more detailed study will aid you in your search for a specific job.

Authors of the articles themselves may well turn out to be important resources. If an article is directly related to your chosen specialty, why not call the author and ask some questions? You'd be amazed how willing many of these professionals will be to talk to you and answer your questions. They may even tell you about job openings at their companies! (But *do* use common sense—authors will not *always* respond graciously to your invitation to "chat about the business." And don't be *too* aggressive here.)

Whether you've interned at a publishing house, majored in English and/or written or edited every college newspaper and magazine in existence, you may still wish to attend one of the book publishing institutes at some of the major colleges across the U.S. We have listed the most well-known and well-respected of these in Appendix C. (Someone already in the industry who wants to learn more so they can move up or to another area of specialization would probably find these courses extremely helpful, too.)

You'll find such research to be a double-edged sword. In addition to helping you get a handle on whether the book business is really right for you, you'll slowly learn enough about particular specialties, publishers, the industry, etc., to actually sound like you know what you're talking about when you hit the pavement looking for your first job. And nothing is better than sounding like a pro...except being one.

BOOKS ARE IT. NOW WHAT?

After all this research, we're going to assume you've reached that final decision—you really *do* want a career in book publishing. It is with this vague certainty that all too many of you will race off, hunting for any publisher willing to give you a job. You'll manage to get interviews at a couple of houses and, smiling brightly, tell everyone you meet, "I want a career in publishing." The interviewers, unfortunately, will all ask the same awkward question—"What *exactly* do you want to do at our house?"—and that will be the end of that.

It is simply not enough to narrow your job search to a specific industry. And so far, that's all you've done. You must now establish a specific career objective—the job you want to start, the career you want to pursue. Just knowing that you "want to get into book publishing" doesn't mean anything to anybody. If that's all you can tell an interviewer, it demonstrates a lack of research into the industry itself and your failure to think ahead. Do you want to start as an editorial assistant, hoping to work your way up the ladder to editor-in-chief, or catch on as a sales rep, with VP-sales your eventual goal? The two entry-level positions are completely different. They require different skills and educational backgrounds.

Interviewers will *not* welcome you with open arms if you're still vague about your career goals. If you've managed to get an "informative interview" with an executive whose company currently has no job openings, what is he supposed to do with your resume after you leave? Who should he send it to for future consideration? Since *you* don't seem to know exactly what you want to do, how's *he* going to figure it out? Worse, he'll probably resent your asking him to function as your personal career counselor.

Remember, the more specific your career objective, the better your chances of finding a job. It's that simple and that important. Naturally, before you declare your objective to the world, check once again to make sure your specific job target matches the skills and interests you defined in your self evaluation. Eventually, you may want to state such an objective on your resume and "To obtain an entry-level position as an assistant editor at a major Trade publishing house" is quite a bit better than "I want a career in publishing." Do not consider this step final until you can summarize your job/career objective in a single, short, accurate sentence.

CHAPTER TWENTY ONE

Targeting Publishers And Networking For Success

If you've spent the time and effort going through the self-evaluation process in the previous chapter, you're now sure—you *know* what you want to do. The next question: Where are you going to get a job doing it? There are thousands of book publishers, ranging in size from the biggest (Simon & Schuster, Random House, McGraw-Hill, etc.) to the smallest (a plethora of "small press" publishers). Small or large? New York or Oshkosh? Just which of the publishers is the right one for you?

YOUR IDEAL PUBLISHER PROFILE

Let's establish some criteria to evaluate potential employers. This will enable you to identify your target houses, the places you'd really like to work. (This process, as we've pointed out, is not publishing-specific; the same steps, with perhaps some research resource variations, are applicable to any job, any company, any industry. But for this volume, we are now specifically concerned with jobs in the book business. If you are primarily interested in working for a newspaper, see the brand-new second edition of our <u>Newspapers Career Directory</u>. And for you aspiring magazine editors, designers and advertising salespeople—the third edition of our Magazines Career Directory is also available.)

Take another sheet of blank paper and divide it into three vertical columns. Title it "Book Publisher—Ideal Profile." Call the left-hand column "Musts," the middle column "Preferences," and the right-hand column "Nevers."

We've listed a series of questions below. After considering each question, decide whether a particular criteria *must* be met, whether you would simply *prefer* it or *never* would consider it at all. If there are other criteria you consider important, feel free to add them to the list below and mark them accordingly on your Profile.

1. What are your geographical preferences? (Possible answers: U.S., Canada, International, Anywhere). If you only want to work in the U.S., then "Work in United States" would be the entry in the "Must" column. "Work in Canada or Foreign Country" might be the first entry in your "Never" column. There would be no applicable entry for this question in the "Preference" column. If, however, you will consider working in two of the three, then your "Must" column entry might read "Work in U.S. or Canada," your "Preference" entry—if you preferred one over the other—could read "Work in U.S.," and the "Never" column , "Work Overseas."

2. If you prefer to work in the U.S. or Canada, what area, state(s) or province(s)? If Overseas, what area or countries?

3. Do you prefer a large city, small city, town, or somewhere as far away from civilization as possible?

4. In regard to question 3, any specific preferences?

5. Do you prefer a warm or cold climate?

6. Do you prefer a large or small publishing company? Define your terms (by number of titles, in print, income, employees, offices, etc.).

7. Do you mind relocating right now? Do you want to work for a publisher with a reputation for *frequently* relocating top people?

8. Do you mind travelling frequently? What percent do you consider reasonable? (Make sure this matches the normal requirements of the job specialization you're considering.)

9. What salary would you *like* to receive (put in the "Preference" column)? What's the *lowest* salary you'll accept (in the "Must" column)?

10. Are there any benefits (such as an expense account, medical and/or dental insurance, company car, etc.) you must or would like to have?

11. Are you planning to attend graduate school at some point in the future and, if so, is a tuition reimbursement plan important to you?

12. Do you feel a formal training program necessary?

13. What kind of books (general Trade, scholarly, children's, elhi, college, medical, scientific/technical, etc.) would you prefer to work on?

14. Do you want to work only for a particular publisher? (If you're narrowing your search this much already, you better hope they publish a *lot* of books!)

It's important to keep revising this new form, just as you should continue to update your Self-Evaluation Form. After all, it contains the criteria by which you will judge every potential employer. It may even lead you to avoid interviewing at a specific house (if, for example, they're located in a state on your "never" list!). So be sure your "nevers" aren't frivolous. Likewise, make your "musts" and "preferences" at least semi-realistic. If your "must" salary for a position as an assistant editor is $30,000, you will wind up eliminating every house out there!

Armed with a complete list of such criteria, you're now ready to find all the publishers that match them.

TARGETING INDIVIDUAL PUBLISHERS

To begin creating your initial list of targeted publishers, start with the *Job Opportunities Databank* (Section IV). We've listed virtually every major publisher, most of which completed questionnaires we supplied, providing us (and you!) with a plethora of data concerning their overall operations, hiring practices, and other important information on entry-level job opportunities. This latter information includes key contacts (names), the average number of entry-level people they hire each year, along with complete job descriptions and requirements.

This section also includes lists of publishers offering salaried and non-salaried internships, or some of each, and those with formal training programs for "new hires." All of the detailed information in these two chapters was provided by the publishers themselves. To our knowledge, it is available only in this Career Directory.

We have attempted to include information on those major publishers that represent most of the entry-level jobs out there. But there are, of course, many other publishers of all sizes and shapes that you may also wish to research. In the next section, we will discuss some other reference books you can use to obtain more information on the publishers we've listed, as well as those we haven't.

OTHER REFERENCE TOOLS

In order to obtain some of the detailed information you need, you will probably need to do further research, either in the library or by meeting and chatting with people familiar with the publishing houses

As we've already mentioned, more than once, you should consider Literary Marketplace —available from R. R. Bowker (245 West 17th St., New York, NY 10011)—the natural companion to this Career Directory. It lists all of the houses we've featured in Section IV (plus hundreds more) and offers a plethora of additional listings of companies and services allied with the book business. If a listing in chapter 24 instructs you to contact "department heads," for example, regarding employment opportunities, those names would most likely be included in the house's LMP entry. (If you are not interested in working in the U.S. or Canada and are searching for a job overseas, another Bowker publication—International Literary Marketplace— is an invaluable source. It lists more than 9,000 publishers in 160 countries. Check you library—it costs $65.00.)

For more general research (pertinent to all publishers,), you might want to start with How To Find Information About Companies (Washington Researchers, 1985); the Encyclopedia of Business Information Sources (Gale Research, Book Tower, Detroit, MI 48226); and/or the Guide to American Directories (B. Klein Publications, P.O. Box 8503, Coral Springs, FL 33065), which lists directories for over 3,000 fields.

If you want to work for one of the associations which serves the book publishing/selling industry (or the fields with which it's most closely allied), we've listed all those in Appendix A. Other associations may be researched in the Encyclopedia of Associations (Gale Research Co.) or National Trade and Professional Associations of the United States (Columbia Books, Inc., 777 14th St., NW, Suite 236, Washington, DC 20005).

There are, in addition, some general corporate directories which may give you additional information on major publishers. (But do remember: Most publishers are not major, not publicly owned companies, and, therefore, not particularly forthcoming with information or listed in such all-inclusive reference books.) These volumes should all be available in the reference (and/or business) section of your local library:

*Dun and Bradstreet's family of corporate reference resources: the Million Dollar Directory (160,000 companies with a net worth of more than $500,000), Top 50,000 Companies (those with a minimum net worth of just under $2 million), and Business Rankings (details on the top 7,500 firms). A new volume from Dun's —Reference Book of Corporate Managements/America's Corporate Leaders— provides detailed biographical data on the principal officers and directors of some 12,000-odd corporations. Who says you can't find out about the quirks and hobbies of the guy you're interviewing with? All of these volumes are available in most libraries or from Dun's Marketing Services (3 Century Drive, Parsippany, NJ 07054).

*Standard & Poor's Register of Corporations, Directors and Executives includes corporate listings for over 45,000 firms and 72,000 biographical listings. (Available from Standard and Poor's, 25 Broadway, New York, NY 10004.)

*Moody's Industrial Manual (Available from Moody's Investors Ser-vice, Inc., 99 Church St., New York, NY 10007.)

*Thomas's Register of American Manufacturing (Thomas Publishing Company, 1 Penn Plaza, New York, NY 10001.)

*Ward's Business Directory, a three-volume reference work that includes listings of nearly 100,000 companies, the majority of them privately-held, and details that are usually most difficult to acquire about such firms (number of employees, annual sales, etc.). Published by Information Access Company.

Primary sources which should be utilized from now on to complete your research are The *Wall Street Journal, Barron's, Dun's Business Month, Business Week, Forbes, Fortune* and *Inc.* Naturally, the trade magazines which you've been studying (and to which you've already subscribed) like *Publishers Weekly*, offer a steady stream of information. Become as familiar as possible with the publishing companies, authors, jargon, topics covered and the industry.

One last note on potential sources of leads. The Oxbridge Directory of Newsletters (available from Oxbridge Communications, 183 Madison Ave., Suite 1108, New York, NY 10016) lists thousands of newsletters in a plethora of industries and might well give you some ideas and names. And the Professional Exhibits Directory (Gale Research Co.) lists more than 2,000 trade shows and conventions. Such shows are excellent places to "run into" sales reps, editors, etc. and offer unexpected opportunities to learn about the business "from the horse's mouth."

NETWORKING FOR SUCCESS

You're now as prepared as any Boy or Girl Scout in history. You know not only the field you want to enter, but an exact job title, summarized in a concise career objective. You know whether you're heading for a general Trade house or a university press. And you have a complete preliminary list of houses, with detailed data on each, that reflects your own needs, wants and goals.

It's time to start *networking*, telling everybody you know and everybody *they* know exactly the kind of job you're looking for. Faster than you expect, you will begin to develop a network of friends, relatives, acquaintances and contacts. It is most likely that the skillful use of this network and *not* the more traditional approach to job hunting—studying the want ads and sending out resumes to PO Box Numbers—is going to be the key factor in landing a first job.

Why? Because on any day of the week, the vast majority of available jobs, perhaps as high as 85% of all the jobs out there waiting to be filled, are not advertised anywhere. Many of those jobs that are advertised only remain in the classifieds for a day or two. After that, they're pulled and, for the next few weeks, various company personnel sift through resumes while the job is still sitting there, unfilled, just waiting for the right applicant to grab it!

There are some things to keep in mind while you prepare to crack what others have labeled "the hidden job market." First and foremost, remember that there are *always* jobs out there. Nearly 20% of all the jobs in the United States (and probably many more in publishing, a notoriously fluid field) change hands every year, good years and bad. People retire, move on to another job or industry, get promoted. Companies expand. The result is near-constant movement in the job market, if only you know where to look.

Second, people in a company will generally know about a job opening weeks before the outside world gets a clue, certainly before (if) it shows up in a newspaper ad.

Third, just knowing that this hidden market exists is an asset a lot of your colleagues (hereafter, let's just consider them competitors) don't have.

Last, but by no means least, your industry and company research has already made you a most knowledgeable graduates. This will undoubtedly work to your advantage.

CREATING THE IDEAL NETWORK

As in most endeavors, there's a wrong way and a right way to network. The following tips will help you construct a wide-ranging, information-gathering, interview-generating group—your very own network.

Diversify

Unlike the Harvard or Princeton Universities networks—confined to former graduates of each school—*your* network should be as diversified and wide-ranging as possible. You never know who might be in a position to help, so don't limit your group of friends. The more diverse they are, the greater the variety of information they may supply you with.

Don't Forget...

...to include everyone you know in your initial networking list: friends, relatives, social acquaintances, classmates, college alumni, professors, teachers; your dentist, doctor, family lawyer, insurance agent, banker, travel agent; elected officials in your community; ministers; fellow church members; local tradesmen; local business or social club officers. And everybody *they* know!

Be Specific

Make a list of the kinds of assistance you will require from those in your network, then make specific requests of each. Do they know of jobs at their company? Can they introduce you to the proper executives? Have they heard something about or know someone at the company you're planning to inter-view with next week?

The more organized you are, the easier it will be to target the information you need and figure out who might have it. Calling everyone and simply asking for "whatever help you can give me" is unfair to the people you're calling and a less-effective way to garner the information you need.

Know The Difference...

...between an **informational** interview and a **job** interview. The former requires you to cast yourself in the role of information-gatherer; *you* are the interviewer and knowledge is your goal—about an industry, company, job function, key executive, etc. Such a meeting with someone already doing what you soon *hope* to be doing is by far the best way to find out everything you need to know...before you walk through the door and sit down for a formal job interview, at which time your purpose is more sharply-defined: to get the job you're interviewing for.

If you learn of a specific job opening during an informational interview, you are in a position to find out details about the job, identify the interviewer and, possibly, even learn some things about him or her. In addition, presuming you get your contact's permission, you may be able to use his or her name as a referral. Calling up the interviewer and saying, "Joan Smith in your Editorial department suggested I contact you regarding openings for assistant editors" is far superior to "Hello. Do you have any job openings in your house?"

(In such a case, be careful about referring to a specific job opening, even if your contact told you about it. It may not be something you're supposed to know about. By presenting your query as an open-ended question, you give your prospective employer the option of exploring your background without further commitment. If there is a job there and you're qualified for it, you'll find out soon enough.)

Don't Waste A Contact

Not everyone you call on your highly-diversified networking list will know about a job opening. It would be surprising if each one did. But what about *their* friends and colleagues? It's amazing how everyone knows someone who knows someone. Ask—you'll find that someone.

Value Your Contacts

If you've taken our admonitions about record keeping to heart, this is where you'll begin to appreciate the dividends. If someone has provided you with helpful information or an introduction to a friend or colleague, keep him or her informed about how it all turns out. A referral that's panned out should be reported to the person who opened the door for you in the first place. Such courtesy will be appreciated...and may lead to more contacts. If someone has nothing to offer today, a call back in the future is still appropriate and may yet pay off.

The lesson is clear: Keep your options open and your contact list alive. Keeping detailed records of your network—who you spoke with, when, what transpired, etc.—will certainly help you keep track of your overall progress and organize what can be a complicated and involved process.

Organizing Your Home Office

With so many other people working for you, you must carefully and completely organize your own personal employment office. If you've already started filing detailed company data in separate folders, you're already a step ahead.

We suggest preparing a separate folder for each person you're working with, along with a centralized phone list. Throughout your job search, be prepared to keep accurate and organized records every step of the way. Keep copies of your research notes, photocopy every letter you mail, and keep detailed notes of telephone conversations. Always send off a timely and polite thank-you note to those helping out. That simple gesture will demonstrate a degree of professionalism and good manners often overlooked by students.

If you can afford one, consider purchasing a telephone answering machine. An employer who may have seen and liked your resume—one who's even willing to interview you—will rarely call more than once to set up an appointment.

IF THE PROCESS SCARES YOU

Some of you will undoubtedly be hesitant about, even fear, the networking process. It is not an unusual response—it is very human to want to accomplish things "on your own," without anyone's help. Understandable and commendable as such independence might seem, it is, in reality, an impediment if it limits your involvement in this important process. Networking has such universal application because *there is no other effective way to bridge the gap between job applicant and job*. Employers are grateful for its existence. You should be, too.

Whether you are a first-time applicant or reentering the work force now that the children are grown, the networking process will more than likely be your point of entry. Sending out mass mailings of your resume and answering the help-wanted ads may well be less personal (and, therefore, "easier") approaches, but they will also be far less effective. The natural selection process of the networking phenomenon is your assurance that water does indeed seek its own level—you will be matched up with publishers and job opportunities in which there is a mutual fit.

CHAPTER TWENTY TWO

Preparing Resumes And Cover Letters

Your resume is a one- or two-page summary of you—your education, skills, employment experience and career objective(s). It is not a biography, but a "quick and dirty" way to identify and describe you to potential employers. Most importantly, its real purpose is to sell you to the publisher you want to work for. It must set you apart from all the other applicants (those competitors) out there. So, when you sit down to formulate your resume, remember you're trying to present the pertinent information in a format and manner that will convince an executive to grant you an interview, the prelude to any job offer. (If you feel you need more help in resume preparation, or even in the entire job search area, we recommend Your First Resume by Ronald W. Fry,. a brand-new publication now available from The Career Press. See the coupon in back of this book to order.)

AN OVERVIEW OF RESUME PREPARATION

• **Know what you're doing**—your resume is a personal billboard of accomplishments. It must communicate your worth to a prospective employer in specific terms.

- **Your language should be action-oriented,** full of "doing"-type words. And less is better than more—be concise and direct. Don't worry about using complete sentences.

- **Be persuasive.** In those sections that allow you the freedom to do so, don't hesitate to communicate your worth in the strongest language. This does not mean a numbing list of self-congratulatory superlatives; it does mean truthful claims about your abilities and the evidence (educational, experiential) that supports them.

- **Don't be cheap or gaudy.** Don't hesitate to spend the few extra dollars necessary to present a professional-looking resume. Do avoid outlandish (and generally ineffective) gimmicks like over-sized or brightly-colored paper.

- **Find an editor.** Every good writer needs one, and you are writing your resume. At the very least, it will offer you a second set of eyes proofreading for embarrassing typos. But if you are fortunate enough to have a professional in the field—a recruiter or personnel executive—critique a draft, grab the opportunity and be immensely grateful.

- **If you're the next Michaelangelo,** so multi-talented that you can easily qualify for jobs in different career areas, don't hesitate to prepare two or more completely different resumes. This will enable you to change the emphasis on your education and skills according to the specific career objective on each resume, a necessary alteration that will correctly target each one.

- **Choose the proper format.** There are only three we recommend— chronological, functional and combination—and it's important you use the one that's right for you.

THE RECORDS YOU NEED

The reason for organizing records is to be more efficient and accurate when you sit down to prepare the ingredients for your resume. Records do NOT belong scattered throughout the household or dumped into the family "record file" in a kitchen drawer. Organizing your records in a single location, filed by topic, will save you time, energy and stress.

So start by deciding upon a single location in which to store your personal records. Develop a good filing system and, if you don't own a file cabinet, consider buying one of two products available at most stationery or office supply stores: an expandable pocket portfolio or a solid plastic file box (sturdier, but less compact). In either container, designate a separate folder for each of the following categories of important documents:

REPORT CARDS—Along with actual report cards, you might save samples of your work— especially in courses pertinent to your career objective. The actual work easily records interests, talents, difficulties and accomplishments.

TRANSCRIPTS/GPA/CLASS RANK—Transcripts are your school's official record of your academic history. They are generally kept in the guidance office (high school) or registrar's office (college). Make sure honors courses are noted in the transcript.

The GPA (Grade Point Average) is usually found on the transcript. Many schools generally calculate this by computing credits times a numerical grade equivalent (often "A" = 4.0, "B" = 3.0, etc.). Class rank is simply a listing of GPAs, from highest to lowest. Example: 75/306 (75th out of a class of 306 students).

ACTIVITY RECORDS—This should be a comprehensive list of sports, clubs, honor societies and other extracurricular or special activities in which you've participated, either inside or outside school. Make sure you list any leadership positions held

AWARDS/HONORS—List award name, date received and significance of the award. Example: Peabody Scholar, 1987, awarded to Jefferson High School senior who demonstrates musical prowess and an interest in pursuing a musical career.

WORK/VOLUNTEER RECORDS—List each job title, dates of employment, business name, address and phone number, name of immediate supervisor, responsibilities. Any work experience, from babysitting to lawn mowing, should be listed. Also list any volunteer work, even if it was only for one day. You may wish to keep a separate folder for Letters of Recommendation from any of these employers.

MILITARY RECORDS—Include complete military history, if pertinent.

TRAVEL RECORDS—Keep a list of your travel experiences and, perhaps, some personal reactions to each trip. Travel experience helps demonstrate that you are well-rounded, and the written reactions might prompt responses to interview questions.

THIS IS NOT THE TIME OR PLACE TO BE MODEST! Keep track of all your accomplishments, no matter how trivial they may seem to you. Brainstorm about what you've gained from your experiences and be sure you are able to talk about what you've accomplished. You probably have more to offer than you think!

From this growing collection of records and achievements, you will begin to get a clearer picture of what you really have to offer the world.

Once you have this information in hand, you have a lot of options about what to include or leave out. In general, we suggest you always include the following data:

1. Your name, address and telephone number.
2. Pertinent work history
3. Pertinent educational history
4. Academic honors
5. Memberships in professional organizations.
6. Contributions to professional publications.

You have the option of including the following:

1. Your career objective
2. Personal data (marital status, etc.)
3. Hobbies
4. Feelings about travel and/or relocation
5. Military service history

And you should *never* include the following:

1. Why you left past jobs
2. Photographs or illustrations (of yourself or anything else!)
3. References
4. Past salaries or present salary objectives/requirements

CHRONOLOGICAL AND FUNCTIONAL RESUMES

The two standard resume formats are chronological, arranged by date (last job first), and functional, which emphasizes skills rather than the sequential history of your experiences. Generally, since students have yet to develop specific, highly employable skills or the experience to indicate proficiency in specific job functions, they should use the chronological format. A bit of sales, a touch of writing, and a smidgen of research will not impress anyone on a functional resume. The latter is useful, however, if you have a great deal of pertinent job expertise, since it emphasizes qualifications and abilities in terms of job titles and responsibilities. Dates are usually omitted (though we personally feel that leaving dates out altogether lessens the effectiveness of any resume. We'd find a way to include dates—perhaps in a brief, chronological, job history section.) At the end of this chapter are examples of both.

(There are other kinds of resumes—analytical, synoptic, "creative" approaches that defy easy classification. None of these are as efficient or easily understood and accepted as the two basic formats. And none of them are at all adaptable to an entry-level candidate. So stick with the chronological or, in exceptional cases, the functional.)

GUIDELINES FOR RESUME PREPARATION

Your resume should be limited to a single page if possible, two at most. It should be printed, not xeroxed, on 8 1/2" x 11" white, cream or ivory stock. The ink should be black or, at most, a royal blue. Don't scrimp on the paper quality—use the best bond you can afford. And since printing 100 or even 200 copies will cost little more than 50, tend to overestimate your needs and opt for the highest quantity you think you may need.

When you're laying out the resume, try to leave a reasonable amount of "white space"— generous margins all around and spacing between entries. A resume is not a complete biography and anything that is not, in some way, a qualification for the type of position you're seeking should be omitted.

Be brief. Use phraseology rather than complete sentences. Your resume is a summary of your talents, not an English Lit paper. Choose your words carefully and use "power words" whenever possible. "Organized" is more powerful than "put together;" "supervised" better than "oversaw;" "formulated" better than "thought up." Strong words like these can make the most mundane clerical work sound like a series of responsible, professional positions. And, of course, they will tend to make your resume stand out. Here's a "starter list" of words which you may want to use in your resume:

achieved	administered	advised	analyzed
applied	arranged	budgeted	calculated
classified	communicated	completed	computed
conceptualized	coordinated	critiqued	delegated
determined	developed	devised	directed
established	evaluated	executed	formulated
gathered	generated	guided	implemented
improved	initiated	instituted	instructed
introduced	invented	issued	launched

lectured	litigated	lobbied	managed
negotiated	operated	organized	overhauled
planned	prepared	presented	presided
programmed	promoted	recommended	researched
reviewed	revised	reorganized	regulated
selected	solved	scheduled	supervised
systematized	taught	tested	traced
trained	updated	utilized	wrote

An important suggestion: When you've completed writing and designing your resume, have a couple of close friends or family members proofread it for typographical errors *before* you send it to the printer. For some reason, the more you check it yourself, the less likely you'll catch the errors you missed the first time around. A fresh look from someone not as familiar with it will catch these glaring (and potentially embarrassing) errors before they're duplicated a couple of hundred times.

PREPARING COVER LETTERS

A cover letter should be included with each resume you send out. It may be addressed to a particular individual your networking has identified (or with whom you've already met or spoken) or sent in response to a newspaper ad (even those that refer you solely to post office boxes). Whatever the case, each cover letter should be personalized—targeted to the individual company, executive and position. To our mind—and most executives with whom we've talked seem to agree—the cover letter tells them more about a candidate, and is, therefore, more important from your standpoint, than the resume.

Each cover letter should be error-free, neatly typed, and correctly formatted. Such a letter should probably never be handwritten. A handwritten note screams of informality, so don't use one unless that's the precise impression you're trying to convey. Students, in particular, sometimes send out cover letters reminiscent of letters home from camp, complete with the requisite stains from lunch. That is both unprofessional (you *are* trying to impress them with your professionalism) and downright offensive to any potential employer. These letters should be business letters. If you are unfamiliar with the correct way to format such a letter—and, sadly, far too many of you *are*—study the examples we've included (and, if necessary, go to your local library and study the appropriate books in the business section).

Address each letter to the proper person at the publishing company (i.e., don't write to the editor-in-chief to find a job in field sales). If you intend to send out a series of "blind" cover letter/resume packages to a number of houses —those where you're not sure of any job openings—the personnel office is usually *not* the place to direct an unsolicited resume. When we surveyed the major book publishers to compile data for the new edition of this Career Directory, only a small minority of the respondents suggested contacting personnel first. Generally, the smaller the publishing company, the more often they counseled students to "go right to the top"—the president or chief executive officer. The larger companies generally directed entry-level applicants to the appropriate department heads. (The rest either didn't list a particular preference or referred students to other specific executives, by name). The *Job Opportunities Databank* in Section IV, which details the extensive data we received from publishers, lists the name and title of the specific individual each house recommended you initially contact.

Some newspaper or trade magazine ads will not include a contact name, but will instruct you to send your resume to a post office box. In this case (and this case only), "Dear Sir:" is an appropriate salutation. And if the ad lists a series of instructions ("write, don't call;" "send letter including salary requirements; send unreturnable copy sample;" etc.), follow them <u>exactly</u>. Don't call; don't ask for your sample back. Failing to follow precise instructions (they are there for a *reason*) could mean you already failed their "pre-screening interview." You'll have lost the job before you even started chasing it!

The Correct Format

First paragraph: State the reason for the letter, the specific job or type of work for which you're applying, and where (or from whom) you learned of the opening.

Second paragraph: Indicate why you're interested in their company and that particular position and, more important, what you have to offer them. Without repeating information from your resume verbatim, explain the appropriate academic or work experiences that specifically qualify you for the position.

Third paragraph: Refer him to the resume you've enclosed and add anything else you feel it's important he know about you.

Final paragraph: Indicate your desire to meet for a personal interview and your flexibility as to the place and time. Try to close the letter with a statement or question that will encourage him to take some action. Instead of "looking forward to hearing" from him, tell him when he should expect to hear from you. Otherwise, be prepared to *not* hear from him. Publishing executives get streams of letters, and can't *(don't)* answer most of them.

Try to personalize each letter you write—mention the company's name whenever and wherever you have the chance. Refer to some of their specific book titles or authors, trade advertisements, awards, or anything else your research has uncovered. Executives at the top publishing companies receive hundreds of applications, letters and unsolicited resumes from students and others looking for jobs...*weekly*. They can spot a "form letter" a mile away. Take this opportunity to show them that you are, in fact, serious about working at their company and that you've taken the time to learn something about them. And don't hesitate to demonstrate the fruits of your research in your letters.

Don't make a common mistake and simply recopy half your resume into the body of the cover letter. The letter offers you the opportunity to be a little creative, compensate for some glaring weakness or omission in your resume, and make a good, professional first impression. If the cover letter doesn't "sell" them, they may never even bother looking at the resume.

Two sample cover letters are reproduced at the end of this chapter (after some sample resumes). Cover Letter 1 might have been written in response to a small "want ad" in *Publishers Weekly,* one that didn't identify the publisher and directed all inquiries to a PO Box number. Letter 2 is one we'd write to the marketing director at a publisher one of our contacts told us might be hiring two or three new people for their Marketing/Sales Training Program.

SAMPLE RESUME #1: CHRONOLOGICAL

GILDA H. RADNER

HOME ADDRESS:	**SCHOOL ADDRESS:**
80 Stemmons Freeway,	4240 Hill St.,
Dallas, TX 87540	Los Angeles, CA 90410
(214)788-0000	(213)001-0100

JOB
OBJECTIVE

A position offering challenge and responsibility in book publishing marketing research, advertising or promotion

EDUCATION

U.C.L.A.

1984-1988 Graduating in June, 1988, with a B.A. degree in Marketing. Deans List four years; Summa cum laude.

Fields of study include: marketing and advertising theory, research, business law, economics, mass communications, statistical analysis and research methodology.

Graduate courses in advertising theory and policies, consumer behavioral theory, sales management.

1979-1983 Greg Wright High School, Los Angeles, Calif. National Honor Society. Senior Class President. United Way Club Head Fund Raiser.

WORK
EXPERIENCE
(SUMMERS)

1987: JIM CANNON , INC., Los Angeles, Ca. Administrative assistant in Research Department. Trained in behavioral research techniques. Responsible for record keeping, expense reports, public relations, lab report dissemination, correspondence.

1984 - 1986: KISCHTRONICS, San Diego, Ca. Basic sales and management training at this major research and development facility. Duties included billing, inventory control, shipping and distribution, lab maintenance and delivery schedules.

SAMPLE RESUME #2: FUNCTIONAL

JIM BEAM
76 Cortlandt St.,
New York, NY 10017
(212)555-1111

Career Objective: A position as a Trade book sales representative

SUMMARY

I am completing my degree in journalism, specializing in marketing, at University State. Last summer, I interned as an assistant account executive (with copywriting responsibilities) for a local advertising agency. I also have one year's experience selling advertising space (and supervising a staff of three salespeople) on my college newspaper. Both jobs have convinced me I will be successful in book sales.

EXPERIENCE

Summer, 1985 & 86: Intern, Kay Silver & Associates, Inc.
Summer, 1984 : Intern, Committee to Re-elect Kim Kerr

1985/86 school year:Ad Director, *The Daily Planet*
1986/87 school year:Salesman, Joe's University Book Store.

EDUCATION

B.A. Journalism (Marketing) University State - June, 1987
(summa cum laude).

PROFESSIONAL MEMBERSHIPS AND BUSINESS SKILLS

Member of the young Professionals Division of the Advertising Club of New York. Skills: Sales, media placement, typing (50 wpm), word processing, computer literate.

PERSONAL

Age: 21. Health: Excellent. Language Skills: Fluent (read/write/speak) in German and French.

References Available Upon Request

COVER LETTER 1

May 6, 1988

Bill Killpatrick
422 W. 22nd St.,
New York, NY 10000
(212)888-1111

Post Office Box 1000
<u>Publishers Weekly</u>
205 E. 42nd Street,
New York, New York 10017

Dear Sir:

The entry-level Trade book sales position briefly outlined in your May 5th <u>PW</u> advertisement is very appealing to me. Please accept this letter and the attached resume as my application for this position.

While majoring in journalism (with a marketing emphasis) at Stein University, I worked on a number of projects which required the communication skills you specified in your ad. In addition, as advertising director for the <u>Daily Planet</u>, and a summer intern for a local advertising agency, I demonstrated the sales and interpersonal skills such a position requires.

I am especially excited about the possibility of covering the Midwest region , as your ad indicates this new employee would. As I was born and raised in Indiana, I am already familiar with and enjoy Chicago, St. Louis, Minneapolis, and the other major cities this territory encompasses.

I would like to meet with you at your convenience to discuss this position and my qualifications for it in more detail. I will be in Chicago for other interviews the week of May 27th. I will call you the week of May 14th, to see if we can set up an appointment for that week.

Thank you for your time. I look forward to meeting with you.

Sincerely yours,

Bill Killpatrick

COVER LETTER 2

May 6, 1988

Tim Carhart
44 Overview Circle,
Fargo, North Dakota
(718)888-0101

Ms. Pamela Cummings
Advertising Director
Print 'Em & Sell 'Em Publications, Inc.
2435 Dyer Street,
Kokomo, IN 46254

Dear Ms. Cummings:

I recently met your colleague, Arthur Hyman, at a seminar sponsored by <u>Publishers Weekly</u> magazine. He mentioned you were considering hiring two or three entry-level people for your Marketing/Sales Training Program and suggested I contact you.

Ms. Cummings, it has been my dream to work at a major publisher on a respected consumer publication. If at all possible, I had hoped to be accepted in a well-respected, formal advertising sales training program.Your training program is the best in the industry.

And I'm the right person for you to hire. While majoring in journalism (with a marketing emphasis) at University State, I worked on a number of projects, two of which simulated marketing problems you had to solve for your recent publication of <u>Lose 100 Lbs. and Make a Million Dollars in Just 18 Days!</u> In addition, as ad director for the <u>Centennial</u> and, this past summer, working as an account services intern for a local agency, I clearly demonstrated my sales, communication and interpersonal skills.

Ms. Cummings, I will be returning home to Indiana in one week and would like to meet with you soon thereafter to discuss this opportunity in more detail. I will call you on May 14th to schedule an appointment. I look forward to talking with you then.

Sincerely yours,

Tim Carhart

CHAPTER TWENTY THREE

Questions For You,
Questions For Them

Well, the days of research, preparation, chart-making, form-filling and resume-printing worked. They're lining up to meet you! So it's time to prepare once again—for the interviewing process that will inevitably determine the job offers you actually get.

Interviews shouldn't scare you. After all, the very concept of two (or more) persons meeting to determine if they are right for each other is a good one. As important as research, resumes, letters and phone calls are, they are inherently impersonal. The interview is your chance to really see and feel the company firsthand—"up close and personal;" so think of it as a positive opportunity—your chance to succeed.

This chapter will focus on the kinds of questions you are likely to be asked, how to answer them and the questions you should be ready to ask your-self. By removing the workings of the interview process from the "unknown" category, you will reduce the fear it engenders. (If you feel you need more help with interviewing, we suggest Interview For Success by Drs. Caryl & Ron Krannich, a brand-new edition of which is now available through The Career Press.

GETTING ORGANIZED, GETTING STARTED

Start by setting up a calendar on which you can enter and track all your scheduled appointments. When you schedule an interview with a publisher, ask them how much time you should allow for the appointment. Some companies require all new applicants to fill out numerous forms and/or complete a battery of intelligence or psychological tests—all before the first interview. If you've only allowed an hour for the interview—and scheduled another at a nearby house ten minutes later—the first time you confront a three-hour test series will effectively destroy any schedule.

Some companies, especially if the first interview is very positive, like to keep applicants around to talk to other executives. This process may be planned or, in a lot of cases, a spontaneous decision by an interviewer who likes you and wants you to meet some other key decision makers. Other companies will tend to schedule such a series of second interviews on a separate day. Find out, if you can, how the publisher you're planning to visit generally operates. Other-wise, especially if you've traveled to New York or another city to interview with a number of companies in a short period of time, a schedule that's too tight will fall apart in no time at all.

If you need to travel out-of-state to interview with a publisher, be sure to ask if they will be paying some or all of your travel expenses. (It's generally expected that you'll be paying your own way to companies within your home state.) If the publisher doesn't offer—and you don't ask—presume you're paying the freight.

Even if the publisher agrees to reimburse you, make sure you have enough money to pay all the expenses yourself. While some companies may reimburse you immediately, handing you a check as you leave the building, the majority may take from a week to a month to forward you an expense check.

PRE-INTERVIEW RESEARCH

The research you did to find these publishing companies is nothing compared to the research you need to do now that you're beginning to narrow your search. If you followed our detailed suggestions when you started targeting these publishers in the first place, you've already amassed a lot of information about them. If you didn't bother to do the research *then*, you sure better decide to do it *now*. Study each publishing company as if you were going to be tested on your detailed knowledge of their organization and operations. Here's a complete checklist of the facts you should try to know about each company you plan to visit for a job interview:

The Basics

1. The address of (and directions to) the office you're visiting.
2. Headquarters location (if different).
3. Some idea of domestic and international branches.
4. Relative size (compared to other houses.
5. Annual sales and income (last two years).
6. Subsidiary companies; specialized divisions.
7. Departments (overall company structure).
8. Number of books in print; number of new titles (last two years)

The Extras

1. The history of the company (including specialties, honors and awards, famous names, etc.).
2. Names, titles and backgrounds of top management.

3. Major authors associated with the house.

4. Existence (and type) of training program.

5. Relocation policy.

6. Relative salaries (compared to other publishers).

7. Recent developments concerning the company or its major authors (from your trade magazine and newspaper reading).

8. Everything you can learn about the career, likes and dislikes of the person(s) interviewing you.

The amount of time and work necessary to be *this* well-prepared for an interview is considerable. It will not be accomplished the day before the interview. You may even find some of the information you need to be unavailable on short notice. (Is it really so important to do all this? Well, *some*body out there is going to. And if you happen to be interviewing for the same job as that other, well-prepared, knowledgeable candidate, who do *you* think will impress the interview more?)

If you give yourself enough time, most of this information is surprisingly easy to obtain. In addition to the detailed information in the *Job Opportunities Databank* (Section IV) of this Career Directory and the other reference sources we covered in the earlier chapters of this job search section, the publishing company itself can supply you with a great deal of data. A company's Annual Report—which all publicly-owned companies must publish yearly for their stockholders—is a virtual treasure trove of information. Write each house and request copies of their last two Annual Reports. A comparison of sales, income and other data over this period may enable you to infer some interesting things about the company's overall financial health and growth potential. Many libraries also have collections of annual reports from major corporations. Also, each house has a catalogue that it prepares (primarily) for its wholesalers and retail book buyers, sometimes as often as quarterly. These will help you be current on big-name authors, new releases, best-sellers in the works, etc.

Attempting to learn about your interviewer is a chore, the importance of which is underestimated by most applicants (who then, of course, don't bother to do it). Being one of the exceptions may get you a job. Use the biographical references mentioned earlier in this section. If he is listed in any of these sources, you'll be able to learn an awful lot about his background. In addition, find out if he's written any articles that have appeared in the trade press or, even better, books on his area(s) of expertise. Referring to his own writings during the course of an interview, without making it *too* obvious a compliment, can be very effective. We all have egos and we all like people to talk about us. The interviewer is no different from the rest of us. You might also check to see if any of your networking contacts worked with him at his current (or a previous) house and can help "fill you in."

THE DAY OF THE INTERVIEW

On the day of the interview, wear a conservative business suit (not a sports coat, not a "nice" blouse and skirt).

It's not unusual for resumes and cover letters to head in different directions when a company starts passing them around to a number of executives. If you sent them, both may even be long gone. So bring along extra copies of your resume and your own copy of the cover letter that originally accompanied it. Whether or not you make them available, we suggest you prepare a neatly-typed list of references (including the name, title, company, address and phone number of each person). You may want to bring along a copy of your college transcript, especially if it's something to brag about. (Once you get your first job, you'll probably never use it—or be asked for it—again, so enjoy it while you can!) And, if appropriate or required, make sure you bring samples of your work (e.g., your art portfolio or "clippings file").

Plan to arrive fifteen minutes before your scheduled appointment. If you're in an unfamiliar city, or have a long drive to the company, allow extra time for the unexpected delays that seem to occur with mind-numbing regularity on days like this. Arriving early will give you some time to check your appearance, catch your breath, check in with the receptionist, learn how to correctly pronounce the interviewer's name, and get yourself organized and battle-ready.

Arriving late does not make a sterling first impression. If you are only a few minutes late, it's probably best not to mention it or even excuse yourself. With a little luck, everybody else is behind schedule and no one will notice. However, if you're more than fifteen minutes late, have an honest (or serviceable) explanation ready and offer it at your first opportunity. Then drop the subject as quickly as possible and move on to the interview.

When you meet the interviewer, shake hands firmly. People pay attention to hand-shakes. Ask for a business card. This will make sure you get the name and title right when you write your follow-up letter. You can staple it to the company file for easy reference as you continue your networking.

Try to maintain eye contact with the interviewer as you talk. This will indicate you're interested in what he has to say. Sit straight. Keep your voice at a comfortable level, and try to sound enthusiastic (without imitating a high school cheerleader). Be confident and poised, and provide direct, accurate and honest answers to his trickiest questions. And, as you try to remember all this, just be yourself and try to act like you're comfortable and enjoying yourself!

Interviews are sometimes conducted over lunch, though this is not usually the case with entry-level people. If it does happen to you, though, try to order something in the middle price range, neither filet mignon nor a cheeseburger. Do not order alcohol. If your interviewer orders a carafe of wine, you may share it. Otherwise, alcohol should be considered *verboten*, under any and all circumstances. Then hope your mother taught you the correct way to eat and talk at the same time. If not, just do your best to maintain your poise.

There are some things interviewers will always view with displeasure—street language, complete lack of eye contact, insufficient or vague explanations or answers, a noticeable lack of energy, poor interpersonal skills (i.e., not listening or the basic inability to carry on an intelligent conversation) and a demonstrable lack of motivation.

Before you allow an interview to end, summarize why you want the job, why you are qualified and what, in particular, you can offer their company. Then, take some action. If the interviewer hasn't told you about the rest of the interview process and/or where you stand, ask him. Will you be seeing other people that day? If so, ask him for some background on the other people with whom you'll be interviewing. If there are no other meetings that day, what's the next step? When can you expect to hear from them about coming back?

When you return home, file all the business cards, copies of correspondence, and notes from the interview(s) with each company in the appropriate files. Finally, but most importantly, ask yourself which publishers you really want to work for and which you are no longer interested in. This will quickly determine how far you want the process at each house to develop before you politely tell them to stop considering you for the job.

Immediately send a thank-you letter to each executive you met. These should, of course, be neatly-typed business letters, not handwritten notes (unless you are most friendly, indeed, with the interviewer and want to *stress* the "informal" nature of your note). If you are still interested in pursuing a position at their company, tell them in no uncertain terms. Reiterate why you feel you're the best candidate and tell each of the executives when you hope (expect?) to hear from them.

QUESTIONS EVERY INTERVIEWER KNOWS...AND MOST USE

Preparing for your interviews by learning about the publishing company is a key first step. Preparing to deal with the questions the interviewer will throw at you is a necessary second one. Don't go in "cold," oblivious to what's going to occur when you walk into his office. There are certain questions we can almost guarantee will be asked during any first interview. Study the list of questions (and hints) that follow, and prepare at least one solid, concise answer that you can trot out on cue. Practice with a friend until your answers to these most-asked questions sound intelligent, professional and, most important, unmemorized and unrehearsed.

"Why do you want to be in book publishing?" Using your knowledge and understanding of the book industry, explain why you find the business exciting, and where and how you see yourself fitting in.

"Why do you think you'll be successful in this business?" Using the information from your self evaluation and the research you did on that particular company, formulate an answer which marries your strengths to theirs and to the characteristics of the position for which you're applying.

"Why did you choose our company?" This is an excellent opportunity to explain the extensive process of research and education you've undertaken. Tell them about your strengths and how you match up with their company. Emphasize specific things about their firm that led you to seek an interview. Be a salesperson—be convincing.

"What can you do for us?" Construct an answer that essentially lists your strengths, the experience you have which will contribute to your job performance and any other unique qualifications that will place you at the head of the applicant pack. Be careful: This is a question specifically designed to <u>eliminate</u> some of that pack. Sell yourself. Be one of the few called back for a second interview.

"What position here interests you?" If you're interviewing for a specific position, answer accordingly. If you want to make sure you don't close the door on other opportunities of which you might be unaware, you can follow up with your own question: "I'm here to apply for your Editorial Training Program. Is there another position open for which you feel I'm qualified?"

If you've arranged an interview with a house without knowing of any specific openings, use the answer to this question to describe the kind of work you'd like to do and why you're qualified to do it. Avoid a specific job title, since they will tend to vary from house to house. If you're on a first interview with the personnel department, just answer the question. They only want to figure out where to send you.

"What are your strengths and weaknesses?" and **"What are your hobbies (or outside interests)?"** Both questions can be easily answered using the data you gathered to complete the self-evaluation process. Be wary of being too forthcoming about your glaring faults (nobody expects you to volunteer every weakness and mistake), but do *not* reply, "I don't have any." They won't believe you and, what's worse, *you* won't believe you. After all, you did the evaluation—you know it's a lie!

"What are your career goals?"...Which is why we suggested you think about such things in the first place. Tell them what you want to do.

"What jobs have you held and why did you leave them?" Or the direct approach, "Have you ever been fired?" Take the opportunity to expand on your resume, rather than precisely answering the question by merely recapping your job experiences. In discussing each job, point out what you liked about it, what factors led to your leaving, and how the next job added to your continuing professional education. If you have been fired, say so. It's very easy to check.

"What are your salary requirements?" If they are at all interested in you, this question will probably come up. The danger, of course, is that you may price yourself too low or, even worse, right out of a job you want. Since you will have a general idea of industry figures for that position (and may even have an idea of what that house tends to pay new people for the position), why not refer to a *range* of salaries, such as "$16,000 - $19,000?"

If the interviewer doesn't bring up salary at all, it's doubtful you're being seriously considered, so you probably don't need to even bring the subject up. (If you know you aren't getting the job or aren't interested in it if offered, you may try to nail down a salary figure in order to be better prepared for the next publisher interview).

"Tell me about yourself." Watch out for this one! It's often one of the first questions asked. If you falter here, the rest of the interview could quickly become a downward slide to nowhere. Be prepared, and consider it an opportunity to combine your answers to many of the previous questions into one concise description of who you are, what you want to be and why that publisher should take a chance on you. Summarize your resume—briefly—and expand on particular courses or experiences relevant to the company or position. Do not go on about your hobbies or personal life, your dog, where you spent your summer vacation, etc. None of that is particularly relevant to securing that job. You may explain how that particular job fits in with your long-range career goals and talk specifically about what attracted you to their company.

The Not-So-Obvious Questions

Every interviewer is different and, unfortunately, there are no rules saying he has to use all or any of the "basic" questions. But we think the odds are against his avoiding *all* of them. Whichever of these he includes, be assured most interviewers do like to come up with questions that are "uniquely theirs." It may be just one or a whole series—questions he's developed over the years that he feels help separate the wheat from the chaff.

You can't exactly prepare yourself for questions like, "What would you do if...(fill in the blank with some obscure occurrence)?," "Tell me about your father," or "What's your favorite ice cream flavor?" Every interviewer we know has his or her favorites and all of these questions seem to come out of left field. Just stay relaxed, grit your teeth (quietly) and take a few seconds to frame a reasonably intelligent reply.

Some questions may be downright inappropriate. Young women, for example, may be asked about their plans for marriage and children. Don't call the interviewer a chauvinist (or worse). And don't point out that the question may be a little outside the law. (The nonprofessional interviewer may not realize such questions are illegal, and a huffy response may confuse —and anger—him.) Whenever any questions are raised about your personal life—and this question surely qualifies—it is much more effective to respond that you are very interested in the position and have no reason to believe that your personal life will preclude you from doing an excellent job.

"Do you have any questions?" It's the fatal twelfth question on our list—often the last one an interviewer throws at you—after an hour or two of grilling. Unless the interview has been very long and unusually thorough, you probably *should* have questions about the job, the company, even the industry.

Preparing yourself for an interview means more than having answers for some of the questions an interviewer may ask. It means having your *own* set of questions—at least five or six—for the interviewer. The interviewer is trying to find the right person for the job. *You're* trying to find the right job. So you should be just as curious about him and his company as he is about you. Here's a short list of questions you may consider asking on any interview:

1. What will my typical day be like?
2. What happened to the last person who had this job?
3. Given my attitude and qualifications, how would you estimate my chances for career advancement at your company?
4. Why did you come to work here? What keeps you here?
5. If you were I, would you start here again?
6. How would you characterize the management philosophy of your firm?
7. What characteristics do the successful_____ at your company have in common (fill in the blank with an appropriate title, such as "editors," "sales reps," etc.)?
8. What's the best (and worst) thing about working here?
9. On a scale of 1 to 10, how would you rate your company in terms of salaries, benefits, and employee satisfaction, in comparison to others your size?

Other questions about the company or position will be obvious—they're the areas your research hasn't been able to fill in. Ask the interviewer. But be careful and use common sense. No one is going to answer highly personal, rude or indiscreet questions. Even innocent questions might be misconstrued if you don't think about the best way to pose them—*before* they come trippingly off your tongue.

Unless you're interviewing with the Personnel (or Human Resources) department, remember that most, if not all, of the executives you'll be meeting will *not* be professional interviewers. Which means they might well spend more time talking about themselves than the company, the position or you. If that happens, use it as an opportunity to create an informal dialogue. Such a "conversational approach" is often a more productive way of finding out important information, and selling yourself, than a straightforward question and answer session anyway.

No job search is an easy one. They all require time, energy, research and more than a modicum of luck. And jobs at "big name" publishing companies are never easy to get. The detailed job search process we've outlined in these chapters is complicated, time-consuming and, we expect, far more involved than most of you will like. None of you will precisely follow each recommended step. But, hopefully, you will come to understand why we've made each recommendations and find them helpful in your own search.

Because the extra work you do now *will* pay off in the long run. The more time and effort you put into your career *now*—as you're just starting out—the more likely you'll end up at the right publisher, in the right department, heading in the right direction, and well on your way to achieving the personal goals you set. ***Good luck!***

SECTION IV

Job Opportunties Databank

CHAPTER TWENTY FOUR

Entry-Level
Job Listings

There are two chapters in this section. This one includes information on the book publishers we surveyed regarding entry-level job opportunities; chapter 25 includes internship and training program information on these publishers. This information was compiled by our staff through direct mail questionnaires and telephone calls and represents data that is completely unavailable anywhere else. (We have, however, recently published the first two volumes of our brand-new **Internship Series**. Those of you interested in journalism internships should, therefore, also consult **Internships, Volume 2: Newspaper, Magazine and Book Publishing,** which includes more information on the publishers listed in these two chapters, as well as those newspaper and magazine publishers listed in the *Job Opportunities Databanks* of our other two publishing Career Directories.)

As should be obvious, this is not a complete listing of U. S. book publishers. However, it *is* a most substantial list of those publishers *offering entry-level opportunities and/or internships* and, as a matter of fact, includes listings for virtually every major general trade house (Simon & Schuster, Random House, Doubleday, Harper & Row, etc.), educational publishers (McGraw-Hill, D. C. Heath, Houghton Mifflin, Grolier, etc.), paperback publishers (Ballantine, Bantam, Pocket Books, Warners, etc.), a plethora of medium-sized houses (Alfred A. Knopf, Crown, St. Martins, etc.), a representative sampling of scholarly, medical and technical publishers (Van Nostrand Reinhold, Addison Wesley, Marcel Dekker), major university presses, other specialized publishers and small trade houses. And a selection of major **Canadian** houses, as well.

With these listings as a guide, you should be able to get a better feel for the possibilities out there. You can then use a reference book like Literary Marketplace (from R.R. Bowker) to find other houses that match those listed here in size or location. But even if you just stick with this list, you will be working with the publishers that will probably end up hiring the majority of entry-level candidates.

Most of the information should be self-explanatory.

"Average Entry-level Hiring" is that house's best estimate of anticipated need for new people each year. How accurate is it? Not very. For example, in the first edition of this volume, published in 1986, Addison-Wesley indicated they would be hiring 10 entry-level people in 1986. Yet in the 1987 edition, they noted that they had actually hired **76 entry-level people!** And are now indicating 20 as an "average.". So use this figure as an *indicator* at best.

Two important points: 1) A "?" following the "average entry-level hiring" entry means *they tend to hire entry-level people;* **they were just unable to come up with any specific number. 2) If the publisher indicates they do not plan to hire any entry-level people, they may still have listed "Opportunities." In this case, these should not be considered actual jobs, merely the positions they consider entry-level...whether or not they currently have openings.**

If the publishers themselves had any specific suggestions, we've included them. These will help you get a head start on other applicants—you'll know what the houses want you to do!

Whenever we couldn't confirm the accuracy of an entry, we merely entered "NA"— Not Available.

Oh, and don't forget the second chapter of this section—it lists all of the book publishers we've identified that offer internships and/or training programs.

ABBEVILLE PRESS, INC.
Listing deleted at Publisher's request.

ABINGDON PRESS
201 Eighth Ave.
Nashville, TN 37202
615-749-6000
EMPLOYMENT CONTACT: Cindy Knight, Employment Supervisor
TYPES OF PUBLISHING: General, Religious
TITLES IN PRINT: 184
TOTAL EMPLOYEES: 1,399
AVERAGE ENTRY-LEVEL HIRING: 300
OPPORTUNITIES: Clerical (bookkeeping), Editorial, Production Depts. No specific requirements available.

HARRY N. ABRAMS, INC.
A Division of The Times Mirror Company
100 Fifth Avenue
New York, NY 10011
212-206-7715
EMPLOYMENT CONTACT: Ellie Giannasco, Personnel Manager
TYPES OF PUBLISHING: Trade and art/illustrated
TITLES IN PRINT: 140
TOTAL EMPLOYEES: 150
AVERAGE ENTRY-LEVEL HIRING: 0
OPPORTUNITIES: Editorial Asst.—College degree; typing, filing, knowledge of publishing. Marketing Asst.—College degree; clerical skills, publishing background. Publicity Asst.—College degree; clerical skills, good phone contact. Production Asst.—College degree; typing, filing, secretarial background.

ACADEMIC PRESS

See listing for Harcourt Brace Jovanovich

ACROPOLIS BOOKS, LTD.

Colortone Bldg
2400 17th St. NW
Washington, DC 20009
202-387-6805
EMPLOYMENT CONTACT: Alphonse J. Hackl, President
TYPES OF PUBLISHING: Non Fiction
TITLES IN PRINT: 300
TOTAL EMPLOYEES: 65
AVERAGE ENTRY-LEVEL HIRING: 1
OPPORTUNITIES: Art Dept., Clerical (bookkeeping). No requirements specified.

ADDISON-WESLEY PUBLISHING COMPANY, INC.

Rt. 128
Reading, MA 01867
617-944-3700
EMPLOYMENT CONTACT: Roger L. Drumm, Corporate Recruiter
TYPES OF PUBLISHING: Audio/Visual, College Text, Elhi, Professional, Reference, Scholarly, Scientific/Technical, Software, Trade (Hardcover) Trade (Paperbound), Training.
TITLES IN PRINT: 5,700
TOTAL EMPLOYEES: 1,292
AVERAGE ENTRY-LEVEL HIRING: 20
OPPORTUNITIES: All of the following positions require a college degree or equivalent experience, preferably with a liberal arts major, plus those other skills specified: College Field Sales—Leadership, verbal communications skills. Editorial Asst. or Promotion Asst.—Word processing, organization. Telemarketing Sales or Sales Asst. —Strong communication skills, organization, minimal production experience. Marketing Asst. —Word processing, written and verbal communication skills.
SUGGESTIONS: "Conduct extensive research before contacting publishers. Use local sources (i.e., on-campus authors, faculty, bookstore managers, trade buyers, design schools). Also consult publisher's catalog to determine the nature of its publishing programs. Contact Publishing Institutes (e.g., Stanford, Howard University, UC Berkeley, Denver, Radcliffe, Rice, CUNY, Hofstra, etc.) Visit trade shows, academic conventions."—Mr. Drumm

AD-LIB PUBLICATIONS

51 N Fifth St, PO Box 1102
Fairfield, IA 52665-1102
515-472-6617
EMPLOYMENT CONTACT: John Kremer, Publisher
TYPES OF PUBLISHING: Business and Professional
TITLES IN PRINT: 7
TOTAL EMPLOYEES: 3
AVERAGE ENTRY-LEVEL HIRING: 1
OPPORTUNITIES: Data Entry—High school graduate; typing. Database Managers/Editors—College degree; typing, detail oriented. Publicist—College degree; writing.

ALASKA NORTHWEST PUBLISHING COMPANY

130 Second Ave South
Edmonds, WA 98020
206-774-4111
EMPLOYMENT CONTACT: Rick Paul, Associate Publisher
TYPES OF PUBLISHING: Audio/Visual, Trade (Hardcover), Trade (Paperbound) (plus monthly consumer magazine, annual travel guides.)
TITLES IN PRINT: 80
TOTAL EMPLOYEES: 40
AVERAGE ENTRY-LEVEL HIRING: 0
OPPORTUNITIES: All positions require experience.

ALFRED PUBLISHING

Box 5964, 15335 Morrison St.
Sherman Oaks, CA 91413
818-891-5999
EMPLOYMENT CONTACT: Sandy Feldstein, Vice President
TYPES OF PUBLISHING: Educational, Trade, Music, Software
TITLES IN PRINT: 5,000
TOTAL EMPLOYEES: 75
AVERAGE ENTRY-LEVEL HIRING: 7
OPPORTUNITIES: Clerical, Sales, Keypunch, Shipping & Receiving. No requirements specified.

ALLYN & BACON, INC.
A Subsidiary of Simon & Schuster, Inc.
7 Wells Ave.
Newton, MA 02159
617-455-1200
EMPLOYMENT CONTACT: Stacey Liebertal, VP-Human Resources
TYPES OF PUBLISHING:
TITLES IN PRINT: 300
TOTAL EMPLOYEES: 300
AVERAGE ENTRY-LEVEL HIRING: 40-50
OPPORTUNITIES: Clerical, Administration, Editorial. No specified requirements.

AMACOM BOOK DIVISION
(American Management Association)
135 West 50th St.
New York, NY 10020
212-903-8018
EMPLOYMENT CONTACT: George Harmon, Personnel Director
TYPES OF PUBLISHING: Trade non fiction—management and business.
TITLES IN PRINT: 300
TOTAL EMPLOYEES: 700+
AVERAGE ENTRY-LEVEL HIRING: 15-20
OPPORTUNITIES: Clerk, Marketing Asst., plus entry-level jobs in Personnel, Customer Service and Accounting.

AMERICAN LIBRARY ASSOCIATION
50 East Huron St.
Chicago, IL 60611
312-944-6780
EMPLOYMENT CONTACT: Paul A. Hobaso, Asst. Director of Marketing
TITLES IN PRINT: 200
TOTAL EMPLOYEES: 200
AVERAGE ENTRY-LEVEL HIRING: 4-5
OPPORTUNITIES: In all departments.

AMERICAN PHILOSOPHICAL SOCIETY
104 South Fifth St
Philadelphia, PA 19106
215-627-0706
EMPLOYMENT CONTACT: Carole N. Le Faivre, Associate Editor
TYPES OF PUBLISHING: Scholarly
TOTAL EMPLOYEES: 4
AVERAGE ENTRY-LEVEL HIRING: 0

ASPEN PUBLISHING, INC.
1600 Research Blvd.
Rockville, MD 21658
301-251-5000
EMPLOYMENT CONTACT: Bill Hingst, Public Relations Dept.
TYPES OF PUBLISHING: Healthcare, Nursing, Medical
TITLES IN PRINT: 600
TOTAL EMPLOYEES: 47
AVERAGE ENTRY-LEVEL HIRING: 3
OPPORTUNITIES: Clerk—High school graduate. Editorial Dept.—College degree. No other requirements specified.

ASHLEY BOOKS, INC.
30 Main St
Port Washington, NY 11050
516-883-2221
EMPLOYMENT CONTACT: Joan Calder, Vice President
TYPES OF PUBLISHING: College Text, Elhi, Professional, Religious, Scholarly, Scientific/Technical, Trade (Hardcover), Trade (Paperbound), (Health field fiction & non-fiction)
TITLES IN PRINT: 390
TOTAL EMPLOYEES: 200
AVERAGE ENTRY-LEVEL HIRING: 3
OPPORTUNITIES: Assistants in all Departments—English or History major helpful (however all majors will be considered if person can apply themselves with enthusiasm and really wishes to learn publishing), writing and typing skills. "Any applicant must be a self-starter and a well-organized person."
SUGGESTIONS: "Call and make an appointment to see Joan Calder. It would be helpful to bring a resume."

ATHENEUM PUBLISHING
115 Fifth Ave.
New York, NY 10003
212-702-2000
EMPLOYMENT CONTACT: Susan Leon, Senior Editor
TYPES OF PUBLISHING: Fiction, non-fiction and poetry; drama, sports, paperback, mystery
TITLES IN PRINT: 1,200
TOTAL EMPLOYEES: 75
AVERAGE ENTRY-LEVEL HIRING: 2-3

OPPORTUNITIES: Assistants in Advertising, Sales and Clerical Depts.

BALLANTINE/DEL REY/FAWCETT BOOKS
See listing for Random House

BALLINGER PUBLISHING COMPANY
Listing deleted at Publisher's request

BANTAM BOOKS, INC.
666 Fifth Avenue
New York, NY 10103
212-765-6500
EMPLOYMENT CONTACT: Terri Gioia, Personnel Manager
TYPES OF PUBLISHING: Paperback
TOTAL EMPLOYEES: 1,900
AVERAGE ENTRY-LEVEL HIRING: 10
OPPORTUNITIES: Clerks in Bookkeeping Dept (will train). Art Dept—Prefer 2 years experience.

BARRON'S EDUCATIONAL SERIES, INC.
250 Wireless Blvd.
Hauppauge, NY 11788
516-434-3311
EMPLOYMENT CONTACT: Don Musner, Personnel Manager

BEEKMAN PUBLISHERS, INC.
PO Box 888
Woodstock, NY 12498
914-679-2300
EMPLOYMENT CONTACT: Joanne Michaels, Vice President
TYPES OF PUBLISHING: Professional, Reference, Scientific/Technical, Reprints
TOTAL EMPLOYEES: 5
AVERAGE ENTRY-LEVEL HIRING: 0

ROBERT BENTLEY, INC.
1000 Massachusetts Ave
Cambridge, MA 02138
617-547-4170
EMPLOYMENT CONTACT: D. Waite, Personnel Manager
TYPES OF PUBLISHING: College Text, Professional, Reference, Scientific/Technical.
TITLES IN PRINT: 135
TOTAL EMPLOYEES: 11
AVERAGE ENTRY-LEVEL HIRING: 2

OPPORTUNITIES: Asst Production Editor— College degree. No other requirements specified.
COMMENTS: "Interest and organizing ability are important."

BERKLEY PUBLISHING GROUP
See Listing for Putnam Berkley Group

BIRCH TREE GROUP LTD
180 Alexander St.
Princeton, NJ 08540
609-683-0090
EMPLOYMENT CONTACT: Janet James, Office Manager
TYPES OF PUBLISHING: Educational Music Methods
TITLES IN PRINT: 250
TOTAL EMPLOYEES: 30-35
AVERAGE ENTRY-LEVEL HIRING: 2-5
OPPORTUNITIES: No entry-level openings at this time. Experienced help only.

BRANDEN PUBLISHING COMPANY
17 Station St, Box 843
Brookline Village, MA 02147
617-734-2045
EMPLOYMENT CONTACT: Adolph Caso, President
TYPES OF PUBLISHING: Children's, College Text, Professional, Reference, Religious, Scholarly Scientific/Technical, Software, Trade (Hardcover), Trade (Paperbound).
TITLES IN PRINT: 260
TOTAL EMPLOYEES: 8
AVERAGE ENTRY-LEVEL HIRING: 2
OPPORTUNITIES: Tends to hire graduate students only. Opportunities not particularly good at this time.

BRIDGE PUBLISHING, INC.
2500 Hamilton Blvd.
South Plainfield, NJ 07080
201-754-0745
EMPLOYMENT CONTACT: Stephen R. Clark, Executive Editor
TYPES OF PUBLISHING: Trade (Paperbound), Mass Market Paperback, Religious.
TITLES IN PRINT: 215
TOTAL EMPLOYEES: 10
AVERAGE ENTRY-LEVEL HIRING: 0

BRUNNER/MAZEL, INC.
19 Union Square West
New York, NY 10003
212-924-3344
EMPLOYMENT CONTACT: Mark Tracten,
President
TYPES OF PUBLISHING: Scientific/Technical
TITLES IN PRINT: 20
TOTAL EMPLOYEES: 25
AVERAGE ENTRY-LEVEL HIRING: 1-2
OPPORTUNITIES: Entry-level positions in
Editorial, Production and Clerical Depts. No
educational or skill requirements specified.

BUTTERWORTH PUBLISHERS
80 Montvale Ave.
Stoneham, MA 02180
617-438-8464
EMPLOYMENT CONTACT: Eric. J. Newman, Chief
Executive-STM Publisher
TYPES OF PUBLISHING: College, Professional,
Reference, Scientific/Technical.
TOTAL EMPLOYEES: 40
AVERAGE ENTRY-LEVEL HIRING: 2

CAMBRIDGE UNIVERSITY PRESS
32 E 57th St
New York, NY 10022
212-688-8885
EMPLOYMENT CONTACT: Carol D. New,
Personnel Manager
TYPES OF PUBLISHING: Children's, College Text,
Professional, Reference, Religious, Scholarly,
Scientific/Technical, Software.
TITLES IN PRINT: 9,000
TOTAL EMPLOYEES: 834
AVERAGE ENTRY-LEVEL HIRING: 5-6
OPPORTUNITIES: Editorial Asst.—College
degree, 60 WPM typing, and computer skills.
"This is a promotable position—average life of
an editorial assistant is nine months to two years."
COMMENTS: "Applicants are tested for typing
skills, spelling and grammar."

THE CAREER PRESS INC.
62 Beverly Rd., PO Box 34
Hawthorne, NJ 07507
201-427-0229
EMPLOYMENT CONTACT: Richard Start, Asst. to
the President

TYPES OF PUBLISHING: Reference, Educational
(Hardcover and Paperbound)
TITLES IN PRINT: 16
AVERAGE ENTRY-LEVEL HIRING : 1
OPPORTUNITIES: Assistant Editor—College
degree (major unimportant), excellent typing (50
wpm absolute minimum), good organizational,
communication, grammar, spelling, composition
skills. Good "team spirit." Hard worker. Word
processing experience and knowledge of publishing business preferred (any college publication
experience a plus); PC experience a definite plus.
COMMENTS: Cover letters and resumes only, <u>no
phone calls.</u>

CAROLRHODA BOOKS, INC.
241 First Avenue North
Minneapolis, MN 55401
612-332-3344
EMPLOYMENT CONTACT: Emily Kelley,
Editorial Director
TYPES OF PUBLISHING: Children's, Trade
(School & Library editions)
AVERAGE ENTRY-LEVEL HIRING : 0

CATHOLIC UNIVERSITY OF AMERICA PRESS
620 Michigan Ave NE
Washington, DC 20064
202-635-5052
TYPES OF PUBLISHING: Professional, Reference,
Religious, Scholarly
TITLES IN PRINT: 194
TOTAL EMPLOYEES: 8
AVERAGE ENTRY-LEVEL HIRING: 2-8
OPPORTUNITIES: Editorial Asst., Marketing
Asst., Advertising Asst. No educational or skill
requirements specified.

**CBS EDUCATIONAL & PROFESSIONAL
PUBLISHING**
A Division of Harcourt Brace Jovanovich Inc.
Orlando, FL 32887
305-345-2000
EMPLOYMENT CONTACT: James Brescia,
Director of Personnel
TYPES OF PUBLISHING: College Text, Elhi,
Scientific/Technical, Software, Medical
TOTAL EMPLOYEES: 2,100
AVERAGE ENTRY-LEVEL HIRING: ?
OPPORTUNITIES: Editorial Asst., Marketing
Asst., Sales Asst., Advertising Asst., Sales

Representative, Junior Copywriter, Production Asst.—All these positions require a college degree. Junior Financial Analyst—College degree (BA accounting or finance). Junior Accountant—College degree (BA accounting). Secretary—High school or college graduate. No other requirements specified.
Note: This information has not been updated for this edition.

CHILDRENS PRESS
A Division of Regensteiner Publishing. Enterprises.
5440 North Cumberland Ave.
Chicago, IL 60656
312-693-0800
EMPLOYMENT CONTACT: Roy Spahr, VP & General Manager
TYPES OF PUBLISHING: Children's, El/Hi, Trade (Paperbound).
TITLES IN PRINT: 1,500
TOTAL EMPLOYEES: 150
AVERAGE ENTRY-LEVEL HIRING: 3-4
OPPORTUNITIES: Both of the following positions require a 4 year college degree: Photo Editor, Junior Editor. No other requirements specified.

CHILTON BOOKS
Listing deleted at Publisher's request

CLYMER PUBLICATIONS
12860 Muscatine St
Arleta, CA 91333-4520
818-767-7660
EMPLOYMENT CONTACT: Judy McNeil, Vice President
TYPES OF PUBLISHING: Do-it yourself repair manuals
TITLES IN PRINT: 200
TOTAL EMPLOYEES: 35
AVERAGE ENTRY-LEVEL HIRING: 1-2
OPPORTUNITIES: Production Coordinator—Some college, strong interest in book production. Editorial Assistant—Some college, strong knowledge of engine mechanics, basic editorial skills.

COLEMAN PUBLISHING
99 Milbar Blvd
Farmingdale, NY 11735
516-293-0383
EMPLOYMENT CONTACT: Saul Steinberg, Director
TYPES OF PUBLISHING: Audio/Visual, Children's Reference, Religious
TITLES IN PRINT: 200
TOTAL EMPLOYEES: 25
AVERAGE ENTRY-LEVEL HIRING: 1-2

CPI (CONTEMPORARY PERSPECTIVES, INC.)
145 E 49th St
New York, NY 10017
212-753-3800
EMPLOYMENT CONTACT: Sherry Olan, VP of Production
TYPES OF PUBLISHING: Elhi, Software.
TITLES IN PRINT: 150
TOTAL EMPLOYEES: 20
AVERAGE ENTRY-LEVEL HIRING: 3-5
OPPORTUNITIES: "CPI is a small educational publishing developer, hiring on an as-needed basis for various editorial/production positions. We also use a lot of freelancers." No specific titles/positions described.

CROSSROAD/UNGAR/CONTINUUM
370 Lexington Ave
New York, NY 10017
212-532-3650
TYPES OF PUBLISHING: College Text, Professional, Reference, Religious, Scholarly, Trade (Hardcover), Trade (Paperbound)
TITLES IN PRINT: 1,000
TOTAL EMPLOYEES: 20
AVERAGE ENTRY-LEVEL HIRING: ?
OPPORTUNITIES: Editorial Asst, Promotion Asst, Sales Asst, Production Asst, Administrative Asst—All require a college degree, typing and word processing skills.

CROWN PUBLISHERS, INC.
225 Park Avenue South
New York, NY 10003
212-254-1600
EMPLOYMENT CONTACT: Linda Torrcaco, Employment Manager
TYPES OF PUBLISHING: Audio/Visual, Children's, Software, Trade (Hardcover).

TOTAL EMPLOYEES: 1,500

AVERAGE ENTRY-LEVEL HIRING: 75

OPPORTUNITIES: All of the following require a college degree (BA preferred) plus typing (30-40 wpm). PC or CRT familiarity a plus, prior office experience or intern program helpful: Publicity Asst., Editorial Asst., Marketing/Production Asst., Production Asst., Sales Asst.

HARRY CUFF PUBLICATIONS LTD
1 Dorset St

St. John's, Newfoundland, Canada A1B 1W8

709-726-6590

TYPES OF PUBLISHING: Children's, College Text, Professional, Scholarly, Trade (Paperbound).

TITLES IN PRINT: 50

TOTAL EMPLOYEES: 6

AVERAGE ENTRY-LEVEL HIRING: 0

MARCEL DEKKER, INC.
270 Madison Ave

New York, NY 10016

212-696-9000

EMPLOYMENT CONTACT: Stacey Miller, Personnel Recruiter

TYPES OF PUBLISHING: College Text, Elhi, Professional, Reference, Scholarly, Scientific/Technical, Software, Trade (Hardcover), Trade (Paperbound).

TITLES IN PRINT: 2,215

TOTAL EMPLOYEES: 372

AVERAGE ENTRY-LEVEL HIRING: 12-15

OPPORTUNITIES: Editorial Asst.—College degree (preferred); experience on school publication, P/T office background. Production Asst or Journal Production Editor—College degree (preferred); P/T office experience, typing (40 wpm) and work on school publication a plus. Promotion Asst.—College degree (English preferred); 60 wpm, P/T office experience. Administrative Asst.—College degree or Secretarial School; 60 wpm, P/T office experience. Art Asst.—Some college, art school a must; paste-up experience and portfolio. Marketing Asst.- College degree (BA Liberal Arts preferred); 50 wpm, p/t office experience. Clerks in Bookkeeping Dept.—High school graduates.

SUGGESTIONS: "Please send cover letter with salary requirements and resume."

DEVIN-ADAIR, PUBLISHERS INC.
6 N Water St

Greenwich, CT 06830

203-531-7755

EMPLOYMENT CONTACT: Roger H. Lourie, Managing Editor

TYPES OF PUBLISHING: Professional, Trade (Hardcover), Trade (Paperbound)

TITLES IN PRINT: 500

TOTAL EMPLOYEES: 10

AVERAGE ENTRY-LEVEL HIRING: 1

OPPORTUNITIES: Clerks—High School graduate a plus. Editorial or Sales Asst.—College degree preferred. No other requirements specified.

DIAL BOOKS FOR YOUNG READERS
A Division of E. P. Dutton

2 Park Ave.

New York, NY 10016

212-725-1818

EMPLOYMENT CONTACT: Shelly Sadler, , Personnel Dept.

TYPES OF PUBLISHING: General Trade, Fiction and Non-Fiction (Hardcover and Paperback).

TITLES IN PRINT: 500

TOTAL EMPLOYEES: 600

AVERAGE ENTRY-LEVEL HIRING: 3-5

OPPORTUNITIES: Entry-level positions in Personnel, Accounting and Customer Service Depts. No requirements specified.

DIMENSION BOOKS INC.
Listing deleted at Publisher's request

DODD, MEAD & COMPANY
71 Fifth Ave.

New York, NY 10003

212-627-8444

EMPLOYMENT CONTACT: Eileen Dlutman, Office Manager

TYPES OF PUBLISHING: General Trade (Children's and Adult)

TITLES IN PRINT: 100

TOTAL EMPLOYEES: 50

AVERAGE ENTRY-LEVEL HIRING: 5-7

OPPORTUNITIES: Editorial Asst.—High school graduate, typing 50 wpm.

DOUBLEDAY & COMPANY, INC.
666 Fifth Ave.
New York, NY 10017
212-984-7561
EMPLOYMENT CONTACT: Peggy Hellberg,
Director of Personnel
TYPES OF PUBLISHING: Children's, General
Trade (Hardcover), Mystery, Religious, Science
Fiction.
TITLES IN PRINT: 4,000+
TOTAL EMPLOYEES: 275
AVERAGE ENTRY-LEVEL HIRING: 72***
OPPORTUNITIES: Editorial secretary—BA or BS,
typing 50 wpm. Publicity Secretary—BA or BS,
typing 50 wpm. Marketing Secretary—Business
degree, typing 50 wpm. Production clerk—BA or
BS, typing 50 wpm. Media Assistant—Business
degree, light typing.
***Important Note: As of 2/1/88, complete hiring
freeze was in effect. Check with contact before
sending resumes.

DUNDURN PRESS LTD
1558 Queen St E
Toronto, Ontario, Canada M4L 1E8
416-461-1881
EMPLOYMENT CONTACT: Kirk Howard,
President
TYPES OF PUBLISHING: Reference, Scholarly,
Trade (Hardcover), Trade (Paperbound).
TITLES IN PRINT: 125
TOTAL EMPLOYEES: 6
AVERAGE ENTRY-LEVEL HIRING: 1
OPPORTUNITIES: Editorial Asst., Clerk,
Production Dept. Asst. No requirements specified.

THE DUSHKIN PUBLISHING GROUP, INC.
Sluice Dock
Guilford, CT 06437
203-453-4351
EMPLOYMENT CONTACT: Don Young,
Administrative Manager
TYPES OF PUBLISHING: College Text, El/Hi,
Reference.
TITLES IN PRINT: 80
TOTAL EMPLOYEES: 40
AVERAGE ENTRY-LEVEL HIRING: 1
OPPORTUNITIES: Word Processor—High school
graduate. Order Entry Clerk—High school
graduate. Editorial Asst.—College degree. No
other requirements specified.

EDITION FIDES
5710 Ave Decelles
Montreal, Quebec Canada H3S 2C5
514-735-6406
EMPLOYMENT CONTACT: Mr. Raymond Lapres
TYPES OF PUBLISHING: Children's, College Text,
Elhi, Mass Market Paperback, Professional,
Reference, Religious, Scientific/Technical, Trade
(Hardcover), Trade (Paperbound).
TOTAL EMPLOYEES: 18
AVERAGE ENTRY-LEVEL HIRING: 1-2
OPPORTUNITIES: PR Religious Sector—College
degree; knowledge of religious studies, good PR.
Publishing Asst—College degree; very good
knowledge of French and religious studies.

ENCYCLOPAEDIA BRITANNICA
310 South Michigan Ave
Chicago, IL 60604
312-347-7284
EMPLOYMENT CONTACT: Joan K. Downey,
Personnel Manager
TYPES OF PUBLISHING: Reference
TOTAL EMPLOYEES: 1,031
AVERAGE ENTRY-LEVEL HIRING: ? (1986 Entry-
Level Hiring = 32)
OPPORTUNITIES: Asst. Copy Editor Trainee—
Some college, proofreading experience on student
publications. Research Specialist—College
degree (Science), research ability, excellent
reading skills, knowledge of library procedures &
computer searching. Editorial Asst.- College
degree, proofreading experience on student
publication, typing (45 wpm). Asst. Librarian—
MLS Degree; familiarity with AACR2, OCLC,
NEXIS essential, reading knowledge of at least
one foreign language. Many clerical (business)
positions, too numerous to list.

FABER & FABER, INC.
50 Cross St
Winchester, MA 01890
617-721-1427
EMPLOYMENT CONTACT: Thomas Kelleher,
Vice President
TYPES OF PUBLISHING: Children's, Trade
(Hardcover), Trade (Paperbound).
TITLES IN PRINT: 800
TOTAL EMPLOYEES: 8
AVERAGE ENTRY-LEVEL HIRING: 0

FACTS ON FILE, INC.
460 Park Ave. South
New York, NY 10016
212-683-2244
EMPLOYMENT CONTACT: Henry Grant,
Personnel Manager
TYPES OF PUBLISHING: Reference
TITLES IN PRINT: 800
TOTAL EMPLOYEES: 90
AVERAGE ENTRY-LEVEL HIRING: 13-14
OPPORTUNITIES: Clerical. No requirements
specified.

F & W PUBLICATIONS INC.
1507 Dana Ave.
Cincinnati, OH 45207
513-531-2222
EMPLOYMENT CONTACT: Kathy Schneider,
Personnel Manager
TYPES OF PUBLISHING: Books—art and writing
titles and directories; book clubs; magazines;
home study courses.
TITLES IN PRINT: 300
TOTAL EMPLOYEES: 160
AVERAGE ENTRY-LEVEL HIRING: 10-15
OPPORTUNITIES: Editorial assistants, Circulation and Marketing assistants, copywriter,
clerical/order processing (including some accounts
receivable), Telemarketing. No requirements
specified.
SUGGESTIONS: "Send work/writIng samples,
when appropriate, with resume."

FARRAR, STRAUS & GIROUX, INC.
19 Union Square W
New York, NY 10003
212-741-6900
EMPLOYMENT CONTACT: Peggy Miller, Office
Manager
TYPES OF PUBLISHING: Children's, Trade
(hardcover), Trade (Paperbound)
TITLES IN PRINT: 300
TOTAL EMPLOYEES: 80
AVERAGE ENTRY-LEVEL HIRING: 0

FODOR'S TRAVEL GUIDES
See listing for Random House

GALE RESEARCH COMPANY
Book Tower
Detroit, MI 48226
313-961-2242
EMPLOYMENT CONTACT: Ronald L. Frederick,
VP Personnel
TYPES OF PUBLISHING: Indexes, encyclopedias,
directories.
TITLES IN PRINT: 4,000
TOTAL EMPLOYEES: 560
AVERAGE ENTRY-LEVEL HIRING: 15-20
OPPORTUNITIES: Editorial Assistants, Clerks—
High school graduates. No other requirements
specified.

GARDEN WAY/STOREY PUBLISHING
A Division of Storey Communications, Inc
Schoolhouse Rd
Pownal, VT 05261
802-823-5871
EMPLOYMENT CONTACT: Martha M. Storey,
Vice President
TYPES OF PUBLISHING: Trade (Paperback)
TITLES IN PRINT: 225
TOTAL EMPLOYEES: 32
AVERAGE ENTRY-LEVEL HIRING: 4-5
OPPORTUNITIES: Asst. Editor—College degree
(BA preferred); typing. Production—Paste-up
experience. Business Office Asst.—general
accounting.

GARLAND PUBLISHING
136 Madison Avenue
New York, NY 10016
212-686-7492
EMPLOYMENT CONTACT: Pat Musto, Personnel
Manager
TYPES OF PUBLISHING: College Text,
Professional, Reference, Religious, Scholarly.
TITLES IN PRINT: 5,000
TOTAL EMPLOYEES: 80
AVERAGE ENTRY-LEVEL HIRING: 1
OPPORTUNITIES: Marketing Asst., Advertising
Dept.—College degree.

WARREN H. GREEN, INC.
8356 Olive Blvd
St. Louis, MO 63132
314-991-1335
EMPLOYMENT CONTACT: Dr. Warren H. Green,
President
TYPES OF PUBLISHING: Professional, Scholarly.
TITLES IN PRINT: 260
TOTAL EMPLOYEES: 8
AVERAGE ENTRY-LEVEL HIRING: 0
COMMENTS: "We publish clinical medicine and
medical research books. This requires B.S. or M.S.
degrees AND publishing experience and strength
in medical terminology, physics, chemistry,
math and statistics."

GREENWOOD PRESS
Box 5007, 88 Post Rd.
Westport, CT 06881
203-226-3571
EMPLOYMENT CONTACT: Simon Knott, Personnel
and Office Manager
TYPES OF PUBLISHING: Professional and
advertising books.
TITLES IN PRINT: 10,000
TOTAL EMPLOYEES: 89
AVERAGE ENTRY-LEVEL HIRING: 5-6
OPPORTUNITIES: Advertising Dept.—College
degree. Clerks—High school graduates. No other
requirements specified.

GROLIER INC.
Sherman Turnpike
Danbury, CT 06816
203-797-3500
EMPLOYMENT CONTACT: Ann Graves, Personnel
Manager
TYPES OF PUBLISHING: English and foreign-
language encyclopedias, reference books, reading
programs and children's books.
TITLES IN PRINT: 3,500
TOTAL EMPLOYEES: 1,000
AVERAGE ENTRY-LEVEL HIRING: 4-5
OPPORTUNITIES: Clerks. No requirements
specified.

GUERNICA EDITIONS
PO Box #633, Station N.D.G.
Montreal, Quebec, Canada H4A 3R1
514-256-5599
EMPLOYMENT CONTACT: Antonio D'Alfonso,
Director of Literature
TYPES OF PUBLISHING: Children's, College Text,
Mass Market Paperback, Reference, Scholarly,
Trade (Hardcover), Trade (Paperbound)
TITLES IN PRINT: 80
TOTAL EMPLOYEES: 3
AVERAGE ENTRY-LEVEL HIRING: 10
OPPORTUNITIES: University student with
literary background

G. K. HALL & COMPANY
A Division of Macmillan, Inc.
70 Lincoln St.
Boston, MA 02111
617-423-3990
EMPLOYMENT CONTACT: Anna Michaud,
Personnel Manager
TYPES OF PUBLISHING: Reference, popular
fiction—books and cassettes.
TITLES IN PRINT: 3,000
TOTAL EMPLOYEES: 130
AVERAGE ENTRY-LEVEL HIRING: 10-15
OPPORTUNITIES: Clerks and Order Dept.—High
school graduates. Production, Marketing, Editor-
ial Depts.—College degree preferred. No other
requirements specified.

HARCOURT BRACE JOVANOVICH, INC.
Orlando, FL 32887
305-345-3178
EMPLOYMENT CONTACT: Carol Winstead,
Employment Supervisor
OPPORTUNITIES: In every area, editorial to
data processing.
COMMENTS: Offices across the country. contact
headquarters in Orlando for name and address of
office in your area.

HARPER & ROW PUBLISHERS, INC.
10 E 53rd St
New York, NY 10022
212-207-7000
EMPLOYMENT CONTACT: Joan Maniscalco,
Assistant Personnel Manager
TYPES OF PUBLISHING: Children's College Text,
Mass Market Paperback, Professional, Reference,

Religious, Scientific/Technical, Trade (Hardcover) Trade (Paperbound).
TOTAL EMPLOYEES: 1,800
AVERAGE ENTRY-LEVEL HIRING: 3-5
OPPORTUNITIES: Secretary, Secretary Asst., Production Asst.—Good typing, excellent English skills. Copywriters—Portfolio to show. Clerks—Good typing, good English skills. Contract Asst.—College degree; good typing, good English skills.

D.C. HEATH & COMPANY
A Division of Raytheon Company
125 Spring St
Lexington, MA 02173
617-862-6650
EMPLOYMENT CONTACT: Janet Kenneally, Personnel Dept.
TYPES OF PUBLISHING: College Text, Elhi, Professional, Scholarly, Trade (Hardcover).
TOTAL EMPLOYEES: 740
AVERAGE ENTRY-LEVEL HIRING: 60
OPPORTUNITIES: Sales Representatives—College degree; sales experience helpful. Editorial Asst.—College degree. Asst. Editors—College degree; teaching experience in specific fields or publishing experience.

HENRY HOLT & COMPANY
521 Fifth Ave., 6th floor
New York, NY 10175
212-599-4455
EMPLOYMENT CONTACT: Bernie Richardson, Director of Personnel
TYPES OF PUBLISHING: General trade—adult and juvenile.
TITLES IN PRINT: 1,100
TOTAL EMPLOYEES: 99
AVERAGE ENTRY-LEVEL HIRING: 30
OPPORTUNITIES: Marketing Asst.—College degree preferred. Clerical—High school graduate.No other requirements specified.

HOUGHTON MIFFLIN COMPANY
1 Beacon St
Boston, MA 02108
617-726-5000
EMPLOYMENT CONTACT: Denise Kagan, Personnel
TYPES OF PUBLISHING: Children's, College Text, Elhi, Reference, Software, Trade (Hardcover), Trade (Paperbound).

TOTAL EMPLOYEES: 840
AVERAGE ENTRY-LEVEL HIRING: 40-75
OPPORTUNITIES: Administrative Secretary—High school graduate (business/ secretarial courses); typing, filing, organizational skills, willingness to learn word processing and/or dictaphone, 1 year office experience. Administrative Asst.—High school graduate (advanced business/secretarial courses); typing, filing, organizational skills, willingness to learn word processing and/or dictaphone. Editorial Asst.—College degree (BA, BS or equivalent); previous publishing experience. Associate Editor—College degree (BA/BS or equivalent required; MA/MS or equivalent preferred); teaching experience.
COMMENTS: "Of the 42 entry-level hires in 1986, half of these employees were hired for straight secretarial positions. The balance of the positions is split between non-editorial assistant and support positions and associate or assistant editorial slots. These latter are often filled by those with some publishing experience or career changers, in spite of the 'entry-level' status. There is no defined entry-level as such with the exception of one or two editing assistant job titles. All positions that do function as entry-level do so because of unplanned opportunity with the job, but made possible by the location of the position in an editorial or production department. The incumbent's academic preparation and/or prior experience in positions such as teaching is often a contributing factor."

HUMAN KINETICS PUBLISHERS
1607 North Market St., PO Box 5076
Champaign, IL 61820
217-351-5076
EMPLOYMENT CONTACT: Mary T. Krzysik, CPS, Executive Secretary
TYPES OF PUBLISHING: Audio/Visual, College Text, Professional, Reference, Scholarly, Scientific/Technical, Trade (Hardcover), Trade (Paperbound)
TITLES IN PRINT: 250
TOTAL EMPLOYEES: 70
AVERAGE ENTRY-LEVEL HIRING: 10
OPPORTUNITIES: Asst. Editor—College degree (BS Journalism or English); excellent organizational and interpersonal skills, knowledge of copy editing and proofreading procedures. Receptionist/Typist—High school graduate; initiative, typing 50-60 wpm, word processing,

good communication skills. Mail Clerk/Errands—High school graduate; previous mailroom experience, organizational skills, initiative. Asst Bookkeeper—High school graduate; education or experience in accounts receivable, computer experience. Paste-Up Artist—High school graduate, BS in Art & Design; understanding of graphic arts techniques, standards and procedures, attention to detail. Typesetter—High school graduate; knowledge of typesetting and graphic arts techniques. ACEP Services Asst.—High school graduate, BS or attendance at college; excellent organizational, computer communication, & secretarial skills. Packing Clerk—High school graduate. Invoice/Fulfillment Clerk -- High school graduate; communication, organizational and typing skills; math ability. Marketing Assistant-Special Sales—College degree (BA or BS).

COMMENTS: "The positions listed above are what we consider entry-level positions. Other positions that may become available require an M.S. or Ph.D degree in the fields of physical education and sports medicine. We hire <u>only non-smokers</u>. All applicants should submit a resume and a cover letter."

HUMAN SCIENCES PRESS, INC.
72 Fifth Ave
New York, NY 10011
212-243-6000
EMPLOYMENT CONTACT: Sheldon R. Roen Ph.D., Chairman
TYPES OF PUBLISHING: Children's, College Text, Professional, Religious, Scholarly, Trade (Hardcover), Trade (Paperbound), Professional Journals.
TITLES IN PRINT: 600
TOTAL EMPLOYEES: 20
AVERAGE ENTRY-LEVEL HIRING: 3-4
OPPORTUNITIES: Marketing—College degree; typing, ambitious. Data Entry—High school graduate; fast typing, dedication.

IOWA STATE UNIVERSITY PRESS
2121 South State Ave.
Ames, IA 50010
515-294-5280
EMPLOYMENT CONTACT: Richard R. Kinney, Director
TYPES OF PUBLISHING: Professional and college books in a wide variety of educational disciplines
TOTAL EMPLOYEES: 35

AVERAGE ENTRY-LEVEL HIRING: 3-4
OPPORTUNITIES: Editorial and Marketing & Sales Depts., Proofreaders—Prefer candidates with Ba, MA and PhD. Some editorial experience a plus.

RICHARD D. IRWIN, INC.
A Subsidiary of Dow Jones & Co, Inc.
1818 Ridge Rd
Homewood, IL 60430
312-798-6000
EMPLOYMENT CONTACT: Personnel
TYPES OF PUBLISHING: College Text, Professional, Trade (Hardcover).
TITLES IN PRINT: 750
TOTAL EMPLOYEES: 400
AVERAGE ENTRY-LEVEL HIRING: 40-50
OPPORTUNITIES: Sales—College degree (but MBA preferred); strong people skills, self-starters. Production Editor—College degree (English or Journalism): strong writing style; sensitivity. Advertising Copywriter—Same requirements.
SUGGESTIONS: "A cover letter describing interest in book publishing, resume and work samples if appropriate."

KLUWER ACADEMIC PUBLISHERS
101 Philip Drive
Norwell, MA 02061
617-871-6600
EMPLOYMENT CONTACT: Mrs. Patricia Glavin
TYPES OF PUBLISHING: Scholarly, business and professional, scientific/technical/medical books and journals.
TITLES IN PRINT: 800
TOTAL EMPLOYEES: 60
AVERAGE ENTRY-LEVEL HIRING: 10-12
OPPORTUNITIES: Marketing Assistants—College degree, some publishing (especially direct mail) experience helpful.

ALFRED A. KNOPF INC.
A Subsidiary of Random House
201 East 50th St.
New York, NY 10022
212-751-2600
EMPLOYMENT CONTACT: Christine Names, Personnel Director (Random House)
TYPES OF PUBLISHING: Books for the General Reader

TITLES IN PRINT: 1,000
TOTAL EMPLOYEES: 70
AVERAGE ENTRY-LEVEL HIRING: 4
OPPORTUNITIES: Entry-level positions in
Editorial, Publicity, Production, Design. No
specific educational or skill requirements
submitted.

JOHN KNOX PRESS

A subsidiary of Presbyterian Publishing House
341 Ponce de Leon Ave, NE
Atlanta, GA 30365
404-873-1549
EMPLOYMENT CONTACT: Vicki Miller,
Personnel Officer
TYPES OF PUBLISHING: College Text,
Professional, Reference, Religious, Scholarly,
Trade (Hardcover), Trade (Paperbound).
TITLES IN PRINT: 226
TOTAL EMPLOYEES: 9
AVERAGE ENTRY-LEVEL HIRING: 2*
OPPORTUNITIES: Copy editor (freelance)—
College degree; graduate work/degree
(especially in religion), copy editing/proof-
reading experience. *There is also a chance we
will need freelancers from time to time.
*COMMENTS: "Turnover in John Knox Press is
very low; I last recruited for a position there in
1983; openings are more frequent in other divi-
sions of the Publishing House, and an entry-level
person might do better to apply to one of these."
—Vicki Miller, Personnel Officer, Presbyterian
Publishing House.

PETER LANG PUBLISHING INC.

62 West 45th St.
New York, NY 10036
212-302-6740
EMPLOYMENT CONTACT: Brigitte McDonald,
Office Manager
TYPES OF PUBLISHING: Scholarly
TITLES IN PRINT: 50
TOTAL EMPLOYEES: 6
AVERAGE ENTRY-LEVEL HIRING: 0

LEA & FEBIGER

600 S Washington Square
Philadelphia, PA 19106
215-922-1330
EMPLOYMENT CONTACT: Robert N. Spahr,
Partner

TYPES OF PUBLISHING: Medical and scientific
TITLES IN PRINT: 500
TOTAL EMPLOYEES: 55
AVERAGE ENTRY-LEVEL HIRING: 2-3
OPPORTUNITIES: Copy Editor—College degree
(B.A. English preferred); good language skills &
excellent grasp of grammar, basic elements of
style and composition. Secretary (Advertising
Department)—College degree (preferred); typing
skills. Order Clerk—High school graduate;
typing skills.

LERNER PUBLICATIONS COMPANY

241 First Ave N
Minneapolis, MN 55401
612-332-3344
EMPLOYMENT CONTACT: Nancy Campbell,
Editor
TYPES OF PUBLISHING: Children's.
TITLES IN PRINT: 687
TOTAL EMPLOYEES: 70
AVERAGE ENTRY-LEVEL HIRING: 12
OPPORTUNITIES: Editorial Assistant—College
degree.Marketing Assistant—College degree,
enthusiastic.

LITTLE, BROWN AND COMPANY

A Subsidiary of Time Inc.
34 Beacon Street
Boston, MA 02106
617-227-0730
EMPLOYMENT CONTACT: Rebecca Parker,
Human Resources Representative
TYPES OF PUBLISHING: Children's, Professional,
Reference, Trade (Hardcover)
TOTAL EMPLOYEES: 645
AVERAGE ENTRY-LEVEL HIRING: 0-10
OPPORTUNITIES: All of the following positions
require previous office experience (including 45-65
wpm) and a demonstrated interest in publishing.
The level of position would be commensurate
with experience of candidate. There are no
educational requirements for these office
positions: Secretary Assistant, Editorial Asst.,
Administrative Asst. "These are basically all
the same. While Editorial might *sound* better,
Secretarial position would probably be a better
entry-level path. There is definitely room for
good people to get ahead."
SUGGESTIONS: "A letter of inquiry, along with a
resume, should initially be forwarded to the

Human Resources Dept. Special areas of interest, typing (and other special skills), and salary history/or requirements should be included.

LONGMAN, INC.
95 Church St.
White Plains, NY 10601
914-993-5000
EMPLOYMENT CONTACT: Karen O'Brien, Asst. Vice President
TYPES OF PUBLISHING: College, Children's, Elhi, Professional, Reference, Scientific/Technical.
TITLES IN PRINT: 3,000
TOTAL EMPLOYEES: 115
AVERAGE ENTRY-LEVEL HIRING: 3-5
OPPORTUNITIES: Editorial Asst., Marketing Asst., Adminstration Dept.—All require college degree, good written communications skills.

LOUISIANA STATE UNIVERSITY PRESS
Baton Rouge, LA 70893
504-388-6294
EMPLOYMENT CONTACT: Personnel Manager
TYPES OF PUBLISHING: Scholarly, Trade (Hardcover), Trade (Paperbound).
TITLES IN PRINT: 800
TOTAL EMPLOYEES: 30
AVERAGE ENTRY-LEVEL HIRING: 0

McDOUGAL, LITTELL & COMPANY
1560 Sherman Ave.
Evanston, IL 60204
312-869-2300
EMPLOYMENT CONTACT: Kathy Mattox, Personnel Director
TYPES OF PUBLISHING: Children's, Elhi
TITLES IN PRINT: 150
TOTAL EMPLOYEES: 300
AVERAGE ENTRY-LEVEL HIRING: 3-5
OPPORTUNITIES: Personnel Clerical—High school graduate (minimum); typing, general office skills. Production Asst.—High school graduate (minimum); organizational skills, figure aptitude. Sales Asst.—College degree; communication skills. Accountant—College degree (or high school plus experience). Administrative Asst.—High school graduate (minimum); office experience. Advertising Asst.—College degree; communication skills.

Asst. Editor—College degree; teaching experience.
SUGGESTIONS: "Send resume"

McFARLAND AND COMPANY, INC.
Box 611
Jefferson, NC 28640
919-246-4460
EMPLOYMENT CONTACT: Rhonda Herman, Business Manager
TYPES OF PUBLISHING: Film Reference and scholarly monographs
TITLES IN PRINT: 47
TOTAL EMPLOYEES: 150
AVERAGE ENTRY-LEVEL HIRING: ?
OPPORTUNITIES: Clerical.

McGRAW-HILL BOOK COMPANY
1221 Avenue of the Americas
New York, NY 10020
212-512-3333
EMPLOYMENT CONTACT: William Leonard, Manager of Corporate Recruitment
TYPES OF PUBLISHING: Children's, College Text, Elhi, Mass Market Paperback, Professional, Reference, Religious, Scholarly, Scientific/Technical, Software, Trade (Hardcover).
TITLES IN PRINT: 20,808
TOTAL EMPLOYEES: 15,000
AVERAGE ENTRY-LEVEL HIRING: 10-15
OPPORTUNITIES: Clerical—H.S./Business School graduate; math aptitude. Entry Secretary—H.S./College/Business School graduate; typing, steno, word processing.

DAVID McKAY COMPANY, INC.
See listing for Random House

MACMILLAN PUBLISHING COMPANY
A subsidiary of MacMillan, Inc.
866 Third Avenue
New York, NY 10022
212-702-2000
EMPLOYMENT CONTACT: Ms. Amryl W. Holloway, Manager of Staffing and Employment Relations
TYPES OF PUBLISHING: Children's, College Text, Elhi, Mass Market Paperback, Professional, Reference, Religious, Scholarly, Software,

Scientific/Technical, Trade (Hardcover), Trade (Paperbound), and Music Books.

TITLES IN PRINT: 26,000

TOTAL EMPLOYEES: 2,300

AVERAGE ENTRY-LEVEL HIRING: 50-60

OPPORTUNITIES: Assistantships in Editorial, Production, Marketing, Subsidiary Rights, Publicity, Contracts and Permissions. All positions require a college degree and some prior general office experience (or an equivalent combination of education and experience), excellent organizational, communication and written skills (grammar, punctuation, spelling, etc.), accurate typing (minimum 45 wpm). Exposure to personal computers always a plus. Recommended areas of study: English, Communications, History, Journalism, Marketing, Advertising, Art/Design. Some entry-level assistantships are titled "Secretary," depending on the department. Some positions may require good figure aptitude and/or bookkeeping skills.

MASTERY EDUCATION
85 Main St
Watertown, MA 02172
617-926-0329
EMPLOYMENT CONTACT: Elena Wright, Managing Editor
TYPES OF PUBLISHING: Elhi
TITLES IN PRINT: 107
TOTAL EMPLOYEES: 63
AVERAGE ENTRY-LEVEL HIRING: 5-7
OPPORTUNITIES: Trainee or Work/study opportunities for experienced paste-up/layout, word processor and Proofing Asst.—Coursework or experience required.

MAYFIELD PUBLISHING COMPANY
1240 Villa St.
Mountain View, CA 94041
415-960-3222
EMPLOYMENT CONTACT: Pamela Trainer
TYPES OF PUBLISHING: College Text.
TITLES IN PRINT: 140
TOTAL EMPLOYEES: 32
AVERAGE ENTRY-LEVEL HIRING: 4-6
OPPORTUNITIES: Editorial Asst—College degree (preferred); good English language skills, typing (50 wpm), word processing skills helpful, but not mandatory. Clerks—High school graduates.
year.

MEREDITH CORPORATION
1716 Locust St.
Des Moines, IA 50336
515-284-3000
EMPLOYMENT CONTACT: Denise Rock, Personnel Director
TYPES OF PUBLISHING: Hardcover and Paperback Trade, Cookbooks
TITLES IN PRINT: 100
TOTAL EMPLOYEES: 3,000
AVERAGE ENTRY-LEVEL HIRING: 12-15
OPPORTUNITIES: Editorial Asst., Clerk/Typist. No requirements specified.

MERRIAM-WEBSTER INC.
A Subsidiary of Encyclopaedia Britannica
47 Federal St, PO Box 281
Springfield, MA 01102
413-734-3134
EMPLOYMENT CONTACT: Dr. Frederick C. Mish, Editorial Director
TYPES OF PUBLISHING: Reference.
TITLES IN PRINT: 33
TOTAL EMPLOYEES: 59
AVERAGE ENTRY-LEVEL HIRING: 0
OPPORTUNITIES: Editorial Asst.—College degree (Bachelor's with excellent academic record); native speaker of English, strong interest in English and language generally, well-developed writing skills.

MERRILL PUBLISHING COMPANY
A subsidiary of Bell & Howell Company
936 Eastwind Drive
Westerville, OH 43081
614-890-1111
EMPLOYMENT CONTACT: James Green
TYPES OF PUBLISHING: College Text, Elhi
TITLES IN PRINT: 4,000
TOTAL EMPLOYEES: 500
AVERAGE ENTRY-LEVEL HIRING: 6-8
OPPORTUNITIES: Associate Editorial Asst., Customer Service Clerks, Microfilm Clerks— High school graduate; typing, grammar, spelling. Warehouse Workers—No specific education or experience required.

WILLIAM MORROW & CO, INC.
A subsidiary of the Hearst Corporation
105 Madison Ave
New York, NY 10016
212-889-3050
EMPLOYMENT CONTACT: Mrs. Barbara E.
Spence, Personnel Director
TYPES OF PUBLISHING: Children's, Non-Fiction,
Travel, Fiction
TITLES IN PRINT: 2,300
TOTAL EMPLOYEES: 150
AVERAGE ENTRY-LEVEL HIRING: 18
OPPORTUNITIES: Editorial Asst./Secretary,
Clerk Typist, Department Aide, Mail Clerk.

THE C.V. MOSBY COMPANY
A Subsidiary of Times Mirror
11830 Westline Industrial Drive
St. Louis, MO 63146
314-872-8370
EMPLOYMENT CONTACT: Lucy Morgan,
Employment & Training Specialist
TYPES OF PUBLISHING: College Text,
Professional, Reference, Scientific/Technical,
Software.
TITLES IN PRINT: 2,000
TOTAL EMPLOYEES: 600
AVERAGE ENTRY-LEVEL HIRING: 10-20
OPPORTUNITIES: Editorial Asst.—College
degree (preferred)in English or Sciences; clerical
skills & phone communication skills. Asst.
Editor—College degree (English or Sciences
preferred), basic knowledge of publishing,
specialized (i.e., nursing) knowledge. Production
Editor trainee—College degree (English), prefer
technical editing certificate; editing and
production skills. Customer Service Representative—Some college; extensive phone experience.
Sales Service Representative, TelemarketIng
Representative—College degree (preferred);
sales background preferred. Bookkeeping—High
school graduate; CRT, typing, adding machine.
Credit Collection Rep.—High school graduate;
bookkeeping or credit training required.

THOMAS NELSON PUBLISHERS
Elm Hill Pike at Nelson Place
Nashville, TN 37214
615-889-9000
EMPLOYMENT CONTACT: Susan Andrews,
Assistant to Vice President

TYPES OF PUBLISHING: Audio/Visual,
Children's, Mass Market Paperback, Paperback
Trade, Reference,. Religious, Romance novels.
TOTAL EMPLOYEES: 235
AVERAGE ENTRY-LEVEL HIRING: 3-5

NELSON-HALL PUBLISHERS
111 N Canal St
Chicago, IL 60606
312-930-9446
EMPLOYMENT CONTACT: Stephen Ferrara, Vice
President-Personnel
TYPES OF PUBLISHING: Audio/Visual, College
Text, Elhi, Professional, Reference, Religious,
Scholarly, Scientific/Technical, Software, Trade
(Hardcover), Trade (Paperbound)
TITLES IN PRINT: 1,200
TOTAL EMPLOYEES: 40
AVERAGE ENTRY-LEVEL HIRING: 2-3
OPPORTUNITIES: "College degree a minimum
requirement for candidates."

NEW YORK UNIVERSITY PRESS
7O Washington Square South
New York, NY 10012
212-998-2575
EMPLOYMENT CONTACT: Colin Jones, Director
TYPES OF PUBLISHING: College Text,
Professional, Reference, Scholarly
TITLES IN PRINT: 550
TOTAL EMPLOYEES: 5
AVERAGE ENTRY-LEVEL HIRING: 1-2
OPPORTUNITIES: Acquisition Editor—College
degree (BA or MA preferred); three years
publishing experience, not necessarily editorial.
Editorial Asst.—College degree (BA preferred);
fast typist, no experience in publishing.

NORTH-SOUTH INSTITUTE
55 Murray St.
Ottawa, Canada K1N 5M3
EMPLOYMENT CONTACT: Max Brem, Senior
Editor
TYPES OF PUBLISHING: Professional, Trade
(Paperbound).
TITLES IN PRINT: 27
AVERAGE ENTRY-LEVEL HIRING: 0

W.W. NORTON & COMPANY, INC.
500 Fifth Avenue
New York, NY 10110
212-354-5500
EMPLOYMENT CONTACT: Marc W. Spaeth
TYPES OF PUBLISHING: College Text,
Professional, Trade (Hardcover), Trade
(Paperbound).
TITLES IN PRINT: 3,000+
TOTAL EMPLOYEES: 260
AVERAGE ENTRY-LEVEL HIRING: 4
OPPORTUNITIES: College Sales—College degree;
driving. Editorial Asst.—College degree; typing.
Accounting/Clerical—High school or college
degree; typing, bookkeeping. Trade Sales—
College degree; retail bookstore experience or
sales experience with another publisher.
SUGGESTIONS: "Send resume—if no response
follow up with a phone call."

THE ORYX PRESS
2214 N Central at Encanto
Phoenix, AZ 85004
602-254-6156
EMPLOYMENT CONTACT: Deborah Sterkowitz,
Personnel Director
TYPES OF PUBLISHING: Professional, Reference,
Scholarly, Scientific/Technical, Software.
TITLES IN PRINT: 250
TOTAL EMPLOYEES: 45
AVERAGE ENTRY-LEVEL HIRING: 2-3
OPPORTUNITIES:Entry-level positions are in
Customer Service.

OXFORD UNIVERSITY PRESS
200 Madison Ave
New York, NY 10016
212-679-7300
EMPLOYMENT CONTACT: Nancy O'Connor,
Personnel Manager
TYPES OF PUBLISHING: College Text,
Professional, Reference, Scholarly, Trade
(Hardcover), Trade (Paperbound), and ESL.
TOTAL EMPLOYEES: 280
AVERAGE ENTRY-LEVEL HIRING: 12
OPPORTUNITIES: Editorial Asst.—College
degree: typing, PC. Marketing Asst.—College
degree; typing, PC.
COMMENTS: "Typing (min 45/50 wpm), PC/word
processing experience definitely a plus."

PANTHEON BOOKS
A Subsidiary of Random House
201 E 50th St, Ste 4
New York, NY 10022
212-751-2600
EMPLOYMENT CONTACT: Diane Wachtell,
Personnel Manager
TYPES OF PUBLISHING: Trade (Hardcover),
Trade (Paperbound).
TITLES IN PRINT: 500
TOTAL EMPLOYEES: 22
AVERAGE ENTRY-LEVEL HIRING: 3-5
OPPORTUNITIES: Editorial Rights or Publicity
Asst.—College degree; typing, organization,
experience, editorial interest.

PERGAMON PRESS
Fairview Park
Elmsford, NY 10523
914-592-7700
EMPLOYMENT CONTACT: D. Pappalardo,
Personnel Director
TYPES OF PUBLISHING: Scholarly,
Scientific/Technical, Software.
TITLES IN PRINT: 2,000
TOTAL EMPLOYEES: 250
AVERAGE ENTRY-LEVEL HIRING: 2-3
OPPORTUNITIES: All of the following must have
knowledge of word processing or personal
computers: Editorial Asst—College degree (BA
preferred). Production Asst.—College degree (BA
preferred). Entry Accountant—College degree
(BBA preferred). Secretary—Associate's degree.

PLENUM PUBLISHING
233 Spring St.
New York, NY 10013
212-620-8000
EMPLOYMENT CONTACT: Mark Shaw,
Production Department
TYPES OF PUBLISHING: Scientific/Technical
TOTAL EMPLOYEES: NA
AVERAGE ENTRY-LEVEL HIRING: 5
OPPORTUNITIES: Editorial Asst—College degree
(minor in science preferred), typing helpful.

POCKET BOOKS
A Division of Simon & Schuster, Inc.
1230 Ave. of the Americas
New York, NY 10020
212-698-7000
EMPLOYMENT CONTACT: Personnel Department
TYPES OF PUBLISHING: Trade and Mass Market
Paperbacks.
TITLES IN PRINT: 1,500
TOTAL EMPLOYEES: 600
AVERAGE ENTRY-LEVEL HIRING: ?
OPPORTUNITIES: Clerical

PRENTICE HALL, INC.
See listing for Simon & Schuster, Inc.

PRICE/STERN/SLOAN PUBLISHERS, INC.
360 N. La Cienega Blvd
Los Angeles, CA 90048
213-657-6100
EMPLOYMENT CONTACT: Spencer Humthrey,
Associate Editor
TYPES OF PUBLISHING: Children's, Trade
(Hardcover), Trade (Paperbound)
TITLES IN PRINT: 300
TOTAL EMPLOYEES: 180
AVERAGE ENTRY-LEVEL HIRING: 3-4

PSG PUBLISHING COMPANY, INC.
545 Great Neck Rd., PO Box 6
Littleton, MA 04160
617-486-8971
EMPLOYMENT CONTACT: Dr. Frank N.
Paparello, President & Publisher
TYPES OF PUBLISHING: Medical, Dental,
Healthcare
TITLES IN PRINT: 200
TOTAL EMPLOYEES: 20
AVERAGE ENTRY-LEVEL HIRING: 1-2

THE PUTNAM BERKLEY GROUP
200 Madison Ave
New York, NY 10016
212-576-8900
EMPLOYMENT CONTACT: Grace Heelan,
Production Manager
TYPES OF PUBLISHING: Children's, Trade
(Hardcover), Trade (Paperbound), (General
Fiction and Non-Fiction).
TOTAL EMPLOYEES: 500

AVERAGE ENTRY-LEVEL HIRING: 75
OPPORTUNITIES: Editorial Asst., Publicity Asst.,
Sales Asst., Sub Rights Asst., Contracts Asst.,
Production Asst.—College degree; good typing
and office skills, light office experience
preferred.

RAND McNALLY & COMPANY
8255 Central Park Avenue
Skokie, IL 60076
312-673-9100
EMPLOYMENT CONTACT: David Kornhauser,
Employment Manager
TYPES OF PUBLISHING: Maps and atlases, travel
books, reference, educational software.
TITLES IN PRINT: 500
TOTAL EMPLOYEES: 800
AVERAGE ENTRY-LEVEL HIRING: 20-40
OPPORTUNITIES: Editorial Asst., Publicity Asst.,
Sales Asst., Production Asst.—College degree
(preferred); good typing and office skills, light
office experience a plus.

RANDOM HOUSE, INC.
201-E. 50th St
New York, NY 10022
212-572-2236
EMPLOYMENT CONTACT: Shari Garfinkel,
Senior Personnel Recruiter
TYPES OF PUBLISHING: Trade book publisher;
adult, juvenile, mass market (paperback),
textbooks (college), El/Hi, Reference,
Audio/Visual, Video, Religious, Software
TITLES IN PRINT: 1,700+
TOTAL EMPLOYEES: 2,458
AVERAGE ENTRY-LEVEL HIRING: 150+
OPPORTUNITIES: Editorial Asst.—College
degree (or equivalent experience); writing skills,
typing (50 wpm). Production Asst.—College
degree (or equivalent experience); good with
numbers, organized and detail-oriented, accurate
typing (35 wpm). Publicity Asst.—College degree
(or equivalent experience); written and oral
communication skills, sales orientation, typing
(50 wpm). Sub-Rights Asst.—College degree (or
equivalent experience); sales "personality" and
negotiating skills, typing 50 wpm. Secretary—
Some college and/or office experience; typing (50-
70 wpm), strong English language skills, organized and detailed oriented. Sales Assistant —
College degree or equivalent experience; comfort

with numbers, sales orientation, typing (50 wpm), strong people skills. Other areas for entry-level opportunities include: Contracts, Copyright/Permissions, Circulation, Design.

RODALE PRESS, INC.
33 E. Minor St.
Emmaus, PA 18049
215-967-5171
EMPLOYMENT CONTACT: John VolanskiPersonnel Dept.
TYPES OF PUBLISHING: Popular science, gardening and health books
TITLES IN PRINT: 250
TOTAL EMPLOYEES: 950
AVERAGE ENTRY-LEVEL HIRING: 10
OPPORTUNITIES: Publishing Dept.—College grad. Editorial Asst., Clerical Dept.—High school graduate. No other requirements specified.

ST. MARTIN'S PRESS
175 Fifth Avenue
New York, NY 10010
212-674-5151
EMPLOYMENT CONTACT: Maria Fornario, Director of Personnel.
TYPES OF PUBLISHING: College, Mass Market Paperback, Reference, Trade (Hardcover), Trade (paperbound).
TITLES IN PRINT: 3,100
TOTAL EMPLOYEES: 300
AVERAGE ENTRY-LEVEL HIRING : 5-8
OPPORTUNITIES: Assistants in Editorial, Production, Subsidiary Rights, Publicity, Sales/Marketing, Advertising, Contracts, Design—All require a B.A. in Liberal Arts or the Social Sciences, plus some related experience (on campus or an internship); excellent written and verbal communications skills; the ability to deal with detailed information; copywriting, editing, proofreading skills, where appropriate; a strong commitment to the book publishing industry; office procedure skills (i.e., typing, recordkeeping, etc.).

HOWARD W. SAMS & CO., INC.
4300 West 62nd St.
Indianapolis, IN 46268
317-298-5400
EMPLOYMENT CONTACT: James Hill, Manager-Book Dept.

TITLES IN PRINT: 385
TOTAL EMPLOYEES: 260
AVERAGE ENTRY-LEVEL HIRING: 3-4
OPPORTUNITIES: Editorial Asst.—College degree (in English or Language preferred). Sales Representative—College degree (in Business or Marketing preferred). Project Coordinator—College degree (BS in Management Science).

W.B. SAUNDERS COMPANY
210 W Washington Square
Philadelphia, PA 19105
215-574-4797
EMPLOYMENT CONTACT: Patricia McKeever, Personnel Director
TYPES OF PUBLISHING: Professional, Scientific/Technical, Software, (Medical Books & Periodicals)
TITLES IN PRINT: 800
TOTAL EMPLOYEES: 400
AVERAGE ENTRY-LEVEL HIRING: 3-5
OPPORTUNITIES: Production Editor Trainee—College degree; copy editing/proofreading. Proofreader—College degree; proofreading technical language (medical preferred). Sales Asst.—College degree; communication skills.

SCHOLASTIC, INC.
730 Broadway
New York, NY 10003
212-505-3000
EMPLOYMENT CONTACT: Julius James, Recruiter.
TYPES OF PUBLISHING: Children's, Elhi, Software, Trade (Paperbound)
TOTAL EMPLOYEES: 450
AVERAGE ENTRY-LEVEL HIRING: 3-5

SHAMBHALA PUBLICATIONS, INC.
300 Massachusetts Ave.
Boston, MA 02115
617-424-0030
EMPLOYMENT CONTACT: Samuel Bercholz, President
TYPES OF PUBLISHING: Trade; art, literature, religion, philosophy, science.
TITLES IN PRINT: 150
TOTAL EMPLOYEES: 15
AVERAGE ENTRY-LEVEL HIRING: 1-2

SIMON & SCHUSTER, INC.
1230 Avenue of the Americas
New York, NY 10020
212-698-7000
EMPLOYMENT CONTACT: Joseph Kelly,
Employee Relations Manager
TYPES OF PUBLISHING: Audio/Visual,
Children's, College, Elhi, Mass Market
Paperback, Professional, Reference,
Scientific/Technical, Trade (Hardcover), Trade
(Paperbound).
TITLES IN PRINT: 7,000-8,000
TOTAL EMPLOYEES: 8,500
AVERAGE ENTRY-LEVEL HIRING: 25-50

W.H. SMITH PUBLISHERS INC.
A Subsidiary of W.H. Smith & Son Holdings
112 Madison Avenue
New York, NY 10016
212-532-6600
EMPLOYMENT CONTACT: Shannon A. White,
Administrative Assistant to the President
TYPES OF PUBLISHING: Software, Trade
(Hardcover), Promotional.
TITLES IN PRINT: 2,000
TOTAL EMPLOYEES: 120
AVERAGE ENTRY-LEVEL HIRING: 3-4
OPPORTUNITIES: Invoice Control Clerk—High
school graduate; mature-mInded, filing exper-
ience. Customer Analyst—College degree
(preferred); some experience. Accounting Clerk—
Accounting courses (degree preferred); PC exper-
ience. Assistant to the Publisher—College
degree; typing, PC input, experience with
publishing industry.
SUGGESTIONS: "Send resumes first."

SOUTH-WESTERN PUBLISHING COMPANY
5101 Madison Rd
Cincinnati, OH 45227
513-271-8811
EMPLOYMENT CONTACT: Nancy C. Noschang,
Vice President/Executive Editor
TYPES OF PUBLISHING: Audio/Visual, College
Text, Elhi, Professional, Software.
TITLES IN PRINT: 600
TOTAL EMPLOYEES: 650
AVERAGE ENTRY-LEVEL HIRING: 3-5

OPPORTUNITIES: Editorial Associate—College
degree (in English): 30 wpm typing, personal
computer experience. Photo Researcher—College
degree (in journalism). Staff Designer—College
degree (in design art). Experience a plus in latter
two positions.
SUGGESTIONS: "Written application including
collegiate transcript."

SPRINGER-VERLAG NEW YORK, INC.
175 Fifth Ave
New York, NY 10010
212-460-1500
EMPLOYMENT CONTACT: Cathy Adams,
Personnel Manager
TYPES OF PUBLISHING:
Scientific/Technical/Medical—Publishers of
books, journals and magazines.
TOTAL EMPLOYEES: 1,200 (200 in U.S., 1,000
international)
AVERAGE ENTRY-LEVEL HIRING: ?
OPPORTUNITIES: Promotion Asst, Production
Asst, Personnel Asst., Editorial Asst., etc.—
College degree; six months general office
experience required (summer jobs acceptable);
typing 45 wpm; demonstrated interest in position
areas listed above; excellent written and good
oral communication skills; knowledge of personal
computers a plus.
SUGGESTIONS: "We like applicants to send
resumes before a decision is made to interview
them. We like people to specify the area of
publishing they are in interested in."

STEMMER HOUSE PUBLISHERS, INC.
2627 Caves Rd
Owings Mills, MD 21117
301-363-3690
EMPLOYMENT CONTACT: Barbara Holdridge,
President
TYPES OF PUBLISHING: Audio/Cassettes,
Children's, Trade (Hardcover), Trade
(Paperbound).
TITLES IN PRINT: 156
TOTAL EMPLOYEES: 4
AVERAGE ENTRY-LEVEL HIRING: 1-2
OPPORTUNITIES: Editorial—College degree
(BA); proofreading. Art—College degree (BA or
BFA required); interest in books. Clerical—

College or business school degree; data processing experience
SUGGESTIONS: "Send letter; no phone calls please."

STERLING PUBLISHING COMPANY. INC.
2 Park Avenue
New York, NY 10016
212-532-7160
TYPES OF PUBLISHING: Children's, Reference, Trade (Hardcover), Trade (Paperbound).
TITLES IN PRINT: 500
TOTAL EMPLOYEES: 45
AVERAGE ENTRY-LEVEL HIRING: 1-2
OPPORTUNITIES: Editorial Dept.—College degree (BA), some experience preferrred.

TAB BOOKS INC.
Blue Ridge
Summit, PA 17214
717-794-2191
EMPLOYMENT CONTACT: Katherine Holtz, Personnel Dept.
TYPES OF PUBLISHING: Technical books
TITLES IN PRINT: 1,200
TOTAL EMPLOYEES: 170
AVERAGE ENTRY-LEVEL HIRING: 2
OPPORTUNITIES: Clerical Assts., Shipping, Advertising Depts.—College degree, will train.

JEREMY P. TARCHER, INC.
9110 Sunset Blvd., Ste. 250
Los Angeles, CA 90069
213-273-3274
EMPLOYMENT CONTACT: Pat Bryer, Personnel Administrator
TYPES OF PUBLISHING: Trade (Hardcover), Trade (Paperbound).
TOTAL EMPLOYEES: 15
AVERAGE ENTRY-LEVEL HIRING: 1
OPPORTUNITIES: Editorial Asst.—College degree. No other requirements specified.

TIME-LIFE BOOKS, INC.
777 Duke St
Alexandria, VA 22314
703-838-7000
EMPLOYMENT CONTACT: Tom Swiger, Director of Personnel Administration

TYPES OF PUBLISHING: Non-fiction (art, cooking, health, photography, science, gardening, home maintenance)
TITLES IN PRINT: 100
TOTAL EMPLOYEES: 290
AVERAGE ENTRY-LEVEL HIRING: 1-2
OPPORTUNITIES: Writers, Researchers, Designers, Accounting Assistants—College degree (BA or BS), 2-3 years experience required for all positions.

TIMES BOOKS
See listing for Random House

TRANSACTION PUBLISHERS
Rutgers University
New Brunswick, NJ 08903
201-932-2280
EMPLOYMENT CONTACT: Scott Bramson, Senior Vice President
TYPES OF PUBLISHING: Professional, Reference, Scholarly, Social Scientific/Technical.
TITLES IN PRINT: 1,700
TOTAL EMPLOYEES: 24
AVERAGE ENTRY-LEVEL HIRING: 3-4
OPPORTUNITIES: Copy-Editing, Asst. Book Editor—College degree; preferably major in social science or communication. Proofreader—College degree; languages or English major.

UNIVERSITY OF CHICAGO PRESS
5801 Ellis Ave.
Chicago, IL 60637
312-702-7700
EMPLOYMENT CONTACT: Virginia Allen, Assistant to Director
TYPES OF PUBLISHING: Scholarly, non-fiction
TITLES IN PRINT: 300
TOTAL EMPLOYEES: 200
AVERAGE ENTRY-LEVEL HIRING: 4-6

UNIVERSITY OF HAWAII PRESS
2840 Kolowalu St
Honolulu, HI 96822
808-948-8255
EMPLOYMENT CONTACT: William Hamilton, Director
TYPES OF PUBLISHING: Children's, College Text, Reference, Scholarly, Trade (Hardcover), Trade (Paperbound).
TITLES IN PRINT: 700

TOTAL EMPLOYEES: 26

AVERAGE ENTRY-LEVEL HIRING: 1-2

OPPORTUNITIES: Editor I—College degree (or equivalent); better than average knowledge of English usage, knowledge of publication procedures, familiarity with computers. Production Asst.—College degree (or equivalent); familiarity with production procedures.

UNIVERSITY OF ILLINOIS PRESS

54 E Gregory Dr
Champaign, IL 61820
217-333-0950

EMPLOYMENT CONTACT: Jan Palumbo, Asst. Director

TYPES OF PUBLISHING: Scholarly, Trade (Hardcover), Trade (Paperbound).

TITLES IN PRINT: 1094

TOTAL EMPLOYEES: 40

AVERAGE ENTRY-LEVEL HIRING: 1-2

OPPORTUNITIES: Copy Editor—College degre; 2-3 years editorial experience.

UNIVERSITY OF NEW MEXICO PRESS

Journalism Building
Albuquerque, NM 87131
505-277-2346

EMPLOYMENT CONTACT: David V. Holtby, Associate Director

TYPES OF PUBLISHING: Professional, Scholarly.

TITLES IN PRINT: 372

TOTAL EMPLOYEES: 20

AVERAGE ENTRY-LEVEL HIRING: 1-2

OPPORTUNITIES: Production Asst—College degree (graphic or fine Arts); experience in paste-up. Marketing Asst—College degree (journalism or advertising). Editorial Asst.—College degree (liberal arts); experience in copy editing. Sales Asst.—College degree (liberal arts or business); sales or bookstore experience. Order Fulfillment Asst—College (2-year) degree (liberal arts or business); sales or bookstore experience.

UNIVERSITY OF NORTH CAROLINA PRESS

Box 2288
Chapel Hill, NC 27515-2288
919-966-3561

EMPLOYMENT CONTACT: Matthew Hodgson, Director

TYPES OF PUBLISHING: University press

TITLES IN PRINT: 450

TOTAL EMPLOYEES: 30

AVERAGE ENTRY-LEVEL HIRING: 1-3

UNIVERSITY OF OKLAHOMA PRESS

1005 Asp Ave
Norman, OK 73019
405-325-5111

EMPLOYMENT CONTACT: Mary Ann Langenback, Secretary to Director

TYPES OF PUBLISHING: College Text, Elhi, Scholarly, Trade (Hardcover), Trade (Paperbound)

TITLES IN PRINT: 743

TOTAL EMPLOYEES: 25

AVERAGE ENTRY-LEVEL HIRING: 1-2

UNIVERSITY OF WASHINGTON PRESS

PO Box 50096
Seattle, WA 98145
206-543-4050

EMPLOYMENT CONTACT: Juanita B. Pike, Program Manager

TYPES OF PUBLISHING: Audio/Visual, Reference, Scholarly, Trade (Hardcover) Trade (Paperbound)

TITLES IN PRINT: 1,300

TOTAL EMPLOYEES: 30

AVERAGE ENTRY-LEVEL HIRING: 1-2

COMMENTS: "We employ students on a regular basis."

UNIVERSITY PRESS OF AMERICA, INC.

4720 Boston Way
Lanham, MD 20706
301-459-3366

EMPLOYMENT CONTACT: James E. Lyons, Publisher

TYPES OF PUBLISHING: College, professional

TITLES IN PRINT: 3,000

TOTAL EMPLOYEES: 50

AVERAGE ENTRY-LEVEL HIRING: 3-5

UNIVERSITY PRESS OF NEW ENGLAND

3 Lebanon St
Hanover, NH 03755
603-646-3349

EMPLOYMENT CONTACT: Thomas McFarland, Director

TYPES OF PUBLISHING: Scholarly, Trade (Hardcover), Trade (Paperbound).

TITLES IN PRINT: 250
TOTAL EMPLOYEES: 15
AVERAGE ENTRY-LEVEL HIRING: 1

UNIVERSITY PRESS OF VIRGINIA
PO Box 3608 University Station
Charlottesville, VA 22903
804-924-3468
EMPLOYMENT CONTACT: Jerry N. Showalter,
Managing Editor
TYPES OF PUBLISHING: Scholarly.
TITLES IN PRINT: 703
TOTAL EMPLOYEES: 15
AVERAGE ENTRY-LEVEL HIRING: 1-2

VAN NOSTRAND REINHOLD
115 Fifth Avenue
New York, NY 10003
212-254-3232
EMPLOYMENT CONTACT: Linda Watson,
Personnel Manager
TYPES OF PUBLISHING: College, Professional,
Reference, Scientific/Technical.
TITLES IN PRINT: 2,100
AVERAGE ENTRY-LEVEL HIRING: 2-5
OPPORTUNITIES: Junior copywriter—BA;
creative writing and research abilities; one year
experience. Junior Manuscript Editor (Technical)
—BS; proficient in English; meticulous eyes for
detail; 6 months-1 year prior book publishing
experience; knowledgeable in subject area. Editorial Assistant—High school or BA; good command
of English language; detail-minded; 6 months-1
year experience desired, but not required. Promotion Assistant—High school or BS; prior adver-
tising/promotion experience required; some
knowledge of space sales/mailing lists essential.
Junior Designer—Art degree; knowledge of type,
specs, design, art production required. Junior
Accountant—6 months-1 year experience with
bank reconciliations, posting, journal entries, etc.
Production Assistant—High school (plus some
college preferred); general; clerical skills;
detail-oriented. Accounts Payable Clerk—High
school (plus some college preferred); good figure
aptitude; strong clerical background; detail-
oriented; familiar with computerized AP system;
1-2 years experience required. Inventory Assistant
—High school grad; general clerical, typing,
light bookkeeping; 6 months-1 year experience
required. Junior Editor—BA; proficient in
English; meticulous eyes for detail; must have

knowledge of subject area. Clerk-Typist—High
school grad; typing; good command of English
language; knowledge of general office procedures;
Art Assistant—High school grad; general
clerical, typing, basic knowledge of art
production.

VIKING PENGUIN INC.
40 W 23rd St
New York, NY 10010
212-337-5200
EMPLOYMENT CONTACT: Personnel Manager
TYPES OF PUBLISHING: Trade books
TITLES IN PRINT: 5,000
TOTAL EMPLOYEES: 160
AVERAGE ENTRY-LEVEL HIRING: 25-30
OPPORTUNITIES: Editorial Asst—College degree
(English or related); good typing, internship a
plus. Advertising & Promotion Asst.—College
degree; typing, writing skills and/or some
experience in graphics or layout (i.e. school
newspaper). Production Asst—High school or
College degree; typing, math skills. Contracts
Asst—College degree; good typing, office
experience helpful. Publicity Asst—College
degree; good typing, writing skills. Children's
Books Asst—College degree; good typing and
writing skills; courses related to children's books
helpful.
SUGGESTIONS: "We welcome resumes from
interested applicants."

WADSWORTH INC.
10 Davis Dr.
Belmont, CA 94002
415-595-2350
EMPLOYMENT CONTACT: Cindy McCann,
Corporate Manager-Human Resources
TITLES IN PRINT: 1992
TOTAL EMPLOYEES: 580
AVERAGE ENTRY-LEVEL HIRING: 6-10

J. WESTON WALCH, PUBLISHER
PO Box 658
Portland, ME 04104
207-772-2846
EMPLOYMENT CONTACT: Richard S. Kimball,
Managing Editor
TYPES OF PUBLISHING: Audio/Visual, Elhi.
TITLES IN PRINT: 1,000
TOTAL EMPLOYEES: 80

AVERAGE ENTRY-LEVEL HIRING: 0
OPPORTUNITIES: Editorial Asst—College
degree; education or experience in acquisitions,
pre-press production, or computer software
development.

WALKER & COMPANY
720 Fifth Ave.
New York, NY 10019
212-265-3632
EMPLOYMENT CONTACT: Mary A. C. Fiske,
Asst. to President
TYPES OF PUBLISHING: Adult and juvenile fiction
and non-fictin, hardover and paperback
TITLES IN PRINT: 100
TOTAL EMPLOYEES: 30
AVERAGE ENTRY-LEVEL HIRING: 2

WARNER BOOKS, INC.
A Division of Warner Publishing Inc.
666 Fifth Avenue
New York, NY 10103
212-484-2900
EMPLOYMENT CONTACT: Laura Tinio, Asst.
Human Resources Manager
TYPES OF PUBLISHING: Audio/Visual,
Children's, Mass Market Paperback, Profes-
sional, Scholarly, Scientific/Technical, Trade
(Hardcover), Trade (Paperbound).
TITLES IN PRINT: 1,500
TOTAL EMPLOYEES: 87
AVERAGE ENTRY-LEVEL HIRING: 15
OPPORTUNITIES: Editorial Asst.—College
degree (prefer BS in English); typing, clerical and
phone skills. Secretary—High school or business
school training preferred; some office experience,
typing (50 wpm), good communication skills.

WARREN, GORHAM & LAMONT, INC.
One Penn Plaza
New York, NY 10119
212-971-5033
EMPLOYMENT CONTACT: Judith Damore,
Manager, Recruitment and Employee Relations
TYPES OF PUBLISHING: Professional books,
periodicals and magazines in the fields of
accounting, banking and financial, law, real
estate, etc.
TITLES IN PRINT: 250
TOTAL EMPLOYEES: 600
AVERAGE ENTRY-LEVEL HIRING: 45

OPPORTUNITIES: "We offer opportunities in the
areas of Editorial, Marketing, New Product
Development, Finance, Human Resources and
Management Information Systems (MIS). These
entry-level positions provide an exposure to the
functional area, as well as an introduction to the
publishing industry. All positiosns also provide
excellent learning and growth potential."

FRANKLIN WATTS INC.
387 Park Ave. South
New York, NY 10016
212-686-7070
EMPLOYMENT CONTACT: Sandra Beach,
Personnel Dept.
TYPES OF PUBLISHING: Adult, Juvenile, Trade,
School and Library
TITLES IN PRINT: 2,000
TOTAL EMPLOYEES: 70
AVERAGE ENTRY-LEVEL HIRING: 4-6
OPPORTUNITIES: Clerical, Editorial Asst.—
High school graduates. No other requirements
specified.

SAMUEL WEISER, INC.
PO Box 612
York Beach, ME 03910
207-363-4393
EMPLOYMENT CONTACT: B. Lundsted, Vice
President
TYPES OF PUBLISHING: Trade (Paperbound),
(new age books, oriental philosophy, alternative
healing, and religions of the world)
TITLES IN PRINT: 400
TOTAL EMPLOYEES: 14
AVERAGE ENTRY-LEVEL HIRING: 1-2
OPPORTUNITIES: "Production people could use a
college degree, but the emphasis is on being able
to write copy, spell, types quickly, and have some
understanding of the material we publish. Understanding in this case does not mean that one has
to specialize in knowing all facets of the occult,
but an interest in the subject matter would certainly make the work more fun. New employees
need to bring a willingness to learn to a new job.
Most of them bring inflated resumes and then
they become difficult to teach, for that can't start
at the beginning when they start the job. Such
people usually last from 3 to 6 months around
here."

COMMENTS: "We accept letters and applications from people who have an interest in the material we publish, who can write, type and think. Working for a small publishing firm is exciting, but it means that employees have to like the work. That's hard to find. Most people want to be stars.

WESTVIEW PRESS
5500 Central Ave.
Boulder, CO 80301
303-444-3541
EMPLOYMENT CONTACT: Miriam Gilbert, VP/Director of College Division
TYPES OF PUBLISHING: Textbooks
TITLES IN PRINT: 2,000
TOTAL EMPLOYEES: 85
AVERAGE ENTRY-LEVEL HIRING: 4
OPPORTUNITIES: Clerical, Sales Asst. No specific requirements available.

JOHN WILEY & SONS INC.
605 Third Ave.
New York, NY 10158
212-850-6000
EMPLOYMENT CONTACT: Susan Fischer, Senior Employment Representative
TYPES OF PUBLISHING: Professional, College, Trade paperback, Technical, Scientific, Medical, Business, Encyclopedias, Software, Cassettes
TITLES IN PRINT: 10,000
AVERAGE ENTRY-LEVEL HIRING: ?
OPPORTUNITIES: All departments, from Clerical to Editorial. No specific requirements available.

WILLIAMS & WILKINS
428 East Preston St
Baltimore, MD 21202
301-528-4000
EMPLOYMENT CONTACT: Paul Shiah, Human Resources Dept.
TYPES OF PUBLISHING: Medical, Allied Health, Nursing.
TITLES IN PRINT: 750
TOTAL EMPLOYEES: 78
AVERAGE ENTRY-LEVEL HIRING: NA
OPPORTUNITIES: Educational Sales Representative—College degree; selling experience. Associate Editors—College degree. Production Sponsors—College degree; manufacturing.

WILLIAMSON PUBLISHING COMPANY
Church Hill Rd, Box 185
Charlotte, VT 05445
802-425-2102
EMPLOYMENT CONTACT: Jack Williamson, Publisher
TYPES OF PUBLISHING: Trade (Paperbound).
TITLES IN PRINT: 20
TOTAL EMPLOYEES: 6
AVERAGE ENTRY-LEVEL HIRING: 1
OPPORTUNITIES: Sales & marketing—College degree; no other requirements specified.

CHAPTER TWENTY FIVE

Internship & Training Program Listings

$\mathbf{M}$any of the publishers listed in the previous chapter also provided us with information about internships and training programs at their houses. We have included that important information in this chapter.

The listings are pretty self-explanatory. Following the name, address and telephone number of the publisher, we listed the data as follows:

Internship Contact: The person in charge of internships, often *different* from the one indicated in the previous chapter as *employment contact*. If there are different contacts for different departments—or for different offices—we've indicated them.

Internships Offered: Salaried, non-salaried or some of each ("Both").

Yearly Number Available: Just a note here—a "?" means they have internships available, but couldn't (or wouldn't) hazard a guess as to an exact number.

Internship Departments: in which internships are offered (not training)

Training Available: Their own words—what kinds of training they offer entry-level hirees.

Departments: in which training is offered (not internships)

If any of the above entries is missing from a particular company's listing,, that's because we were unable to confirm that entry <u>with the company itself</u>. Rather than give you wrong or misleading information, we simply omitted it.

One final note: In order to make available the most extensive and pertinent information on publishing internships—more than space would allow us to include in this volume—we have just published a brand-new volume, **Internships, Volume 2: Newspaper, Magazine and Book Publishing.** Additional data—application procedure, number of applications received, duties and responsibilities of the intern and more—is included for each of the publishers listed in this volume (and all the magazine and newspaper publishers included in our <u>Magazines Career Directory</u> and <u>Newspapers Career Directory</u>).

With the exception of only this new <u>Internships</u> volume, here are *more* listings of *more* publishers offering *more* internships than you'll find in any other publication...anywhere.

ABINGDON PRESS
201 Eighth Ave.
Nashville, TN 37200
615-749-6000
INTERNSHIP CONTACT: Cindy Knight, Employment Supervisor
INTERNSHIPS OFFERED: **Both**
YEARLY NUMBER AVAILABLE: 2-3

HARRY N. ABRAMS, INC.
A subsidiary of the Times Mirror Company
100 Fifth Ave.
New York, NY 10011
212-206-7715
INTERNSHIP CONTACT: Ellie Giannasco, Personnel Manager
INTERNSHIPS OFFERED: **Both**
YEARLY NUMBER AVAILABLE: ?
INTERNSHIP DEPARTMENTS: Editorial, Public Relations, Art.

ACROPOLIS BOOKS LTD.
Colortone Bldg.
2400 17th St. NW
Washington, DC 20009
202-387-6805
INTERNSHIP CONTACT: Alphonse J. Hackl, President
INTERNSHIPS OFFERED: **Salaried**
YEARLY NUMBER AVAILABLE: 1

ADDISON-WESLEY PUBLISHING COMPANY. INC.
Route 128
Reading, MA 01867
617-944-3700
TRAINING AVAILABLE: Training programs consist of specific one- or two-and-a-half-day audio/visual units on the topics of sales and time management techniques spread out over a year to supplement an intensive on-the-job training program.
DEPARTMENTS: Sales, Marketing

AD-LIB PUBLICATIONS
51 N Fifth St, PO Box 1102
Fairfield, IA 52666-1102
515-472-6617
TRAINING AVAILABLE: We incorporate our own three books about book marketing: <u>101 Ways to Market Your Books</u>; <u>Book Marketing Made Easier</u>; and <u>Book Marketing Opportunities: A Directory</u>.
DEPARTMENTS: Marketing

ALLYN & BACON INC.
A Subsidiary of Simon & Schuster
7 Wells Ave.
Newton, MA 02159
617-45-1200
INTERNSHIP CONTACT: Stacey Liebertal, VP Human Resources
INTERNSHIPS OFFERED: **Both**
YEARLY NUMBER AVAILABLE: 2-3

AMACOM BOOK DIVISION
The American Management Association
135 West 50th St.
New York, NY 10020
212-903-8018
INTERNSHIP CONTACT: George Harmon,
Personnel Director
INTERNSHIPS OFFERED: **Non-Salaried (Stipend)**
YEARLY NUMBER AVAILABLE: 5-10
INTERNSHIP DEPARTMENTS: Varied, from
Editorial to Marketing

ASHLEY BOOKS, INC.
30 Main St
Port Washington, NY 11060
516-883-2221
INTERNSHIP CONTACT: Joan Calder, Vice
President
INTERNSHIPS OFFERED: **Non-Salaried**
YEARLY NUMBER AVAILABLE: 2
INTERNSHIP DEPARTMENTS: Editorial, Public
Relations, Clerical
TRAINING AVAILABLE: Interns learn publishing
from every level—editorial, publicity, promo-
tion, marketing, writing copy, assisting in produc-
tion, i.e., doing everything in the publishing
spectrum.
DEPARTMENTS: All

BEEKMAN PUBLISHERS, INC.
PO Box 888
Woodstock, NY 12498
914-679-2300
INTERNSHIP CONTACT: Joanne Michaels, Vice
President
INTERNSHIPS OFFERED: **Non-Salaried**
YEARLY NUMBER AVAILABLE: 1

ROBERT BENTLEY, INC.
1000 Massachusetts Ave
Cambridge, MA 02138
617-547-4170
INTERNSHIP CONTACT: D. Waite, Personnel
Manager
INTERNSHIPS OFFERED: **Both**
YEARLY NUMBER AVAILABLE: 2
TRAINING AVAILABLE: 1-2 trainee positions open
per year. These positions are substantially more

than on-the-job training, but do not usually
involve off-site seminars.
DEPARTMENTS: Editorial/Production

BERKLEY PUBLISHING GROUP
See listing for Putnam Berkley Group

BIRCH TREE GROUP LTD
180 Alexander St
Princeton, NY 08540
609-683-0090
INTERNSHIP CONTACT: Janet James, Office
Manager
INTERNSHIPS OFFERED: **Salaried**
YEARLY NUMBER AVAILABLE: 3-5

BRANDEN PUBLISHING COMPANY
17 Station St, Box 843
Brookline Village, MA 02147
617-734-2045
INTERNSHIP CONTACT: Adolph Caso, President
INTERNSHIPS OFFERED: **Non-Salaried**
YEARLY NUMBER AVAILABLE: 2
INTERNSHIP DEPARTMENTS: Marketing

CAMBRIDGE UNIVERSITY PRESS
32 E 57th St
New York, NY 10022
212-688-8885
INTERNSHIP CONTACT: George Andreou,
Internship Coordinator
INTERNSHIPS OFFERED: **Non-Salaried**
YEARLY NUMBER AVAILABLE: 2
INTERNSHIP DEPARTMENTS: Editorial,
Production, Marketing

THE CAREER PRESS INC.
62 Beverly Rd, PO Box 34,
Hawthorne, NJ 07507
201-427-0229
INTERNSHIP CONTACT: Dick Start, Asst. to the
President
INTERNSHIPS OFFERED: **Both**
YEARLY NUMBER AVAILABLE: 1-2
INTERNSHIP DEPARTMENTS: Editorial,
Marketing/Promotion/Publicity.
COMMENTS: Cover letters/resumes only. No
phone calls, please. Apply by April 15 for
Summer. Any time for school year internships.

CBS EDUCATIONAL & PROFESSIONAL PUBLISHING
Bought by Harcourt, Brace Jovanovich, which offers no internship programs at this time.

CENTER FOR COMMUNICATION INC.
30 Rockefeller Plaza, 53rd Floor
New York, NY 10020
212-265-9130
INTERNSHIP CONTACT: Kim Gantz, Program Director
INTERNSHIPS OFFERED: **Salaried (Travel money)**
YEARLY NUMBER AVAILABLE: 12
INTERNSHIP DEPARTMENTS: Journalism, Advertising, Public Relations, Broadcasting

COLEMAN PUBLISHING
99 Milbar Blvd
Farmingdale, NY 11735
516-293-0383
INTERNSHIP CONTACT: Saul Steinberg, Director
INTERNSHIPS OFFERED: **Non-Salaried**
YEARLY NUMBER AVAILABLE: 2

CROWN PUBLISHERS, INC.
225 Park Avenue South
New York, NY 10003
212-254-1600
INTERNSHIP CONTACT: Linda Torraco, Employment Manager
INTERNSHIPS OFFERED: **Salaried**
YEARLY NUMBER AVAILABLE: 4-6 (per semester)
INTERNSHIP DEPARTMENTS: Editorial, Clerical, Sales

MARCEL DEKKER, INC.
270 Madison Ave
New York, NY 10016
212-696-9000
INTERNSHIP CONTACT: Stacey Miller, Personnel Recruiter
INTERNSHIPS OFFERED: **Non-Salaried**
YEARLY NUMBER AVAILABLE: 2
INTERNSHIP DEPARTMENTS: All

TRAINING AVAILABLE: High school executive internship program—you must be a high school student.

DEVIN-ADAIR, PUBLISHERS INC.
6 N Water St
Greenwich, CT 06830
203-531-7755
INTERNSHIP CONTACT: Roger H. Lourie, Managing Director
INTERNSHIPS OFFERED: **Both**
YEARLY NUMBER AVAILABLE: 2
TRAINING AVAILABLE: Intern program covers the following - _Introduction_: Overall organization of a publishing enterprise, work flow, marketing overview, strategic planning. _Editorial Aspects_: Editorial activities, manuscripts, authors, testimonials, endorsements, authors' network. _Sales_: Retail trade sales, sales communications, bookstore promotion, special sales to organizations. Promotion to academic institutions and libraries, importance of reviews, middlemen (jobbers and wholesalers), direct mail sales, direct response advertising, Trade (bookstore) advertisements. _International Aspects_: Translations, English-language sales, rights, exhibits, USIA, foreign agents. Rights, permissions, royalties. Public relations, publicity, pre- and post-publication publicity. Role of reviewers. Book launch. _Operational Aspects_: Manufacturing and book production, typesetting, book design, cover creation. Warehousing and order fulfillment. Customer service. Responsiveness. Business, finance, accounting & bookkeeping, contracts, budgeting.
DEPARTMENTS: All

DIAL BOOKS FOR YOUNG READERS
A Division of E.P. Dutton
2 Park Ave.
New York, NY 10016
212-725-1818
INTERNSHIP CONTACT: Shelly Sadler, Personnel Department
INTERNSHIPS OFFERED: **Salaried**
YEARLY NUMBER AVAILABLE: 1-2

F & W PUBLICATIONS INC.
1507 Dana Ave.
Cincinnati, OH 45207
513-531-2222
INTERNSHIP CONTACT: Kathy Schneider,
Personnel Manager
INTERNSHIPS OFFERED: **Salaried ($200/week)**
YEARLY NUMBER AVAILABLE: 7-8
INTERNSHIP DEPARTMENTS: Advertising, Art,
Book Club Promotion, Magazine and Book
Editorial, Circulation
TRAINING AVAILABLE: On the job; informal
program beyond orientation.

FABER & FABER, INC.
50 Cross St.
Winchester, MA 01890
617-721-1427
INTERNSHIP CONTACT: Susan Nash, VP
COMMENTS: "We haven't offered internships
yet, but might in the future."

FARRAR, STRAUS & GIROUX, INC.
19 Union Square West
New York, NY 10003
212-741-6900
INTERNSHIP CONTACT: Peggy Miller, Office
Manager
INTERNSHIPS OFFERED: **Non-Salaried**
YEARLY NUMBER AVAILABLE: 1-10
INTERNSHIP DEPARTMENTS: All

GALE RESEARCH CO.
Book Tower
Detroit, MI 48226
313-961-2242
INTERNSHIP CONTACT: Karen Bratton, Senior
Employment Director
INTERNSHIPS OFFERED: **Salaried**
YEARLY NUMBER AVAILABLE: 20-32 (5-8 per
quarter)
INTERNSHIP DEPARTMENTS: Editorial,
Research

GARDEN WAY/STOREY PUBLISHING
Schoolhouse Rd
Pownal, VT 05261
802-823-5811
INTERNSHIP CONTACT: Martha M. Storey, Vice
President

INTERNSHIPS OFFERED: **Non-Salaried**
YEARLY NUMBER AVAILABLE: 1-2
INTERNSHIP DEPARTMENTS: All

GREENWOOD PRESS
Box 5007, 88 Post Rd.
Westport, CT 06881
203-226-3571
INTERNSHIP CONTACT: Carole Bronson, VP
Production
INTERNSHIPS OFFERED: **Salaried**
YEARLY NUMBER AVAILABLE: 1-2

GUERNICA EDITIONS
PO Box 633, Station N.D.G.
Montreal, Quebec, Canada H4A 3R1
514-256-5599
INTERNSHIPS OFFERED: **NA**
YEARLY NUMBER AVAILABLE: ?
INTERNSHIP DEPARTMENTS: Editorial
(preferred), Clerical

HUMAN KINETICS PUBLISHERS
1607 North Market St, PO Box #5076
Champaign, IL 61820
217-351-5076
INTERNSHIP CONTACT: Mary T. Krzysik, CPS,
Executive Secretary
INTERNSHIPS OFFERED: **Salaried**
YEARLY NUMBER AVAILABLE: 1
INTERNSHIP DEPARTMENTS: Editorial

RICHARD D. IRWIN, INC.
1818 Ridge Rd
Homewood, IL 60430
312-798-6000
INTERNSHIP CONTACT: Personnel
INTERNSHIPS OFFERED: **Both**
YEARLY NUMBER AVAILABLE: 10
INTERNSHIP DEPARTMENTS: All (assignment
geared to student';s major, i.e., Art, English,
Business, etc.)

LITTLE, BROWN AND COMPANY
A Subsidiary of Time Inc.
34 Beacon Street
Boston, MA 02106
617-227-0730
INTERNSHIP CONTACT: Rebecca Parker, Human
Resources Dept.

INTERNSHIPS OFFERED: **Salaried**
YEARLY NUMBER AVAILABLE: 5-10
INTERNSHIP DEPARTMENTS: All (assignment geared to student's major, i.e., Art, English, Business, etc.)

MACMILLAN PUBLISHING COMPANY
866 Third Avenue
New York, NY 10022
212-702-2000
INTERNSHIP CONTACT: Amryl W. Holloway, Manager-Staffing and Employee Relations
INTERNSHIPS OFFERED: **Non-Salaried**
YEARLY NUMBER AVAILABLE: 5-7
INTERNSHIP DEPARTMENTS: All

MASTERY EDUCATION
85 Main St
Watertown, MA 02172
617-926-0329
INTERNSHIP CONTACT: Elena Wright, Managing Editor
INTERNSHIPS OFFERED: **Non-Salaried**
YEARLY NUMBER AVAILABLE: 2
INTERNSHIP DEPARTMENTS: Editorial, Professional, Marketing

MERRIAM-WEBSTER INC.
47 Federal St, PO Box #281
Springfield, MA 01102
413-734-3134
TRAINING AVAILABLE: "Open-ended training covering various aspects of the dictionary-making process, such as reading for citations, defining, and cross-referencing.
DEPARTMENTS: Editorial

MERRILL PUBLISHING COMPANY
Internships no longer available. Interested students, however, might be able to be part of freelance staff (proofreading, editorial) if capable of doing an exceptional job.

WILLIAM MORROW & COMPANY, INC.
105 Madison Ave
New York, NY 10016
212-889-3050
INTERNSHIP CONTACT: Mrs. Barbara E. Spence, Personnel Director

INTERNSHIPS OFFERED: **Both** (Summer $100/wk, School-year for college credit only)
YEARLY NUMBER AVAILABLE: 10 (4 summer, 6 during school year.)
INTERNSHIP DEPARTMENTS: All

THE C.V. MOSBY COMPANY
11830 Westline Industrial Dr
St. Louis, MO 63108
314-872-8370
INTERNSHIP CONTACT: Jori Alwell, VP-Human Resouces
INTERNSHIPS OFFERED: **Non-Salaried**
YEARLY NUMBER AVAILABLE: 1-2
INTERNSHIP DEPARTMENTS All, including Human Resources, Sales & Marketing, Production.
TRAINING AVAILABLE: In-house manual and product knowledge seminars DEPARTMENTS: Sales (Field)

THOMAS NELSON PUBLISHERS
Elm Hill Pike at Nelson Place
Nashville, TN 37214
615-889-9000
INTERNSHIP CONTACT: Interviews on college campuses nationwide (one student accepted for each four-five interviewed)
INTERNSHIPS OFFERED: **Commission Sales**
YEARLY NUMBER AVAILABLE: 500
COMMENTS: Summer sales jobs; interns travel to Nashville for training.

NELSON-HALL PUBLISHERS
Internships no longer available.

OXFORD UNIVERSITY PRESS
200 Madison Ave.
New York, NY 10016
212-679-7300
INTERNSHIP CONTACT: Nancy O'Connor, Personnel Manager
INTERNSHIPS OFFERED: **No set internship program; in three years, they have only accepted two people directly from the Pace University Publishing Program.**

POCKET BOOKS
A Division of Simon & Schuster
1230 Ave. of the Americas
New York, NY 10022
212-698-7000
INTERNSHIP CONTACT: Personnel Dept.
INTERNSHIPS OFFERED: NA
YEARLY NUMBER AVAILABLE: 3-7

PRENTICE-HALL, INC.
See listing for Simon & Schuster, Inc.

PRICE/STERN/SLOAN PUBLISHERS, INC.
360 North La Cienega Blvd.
Los Angeles, CA 90048
213-657-6100
INTERNSHIP CONTACT: Spencer Humpthrey,
Associate Editor
INTERNSHIPS OFFERED: **Both**
YEARLY NUMBER AVAILABLE: 1

THE PUTNAM BERKELEY GROUP
200 Madison Ave
New York, NY 10016
212-576-8900
INTERNSHIP CONTACT: Grace Heelan,
Production Manager
INTERNSHIPS OFFERED: **Non-Salaried** (but $500
lunch stipend)
YEARLY NUMBER AVAILABLE: 6
INTERNSHIP DEPARTMENTS: Editorial, Publicity, Production, Managing Editor's Office

RODALE PRESS, INC.
33 E. Minor St.
Emmaus, PA 18049
215-967-5171
INTERNSHIP CONTACT: John Volanski, Personnel
Dept.
INTERNSHIPS OFFERED: **Salaried**
YEARLY NUMBER AVAILABLE: 5-7

SCHOLASTIC, INC.
730 Broadway
New York, NY 10003
212-505-3000
INTERNSHIP CONTACT: Julius James, Recruiter
INTERNSHIPS OFFERED: **Non-Salaried**
YEARLY NUMBER AVAILABLE: 1
INTERNSHIP DEPARTMENTS: All

SIMON & SCHUSTER, INC.
1230 Ave. of the Americas
New York, NY 10022
212-698-7000
INTERNSHIP CONTACT: Barbara Learner,
Manager of Corporate Communications
INTERNSHIPS OFFERED: **Salaried**
YEARLY NUMBER AVAILABLE: 40
INTERNSHIP DEPARTMENTS: Editorial, Sales,
Marketing, Publications, Art & Design, Book
Production

STEMMER HOUSE PUBLISHERS, INC.
2627 Caves Rd
Owings Mills, MD 21117
301-363-3690
INTERNSHIP CONTACT: Barbara Holdridge,
President
INTERNSHIPS OFFERED: **Both**
YEARLY NUMBER AVAILABLE: 1-2
INTERNSHIP DEPARTMENTS: Editorial

JEREMY P. TARCHER, INC.
9110 Sunset Blvd., Suite 250
Los Angeles,CA 90069
213-273-3274
INTERNSHIP CONTACT: Pat Bryer, Personnel
Administrator
INTERNSHIPS OFFERED: **Non-Salaried**
YEARLY NUMBER AVAILABLE: 1

TRANSACTION PUBLISHERS
Rutgers University
New Brunswick, NJ 08903
201-932-2280
INTERNSHIP CONTACT: Scott Bromson, Senior
Vice President
INTERNSHIPS OFFERED: **Non-Salaried**
YEARLY NUMBER AVAILABLE: 1

UNIVERSITY OF ILLINOIS PRESS
64 E Gregory Dr
Champaign, IL 61820
217-333-0950
INTERNSHIP CONTACT: Jan Palumbo, Associate
Director
INTERNSHIPS OFFERED: **Salaried**
YEARLY NUMBER AVAILABLE: 1-2

UNIVERSITY OF NEW MEXICO PRESS
Journalism Building
Albuquerque, NM 87131
505 277-2346
INTERNSHIP CONTACT: David V. Holtby,
Associate Director
INTERNSHIPS OFFERED: **Non-Salaried**
YEARLY NUMBER AVAILABLE: 1-2

**THE UNIVERSITY OF NORTH CAROLINA
PRESS**
Box 2288
Chapel Hill, NC 27515-2288
919-966-3561
INTERNSHIP CONTACT: Matthew Hodgson,
Director
INTERNSHIPS OFFERED: **Non-Salaried**
YEARLY NUMBER AVAILABLE: 1-2

UNIVERSITY PRESS OF AMERICA, INC.
4720 Boston Way,
Lanham, MD 20706
301-459-3366
INTERNSHIP CONTACT: James E. Lyons,
Publisher
INTERNSHIPS OFFERED: **Both**
YEARLY NUMBER AVAILABLE: 1

VIKING PENGUIN INC.
40 W 23rd St
New York, NY 10010
212-337-5200
INTERNSHIP CONTACT: Personnel Manager
INTERNSHIPS OFFERED: **Non-Salaried** (but may
reimburse commutation expenses)
YEARLY NUMBER AVAILABLE: 1-2
INTERNSHIP DEPARTMENTS: Adult Editorial,
Children's books, Design, Managing Editor Depts.

WARREN, GORHAM & LAMONT, INC.
One Penn Plaza
New York, NY 10119
212-971-5033
INTERNSHIP CONTACT: Shawna Kripalani,
Employment Specialist
INTERNSHIPS OFFERED: **Salaried (approx. $225-
$250/week)**
YEARLY NUMBER AVAILABLE: 8
INTERNSHIP DEPARTMENTS: Editorial,
Marketing, Finance, Human Resources

WESTVIEW PRESS
5500 Central Ave.
Boulder, CO 80301
303-444-3541
INTERNSHIP CONTACT: Miriam Gilbert,
VP/Director of College Employment
INTERNSHIPS OFFERED: **Non-Salaried**
YEARLY NUMBER AVAILABLE: 1-2
INTERNSHIP DEPARTMENTS: All, including
Marketing, Sales and Editorial

JOHN WILEY & SONS, INC.
605 Third Ave.
New York, NY 10158
212-850-6000
INTERNSHIP CONTACT: Susan Fisher, Senior
Employment Representative
INTERNSHIPS OFFERED: **Salaried ($225/week)**
YEARLY NUMBER AVAILABLE: 3-4
INTERNSHIP DEPARTMENTS: All
TRAINING AVAILABLE: New hires are on 90-day
probation. Each department has its own program
DEPARTMENTS: All

WILLIAMS & WILKINS
428 East Preston St
Baltimore, MD 21202
301-528-4212
INTERNSHIP CONTACT: Paul Shiah, Human
Resources Dept.
INTERNSHIPS OFFERED: **Both**
YEARLY NUMBER AVAILABLE: 5-10
INTERNSHIP DEPARTMENTS: All
TRAINING AVAILABLE: Overview of publishing
functions, orientation to the particular
department, specific task training for the job at
hand.
DEPARTMENTS: All

SECTION V

Appendices

APPENDIX A

Industry Trade Organizations

AMERICAN BOOKSELLERS ASSOCIATION
122 East 42nd Street, 14th floor
New York, NY 10168
212-867-9060

AMERICAN INSTITUTE OF GRAPHIC ARTS
1059 Third Avenue, 3rd floor
New York, NY 10021
212-752-0813

ASSOCIATION OF AMERICAN PUBLISHERS
220 East 23rd Street, 2nd floor
New York, NY 10010
212-689-8920

ASSOCIATION OF AMERICAN UNIVERSITY PRESSES
One Park Avenue, Suite 1103,
New York, NY 10016
212-889-6040

ASSOCIATION OF CANADIAN PUBLISHERS
70 The Esplanade East,
Toronto, Ontario, Canada M5E 1R2
416-361-1408

ASSOCIATION OF JEWISH BOOK PUBLISHERS
c/o Union of American Hebrew Congregations
838 Fifth Avenue,
New York, NY 10021
212-249-0100

ASSOCIATION OF THE GRAPHIC ARTS
5 Penn Plaza, 20th floor,
New York, NY 10001
212-279-2100

CHICAGO BOOK CLINIC
100 East Ohio St.
Chicago, IL 60611
312-951-8254

CHILDREN'S BOOK COUNCIL
67 Irving Place,
New York, NY 10003
212-254-2666

CHRISTIAN BOOKSELLERS ASSOCIATION
PO Box 200, 2620 Venetucci Boulevard,
Colorado Springs, CO 80901
303-576-7880

COSMEP
PO Box 703
San Francisco, CA 94101

NEW YORK RIGHTS AND PERMISSIONS GROUP
c/o Gale Research Co.
Penobscot Bldg.
Detroit, MI 48226
313-961-2242 ext. 6813 (Jeanne Gough, Production Manager

PUBLISHERS AD CLUB
c/o Belle Blanchard
Doubleday and Company
66 Fifth Ave.
New York, NY 10003
212-765-6506

PUBLISHERS PUBLICITY ASSOCIATION, INC.
c/o Putnam Publishing Group
605 Third Ave.
New York, NY 10158
212-850-6259

SOCIETY FOR SCHOLARLY PUBLISHING
2000 Florida Ave. NW, Ste. 305
Washington, DC 20009
202-328-3555

WOMEN IN COMMUNICATIONS, INC.
Box 9561,
Austin, TX 78766
512-346-9875

WOMEN IN SCHOLARLY PUBLISHING
c/o Stanford University Press
Stanford, CA 94305
415-497-9434

WOMEN'S NATIONAL BOOK ASSOCIATION, INC.
160 Fifth Avenue,
New York, NY 10010
212-675-7804

APPENDIX B

Industry Trade Publications

There are, perhaps surprisingly, few magazines directly (or even *indirectly*) concerned with the business of book publishing. Even those we've listed below are primarily concerned either with book*selling*, primarily to libraries, or specialized publications on graphics, production, etc. Only one—*Publishers Weekly*—can claim to be really about book *publishing* (and publishers).

We've listed a number of publications that are peripheral—those in the advertising and public relations areas, for example. There are probably hundreds more depending on the specific area of publishing you decide to go into. These are the most important and will, at least, offer some initial advice.

ADVERTISING AGE
Crain Communications
740 North Rush Street,
Chicago, IL 60611
312-649-5200

ADWEEK
A/S/M Communications
49 East 21 Street, 11th floor,
New York, NY 10010
212-529-5500

AMERICAN BOOKSELLER
Booksellers Publishing, Inc.
122 East 42nd Street,
New York, NY 10168
212-867-9060

AMERICAN PRINTER
MacLean Hunter Publishing Company
29 North Wacker Dr.
Chicago, IL 60606
312-726-2802

ART DIRECTION
10 East 39th Street, 6th floor,
New York, NY 10016
212-889-6500

ART PRODUCT NEWS
In-Art Publishing Company,
PO Box 117,
St. Petersburg, FL 33731
813-821-6064

BOOKLIST
American Library Association
50 East Huron Street,
Chicago, IL 60611
312-944-6780

BOOKSTORE JOURNAL
(Official publication of the Christian
Booksellers Association)
CBA Service Group, Inc.
PO Box 200, 2620 Venetucci Boulevard,
Colorado Springs, CO 80901
303-576-7880

CREATIVE
Magazines/Creative, Inc.
37 West 39th Street, Suite 604,
New York, NY 10018
212-840-0160

EDUCATIONAL MARKETER
Knowledge Industry Publications, Inc.
701 Westchester Ave.
White Plains, NY 10604
914-328-9157

EP&P THE MAGAZINE FOR ELECTRONIC PUBLISHING
MacLean Hunter Publishing Corp.
300 W. Adams
Chicago, IL 60606

GRAPHIC ARTS MONTHLY
Technical Publishing
249 West 17th St.
New York, NY 10011
212-645-0067

GRAPHIC DESIGN: USA
Kaye Publishing Corp.
120 East 56th Street, Suite 440,
New York, NY 10022
212-759-8813

**LIBRARY JOURNAL
SCHOOL LIBRARY JOURNAL**
R.R. Bowker Company
245 West 17th Street,
New York, NY 10011
212-645-9700

LOCUS: THE NEWSPAPER OF THE SCIENCE FICTION FIELD
Locus Publications, Inc.
Box 13305
Oakland, CA 94661
415-339-9196

MAGAZINE AND BOOKSELLER
North American Publishing Company
322 Eighth Avenue,
New York, NY 10001
212-620-7300

MARKETING NEWS
American Marketing Association
250 South Wacker Drive, Suite 22,
Chicago, IL 60606
312-648-0536 (Association)
312-993-9517 (Editorial)

NICHES
The Independent Publishers League
Drawer 5007
Bend, OR 97708

PRINT AND HOW
R.C. Publications, Inc.
104 Fifth Ave., 9th Floor
New York, NY 10011
212-463-0600

PUBLIC RELATIONS JOURNAL
Public Relations Society of America
33 Irving Place
New York, NY 10003
212-995-2230

PUBLISHERS WEEKLY
R.R. Bowker Company
245 West 17th Street,
New York, NY 10011
212-645-9700

QUILL & QUIRE: THE NEWSMAGA-ZINE OF THE CANADIAN BOOK TRADE
56 The Esplanade, Ste. 213
Toronto, Ontario, Canada M5E 1A7
416-364-3333

SCHOLARLY PUBLISHING
University of Toronto Press
Toronto, Canada M5S 1A6

SMALL PRESS: THE MAGAZINE OF INDEPENDENT IN-HOUSE DESKTOP PUBLISHING
Meckler Publishing Corp.
11 Ferry Lane West
Westport, CT 06880
203-226-6967

UPPER AND LOWER CASE (U&lc)
International Typeface Corporation
2 Dag Hammarskjold Plaza, 3rd floor,
New York, NY 10017
212-371-0699

THE WRITER
120 Boylston Street,
Boston, MA 02116
617-423-3157

WRITERS DIGEST
F & W Publications
1507 Dana Ave.
Cincinnati, OH 45207
513-531-2222

TARGET MARKETING
North American Publishing Company
401 North Broad Street,
Philadelphia, PA 19108
215-238-5300

Book Publishing Courses

There are now quite a few courses available—especially "summer institutes"—for the aspiring book publishing professional. In this appendix, we have listed the most well-known/well-respected. We have also listed some (but by no means all) of the best-known degree programs. For a more complete listing of the latter, consult <u>Guide to Book Publishing Courses</u> (Peterson's Guides, 1979). We have also omitted courses/programs primarily for writers. Where available, we have included the following information:

1. The name, address and phone number of the institution.
2. Who to contact (and/or the program director).
3. A brief description of the course/program offerings.
4. When the program or courses are offered.
5. Approximate length of each course/program.
6. Approximate costs.
7. Application procedure (including pertinent deadlines).
8. College credits awarded.
9. Whether the courses/program are primarily for entry-level people.

ASSOCIATION OF THE GRAPHIC ARTS

(formerly Printing Industries of Metropolitan New York)
5 Penn Plaza,
New York, NY 10001
212-279-2100
Gail Zambrano, Director

Now in its 70th year, the AGA's Evening Schools (three campuses: New York City, Montclair, NJ and Hemstead, Long Island) offer some 40 courses per semester—Spring and Fall. Spring classes begin in February, Fall in October. Most are 10 weeks, one night per week. Cost is around $125 (for members), $200 (for nonmembers) plus $15 registration fee. (They accept resumes to pass on to their 700+ corporate members.)

CITY UNIVERSITY OF NEW YORK, GRADUATE CENTER

Education in Publishing Program
33 West 42nd Street, Room 1206A,
New York, NY 10036
212-575-1493
Barbara Heller, Director, Special Programs
Peg Rivers, Program Administrator

Offers some 25-odd publishing courses in the fall and spring semesters. Most courses are ten weeks (one evening per week) and are aimed at those with some experience in publishing. The entire program is developed from the basic curriculum drawn up by the Education for Publishing Committee of the Association of American Publishers. Application deadline: mid-September for fall (classes begin around October 1st); mid-February for spring (classes begin around March 1st). Certificate issued upon completion of course. Tuition works out to approximately $23 per night (so, for most courses, from $225-$235).

DYNAMIC GRAPHICS EDUCATIONAL FOUNDATION

A subsidiary of Dynamic Graphics, Inc.
6000 N. Forest Park Dr.
Peoria, IL 61614
309-688-8866
Brenn Anderson, Director

A number of continuing education courses, some lectures but primarily "hands-on," each lasting from two to five days. Held in major metropolitan areas throughout the U.S. (though some are available in central Illinois only). Cost of each course: $395 - $900. Some colleges accept continuing education units. Courses in graphics, design, art, production computer graphics, printing, AV, both basic and advanced. Write or call to request complete catalog.

EDITORIAL EXPERTS, INC.

85 South Bragg St., Suite 400
Alexandria, VA 22312-2731
703-642-3040
Andrea Lentz, Manager-Training Div.

Basic, intermediate and advanced workshops in publications skills, including grammar, writing, editing, proofreading, production, publication management, proposal preparation, indexing and newsletters. Professional workshops currently offered in Washington, DC area (only). Majority of courses are 1 day and cost $245. Offered in Fall (October-December), Spring and Summer (March-August). Continuing education units for possible college credit.

FREEHAND

Box 806
Provincetown, MA 02657
617-487-3579
Marian Roth, Director

Courses for women writers and photographers. Term is seven-month residency program.

GEORGE WASHINGTON UNIVERSITY

Publication Specialist Program
801 22nd Street, NW, Suite T-409
Washington, DC 20052
202-994-7273 or 5766
Dee Buchanan, Program Director

Five sessions per year (primarily evenings, some Saturday mornings) covering all aspects of book, magazine and newsletter publishing. Each course last 8 weeks, costs from $290—$305 and is noncredit. Full program—consisting of 10, 20-hour courses (24 continuing education units)—is $2,560. Certificate awarded upon completion of program. Spring program begins first week of February, Fall, last week of September.

HOWARD UNIVERSITY PRESS
Book Publishing Institute
2900 Van Ness St., NW
Washington, DC 20008
202-686-6498
Ambassador Aggrey, Acting Director

Intensive 5-week course, featuring top industry
executives, is a good overview of the business,
covering editorial, design, manufacturing,
marketing and business aspects of book publishing. Accepts 30 students—primarily recent college
grads, but occasional college juniors or those
changing careers—for course running from May 27
to July 2. Cost is $1,500, plus a $35 nonrefundable
application fee that must be received with an
application no later than March 19th.

NEW YORK UNIVERSITY
School of Continuing Education
2 University Place, Room 21
New York, NY 10003
212-598-3571 (Admissions)
Ronald W. Janoff, Director
Carol Myer, Program Coordinator

Offers approximately seven 10 or 12 week book
publishing courses (plus courses and a degree
program in magazine publishing), for both the
entry-level and advanced student, plus occasional
1-day seminars. Courses available in three
semesters—Fall, Spring and Summer) and cost
$240 each (plus $20 registration fee). Seminars,
when offered, generally cost under $100. The
Certificate in Book Publishing is awarded to
those who successfully complete five courses with
a minimum "B" grade point average.

**NEW YORK UNIVERSITY'S SUMMER
PUBLISHING INSTITUTE**
Center for Publishing
48 Cooper Square,
New York, NY 10003
212-477-9142
Ronald Janoff, Director
Carolyn Stark, Program Administrator

Highly respected course is offered each summer:
1988 dates were June 15-July 24. Application
deadline is April 13. Cost is $2,500 (plus $35
application fee). Course limited to 60 students.

NORTHEASTERN UNIVERSITY
Center for Continuing Education
Graphic Arts Program
370 Common Street,
Dedham, MA 02026
617-329-8000
Frank Trocki, Director

Courses in all aspects of book publishing, advertising, design, production and management.
Courses are offered in all four quarters. Most are
for 11 weeks and cost approximately $300 (which
includes registration fee). "Hands-on" courses,
such as Photo Typesetting, may cost a bit more.
Two different types of professional certificates
are available. A *Graphic Arts Newsletter* is
available one month before the start of each
quarter's classes, with details on courses,
registration, etc.

PARSONS SCHOOL OF DESIGN
School of Continuing Education
66 West 12th Street,
New York, NY 10011
212-741-8950
Donal Higgins, Dean

Approximately 50 courses in each of three
semesters (plus half that in the summer quarter).
Ten weeks per class—once per week. In summer,
twice a week for five weeks. Cost: $246 per credit;
$220 per course noncredit. Applications accepted
up to the beginning of each semester.

**RADCLIFFE COLLEGE/HARVARD
UNIVERSITY**
Radcliffe Publishing Courses
6 Ash Street,
Cambridge, MA 02138
617-495-8678
Frank Collins, Director

Radcliffe's 6-week course runs from July 11 to
August 19. Application deadline is March 25th;
cost (including room and board) is $3,475. Course
geared to entry-level candidates and includes
both magazine and book publishing. Accepts
approximately 85 students.

ROCHESTER INSTITUTE OF TECHNOLOGY
School of Printing Management and Sciences
One Lomb Memorial Dr.
Rochester, NY 14623
716-475-2727
Miles Southworth, Director

Classes in newspapers, book production, magazine publishing, typography, printing design, computer use, electronic publishing, management, sales, finishing, bindery and screen printing. 10-week courses are offered quarterly. Tuition is $2,752 (plus fees plus room and board) per quarter; scholarship monies are available. College credit given toward B.S. degree. Write to Admissions Office for application ($35 application fee).

SCHOOL OF THE VISUAL ARTS
Division of Continuing Education
209 East 23rd Street,
New York, NY 10010
212-679-7350 or 683-0600
Stephen Pite, Director of Continuing Education

In addition to its highly respect B.F.A. and M.F.A. programs, the School offers 12-week courses in a number of areas—book, newspaper and magazine design; advertising; production, etc for non-degree candidates. Programs begin in September, January and June. Cost approximately $260 per course (includes registration fee). From entry-level up.

STANFORD UNIVERSITY
Stanford Publishing Course
Stanford Alumni Association
Stanford, CA 94305
415-723-2300
Della van Heyst, Director

Now eleven years old, this two-week course is available for either book or magazine publishing. 1988 dates were July 10th-23rd. Aimed at publishing professionals: average age of participants is 36. Cost is $1,650.

UNIVERSITY OF CALIFORNIA EXTENSION
Certificate Program in Publishing
2223 Fulton St.
Berkeley, CA 94720
415-642-4231
Ruth Majdrakoff, Director

Courses in all major areas of publishing offered on weekends or one night per week for up to 15 weeks, three times each year. Cost is $135 to $250 per course.

UNIVERSITY OF CHICAGO
Publishing Program
Office of Continuing Education
5835 South Kimbark Avenue,
Chicago, IL 60637
312-702-1722 or 1729
Joyce Feucht-Haviar, Director

Approximately one dozen courses offered each semester. Cost between $65 and $200. Geared to entry-level candidates.

UNIVERSITY OF DENVER
Publishing Institute
Graduate School of Arts & Humanities
English Dept.
2075 South University, #D-114
Denver, CO 80208
303-871-2570
Elizabeth Geiser, Director

Four-week summer program accepts 85 students, most recent college graduates. Covers only book publishing (not magazines).

UNIVERSITY OF PENNSYLVANIA
Publishing Institute
3808 Walnut St.
Philadelphia, PA 19104-6136
215-898-6479/93
Sylvia Auerbach, Director

Offered in both Fall and Spring semesters. Fall course offers an overview of book publishing, taught by top pros from New York, Boston and Philadelphia houses. Length: 14 weeks. Cost: $425. Certificate of completion offered. Spring course concentrates more on specialties and includes newspaper and magazine publishing. Length: 8 weeks. Cost: $275. ($650 for both semesters.) Suitable for entry-level to advanced.

UNIVERSITY OF WISCONSIN-MADISON
Communications Programs
222 Lowell Hall
610 Langdon St.
Madison, WI 53703
608-262-3982
Arthur Krival, Chairman

One-day courses in magazine, newspaper and book publishing, costing from $85 to $235 each. Suitable for entry-level to advanced.

INDEX

MAIL ORDER COUPON

Name: _____

Mailing Address: _____

City, State, Zip Code: _____

Telephone:_____ ❏ **CHECK HERE FOR CATALOG**

Quantity	Binding	Title	Price
SERIES TITLES (Add postage and handling)			
_____	Paper	Internships, Vol 1.	$11.95
_____	Paper	Internships, Vol. 2	$11.95
_____	Paper	Advertising Career Directory	$26.95
_____	Paper	Book Publishing Career Directory	$26.95
_____	Paper	Magazines Career Directory	$26.95
_____	Paper	Marketing & Sales Career Directory	$26.95
_____	Paper	Newspapers Career Directory	$26.95
_____	Paper	Public Relations Career Directory	$26.95
_____	Hardcover	Advertising Career Directory	$34.95
_____	Hardcover	Book Publishing Career Directory	$34.95
_____	Hardcover	Magazines Career Directory	$34.95
_____	Hardcover	Marketing & Sales Career Directory	$34.95
_____	Hardcover	Newspapers Career Directory	$34.95
_____	Hardcover	Public Relations Career Directory	$34.95
NON-SERIES TITLES (Prices include postage and handling)			
_____	Paper	College Comes Sooner Than You Think!	$11.95
_____	Paper	Your First Resume Book	$11.95
_____	Paper	High Impact Resumes & Letters	$13.95
_____	Paper	Interview for Success	$11.95
_____	Paper	Complete Guide to Public Employment	$15.50
_____	Paper	Public Schools USA	$14.95
_____	Paper	International Careers: An Insider's Guide	$11.95
_____	Paper	After College: The Business of Getting Jobs	$11.95
_____	Paper	Parenting Through the College Years	$11.95
_____	Paper	What's Next? Career Strategies After 35	$11.95
_____	Paper	Complete Guide to Social Security	$11.95

Total number of Series volumes ordered: _____   Amount : $_____

$2.50 per order plus $1.00 per volume shipping charges $_____

Total number of non-Series volumes: _____   Amount: $_____

Total amount of order. <u>This must be enclosed.</u> $_____

NON-SERIES TITLES

❑ **COLLEGE COMES SOONER THAN YOU THINK! The College Planning Guide For High School Students And Their Families,** by Jill Reilly and Bonnie Featherstone. ISBN 0-934829-24-1, Paper, 6 x 9, 176 pp. $11.95 postpaid.

❑ **YOUR FIRST RESUME: The Comprehensive Preparation Guide for High School and College Students** by Ronald W. Fry. ISBN 0-934829-25-X, Paper, 8 1/2 x 11, 160 pp. (approx.). $11.95 postpaid.

❑ **HIGH IMPACT RESUMES AND LETTERS: How to Communicate Your Qualifications to Employers**, 3rd Edition, by Dr. Ronald L. Krannich and William J. Banis. ISBN 0-942710-20-7, Paper, 8 1/2 x 11, 180 pages. $13.95

❑ **INTERVIEW FOR SUCCESS: A Practical Guide To Increasing Job Interviews, Offers and Salaries,** by Drs. Caryl & Ron Krannich. ISBN 0-942710-19-3, Paper, 6 x 9, Indexed & Illustrated, 165 pages. $11.95 postpaid.

❑ **THE COMPLETE GUIDE TO PUBLIC EMPLOYMENT,** by Drs. Ron and Caryl Krannich. ISBN 0-942710-05-3, Paper, 6 x 9, 512 pages. $15.50 postpaid.

❑ **PUBLIC SCHOOLS USA: A Guide To School Districts,** by Charles Harrison ISBN 0-913589-36-5, Paper, 6 x 9, 256 pages. $14.95 postpaid.

❑ **INTERNATIONAL CAREERS: An Insiders Guide,** by David Rearwin. ISBN 0-913589-28-4, Paper, 6 x 9, 192 pages. $11.95 postpaid.

❑ **AFTER COLLEGE; The Business of Getting Jobs,** by Jack Falvey ISBN 0-913589-17-9, Paper, 6 x 9, 192 pages. $11.95 postpaid.

❑ **PARENTING THROUGH THE COLLEGE YEARS**, by Norman Giddan and Sally Vallongo ISBN 0-913589-37-3, Paper, 6 x 9, 192 pages. $11.95 postpaid.

❑ **WHAT'S NEXT?/Career Strategies After 35,** by Jack Falvey. ISBN 0-913589-26-8 Paper, 6 x 9, 192 pages. $11.95 postpaid.

❑ **THE COMPLETE & EASY GUIDE TO SOCIAL SECURITY AND MEDICARE,** by Faustin F. Jehle. ISBN 0-930045-02-5, Paper, 8 1/2 x 11, 175 pages. $11.95 postpaid.

TO ORDER ANY OF THESE TITLES—OR TO REQUEST A CATALOG—SIMPLY FILL OUT THE ORDER FORM ON THE OPPOSITE PAGE OR CALL **1-800-CAREER-1** TO USE YOUR MASTERCARD OR VISA.

GREAT BOOKS FROM THE CAREER PRESS

TO ORDER ANY OF THESE ACCLAIMED VOLUMES or request a catalog, **CALL 1-800-CAREER-1**. For your convenience, we accept MASTERCARD and VISA.

Or simply check the titles you would like on the coupon on the preceding page, fill out the required information completely, tear out the entire page and send (with full payment if you are ordering books) to: The Career Press, 62 Beverly Rd., PO Box 34, Hawthorne, N.J. 07057.

SERIES TITLES:

❑ **INTERNSHIPS, VOL. 1: ADVERTISING, MARKETING, PUBLIC RELATIONS & SALES,** edited by Ronald W. Fry. ISBN 0-934829-27-6, Paper, 6 x 9, 320 pages (approx.). $11.95.

❑ **INTERNSHIPS, VOL 2: NEWSPAPER, MAGAZINE AND BOOK PUBLISHING,** edited by Ronald W. Fry. ISBN 0-934829-28-4, Paper, 6 x 9, 320 pages (approx.). $11.95.

ADVERTISING CAREER DIRECTORY, 3rd edition, 320 pages, 8 1/2 x 11
❑ Paper — ISBN 0-934829-30-6, $26.95.
❑ Hardcover (cloth) — ISBN 0-934829-40-3, $34.95.

MARKETING & SALES CAREER DIRECTORY, 2nd edition, 320 pages, 8 1/2 X 11.
❑ Paper — ISBN 0-934829-34-9, $26.95.
❑ Hardcover (cloth) — ISBN 0-934829-44-6, $34.95.

PUBLIC RELATIONS CAREER DIRECTORY, 3rd edition, 320 PAGES, 8 1/2 X 11.
❑ Paper — ISBN 0-934829-33-0, $26.95.
❑ Hardcover (cloth) — ISBN 0-934829-43-8, $34.95.

MAGAZINES CAREER DIRECTORY, 3rd edition, 256 pages, 8 1/2 X 11.
❑ Paper — ISBN 0-934829-31-4, $26.95.
❑ Hardcover (cloth) — ISBN 0-934829-41-1, $34.95.

BOOK PUBLISHING CAREER DIRECTORY, 3rd edition, 224 pages, 8 1/2 X 11.
❑ Paper — ISBN 0-934829-32-2, $26.95.
❑ Hardcover (cloth) — ISBN 0-934829-42-X, $34.95.

NEWSPAPERS CAREER DIRECTORY, 2nd edition, 240 pages, 8 1/2 X 11.
❑ Paper — ISBN 0-934829-35-7, $26.95.
❑ Hardcover (cloth) — ISBN 0-934829-45-4, $34.95

Please enclose $2.50 per order and $1.00 per title for each series volume ordered.

* * * MORE BOOKS AND MAIL ORDER COUPON ON PRECEDING PAGES * * *